My Two Lives

My Two Lives

J. J. LEVY

The Book Guild Ltd

First published in Great Britain in 2022 by
The Book Guild Ltd
Unit E2 Airfield Business Park,
Harrison Road, Market Harborough,
Leicestershire. LE16 7UL
Tel: 0116 2792299
www.bookguild.co.uk
Email: info@bookguild.co.uk
Twitter: @bookguild

Typeset in 11pt Minion Pro

Printed on FSC accredited paper
Printed and bound in Great Britain by 4edge Limited

ISBN 978 1914471 971

British Library Cataloguing in Publication Data.
A catalogue record for this book is available from the British Library.

To all the friends I have ever known

To MAC

Prologue

"Have you ever thought back over your life and seen that one choice that defined everything that is to come? That one decision which changed everything? And realised that had you made the other choice, your life would be completely different?"

My granddaughter looks at me questioningly. "What do you mean, Granny?"

"Our lives are defined by the choices we make, my love, by the forks in the path of life. Each decision is like throwing a stone into a pond. There are always ripples. As we move through life, our lives touch others in ways we cannot imagine and cannot foresee."

Grace smiles in return. "Are you feeling nostalgic today?"

I shift slightly in my bed. It's the same one I have slept in for thirty years, but I sleep in it alone now.

I glance around my bedroom through worn and tired eyes; everything is just a little bit blurry. White walls, beige carpet. Bright red curtains block out most of the sunlight, but I can still see it's a wonderful day outside. Photos line every surface, people I see every day, and faces of people who left me a long time ago. This is what happens when you get old. I remember my own grandmother telling me that, decades ago on a fine summer's day. Never before has it felt so real.

I study my granddaughter as she sits next to my bed. Her light brown eyes are wide and kind. Her dark blonde hair curly and loose around her face. She wears a loose summer dress. She is sixteen years old, and looks as young as I once felt.

"I lie here all day, and I think about how my life could have been different had I made the other decision." Grace's brow furrows but she doesn't interrupt. "I wonder if I would have met the same people. Would I have met your grandfather? Would I have died younger? Would I have had an impact on the world?"

Grace smiles kindly and reaches over to take my old, wrinkled hand in her young, smooth one. Her hand is hot. "Granny, you've lived a wonderful life, haven't you?"

"Of course, my dear, I have done so much, had so many exciting adventures. But, sometimes, I can almost imagine the other life, almost see the memories in my mind. The one I didn't choose."

"I don't understand."

I chuckle quietly, drawing air deep into my lungs. "That's because I'm being cryptic. Would you like to hear my stories, love? Or would you prefer to be outside, reading your book in the garden?" I shoot her a wrinkled grin. "I know which one I would choose."

Grace laughs. "Granny, don't be silly. Of course I want to hear your story."

I shake my head. "I said stories. I have more than one. They are full of excitement, love and loss; not for the faint-hearted."

Grace shoots me a look at my veiled challenge; she looks so much like her father when she does that. "Tell me then."

I sit up as straight as my old body will let me, leaning back on the pillows and clearing my throat in an overly dramatic fashion.

"When I was eighteen years old," I begin dramatically, "I had a choice about what I wanted to do with my life, two paths I could take. My life up until that point had been pretty good. My parents were middle class, my father worked hard to support us and we were never short of money or food. My mother raised my brother and myself. We grew up in a small town in southern England. I think I was a typical teenager. I went to school, then college. I had no hard choices to make up until then, it was easy. But what faced me now was the rest of my life. I was working as a checkout assistant in a local supermarket at the weekend, just earning enough to have some extra cash. My entire eighteenth year, I deliberated between two options. I pursued both for a time. I just couldn't make that choice. Did I go to university? I wanted to do that. Or did I join the army? I wanted to do that too. My choice was to go to university or to join the army."

*

Many years previously…

Whenever I work on the checkouts, I watch the people I serve. I see what they buy, and I try to imagine their lives. The businessman with a wedding ring buying flowers, chocolates and condoms. For his wife or for his mistress? The mother pushing a buggy buying ready meals, wine and juice boxes. Was she going home to a partner or would she put the kids to bed, then curl up with the ready-made lasagne and a glass of wine? The kid buying chocolate bars. Did his mother know he spent his pocket money on sweets, and did she care? I liked to think I was an astute observer of human nature. In truth, I was simply trying to entertain myself. The checkouts are not glamorous. I'm trying to distract myself from the other parts of my life. How bored I am living at home. How stifling my parents are. How I wish I could leave and have adventures like everyone else.

I know I have my whole life ahead of me, but it seems so far away right now.

It's a Friday night in March 2003. I've been at sixth form college all day, then I went to the gym, now I'm working the late shift. After the post-work rush, Friday nights are pretty slow. I usually get taken off the checkout to help on the other departments.

"Earth to Emma King." Simon, the checkout supervisor, waves a hand in front of my face and smiles.

I blink and glance up at him in surprise. I had been sitting with my chin in my hand gazing out of the window at the pouring rain outside. "Must have been some pretty deep thoughts there." He smiles as he taps the conveyor belt.

I sit up and stretch. "Not really," I lie. "Just wondering what to have for dinner when I get home."

Simon laughs and leans on the top of the screen. I tuck my fringe behind my ear nervously. I'm pretty sure he fancies me. I'm not that experienced with boys, but there's a look in his eye that makes me wonder. Simon always lets me off the checkout first, always finds me jobs to do near him, and he flirts with me all the time. He's not much older than I am, and he's cute, but I'm too tall, too quiet, and my boobs are tiny. I'm just another awkward 'only just eighteen-year-old'. Who would fancy me?

Janine Marshall, my best friend who I have known forever, says I hide behind my fringe and that's why the boys don't ask me out. My fringe drags across my face diagonally and is the only part of my boring brown, curly and wild hair I like. When I am nervous, I tuck it behind my ears constantly. But I should probably listen to her; she has bright red hair and is tall like me, but actually has a figure and knows how to wear makeup and clothes properly. She always has the boys chasing her and she knows what to do about it. In comparison to her, I have boring brown hair and eyes, my tall and lanky body has no figure to speak of, I don't wear makeup or dress stylishly, and I have annoying freckles on my nose which I really hate.

I had a boyfriend last year who cheated on me spectacularly and said some pretty nasty things when we broke up. Janine calls him all sorts of rude names, but my confidence has taken a major hit, and it wasn't great to begin with. So, I don't really know what to do with the attention from Simon, and I ignore it mostly.

Simon lets me off the till and waits for me to join him, then walks with me along the checkouts towards the supervisor area. "So, what are you doing tomorrow night?" he asks casually.

I shrug. "Working here until seven."

Simon smiles. "Me too, and then…"

His tone makes me look up into his face. I like that he is taller than me; I'm tall for a girl so it doesn't happen very much. "Uh, going home, I think." Wow, I just realised I have an epic social life. I blush and look away.

"Well, it's my birthday on Sunday," Simon says, clearly ignoring my uncoolness, "and some of us are going to the Watchmaker after the store closes tomorrow. Want to join?"

Is he asking me out? The Watchmaker is the pub down the road. I was only eighteen last month, so I'm not experienced with the whole 'legally being able to drink in pubs' thing. Janine and I know an off-licence that sells to underage girls like us, and we'd drink in the park. Janine turned eighteen before me, so for my birthday she took me to a local pub. I got ID'd and could prove I was old enough, which was exciting, but I wouldn't know how to act without her. I shift nervously on my feet as we stop by the supervisor station. "Umm, I dunno." I bite my lip and don't look at him. "I have to drive home." If my beat-up Fiesta makes it. I'm always just a little concerned it won't.

"Don't worry, me too."

I glance up at him. "If it's your birthday, won't you be drinking?" It would surprise me if Simon would do that.

Simon smiles, his light blue eyes studying my face as his dark brown hair falls across his forehead. "I may have one drink, but I need to drive home anyway so that'll be it. It would mean a lot to me if you came."

Wow, my stomach does a weird flip-flop that I don't understand. "Umm. Okay then."

Simon's face lights up. "Great!" His beeper goes off and he glances over my shoulder at one of the checkouts that needs him. "It'll be great, you'll see." He moves away. "Oh, can you tidy up aisle twelve?"

I nod and head towards the aisle. My stomach is churning. I hate social functions without Janine. I rarely go out with any of the others from here, even though I have been invited quite a lot. I just feel awkward and odd. I take a deep breath and begin to work on pulling the stock forward, pushing my fringe behind my ear.

*

A week later and I'm dreading my Friday night shift. I didn't go to the pub on Saturday night; I ran out of the back door as soon as my shift ended. I honestly didn't know what I was going to do until right up until the last minute. It had been busy so Simon hadn't had a chance to talk to me that day, but he kept smiling at me widely. I don't work during the week so now is the first time I will see him. Janine says I took the coward's way out, and she was right.

When I arrive, it's busy, so I check my assigned till, relieve Bev and get to work. I see Simon arrive a few minutes later and take over from the day supervisor. He casts an eye over the department and his gaze meets mine. He shoots me a quick smile then looks away as someone else takes his attention. An hour or so later, it's quietened down as usual. I see Simon walking towards me and I swallow hard.

"Evening, Emma," he greets as he passes. "How was your week?"

"It was fine," I reply. "How was your birthday?"

"Brilliant. It's not every day you turn twenty-one." He starts to turn away.

"Simon, I'm sorry I didn't come out on Saturday night… something came up." That sounds lame even to my ears.

Simon smiles at me. "Don't worry about it." He stops in front of the checkout behind me. "We had a great night, didn't we, Robyn?"

I turn and see another checkout girl behind me. My age, black-haired, blue-eyed, gorgeous, and extremely nice. She smiles flirtatiously at Simon and he grins back.

"We sure did." She looks at me and smiles. "You missed a great party, Emma."

I watch as Simon lets her off the till, and then as they walk away, laughing with each other.

I feel so stupid, and ugly, and awkward. Mostly cowardly.

I slump back into my chair, hardly noticing that a customer has walked up until she clears her throat.

I jump and sit up quickly. "Sorry," I mutter, and begin to process the items on autopilot. Fresh spaghetti, red wine, onions, pasta sauce and mint chocolate ice cream. I state the total.

"Are you okay?" The customer is looking at me with concern. I meet her eyes and nod. She smiles at me in sympathy as she slots her card into the machine. Over her shoulder, I see Simon and Robyn laughing together. I feel a pang of something I don't recognise.

"You know, it doesn't really matter in the end," the customer says quietly as her gaze follows mine. "He doesn't really matter."

I frown at her. "I'm sorry?" The customer takes out her card and grabs her shopping bag as I hand over the receipt.

"Him." She nods her head over her shoulder. "Men generally. Once you figure yourself out, they all come running." She winks. "Take my word for it." She moves away and I follow her with my eyes. I see suddenly she is wearing a military dress uniform. Dark green jacket, straight knee-length skirt, tights and low black heels. She looks smart, confident, sophisticated. That's what I want to be.

*

The woman's words echo in my head for weeks afterwards. Until I realise that I need to sort myself out, find myself, find confidence in myself. Once I have that, nothing else will matter.

I needed to stop being a coward and just go for it.

I made my decision sitting in the car on my way to work. I knew what I would do.

Chapter 1

University Part 1

September 2003

I was scared that the first week of university would be daunting and overwhelming. I had moved to a city I didn't know, with no friends or family nearby. I was living in student accommodation just outside the city centre with strangers. I didn't know if the course I had chosen was right, if everything was worth the massive amount of student loans I'd be paying back for years. Questions ran through my head at speed. What if I would be a physically and socially awkward loser for the rest of my life? What if I made no friends? What if I failed my course?

The first night I move into Birmingham, I head to the kitchen. I share a kitchen with seven others, our rooms are all off one long corridor which circles the building. I peer through the door. There are several guys and girls sitting and leaning in the room, just chatting. I bite my lip, hard. I hate social situations like this; I find them really awkward. But I had made my choice; I had chosen to come here. I need to stop being a coward and take a leap.

Before I can change my mind, I push open the door. All conversation stops as I enter, and everyone looks at me. I feel like a rabbit caught in the headlights.

I smile nervously. "Hi."

A tall, exotic guy smiles widely at me. "You must be forty-seven!"

"Huh?" I reply, and say the first thing that comes into my head. "Actually, I'm eighteen. Good guess, though."

To my delight, this produces laughs all around.

"No, I mean you're in room forty-seven. It's the only one missing," the guy explains.

I laugh. "Yep, that's me. Also known as Emma King."

There is a series of hellos and waves all around. "I'm Edward Lang. I'm room forty-eight."

"Ah, we're neighbours then."

"I'm Laura." A short, pretty redhead introduces herself. Short women always make me feel gawky, giant and awkward, but I shake off the sensation and smile. "Want a drink?" She holds up a bottle of rosé wine.

I don't tend to be a wine drinker, but I don't want to be rude. "Sure, thanks."

Laura pours me a small glass, then holds up her own. "A toast, to us lot who have no idea what we are doing here."

I laugh and toast along with the rest of them. The wine is too sweet.

"So, Emma, what are you studying?" Edward says to me, as conversation breaks off into smaller groups. I'm sitting on top of the table next to Laura, swinging my legs. I notice Edward has lovely bright blue eyes.

"Accountancy," I tell him.

Edward smiles. "I had an uncle who was an accountant, good

money to be made there. But I think he is a lorry driver now…" He trails off and looks thoughtful.

"Well, I like numbers, so I hope it's okay," I reply, not commenting on the money thing. "What about you?"

"Mechanical and civil engineering," he replies. "At least that's the plan. We'll see how I like it."

That was cryptic, but I choose not to ask. "Do you know Birmingham at all?"

"Yep, I'm from Coventry."

"Ah great, you can be the leader tonight then," Laura says with a laugh. "Show us all the best pubs and clubs."

"Well, I'll do my best," Edward says flirtatiously. Laura smiles sweetly back.

"Where are you from, Emma?" Laura asks.

"Hampshire," I reply. "A small country village. I've never lived in the city before."

"How exciting," Laura replies with a smile.

"What about you?"

"South East London," Laura replies. "I worked in the city but I decided I wanted a degree."

I thought Laura seemed slightly older. "What are you doing?"

"English literature."

The evening continues with small talk and drinks, then Edward cooks up some pasta and we all contribute ingredients. After dinner, we head out to a pub.

I think that I am going to enjoy this.

*

My first year at uni was a haze of parties, pubs and drinking. Interspersed with lectures. I had chosen accountancy because numbers always worked for me; I saw patterns and shapes. Maths was easy to me and I enjoyed it. I went out with my flatmates a few times in the early days, but after I mentioned to Laura I could hear her and Edward having sex through the wall, they suddenly weren't so keen to invite me. I didn't mind really; I'd made loads of friends on my course by then.

I found the first year really easy. Probably because of that, I thought the second year would be simple too. It wasn't until late in my second year I realised that I really should have studied more. My second-year grade was abysmal. I pulled myself together in my third year and worked really hard. I still partied and hung out with friends, drank too much and spent too much of my student loan, but my third-year grade was good. Unfortunately, that meant my overall grade wasn't great. So I stayed on to do a Masters for a year to improve my chances of a decent job.

My self-confidence grew; I no longer cared what people thought of me. I dressed how I wanted, and did what I wanted. Like the kitchen that first night, I forced myself to go into social situations which made me uncomfortable, and after a while I realised I was enjoying them. I was no longer a coward. Gone were the days when I would shy away from a party or a pub outing. I made new friends, had several boyfriends and generally had a great time. I worked at a local pub for the first few years to help pay my rent, but the hours were unsociable and I eventually found work in a department store. The work wasn't as entertaining, but it meant I now had evenings free for fun.

In my Master's year, several things happened at once. I had a huge argument with a girl, Meredith, who had become my best friend over the last few years. We were living in a shared house with two other friends. I had walked into the unlocked bathroom while her boyfriend was taking a shower, and he had blatantly suggested I lock the door behind me, get naked and join him. Meredith had not taken kindly to this, and accused me of trying to nick him, which I, of course, denied. I had my own boyfriend, and was not a cheater. While I was willing to forgive and forget her blatant accusations, she was not. It made things very awkward in the house for everyone, and her boyfriend kept giving me creepy looks, so I decided the best thing to do would be to move out.

I moved a few roads over into another house a week before my twenty-second birthday. Just after I moved, my boyfriend broke up with me.

Luckily, I had an awesome friend from work who took me out on my birthday. Bought me cake and presents, and got me extremely drunk. My birthday was on a Sunday.

My alarm went off at 8am on Monday morning. I had only flopped into bed four hours earlier, and it felt like a badger had crawled into my mouth and died overnight. I hit the alarm and blinked into the light from my window. I had a 9am lecture, but I was sorely tempted to roll back over and go to sleep. So far this year, my attendance at lectures had been flawless, and I'd be damned if I was going to let a hangover take that away. So I dragged myself out of bed, popped some painkillers, showered, brushed my teeth really hard and left for my lecture. On the way, I stopped for strong coffee.

Clearly, I was working on slower time today, as I arrived a few minutes late. I crept in the back and flumped down into a chair in the second row from the back, not missing the glare shot my way from Professor Minshull, who was talking to the class.

This unit was about unusual aspects of accountancy, smaller subsets of the larger topic. I glanced at my schedule and saw that today's topic was 'environmental accountancy' and I groaned inwardly at myself. I had got out of bed for this? I cast my gaze over the rest of the class, all eyes on the front and notebooks at the ready. The lecture hall sat around one hundred students, though less than half of that were present now, in old-fashioned ascending seating. From the back, I looked down at the professor and the white board about 2 metres below my height. Even in the semi-darkness, the walls were grey, the seats were grey and the ceiling was grey. The long heavy curtains were black and let in minimal light. The whole place was eerie and reminded me of haunted houses I had visited as a kid, without the skeletons poking out of the walls.

The professor stopped talking then and gestured to a younger man sitting in the front row. A guest lecturer today. I tried to pay attention to him, I really did. It wasn't that the subject matter wasn't interesting; it was just that his presentation skills desperately needed work.

When he calls a break at 10am, I groan to myself and slump my head forward onto the seat in front of me. I need more coffee.

I hear a deep masculine chuckle behind me. "I didn't think it was that bad."

I crack my eyes open and peer under my arm. The most dazzling pair of green eyes I have ever seen look back at me in amusement. I blink and sit up slowly, turning to face the guy sitting behind me. Brushing my fringe off my face as I move. He smiles at my expression, but there is concern there too. "Are you okay?"

"Not really," I reply, then sigh. "Though it's my own doing, to be fair."

The guy's smile grows as his eyes flick over my face. "Out partying on a Sunday, were you?" I notice he has the most amazing voice; it's deep and slightly accented but I can't place it.

I nod, slowly, then shrug. "It was my birthday."

"Well, happy birthday for yesterday then."

"Thanks." He glances down at his notes, and I take a second to study him. About my age, thick black hair, strong jaw covered in stubble, red hoodie and jeans covering long legs. Very attractive. Despite my hungover state, I feel the urge to keep his attention. "Do you not find him irritating too?" I ask. The guy looks up and meets my eyes with a questioning look. I jerk my head slowly towards the front. "The guest lecturer, and his incessant use of his water bottle?"

He chuckles and his brows furrow. "Irritating, no. But I did note the use of the water bottle every other sentence."

I sigh and mutter, "He needs to work on his presentation skills."

The guy laughs and leans forward. "Are you always this grumpy on Monday morning?"

I smile a little. "Not usually. Though I am an evening person really."

The guy's eyes twinkle with mischief. "Good to know. I'm Jon Clemens." He holds out his hand and I take it in formal greeting.

"Emma King. Nice to meet you, Jon."

"And you, Emma." He eyes hold mine for a second, then dart to the front where the annoying lecturer is getting ready to start again. "Try not to be too irritated this time."

I smile and turn back around.

As per instructions, I try not to be too irritated, but another hour of incessant water drinking drives me up the bend. The only thing that keeps me sane is knowing there is an attractive guy behind me that I can talk to at the end. I am so relieved when the water bottle man finally stops and Professor Minshull indicates the class is over. As I stand and gather my books, I take a look over my shoulder.

"Thanks for that, Emma." Jon is still sitting and is now mock glaring at me. "Since you pointed it out, I couldn't help but notice every time he took a drink. Talk about irritating."

"Whoops," I reply with a grimace. "Sorry." Jon shakes his head but he is smiling as he stands.

"How about I make it up to you with lunch?" I ask, coming to the end of the row and standing next to him. I'm pleased to see he is taller than me by a good few inches, at least 6 foot, probably a bit more. A soft soap smell lingers in the air.

Jon winces. "Sorry, I have back-to-back lectures all day." He studies me, his eyes moving over my face. "How about I add you on Facebook? Then you can decide if you really want to have lunch with me."

"And vice versa, huh?" I shrug. "Fair enough."

Jon smiles at my directness. "Emma King, right? I should be able to remember that."

A blond guy walks up to us. "Jon, there you are. Hiding at the back, eh?" He glances at me with undisguised interest. "Hi."

"Hi," I reply back, then look back to Jon. "Well, Jon, it was nice to meet you. See you around." I smile widely, then turn and walk out of the hall, catching up with some friends who had just passed.

I smile to myself. Suddenly I'm very glad I got out of bed this morning.

*

I won't deny being extremely pleased when Jon adds me on Facebook that evening. I spend a good hour or so going through his profile. No obvious girlfriend, which is good. Lots of photos and status updates, usually about nothing very important but almost always funny. Some people seem to be writing on his wall in French, which I find interesting. Some of the photos of him on there are absolutely gorgeous and make a tingle run down my spine. He is a very good-looking guy.

I receive a message from him that night, with a link to a website talking about presentation skills. He has extracted a passage linking drinking water to nerves in presentations, which I find hilarious.

I learn that Jon is in his final year of law and accountancy, a combination degree that I once considered.

After some back-and-forth messaging for a few days, we agree to meet on Friday night for a drink. I'm excited; I love first dates.

That anticipation of finding out about this guy, the chatting and flirting, not knowing how the night is going to end.

We choose a pub for our meeting, so I go for jeans and a vest top, along with my trusty leather jacket. I rarely bother with makeup. I keep my hair long and curly these days; my fringe is cut short but styled to flow down the side of my face. I still have that nervous habit of tucking my fringe behind my ears, which I have never been able to break. I arrive at the pub first and order a few beers; we had previously discussed our choice of pub drinks. Jon arrives several minutes later in jeans and a shirt, which shows off his slender figure. He's not broad-shouldered but he is muscular. Jon looks shocked that I beat him there, which I enjoy.

"I have never been beaten to a venue before," he states in that sexy voice of his, shaking his head as we take a seat. "Girls just don't turn up on time."

"Stereotype much?" I tease. "I can think of many male-related ones if you want to go there."

Jon laughs. His laugh is sexy too, full of energy and promise. "Probably best if we don't."

We clink glasses and take a sip. The cool dark beer slips down my throat and I smile.

"So tell me about your accent," I ask immediately. "I just can't place it."

Jon smiles into his beer. "You think I have an accent?"

"Yeah, a bit. I mean, everyone has an accent, whether it be from northern England or another country. But yours is different somehow. Where are you from?"

"France."

I frown. "Really? But you haven't got a French accent."

Jon leans back, watching me. His bright eyes do an interesting flick over my face. "My mother is French, my dad English. I grew up in northern France speaking both, plus some German and Spanish thrown in too." He shrugs. "I speak both languages without an obvious accent, but of course, I don't have an English accent either."

Intriguing. "Are your parents still in France?"

Jon nods. "Yes, they are both schoolteachers. My elder sister lives in Oxford. My younger brother is still at home." He smiles. "What about you? I detect a southern county upbringing."

I laugh. "You got me there. I come from a small Hampshire village. My father is a builder. I have an older brother who lives in London." I lean forward. "I learnt French at school, but I can't really remember it. I'm terrible at languages. You're lucky to have a gift for them."

"I don't believe that," Jon says slowly. I frown. "You can't be terrible at languages when all you have to base it on is school French. I can teach you, if you want."

I smile. "I would like that, but maybe not while drinking." I hold up my pint glass and Jon laughs.

"*Oui, ma chérie.*" The French words spoken in that sexy voice make my spine tingle, but I try not to show it.

"So why do law and accountancy at Birmingham?" I ask. "Why in the UK and not France?"

Jon sips his beer. "We came here a lot when I was growing up, I like being in the UK. The people, the culture – I prefer it. If I want to practise law it needs to be where I learn it really, but I'm not sure if I want to do pure law. I might prefer accountancy. Perhaps use my language skills. I have kept my options open for both. There are only a few select universities that do the combination degree. I had a choice between Birmingham and Edinburgh."

"So why not Edinburgh?"

Jon shrugs. "I met some people on my open day here. I preferred them so I chose Birmingham." He smiles. "One of them is now one of my closest friends."

"You'll have to make a choice soon," I point out. "Between law and accountancy. You're on the final stretch."

"Yep, I know."

His tone makes me wince. "Sorry, pointing out the obvious." Jon leans forward and takes my hand gently.

"No, I'm sorry, I didn't mean to snap. Everyone keeps telling me the same thing, that's all."

I stare down at our entwined fingers, then up at him. He is staring at me with an intense look on his face. Then he blinks and looks at his empty pint glass.

"So what do you want to do?" I ask softly.

"Many things," he says, equally softly. The mock innocence on his face makes me laugh. Then he grins. "But right now, get another beer."

Jon returns a few minutes later. He seems to carry a pleasant soap smell around with him, and it's more intoxicating than the beer we are drinking.

"Tell me, Emma, what are your dreams?" Jon asks as he sits down.

I'm startled by the question. "My dreams?"

"What do you want out of this life?"

I laugh. "Isn't that a rather deep question for a first date?"

"Perhaps, but I'm a deep kind of guy." Jon's mouth twists into a smirk as his intense eyes study me.

I narrow my eyes at him but can't help smiling in return. "Okay, my dreams – other than winning the lottery?"

Jon nods. "Too obvious, try harder."

I ponder for a moment. "I want to be happy in my life. To have fun and enjoy myself, and to make life a happy place for others too."

"Okay…" Jon replies. "Vague, but okay. Do you have any ambitions? What do you want to do with your life to make it happy?"

"One day I want to have children," I say, before I can stop myself. Uck, children on a first date, way to scare him off.

11

But Jon doesn't look scared. He looks thoughtful. "You think children will make your life happy?"

I shrug. "Maybe, but I hope I can make them happy." I ponder some more. "I want to be successful in my career, and I'm willing to work hard for that. But I won't be happy just working, I need a good life outside of work. Friends, family, a partner I can rely on. I want to see the world." I meet his gaze and Jon has a ghost of a smile on his lips. "I would really like to make a difference somehow, but I have no idea how to do that."

Jon tilts his head as his eyes move over my face. "Perhaps that will come to you along the way."

"Perhaps it will. What about you, Jon? What are your dreams?"

Jon stares off above my head. "I too want children one day, and a wife I can rely on to be my equal in everything, to support me in my choices and love me." He pauses. "I hope I can make a difference in the world, even if it is only small. But I doubt that being a lawyer will be fruitful like that to begin with. Only after I work hard and become successful can I set up my own firm to really help others less fortunate than me." He pauses. "Because whatever we may feel now, whatever the world throws at us, there are always those who are less fortunate than we are."

I stare at him. Clearly, he has thought about this. He smiles then shakes his head. "That was definitely too deep for a first date."

I shake my head in reply. "No, it was the best statement I have ever heard on a first date. So heartfelt and honest." I smile widely. "You're a unique guy, Jon."

Jon nods. "So I've been told." Then he grins at me. "You're pretty cool too."

I shrug and mimic him. "So I've been told."

Our conversation veers towards less serious topics as the night progresses and the beers flow. Jon is enthusiastic about a wide range of topics, and I find myself just enjoying listening to him. I notice it feels so comfortable to be around him already. I've never had that so quickly with someone before.

Then suddenly the pub is calling last orders. Jon and I get up to leave and I sway slightly, Jon grabbing my arm to steady me with a wide grin.

"Beer and gravity don't work well together," he murmurs into my ear with a smile, his hand steady on my arm.

Jon lives a few streets away from me so he walks me to my door. Before any awkwardness sets in, he leans down and kisses me gently, then intensely. The kiss is passionate and makes me light-headed as he runs his hands through my hair and brings me in close to him. His warmth and smell envelope me as my body pushes into his. As he pulls away, I try to catch my breath. I'm about to invite him in when he smiles widely, his eyes flicking over my face, and whispers, "Goodnight, Emma." Then he turns and strides away.

*

The next morning, I'm lounging in bed watching YouTube videos with my housemate. Lorna is dark-skinned, curvy and loves outrageously coloured clothes. I only met her just over a week ago, but we've become good friends already. She is sitting with her back to the wall, her bright pink pyjama top clashing hideously with my blue duvet cover. I have to be at work in two hours; I'm doing the late shift today. Which is unfortunate for me as it looks like a glorious spring day.

As we watch a video where a cat is dancing with a disco ball, giggling hysterically, my mobile starts to ring. I glance at it, intrigued, as I answer.

"Hello."

"Good morning, Emma. It's Jon."

"Hi, Jon." Lorna smiles widely, gives me a double thumbs-up and leaves the room.

"It's not too early, I hope."

"Nope," I reply, leaning back onto the pillow. "I'm still in bed, but I'm awake."

Jon chuckles. "Good to know. And how are you this morning?"

"I'm great," I reply with a smile. "I had a good night, you know."

"So did I." God, his voice is sexy. "Emma, I wanted to know if you had plans today. A few friends and I are planning a walk around the city, take in a few pubs and parks."

I groan. "Oh, I would love to, but I have to work." Stupid work.

Jon sighs. "That's a shame." He pauses. "I realise I didn't ask you where you worked last night."

I smile; he sounds ashamed. "The big department store in the west of the Bullring shopping centre, off Edgbaston Street."

"Do you enjoy it?"

I shrug to myself. "It's fine. The people are fun, the work is dull. But," I grin, "I work in the lingerie department. So I have some very interesting stories."

Jon is silent for a few seconds. "You do, huh?"

"Yep."

"Do you... get to take things home?"

I cover my mouth to stop myself from giggling; he actually sounds a bit flustered. "I do get a twenty-five per cent discount, so my underwear drawer is quite full." I love lingerie, and I love telling blokes about it.

"Well, that is... interesting." Jon laughs. I can imagine his face lighting up, his bright green eyes twinkling. "What time do you finish?"

"7pm."

"Cool, not too late. We will probably be at a pub by that time. Shall I let you know so you can join us if you want?"

I smile. "Yes, please, I can tell you all about my day on lingerie."

Jon chuckles. How can a man have such a sexy voice? "I look forward to it."

We say bye and I hang up. I get up and wander into the kitchen, looking for coffee and breakfast.

"So how is your hot Frenchman from last night?" Lorna is perched on the kitchen counter drinking tea from her huge mug, her long dark legs swinging free. We live in a terraced house, which looks like every other terraced house everywhere. The kitchen is at the far end, which makes it one of the coldest rooms. I'm wearing my gown and slippers, but Lorna always seems so unaffected by the cold. She is wearing pyjama shorts and a strap top in early spring. The kitchen is modern but run-down, as expected in a Birmingham student house.

"Still hot," I reply, making myself a coffee. "He has such a sexy voice." I fan myself and giggle. "I'm meeting him and some of his friends tonight for drinks after work."

"You go, girl," Lorna says. She's always using American slang like that, despite her true London accent. "So you're already meeting the friends, huh?"

I nod and take a sip of the bitter beverage, letting the hot liquid warm me to my toes. I love coffee.

"This guy sounds too perfect," Lorna says, giving me a warning look. "Perfect first date with an amazing kiss, meeting the friends, funny, smart, gorgeous. What's the catch?"

I frown. "Why does there have to be a catch?"

"Honey, there is always a catch with men."

My experience has taught me to agree so I shrug. "It's early days. I haven't found it yet, Lorna, but I hope it's not in his trousers."

Lorna hoots loudly as I leave the room to get ready for work.

*

"So, will this underwear get my wife to sleep with me?" I turn abruptly towards the man as he speaks. I have just helped him pick out something nice for his wife, and am leading him towards the checkouts.

"Excuse me?"

"This underwear." The balding, overweight man holds up the matching bra and thong set in red lace. "That's why I am buying this, you know, so I can sleep with my wife."

Okay… actually not the first time I have had this conversation with a man in this department.

"Sir, I'm not really sure that's an appropriate question to ask me."

The man looks confused. "Why not?"

I raise my eyebrows at him. "Because despite being a sales girl on the lingerie department, I'm a stranger, and a younger woman. Don't you think it's kind of inappropriate to ask me that?"

The man thinks for a moment, then his eyes travel down me in a lazy fashion. The uniform I wear is about as unsexy as you can get. Loose black trousers and a dark green baggy jumper. My long hair is tied in a ponytail. I cross my arms and wait for his eyes to jump back to my face.

When they do, he sees my expectant and exasperated, yet polite, expression and flushes.

"Sorry," he mumbles. He turns and heads towards the tills.

I restrain my smile at his retreating back. At least he wasn't creepy, just kind of sad. I hear a deep laugh to my left and whirl.

Jon is leaning against one of the bra stands nearby, and he is clapping slowly with a wide grin on his face. My stomach flip-flops and I'm struck for a moment at just how gorgeous he is. He is wearing smart shoes, dark jeans and a long-sleeved black t-shirt with a slogan across the front. A dark jacket is slung over one arm. His jawline is clean shaven, and his green eyes are twinkling in laughter. "Nicely handled," he says, walking towards me. "Something tells me that's not the first time you've had a question like that." His eyes study me, and I find myself fascinated by that flick his eyes do. Quickly taking in all my face in one glance.

I shrug, glancing around to make sure my supervisor isn't nearby. "No," I state slowly. "It's not, and he wasn't even creepy, or trying to hit on me," I roll my eyes, "because the lingerie department is the best place to pick up girls."

Jon laughs again and shoves his hands in his pockets. "I can imagine you get some awkward questions."

I shake my head, glancing around again to make sure no one is nearby. "The best one is when a bloke comes up to me asking for my help choosing underwear for his lady, and I ask her size. Sometimes they look confused, then puzzled, then they look down to my chest," I do an impression by staring at Jon's chest in an exaggerated way, "and say, 'a little bit bigger than you.'" I roll my eyes and gesture at myself. "Like that really helps me."

Jon grins widely but keeps his eyes on my face, which is unusual. Usually when I tell that story, the blokes use it as an excuse to look for themselves.

"Hazards of working in lingerie?"

"You could say that. Certainly wasn't in the job description." I give him a curious look. "So what are you doing here, Jon? Looking to buy some lingerie for your lady friend?" My question is teasing.

Jon shakes his head. "At this stage, I wouldn't dare buy lingerie for my lady friend." Our eyes meet and he grins but doesn't elaborate. "I was in the area and thought I would drop by and say hi."

"Ah," I say, genuinely touched. "How nice of you." Over his shoulder, I see my supervisor come onto the shop floor, so I begin to tidy the matching underwear sets next to me.

"Still up for tonight?" Jon shuffles his feet, glancing at what I'm doing.

"Sure am," I reply. "Where do you think you'll be?"

"It's my friend's birthday, and he loves the Barrel on Park Road, so probably there."

I stop tidying. "I don't want to intrude on your friend's birthday."

Jon smiles. "You won't be, there will be loads of people there. Plus, he wants to meet you."

"Have you been talking about me?" I give Jon a coy smile.

"Of course." Jon looks down. "And well, also…" he hesitates, "…I had a nasty break-up late last year, and since then I haven't really been out with anyone, so he's interested."

I study him, immensely curious to know about this other relationship but not wanting to be too nosy. "Sounds great. I'll meet you there when I'm done here."

Jon smiles, then leans over and gently kisses my cheek. That soft smell of soap wafts over me. "I'm really looking forward to it," he whispers, then pulls away, smiles and walks towards the stairs. I watch him leave, before my supervisor glares at me and I turn back to work. Now I am really looking forward to tonight.

*

A little after 7.15pm, I walk into the Barrel, putting my MP3 player into my pocket. I was listening to *Sultans of Swing* as I arrived, one of my favourites. I like this pub; it's stylish and modern and caters for student budgets. It's packed already, hardly surprising as it's Saturday night, but the music is still low enough to just be able to chat. I changed at work, leaving my drab work clothes in my locker and sprucing up a little in a low-cut, knee-length purple dress, short black jacket and black boots. I don't tend to wear makeup, but I put on some eyeliner and let my long hair down. This guy deserves some extra effort. I can't deny I'm excited about seeing him; I have butterflies in my stomach.

I wander along the bar, smiling politely at a few blokes who turn to look at me, but I'm only interested in one guy tonight. There is a large group of students in a back corner, several of them wearing flower garlands, but I don't see Jon, so I start to turn away and head back to look at the other end of the bar. I feel hands take my waist and a large body press to my back. Instantly a pleasant smell of soap wraps around me. I relax as the hands slide across my stomach, and I feel his warm breath on my neck as my pulse kicks up.

"Evening," Jon whispers in my ear. "You look incredible."

I smile and turn in his arms. "Hi."

Before I can say anything else, he is kissing me, right there in the middle of the pub. He presses me tight against him and I can't help but notice how my breasts are crushed against his chest. I love that feeling. I can taste beer and salt on his lips and I smile against him. "I like your style of greeting," I whisper to him.

Jon smiles and gently pushes my hair off my face. "Want a drink?"

I nod, so we head to the bar, where Jon buys a round. He is wearing the same as earlier but now has a flower garland around his neck. The effect is surprisingly attractive.

Jon nods for me to follow him and his tray of beer and leads me to the students I had spotted earlier, who all cheer as he approaches with their beer. I am rapidly introduced to about a dozen people, everyone smiling and happy and clearly on their way to being drunk. The birthday boy is called Rob; I recognise him from the lecture theatre where I met Jon. He has about five multi-coloured garlands around his neck. Rob sweeps me up into a big hug in greeting, and spins me around as I laugh.

"Lovely to meet you, Emma," he gushes, taking a long sip from his beer bottle. "Jon hasn't been able to speak about anyone but you all day, which is really quite annoying." He glares at Jon, who punches him lightly on the arm. "Hopefully, now he can shut up."

"If only I could say the same for you," Jon fires back. "You just talk about shit."

"And if only it was just tonight." A pretty blonde appears at Rob's side and wraps her arm around his waist.

"This is Abbey, Rob's extremely patient girlfriend," Jon introduces. Abbey smiles at me widely.

"How nice to meet you. How was your day at work?"

I smile and shrug. "The same as usual. I spend all day with lingerie."

Rob's face lights up. "Really? Do you try it on in the dressing room?" Abbey punches him lightly in the stomach as I laugh.

"Behave, birthday boy, or no treats for you tonight." Abbey grins at me as Rob looks crestfallen.

"Here." Rob takes off one of his garlands and places it around my neck. "Now you are one of us. Better?" He blinks his eyes innocently at his girlfriend, who smiles up at him adoringly.

"Shots, shots, shots." An older guy named Marvin brings over a tray of shot glasses, which everyone scrambles for. I hang back, as I don't want to drink someone else's shot, but Jon hands me one. "You've got a garland," he says, as if that explains everything. His eyes don't leave mine as everyone takes their shot. I'm wondering how drunk he is. The shot is a sweet, fruity schnapps which goes down way too easily but leaves a sticky taste in my mouth. I quickly take a long drink of beer to get rid of the taste.

Jon puts his arm around my shoulder and pulls me into him.

I wrap my arms around his waist and look up at him. "I'm really glad you're here," he whispers into my hair.

I smile. "Jon, how many drinks have you had?"

He looks back with twinkling mischief in his eyes. "Are you asking because I'm being overly enthusiastic in my affection? Or because you're wondering what we might do later?"

It was both actually, but I won't admit that out loud. I grin instead. "What do you think?"

"Hmm. I think I should be very careful about my next words, huh?"

"Probably a good idea."

Jon just grins and presses a kiss to my mouth. I've never kissed someone this much so soon.

Abbey walks up to us. "Jon, heads up." She nods her head towards the bar, and Jon peers over my head. I feel his whole body tense next to me, and his expression darkens. I try to turn around but he keeps me tight against him.

"Dammit," he mutters. I shoot him a curious look. "My ex-girlfriend just walked in." Ah, whoops. "I'm sorry," he continues, looking down at me. "I didn't know she was going to be here."

"That's okay," I reply. "Do you want to leave?" I pause. "Do you want me to leave?"

"What?" Jon looks confused. "No, we are staying right here." He lets go of me slightly so I can turn.

Abbey is still standing next to us. "She better not cause any trouble on Rob's birthday," I hear her say to Jon.

"Jon, baby!" I hear a slightly shrill posh voice say from across the room. Jon's hand is still on my waist and he tightens his grip. A few of Jon's friends seem to cluster around us. I'm getting the impression that this girl is not well liked.

A blonde wearing high heels and a tiny black dress waltzes up to us. She's very pretty, with bright blue eyes and perfect makeup. She is accompanied by two similarly dressed girls.

"Jon, so lovely to see you. You look fantastic." She stops right in front of us and looks like she is going to hug him but then seems to think better of it. "How are you?"

Jon nods. His expression is relaxed but I can feel the tension in his body under my hand. "Fine, thanks. Didn't expect you in a pub on a Saturday night."

The girl shrugs and smiles broadly at him, leaning into him in a way that accentuates her cleavage. "I like to change things, keep everyone on their toes." She seems to notice me for the first time and her expression hardens. "Who is this?" The look she gives me would make an insecure girl cower, but that's not me anymore.

I smile politely at her. "Hi, I'm Emma," I say, sticking out my hand. "Who are you?"

The girl throws me a fake smile and ignores my hand. "I'm Sarah, I'm sure Jon's mentioned me."

I act confused. "Actually, no, he hasn't. Are you a friend of his?"

Sarah's eyes narrow at me but I keep up my polite expression. "We were more than friends, honey."

I keep up my polite look. "Oh, that's nice." Jon's hand squeezes my waist as Sarah blinks sharply at me before turning her gaze back to Jon.

"Jon, can I see you a minute?" she asks him sweetly, clearly trying to get back the upper hand. "I really need to talk to you about something."

"I'm not interested, Sarah," Jon says simply. There's no malice in his voice now, just wariness.

"You're interrupting Rob's birthday," Abbey says with fire in her eyes. "There's plenty of places to sit in here, Willis. Why don't you go annoy someone else?"

Sarah's eyes flash with indignation as she spins on her 4-inch heels and walks away, her friends following.

"Pleasant girl," I mutter.

"Nicely done," Abbey says to me with a wink. "How to take down Sarah Willis in less than twenty words. We should take lessons." She squeezes Jon's arm, then moves off into the crowd.

"You okay?" Jon asks.

I turn to him in surprise. "Me? Of course. Are you okay?"

Jon smiles at me. "I feel much better after that encounter with her than I have in a long time."

"What happened?" I blurt, then I bite my lip. "Sorry, you probably don't want to talk about it."

Jon sighs, then leads me to a bench that has just been vacated. "No, it's okay. We met on the first day of uni, went out for over two years. Then I found out she had cheated on me, several times, with a guy in her economics class." Jon sighs. "I felt like such an idiot." He glances at me. "That was last year, so I broke up with her. Now she seems intent on getting me back. Shows up at these kind of places even though she hates them. Wears stupid clothing like that," he gestures towards where she has disappeared into the crowds, "which is not her usual style, or at least it wasn't. She is not the person I thought I knew."

"Did you love her?" I ask bluntly, then I wonder if it's too personal.

Jon looks thoughtful. "I thought I did, and what she did hurt a lot, but seeing Rob and Abbey together makes me realise our relationship was all skewed towards her, which isn't what it should be." He smiles at me. "I don't think she made me happy, which is the most important thing."

"I agree." I look back into the pub. "Life is too short to be unhappy."

"Want to get out of here?" Jon says suddenly. "I have some whisky at my place."

I smile slowly. "Let's go."

Jon grins, his eyes twinkling, then leaps up to say goodbye to

Rob and Abbey. They both give us a knowing look as Jon grabs my hand and pulls me out of the pub.

We saunter through the busy Saturday night Birmingham streets towards the suburbs. He has his arm around my shoulder and I cling to his waist as we make small talk. After about twenty-five minutes, we arrive at a terraced house not unlike my own. Jon unlocks the door and gestures me in, flipping the light on. The door opens into a long corridor, with several bedrooms going off to the right.

"One of my housemates isn't very well," he whispers. "I just want to check on her a sec."

"Where's your room?" I ask.

Jon points to the stairs I can see going off to the right before the living room door. "Go up the stairs, turn left, it's the big one at the end of the hall." He grins. "Bathroom is on the right if you need it. I won't be long."

I smile and head up the winding stairs. I'm touched by his compassion for his friend. I walk up the stairs and emerge onto a bland corridor. I go right, use the bathroom, then walk softly down the dark hallway. I can see moonlight on the floor through a crack in a door at the end of the hall, so I don't turn on the light. I push open the bedroom door and it squeaks. Fumbling on the wall, I find a light switch and flip it. The room is bathed in a bright light and I blink and look around.

There's a double bed directly opposite me along the back wall, with unmade chequered red and blue sheets. Across the room from that, under the window, is a desk with a closed laptop, books and a few old coffee mugs. Behind me, near the door, is a small wardrobe. The badly painted walls are covered in drawings and photos. The wall opposite the foot of the bed has a French flag and a British flag tacked to it, with scribbles across both. There are a few items of clothing on the floor, but this is the tidiest student bedroom I'd ever been in. I move into the room and drop my bag onto the desk chair, peeling off my boots as I peer out of the window to the empty street below. My eyes land on a photo above the desk. Jon is in the centre, surrounded by an older man and woman who must be his parents. A younger man and woman stand on either side. His siblings, I would guess. The woman is very pretty, with long dark hair and a colouring similar to Jon. She looks very much like him, the younger guy not so much.

I hear a creak and turn as Jon enters the room, shutting the door slowly behind him. Excitement rumbles through me.

"How is your housemate?" I ask quietly as Jon turns on a bedside lamp and turns off the main light, making the room suddenly very cosy.

"She's okay, fast asleep. I gave her some fresh water." Jon approaches and places two clean glasses on the desk. "Would you like whisky?"

"No," I state firmly. Jon looks at me in surprise. I move to him and wrap my arms around his neck. "I don't want whisky… yet."

Jon chuckles as he leans down and kisses me, gently at first, then passionately, moving to frenzied as I pull his t-shirt off, running my hands over the dark curls on his chest. I've never wanted anyone as much as I want him right now. My body is on fire with his touch. I press my hands against him and push away. He lands heavily on the edge of the bed with an intrigued look on his handsome face. With a grin, I lift my dress over my head in one smooth move. Jon's eyes darken instantly and he whistles softly.

"*Parfait*," Jon mutters in French, and from the look in his eyes, I'm guessing that means he likes it. I'm wearing black lace matching underwear. How could I not after our conversation this morning? "It's a shame it's not going to stay on very long."

I grin and move to him, slowly straddling his lap. He puts his hands on my hips as I rest on his thighs, and gently, taking his time, he runs his fingertips from the waistband of my pants up my stomach, until they slowly come to rest on the tops of my breasts. The sensations make me moan softly.

"You're so beautiful," Jon whispers as he kisses me gently, his face upturned to mine as I run my hands through his soft hair.

Without warning, he flips me onto my back and grins down at me. "But I think you're a bad girl."

"You have no idea," I whisper huskily up at him as he leans down to kiss my throat. Jon pushes his pelvis into me and I shiver at what I can feel through his jeans. "And I think you're the bad one."

Jon chuckles against my neck. "Let's find out, shall we?"

When I wake, I'm confused for a minute about where I am. I crack my eyes open and see an unfamiliar room in front of me. I hear muffled voices from somewhere. My eyes go to two flags on the opposite wall as I feel a warm naked body pressed up against mine and an arm holding me tight.

The night comes back to me. Sex, lots of sex, and whisky, followed by more sex. We couldn't get enough of each other. I smile widely into the pillow. I feel his hand on my tummy move slightly, and his breath on my neck as he stirs behind me.

Jon groans into my back and pulls me in closer. "Good morning," he whispers, kissing my neck just under my hairline.

I smile and roll towards him, murmuring, "Morning." I cover my mouth quickly. "Oops, sorry, morning breath."

Jon chuckles, his eyes still partly closed from sleep. He reaches over me and pulls something out of his bedside table. Then hands me a piece of gum, taking one for himself.

I giggle slightly as I chew. "That's a great drawer you have there." That was where the condoms came from last night. I have an IUS, mostly to control my nasty periods, but you can never be too careful. "Anything else in there I should know about?"

Jon smiles, his face pushed back into his pillow. "The pink fluffy handcuffs." He cracks an eye as I laugh. I rest my head on his shoulder and we doze for a while, legs entwined together, until my phone starts to buzz.

I mutter to myself and slide out of bed, leaving the warmth of the duvet behind. I grab my bag and search for my phone. The alarm is sounding, though I don't usually have it set for Sundays. Then I remember I had agreed to work.

"Dammit," I say.

"What's wrong?" I whirl to find Jon leaning up on his hand, watching me. His eyes take in my naked body with obvious heat, and excitement jumps in my belly.

"I have to work today," I say, moving back to the bed and placing my phone on the table, looking around for my underwear, "which means I should probably leave."

Before I can find my clothing, Jon grabs me by the waist and pulls me back under the duvet. I squeal in surprise as I fall into him, but that doesn't last long as Jon covers my mouth with his in a long drawn-out passionate kiss that leaves me breathless. I press my body up against his, feeling the hard planes of his masculine body against mine.

"You're making it very difficult to leave, Jon," I say against his mouth.

"That's the idea," he mutters with a smile, then proceeds to kiss down my throat. "Do you always work the whole weekend?"

"Not usually," I say breathlessly, as Jon moves further downwards. The duvet is covering his head but I can feel exactly where he is. "Just Saturdays, Wednesdays and Thursdays, but I'm covering for a friend." I moan softly.

"What time do you finish today?" His voice is muffled under the covers.

I squeeze my eyes shut. "Five."

"Good, I'll pick you up and we can go for dinner."

I don't reply, just moan again.

"Emma, did you hear me?"

"Yes, yes, I heard you…"

Jon chuckles, and I realise I'm going to be late for work.

*

From that day forward, Jon and I spend all of our free time together. Apart from lectures, or coursework, or exams, or when I'm working, we are together. I have never spent so much time with one person before, let alone a boyfriend, and I wonder if we'll get sick of each other. Or bored. We don't; in fact, the more time we spend together, the more attached we get. I realise after about two months that I think I am falling in love with him. I've never been in love before. It is a new and scary feeling, so I keep it to myself. I don't know if Jon feels the same. He always seems as enthusiastic to see me as I am to see him, but my previous boyfriends have taught me to be wary.

After deep discussions with me, and a lot of diligent research and soul-searching, Jon had decided to pursue law as a career. He applied for various graduate positions, but I got the impression his heart wasn't really in it. I had a vague idea forming in my mind about that.

We both had numerous exams in June of 2007, so unusually we spent several days and nights apart. Jon was extremely diligent in his studies; he wanted a top-class degree when he graduated. Because my Masters was a year, I still had a few weeks of thesis writing to do, but my lectures and exams had finished a day before Jon's. So I excitedly waited outside his building for him and his classmates, hoping to surprise him after his final exam.

Rob emerges first, takes an exaggerated breath, raises his arms and yells, "Freedom!" at the top of his lungs. I'm standing beside the door, so Jon doesn't see me as he emerges a second later. The excitement in my stomach kicks up as soon as I see him. I like watching him when he doesn't know I am there. He has his red backpack slung over one shoulder and is wearing black jeans, flip-flops and a blue t-shirt. Sunglasses rest on top of his black hair. He looks cool and confident, and he is all mine. Jon claps Rob on the back and laughs loudly. I love the sound of his laugh.

I put my fingers in my mouth and whistle sharply, a trick I learned from my grandfather years ago, and Jon turns at once, a massive grin on his face. Rob waves at me and starts chatting to a group of guys who have emerged behind Jon, as my gorgeous boyfriend makes his way over to me.

"Hey, sexy," Jon greets, before sweeping me up into a passionate embrace. "Been waiting long?"

"I haven't seen you in two days," I pout. "That's way too long."

"Hmm, I agree." Jon kisses me hard.

"Emma, we're off to the Barrel. Bring Jon along when you're done with him," Rob yells. "But don't be too long – it's celebration time!" I peer over Jon's shoulder and wave in agreement.

"I'm so not done with you," Jon murmurs into my ear.

"Your friends are celebrating," I reply, wrapping my arms around his neck. "You should join them."

"We should join them," Jon corrects, then grabs my arm and pulls me around the corner of the building. "But first."

He pushes me hard against the wall and kisses me passionately. I melt into his embrace; I love it when he loses control like this. His hands wander all over my body, kneading my breasts and cupping my arse under my skirt. I return the favour, feeling his warm skin under my palms and dipping below his waistband. Jon's lips caress my throat and I briefly open my eyes to peer up at the sky above. My gaze lands on something I don't expect and I smirk.

"Jon?" I whisper.

"Uh-huh?"

"As much as I like this, and I do," I murmur, "I really don't fancy making a porno in an alley."

Jon stops and pulls away, looking at me with confusion. I point with one finger to the wall opposite us, and Jon follows my gaze.

A security camera, located high on the wall above our heads, is trained directly on us. Jon stares at it for a moment, then bursts into laughter.

"Shall we go to the pub?" I suggest.

Jon pulls my skirt back into place. "Probably a good idea." He adjusts his jeans and grins at me.

Rob, Jon, their other classmates and I spent the rest of the afternoon and evening in the pub. It was rowdy and entertaining. Rob, and Abbey, had become really good friends since I met them. They were both bubbly, happy people, reliable and fun to be around.

It's my round so I gesture to Jon if he wants another, and he smiles and holds up his thumb. Rob waves me away; he has an almost full pint still. I grab my bag and head for the bar. It's early evening, but the pub is crowded with students, and the bar is busy. I wait patiently behind two men, looking for bar space. After they receive their drinks, they do that annoying thing where they stay at the bar to drink them, taking up valuable ordering space.

One of the blokes – a tall, skinny, brown-haired man – turns to see me.

"Sorry, love," he says with a smile, standing aside so I can get to the bar, but only just.

"Thanks, mate," I reply, moving in between the two men.

"Busy, huh?" I look up to see the man is talking to me.

I smile. "Sure is, everyone is celebrating." I glance at the barmaid, trying to get her eye so I can order.

The man leans onto the bar, facing towards me. I can smell beer on his breath and I turn my face away. "So are you celebrating the end of your exams too?"

"Of course, are you?" I wasn't really interested in talking to him but I didn't want to be rude.

"Yep. Finished today, thank God. Exams are a pain in the arse."

I smile politely back at him. "Necessary for that degree, though."

"I guess." He has the air of someone who doesn't really care about that particular fact. He studies my face and smiles. "I'm Dave. Can I buy you a drink?"

I shake my head. "No, thanks, Dave." I finally catch the barmaid's attention and lean over the bar to order in her ear. In the mirror behind her, I see Dave do a quick perusal of me, a smirk on his face. Then he looks up at his friend and leers. I will myself not to react to the creepy vibes that I am getting off him. Someone bumps into Dave from behind and he falls into me just a little too much. I lean back off the bar, shifting my weight backwards as the barmaid starts placing the pints in front of me.

"Looks like you're buying someone else's drink too," Dave comments. There is an undertone to his voice I don't like. "A lovely little thing like you shouldn't have to do that."

I shrug and resist the urge to cringe. "It's my round."

Jon and I share everything, including paying in turn. Neither of us have a great deal of money so it's only fair. Jon doesn't work, so on top of his student loan he has an allowance from his parents. He is extremely strict with his money; everything is budgeted weekly and he never spends any more. It often means that he doesn't go out if he has reached his budget.

"What's your name?" Dave asks. I had hoped my disinterested tone would deter him from further conversation, but apparently not. I watch his face in the mirror. He is staring at me with an annoyed look on his face as I don't answer. I hand over a tenner to the barmaid and wait for my change. I am really not good at confrontation like this, probably because I don't want to be rude, or say something that would make him aggressive, but I also really don't want to talk to him.

"Hey, love, I asked you a question." I turn to look at him as the barmaid hands me my change.

"I'm not sure I want to answer that," I say slowly. "No offence." I grab the two pints off the bar. "Goodbye." I don't wait to see his reaction.

As I walk away, I let out a long breath. Jon meets me partway, relieving me of his pint. "Cheers, baby."

I relax as Jon puts his arm around me and leads me back to Rob. I feel Dave's eyes on me but I don't turn around. I don't enjoy situations like that, especially with drunk strangers who won't take no for an answer. I also don't like that the guy has creeped me out so much. I try to forget about him and enjoy myself, and I pretty much have by the time I have to go to the loo.

The toilets are through a double set of doors, and up a big staircase on the second floor. I am walking down them back to the bar, in my own world, when I spot Dave standing at the bottom. I slow my descent, knowing this is not going to be good.

He looks up at me and smiles creepily, his eyes raking over me from head to toe.

"Hi. Remember me from earlier?" I nod warily. "Look, I'm sorry if I came over a little strong at the bar earlier. I didn't mean to. I was just making small talk."

"Okay," I reply. I am on the bottom step now and I pause. Dave is between me and the doorway back to the bar.

Dave smiles. "So is he your boyfriend?" I raise an eyebrow in question. "The one you bought the drink for?"

"Yeah."

"Does he always make you buy his drinks?" The friendliness in his voice is still there, but that undercurrent in his tone sets off my alarm bells.

"I'm not sure that's any of your business." I step off the bottom step and start to walk around him, but he steps in my way. My heart rate kicks up. "Excuse me, please."

"I'm just making conversation." Dave smiles.

I don't smile back. "I think we are done with this conversation." Once again, I try to step around him and once again, he blocks my route.

"Why are you in such a hurry to run off? And why won't you tell me your name?"

"Because you're creepy," I shoot back, annoyance in my voice. "You need to take a hint and back off."

Dave raises an eyebrow and laughs. "I like you, you're feisty. I'm not a bad guy, you know. Maybe you need to chill out a bit." He steps towards me and I step back immediately.

"Please get out of my way." I feel goose bumps on my skin and hear my pulse in my ears as the adrenaline kicks in. I have never felt this threatened before.

Dave steps towards me again. "All I want to do is talk." He looks me up and down again with a leer that makes me want to take a shower. "At least to start with. We could have lots of fun, you know."

I resist the urge to back up again; I'm almost at the bottom step. "Not on your life, now move out my way."

"Emma? Is everything all right?" Rob has appeared behind the creep, concern and confusion in his eyes.

Dave smirks and it's very creepy. "Emma, huh? Now I know your name."

I step around Dave and this time he doesn't stop me. Rob must have seen the relief on my face because he puts his arm around me and glares behind him at the guy. Together, we walk back to our seats. Something must have shown on my face because Jon immediately stands and looks concerned.

"What's wrong?"

"Emma was being hassled by some guy in the stairway," Rob says before I can reply. He casts a look behind him, where Dave has emerged from the doors and is staring over at us. Jon frowns, pulling me into a hug. I wrap my arms around him and try to fight off the bad feelings that guy has introduced.

"Em?"

I look up at him and smile. "I'm fine. He was talking to me at the bar earlier. I guess he didn't get the hint, because he cornered me in the stairwell." I turn to look at my friend. "Thanks, Rob, I owe you."

Rob smiles and pats me on the back. "Nah, you would have kicked him in the balls in the end."

I laugh, and feel loads better. I look up at Jon. "Can we leave? I want to do some celebrating of our own."

Jon grins and brushes his lips over mine. "Absolutely."

We both finish our drinks quickly and say our goodbyes. I feel relieved to be leaving. As I lead the way towards the exit, holding Jon's hand and pulling him behind me, I see Dave standing with a group of people, next to our exit path. My pulse kicks up again. He sees me approach and smiles creepily.

"Goodnight, Emma," he whispers as I pass. I have the urge to shower again. I feel Jon start to pause but I grip on to his hand tightly. As we reach the exit, I slow. It feels like this creepy guy is chasing me out of a pub I love. Anger surges in my veins. I can't let that happen.

"Wait here," I say to Jon. Before he can protest, I turn and head back to Dave.

He isn't looking in our direction anymore, and turns, startled, as I approach.

"You're a creep." I spit at him; people all around us turn to look at my raised voice. I point a finger at him. "If you ever talk

34

to me again, I will punch your lights out, or kick you in the balls. Whatever I feel like."

I only catch a glimpse of the absolute shock on his stupid face before I turn on my heel and head back towards Jon, who is grinning at me. Grabbing his hand, I move swiftly out of the exit and down the stairs, only slowing when we are on the street and walking away.

"Feel better now?" Jon asks as I exhale hard. He sounds amused, and impressed.

"Much better."

I relax into his embrace as he kisses the top of my head and whispers, "Remind me not to piss you off."

*

I take time off from work the next weekend and join Jon on a trip to see his sister. They had invited us down to Oxford for an ale festival on the Saturday and to stay the whole weekend. I had never met any of his family before so I was a little nervous. Neither of us had a car so we took the train. Jon's sister, Amie, met us at the train station.

Amie is three years older than Jon, and very pretty. She has the same bright green eyes and dark hair, same easy smile and outgoing personality. She lives with her husband, Mike, in a large house about fifteen minutes' walk from the city centre. The house is huge and, I guess, very expensive. Amie is a physics lecturer at Oxford University, and Mike is a lawyer. They clearly earn a lot between them. Mike is lovely; tall and slender with light brown hair and a great big smile on his face, which matches perfectly his strong northern England accent.

They cook us steaks and we sit in the garden in the late-evening sunshine. We drink a few bottles of wine between us, Jon and Amie telling stories of growing up in France.

The next morning, I wake to quiet tapping and bright sunshine. I blink my eyes open to a prettily decorated, unfamiliar guestroom and look around. I see Jon sitting in his underwear at the desk. He has brought his laptop with him. I watch him for a moment, then wrap the duvet around me and stand up. Jon is concentrating so hard, he doesn't hear me approach, jumping as I wrap my arms around his shoulders.

"Morning, gorgeous," I whisper in his ear.

Jon leans back and takes my hands. "Morning. Did I wake you?"

"Nope." I kiss his neck. "Whatcha doing?"

"Looking for jobs." He sighs. "I'm going to apply for that graduate programme I told you about."

"The one in London?"

"Yeah." Jon pauses. "There is another in Birmingham, but the law firm isn't as highly rated. Mike suggests I train in London at one of the big firms, then I can move out after a few years when I'm qualified and have experience."

I nod against his neck. "Jon, you don't sound very happy about this."

"I don't?"

"No." I move around and position myself on his lap, wrapping the duvet around us both. "What is it you really want to do?"

Jon hesitates. "I don't know, Em, but I feel this is what I should do."

"I have an idea," I study him, "but it's wild and unpredictable and might end badly."

Jon raises his eyebrows. "That sounds intriguing. What is it?"

"Instead of doing the usual, graduate from uni then find a job, which is very adult, why don't we go travelling the world?" Jon's eyebrows shoot to his hairline. I continue quickly. "Once we get a job, we'll be on a career path and earning money, which is great, but I want to explore the world first. See what other places and cultures are like." Jon is staring at me. "Maybe we could even work abroad for a while, if we find something. Or, when we come back here, we'll be much wiser and can start the job and adult stuff then."

Jon smiles slowly. "That is wild and unpredictable, but I like it."

"You do?"

Jon nods and leans in to kiss me softly. "Wild and unpredictable, just like you."

I chuckle. "There is one problem, though."

"Yeah?"

"Where do we get the money from?"

Jon pauses. "The money?"

"Yeah." I bite my lip. "I have some savings we could use, but they wouldn't last long. I suppose we could work, but then we couldn't travel as much. I don't know how we would fund it." I frown as another thought enters my head. "Plus, it's a big commitment for us, I guess." Jon looks thoughtful. "Anyway," I kiss his lips quickly, "let's think about it."

Jon smiles. "Okay." There is a knock on the door, and Jon swivels the chair around.

Amie pokes her head in, smiling widely as she sees us. I'm not sure how she manages to look so perfect while wearing zebra pyjamas and whale slippers, but she does.

"Mike's making his famous bacon and hash brown omelettes. Be down in ten or I'm eating yours!" She sticks her tongue out, presumably at Jon rather than me, then quickly closes the door.

"Your sister is pretty amazing," I comment.

Jon grins. "Yes, she is, and Mike's omelettes are even better." He picks me up and throws me on the bed, duvet and all. "Get out of bed, lazybones, or I will eat all of yours." In response, I throw a pillow at him.

The omelettes are amazing, and fill us up enough to head out to a day of ale drinking.

The CAMRA ale and cider festival is held in the town hall in the centre of Oxford. It spans over three rooms on the second floor, and showcases over fifty real ales and ciders, a high number of them locally brewed.

We are standing in the main room which holds casks of fresh ale along one side. Enthusiastic volunteers in red t-shirts exchange tokens for half or full pints over the long table. There are a good number of chairs and tables, with standing room for everyone else. It's busy, but not overly crowded. The intricately crafted ceiling is high above my head, the walls adorned with famous works of art, high up enough that no normal-sized man could damage them. It has an atmosphere that I love as soon as I walk in. The room is full of typical ale drinkers, older men with big beards and bigger bellies, and young male students, a lot of whom know Amie and stop to chat. There are quite a few women enjoying their ale, more than I've seen at ale festivals before. The air is filled with the sounds of glasses clinking, laughter and chat.

We are on our fifth half-pint, and munching on some crackers Mike had thought to bring. I'm staring up at the ceiling, studying it and thinking.

"So, Emma." Amie moves away from where Jon and Mike are discussing cooking and smiles at me. She is slightly shorter than I am, wearing a very pretty purple print dress and brown boots. "I haven't asked you yet. What are your plans after you graduate?"

I take a sip of my ale. "Well, that's a good question," I answer truthfully. "I have applied to a few accounting firms who have graduate programmes, and a few trainee jobs. But I'm not quite sure on location really." My gaze strays to Jon.

Amie smiles in sympathy. "It's a big decision, not just the job but where to move to." She pauses. "I've managed to stay where I went to uni, and now I have a job here, but I remember what a daunting prospect it was back then."

"When did you meet Mike?"

"About five years ago, here in Oxford, but not at university. Mike went to Imperial. We met at the gym." Amie rolled her eyes. "Of all places." I laugh. "So what do you want to do, Emma?"

"I do want to work in accounting. I really enjoyed my degrees, and I've worked really hard on them, but maybe not right away." I pause. "Jon and I were talking this morning about it actually. I thought maybe we could go travelling for a while, before we settled, you know."

Amie's face brightens. "What a good idea!"

Jon and Mike turn at Amie's tone.

"What's a good idea?" Mike asks his wife.

"Emma and Jon might go travelling before they start work. I think that's great, Jon."

Jon grins. "I like it too."

"The only problem is, we don't have the money to do it," I reply with a shake of my head. "Poor students and all."

Amie frowns, then her face lights up and she pats Jon's arm. "You're twenty-three now. You could use that money, you know."

I look at Amie, confused. "What money?"

Amie smiles at me. "Mamie's money. The inheritance money. This is exactly the kind of thing she would have loved you to spend it on, Jon."

I look over at Jon. He has frozen with an odd look on his face, directed straight at his sister. Amie looks at him and frowns, then she glances at me. Her expression suddenly fills with guilt. Mike cringes, taking a sip of his ale to hide it.

"Uh… you haven't told Emma about that, have you?"

Jon slowly shakes his head. Amie looks forlorn as she whispers, "*Je suis désolée, Jonny.*"

"Inheritance money?" I ask slowly, my eyes skipping between the siblings.

There is a pause. "Our French grandmother was rather wealthy. She left us all an inheritance when she died ten years ago. We get it on our twenty-third birthdays," Jon explains, not meeting my eye. "I was twenty-three in January so I have it now."

"Okay…" I say. I'm curious. "Can I ask how much?"

Amie and Jon look at each other for a moment, then Jon nods his head very slightly.

"It's 75,000 Euros," Amie replies. "Each."

My jaw hits the floor. "Each?"

Amie nods. "Plus, our parents got a large sum, and there is 25,000 Euros for each of the first five grandchildren. My mother is the only living child, so it will all come to Jon, Jac and myself eventually."

I am speechless. That is some inheritance. "Wow."

"Yeah." Amie nods. "It's how Mike and I afforded our house here." She catches Jon's gaze and grimaces, then takes her husband's arm. "Uh, Mike, I think I need a refill." Mouthing sorry at Jon, they move off.

Jon hasn't looked at me still. "So, wealthy grandmother, huh?" I try a light tone, but it doesn't work.

"Yeah."

I take a sip of my ale and glance around, waiting for Jon to sort out his thoughts and speak. After a few minutes' silence, he sighs and turns to me. "Look, Emma, I didn't tell you because—"

"It's okay," I interrupt. "Really, Jon, it's fine."

Jon sighs again. "Let me finish, please, Em. As I was saying, I didn't tell you because I was embarrassed."

"Embarrassed? About what?" I know I have interrupted but the statement sounds so absurd to me.

"That I suddenly had loads of money on my twenty-third birthday, and was technically no longer a poor student, but that I continued to act like it."

I tilt my head in confusion. "I don't understand."

Jon sighs and runs his hand through his hair, something he only does when he is stressed. "I've always been so tight with money because despite my parents being quite wealthy I've never really thought I deserved it," he says. "So, yes, they paid my uni fees and give me an allowance, and even though I inherited this money, they've continued to do that. It feels wrong when I have friends who have massive loans, or work jobs to pay their rent. I just feel... embarrassed."

I poke Jon's arm gently. "Don't be embarrassed, Jon, and don't feel bad because you didn't tell me. I understand. If you wanted me to know, you would have told me."

Jon nods. "After what we were talking about this morning, I was going to do exactly that. Then we would at least have more options in our life." He gestures around. "I wasn't going to tell you here, though."

"We would have options in our life?" I repeat, startled. "It's your money Jon. You need to decide what you are going to do with it, in your life."

Jon smiles and raises his hand to stroke my face gently. "Haven't you realised yet, Emma? You are in my life to stay." He leans down so his face is inches from mine. "Because I think I have fallen in love with you."

My breath catches in my throat and I swallow hard. "Jon."

"Yes, Emma?"

"I think I love you too."

*

I met Jon's parents the day we graduated, and Jon met mine. Jon's parents are lovely. His mother, Gaetana, was stunning, even as an older woman. She was petite, had long light grey hair and those bright green eyes. Jon's father, Alfred, was around my height, also greying, with a big smile. I could see where Jon and Amie had got their looks, and personalities, from. Amie, now pregnant, and Jason, my older brother, had both come along for our graduation too, and it was so good to see them both. Jon's younger brother, Jac, had stayed in France.

After the ceremony, we all went for lunch at a restaurant by the river. My parents are not the most social of people, preferring to stay at home with the TV than socialise, but they made an effort to be civil. My father, prevented from grilling Jon in front of his parents, was quiet. A stark difference from Alfred, who was loud and bubbly throughout the meal. My mother was clearly very proud of me for getting two degrees, and talked Gaetana's ear off almost the entire meal.

My mum and dad could be difficult, and my childhood had been strict, but they had supported me when I headed to Birmingham for university, even sending me money for rent in my third year when I needed to study rather than work full time. That financial support had been invaluable.

We ate and drank wine all afternoon. Eventually, the conversation turned to what we were going to do now. My mum had been subtly hinting that I find a job in the south of England, so I could be closer to their home. My father had already asked me what jobs I had applied for. A few weeks ago on the phone, I had vaguely mentioned our idea to my mum, but she had shot it down straight away as idiotic. I had really wanted them to be here today, so I hadn't told them we were actually doing it. I was wary the idea might upset them. I regretted that now as Jon explained our plan to the table.

"We are so looking forward to it," Jon says with a smile. I glance at my mum, who looks confused. "Tomorrow, after celebrating tonight, we will shove our stuff into Amie's car and go down to Oxford," Jon says with a smile at his sister. "Amie and Mike have said we can leave whatever we aren't taking with us at their house. A week Friday, we have tickets booked to Sydney." Amie claps her hands in excitement. "From there, we plan to visit New Zealand, then go around Asia for a few months, maybe even South and North America. We don't know how long we will be gone for, maybe a year. It should be fun." Jon reaches over and takes my hand with a smile. I chance a glance at my father; he is staring at me with irritation on his face. Jason catches my eye and gives me a 'you didn't tell them?' look. I shake my head and wince.

"You should travel around Europe too," Gaetana suggests in her soft French accent, seemingly unaware of the drama playing out on my side of the table. "It's not to be forgotten on your tour of the world." She smiles at her husband. "We got married in Rome, it was wonderful."

Alfred looks over at her and smiles lovingly. "At the end of your tour, you should come and visit us at home," he suggests, then looks at Amie. "We could make it a family event."

Amie smiles. "Yes, we need to come and visit you next year, Papa." She looks at Jon. "We'll Skype about it when you know more."

"You'll love my parents' house," Jon says to me. "We should totally do that."

As the conversation drifts to what Jon's parents are doing on their house, I chance another glance at my parents.

Mum is staring at me in confusion. "You're going away?" she asks quietly.

"I did say on the phone a few weeks ago." It is a cop-out and I know it.

She looks shocked. "You said it was an option, not that you were doing it. Sweetheart, you've worked for four years on your degrees. You'll easily be able to find a job. If you wait a year, you might not find one at all."

"It's what I want to do, Mum." I feel Jon shift next to me, squeezing my hand, and know he was listening.

Mum looks at Jason in concern. "Jason, did you know about this?"

Jason meets my eyes and nods. "Yep."

"And you didn't try to stop her?"

Jason sighs in exasperation. "Emma's twenty-two, Mum. She's an adult. She can do what she wants." He smiles at me. "Plus, I think it's a great idea, wish I had thought of it first."

My father grunts and takes a sip of his wine. He hasn't said anything yet, which is concerning.

I want them to understand. "I just want to see the world," I say. "Before I do all the adult things I am supposed to do. I've worked hard these past few years. I want to have fun for a bit."

My father grunts again and says quietly, "That's just childish."

I sigh and look down at my empty plate. No way will they ever understand. My father stands suddenly. "Come with me, I want to talk about this with you."

Reluctantly, I stand up, releasing Jon's hand and sharing a long look with Jason.

We move off the restaurant patio and along the river a few metres, my mother following us. The weather is warm today, with very little breeze, and I'm glad that I'm not wearing my cap and gown anymore.

Abruptly, my father stops and turns, his arms crossed in front of his chest in what I recognise as his 'no nonsense pose'. Bob King is a broad man, tall and strong, necessary in his business as a house builder. He is used to getting his way, and bosses everyone around, including my mum, Jason and myself. In our childhood, we had wanted for nothing, except some love and understanding from our father, and some strength and wisdom from our mother. Jason had left home as soon as he could, rather than be bullied into entering the family building business. I had ached to leave as well. Without Jason there, everything had been pointed in my direction.

"To start with," he begins, "why did we only just find out about this? In front of strangers. You could at least have had the respect to tell us yourself."

I sigh and lean on the railing. "Because I thought if I told you before, you wouldn't come today in protest, and I wanted you guys here."

Mum gasps. "What? Why would you think that?" She looks appalled. "Of course we would have been here, darling." She looks at her husband. "Wouldn't we, Bob?"

My father grunts, his standard response to my mother. "I'm sorry you had to find out like that," I reply, "but it's what Jon and I want to do."

"I haven't supported you for years for you to ruin your chances of a successful career by running off into the world with a boy who is practically a stranger," he spits out, as if we haven't spoken. "I won't stand for it, Emma. You need to find a job and earn a living, just like everyone else."

"Jon is not a stranger, he's my boyfriend. I love him."

Mum stares at me in shock, her apparent expression of the day. My father shakes his head. "You can't know that," he dismisses. "I agree that the boy has potential, and his parents have clearly done very well for themselves, and seem pleasant." Pretty much a compliment coming from him. "But people don't just go off travelling without some security at home. You have very little money, no job, and if you do this, it's doubtful you will find one. And how do you expect to pay for all this travel anyway?"

I square my shoulders and meet his eye. "That is a risk I am willing to take, and I have enough money to live for a while."

"It is a stupid and unnecessary risk to take. Either you stop this nonsense right now, or I expect you to pay back the money I have given you over the last few years."

I freeze. "What?" I had to have misheard.

My father nods. "Yes. I have it calculated already, the money I gave you for rent in your third and fourth years. I expect it to be paid back immediately." He leans down and looks me in the eye. "But if you stay here, get a job, and work, you don't have to pay it back."

"You can't be serious?" I ask in shock. I never expected him to stoop this low.

"I am, Emma."

"No." Both our heads snap to my mother, who has been standing there, listening to us. "No, Bob, you can't do that."

My father frowns at her and looks confused. "Of course I can."

"But you won't. We may not agree with Emma's decision, but Jason is right. She is an adult, the decision is hers. I won't let you blackmail her. She'll end up hating us. That's not acceptable."

I am shocked. I have never heard my mum stand up to my dad before.

Apparently, my father has never heard it either. "Linda…"

"No. You gave Emma that money to support her studies. What you threaten is underhanded and pathetic."

My father's eyes widen until I think they're going to explode from his head. My mother turns to me with a forced smile.

"You can go back to the table now, darling. We'll be along shortly."

Nodding, still in a state of shock, I walk back to the table. Jon and Jason look up as I sit down.

"You okay, Em?" Jason asks. "What did Dad say?"

I sit down hard, then glance back over my shoulder at them. I can see Mum wagging her finger at Dad, a stern expression on her face. My dad has dropped his arms and is staring at her in shock.

"Mum told Dad off for threatening to take my money," I say slowly, turning back around. "I never knew she had it in her."

Jason looks shocked as well, peering over my shoulder at them with wide eyes.

"I guess your mum is stronger than you think," Jon whispers in my ear. I meet his gaze and nod, still slightly stunned.

"Don't worry, Emma." Gaetana leans across the table and takes my hand. "Being a parent is very hard, but they only want what is best for you in the end. Sometimes, that and what you want do not always coincide, yes?"

I smile at her. "More often than not."

Gaetana smiles sympathetically. "When you have children of your own, you will understand."

Chapter 2

Army Part 1

September 2003

My first impression of being an army cadet was that I just didn't have what it took to make it. I didn't like being shouted at; I didn't like being ordered around; I didn't like that I couldn't have a coffee every morning; I didn't like sharing a room with fourteen girls; I really didn't like showering with fourteen girls.

I thought the food was terrible; the days started at 0500 and often didn't end until after 2000. We ran no matter the weather in big boots that gave me blisters; we sat in stuffy classrooms and were yelled at while wearing stiff and uncomfortable clothes. After two weeks, I knew I had made the wrong decision and was filled with regret. It felt petty, but the one thing that got me through those early days was knowing that if I dropped out, I would have to face my father's smug face when he found out. When I told them my decision, he had laughed, telling me I wasn't cut out to be in the British army. My mother had looked sad and asked me to change my mind.

My older brother, Jason, had been the only one who had supported me. He'd driven me to ATC Pirbright, near Woking, given me a massive hug and told me to go kick some arse.

I had joined the Royal Corps of Engineers as a recruit. The recruiter who had handled my application and assessment centre had said it matched my skill set and qualifications. I could even achieve a degree eventually, paid for by the army. I'd never considered engineering before but I was good with numbers and physics so I agreed. The recruiter had also said that competent female engineers were highly sought-after, both in the army and outside it, but I really wasn't thinking that far ahead. He had suggested I become an officer, but I wasn't interested in being a leader. I could make that decision further down the line if I wanted to.

No matter what corps you apply for, phase 1 training is always the same. The recruit corps was sixty strong: fifteen girls and forty-five boys. Our instructors told us that, on average, only 75% of us would graduate the course. More than half of the girls would drop out. I wasn't sure this statistic was right. Those weren't the figures in their marketing material, but I kept that to myself.

I excelled at the classroom work, especially the technical and mathematical side. The strategic and tactical thinking exercises I was pretty sure I would pick up; that was more to do with experience. It was the physical side I was failing. I thought I had been in a reasonable state of fitness – I had been running and swimming since I was a kid – but I had been very wrong. I had passed the entrance fitness test, though not by much, and I found the runs and training exercises we did exhausting, always finishing near the end and having painful, aching muscles the next day.

When my section commander told us that in a few weeks we had another fitness test, and I needed to pass both the bleep test and the obstacle course in an acceptable time in order to continue, I started to panic. What if they threw me out? So I picked up my pace in the runs, over exerting myself but improving my time. I was constantly exhausted. After the first three weeks, we were given Sunday afternoons off. I spent them running around the base and doing the obstacle course in a panicked effort to ensure I didn't fail.

On my third loop of the course one Sunday, I caught two male recruits watching me from under a tree. It was a cool day, cloudy with occasional rain. I recognised them, though I had never spoken to either. I didn't know any of the others very well, even the girls I shared a room with. There wasn't much chance for socialising and, frankly, I felt awkward around new people anyway.

So I simply ignored them. Across the field, I saw them start the course too and I groaned inwardly. They would catch me up in no time. I had a real problem with my upper body strength, in that I had none. I wasn't a petite girl, my 5"9' height and less than slender body meant I had a lot of weight to carry on my arms. The monkey bars really challenged me. I would make it about halfway across before my shoulders would give out and I'd fall to the ground. My goal today was to make it all the way across. I wasn't going to my bed to rest until I did.

My shoulders burn as I try for the third time in a row. My arms give out and I collapse onto the ground, panting heavily as I crouch. Sweat covers my body and I angrily push my hair off my forehead; the stupid fringe is too short to go into my bun.

I hear the blokes behind me, running up the ladder which leads onto the monkey bars, and I move out of the way. Keeping my back to them, I stretch my shoulders carefully, feeling the muscles twinge. I hear laughter behind me and turn involuntarily to see a tall, dark-haired bloke swing effortlessly along the monkey bars. He comes to the end, glances at me and winks, then continues the course. The guy behind him also completes the bars easily, yelling in a Welsh accent at the other bloke that he is a stinking cheater.

I fume to myself. They make it look so damn easy. Now the bars are clear I start again, but again I fail to make it all the way across.

Cursing myself, I note the two guys are running the course again. I step out of the way, placing my hands on my hips, and watch them with annoyance as they easily swing along the monkey bars.

"How the hell do you do that so easily?" I yell as the first guy finishes. He looks at me, startled, then grins widely.

"It's all about momentum, love," he calls out, making me feel a stab of anger at the word. There is no mistaking this guy is Scottish. "Use your body weight to propel you across the bars. Then it's all about the muscle." He sticks out his arm in a body builder pose, winks at me again and runs off. I glare after him. What an arse.

The Welshman drops off the bars about halfway across and regards me with curiosity. "This is your weakness, huh?"

He catches me by surprise. "Excuse me?"

The Welshman shrugs his wide shoulders. He is only a fraction taller than me. "We've been watching you. Everything else you can do really well. You're the teacher's pet on the academic stuff," he scrunches up his face, "but you can't do the simple monkey bars?"

"Yeah," I admit with a defeated sigh. "If I can't do the monkey bars I can't complete the course, then the rest of that stuff doesn't matter."

"Too right." The Scotsman runs up. "I guess you're just too much of a girl to do it."

I bristle; my anger turns onto him. "That has nothing to do with it."

The Scotsman laughs. "It has everything to do with it." He reaches over and pinches my arm, and I swat away his hand. "You've got girl arms that go with your girl body." He grins. "A mighty fine girl body but it won't get you across the monkey bars."

I look at him in disgust. What a creep. "Let me guess, you are one of these sexiest guys that think girls don't belong in the army?"

The Scot shakes his head. "Nope. I just think if you can't do the monkey bars you don't belong in the army."

I growl at him as he smirks, then without a word I stalk off towards the ladder. I climb it swiftly as his words echo in my head. Use my momentum. The two guys watch me with interest as I pause at the top.

Gritting my teeth, I swing down. Kicking out my legs, I use my body weight to propel my next hand to the bar. Again and again, I move my hands, ignoring the scream in my arms and shoulders. I keep going, my eyes focused on the final bar, until suddenly I am there. I drop to the ground, my arms shaking, feeling like they are about to fall off.

I hear clapping behind me and spin around. The Scotsman and Welshman are grinning broadly at me. They look pleased, and oddly proud.

"Knew you could do it, love."

"Don't call me love," I snap. The Scot holds up his hands, the grin still in place.

"I'm Trent McTavish. I thought that girl comment would fire you up." I look at him in surprise, then it clicks.

"You did that on purpose?"

"Of course he did." The Welshman laughs. "He's an arsehole, and you needed motivation. Nothing like anger towards an arsehole for motivation. I'm Rhys Jones, and you are...?"

"Emma King."

"Ha!" Trent laughs. "A Scot, a Welshman and an English girl called King."

"Sounds like the start of a dirty joke." I pause as they grin at me. "Thanks."

Rhys shrugs. "Ah, think nothing of it, you would have got it eventually."

Trent claps me hard on the back. "Now what do you say we have a race, English?"

*

Trent, Rhys and I become virtually inseparable during the rest of our basic training. So much so that one of the instructors begins to call us the three musketeers. I began to enjoy the training more and more, putting my earlier thoughts of regret way behind me. Trent and Rhys were typical eighteen–year-old boys; cocky, foulmouthed and horny. As such, a lot of our conversations revolved around sex, even if they didn't start out that way. I wasn't a virgin, but I had limited experience, which I was sure showed. However, I found that I also had a rather smutty mind, and my confidence in my body, and what I could do with it, only grew over time. The boys seemed to enjoy my company, especially when I began adding my own feminine inputs to their male conversations. We traded stories, jokes and observations about the world, even when we were covered in mud.

The three of us were a team, the first team I felt I had ever really belonged to. They helped me with my fitness, pushing me past my limits to a pace I never would have tried before, in ways that made it fun. I passed all my fitness tests with flying colours. I helped them with classroom work. Rhys was clever but disinterested, preferring to be outside than studying. Trent clearly wasn't meant for academic achievement, but he was stubborn and tried hard, just about passing the classes.

We graduated our Phase 1 training after fourteen weeks. My parents even turned up for my passing-out parade, much to my surprise. I then said goodbye to Trent and Rhys, as the next phase was corps specific. I was sad to see them go.

I had chosen the role of survey engineer in the Royal Corps of Engineers, so next I completed my military engineer combat course, which lasted for nine weeks, at the Royal School of Military Engineering regiment near Camberley. I found I really had a knack for mechanical and civil engineering, and achieved high marks in both the theory and the practical exercises. After that, I transferred to the Royal School of Military Engineering in Chatham for twenty-seven weeks to complete my Class Two surveyor engineer course. I was one of only three girls in this part of my training.

Almost one year after I joined the army as a recruit, I officially became a private, or sapper. I was finally in the army.

I worked within the engineering teams, headquartered at Chatham for six months. It was there I started to get interested in furthering my engineering skills and took several additional courses to increase my skills set. I was deployed overseas for the first time to Cyprus, working with civilian teams on a wide range of civil engineering projects. Up to this point, I hadn't met any guys who I could have been involved with, let alone that I was interested in. Then I met Edward Lang. He was a University of Birmingham engineering student on a year in industry, sponsored by one of the civil contracting companies we worked with. Edward had dark exotic looks and bright blue eyes. I had noticed him a few times on our sites. He came up to me one evening in a bar where my army colleagues and I were all relaxing, and gave me a cheesy one-liner which had me in stitches for ages. Once I had calmed down, we flirted, and he asked me out for a drink. I looked over at him thoughtfully; he was hot, smart and funny. That old urge to run and cower came back for an instant, but I pushed it down. I was an army engineer, not a coward. I agreed to see him and we went out the next Sunday afternoon, my only time off in the week. Edward and I dated for six weeks, breaking up when I returned to the UK after my seven-month deployment ended. I was sad when I left, but I didn't want a long-distance relationship of any kind. I had the feeling Edward felt the same way.

I was promoted to lance corporal on my return to the UK, which I was ecstatic about. Now I could run some small projects of my own, really honing all my engineering skills. Once I came back from two weeks' leave, I found out my next deployment. Iraq.

To say I was nervous to be heading into a war zone was an understatement. I had met soldiers who had come back from the Middle East, and some of the stories they had told me made me want to turn tail and run.

The British invasion of Iraq as part of the US war on terror in 2003 had hardly gone unnoticed by me. When I had joined the army, I had known this might be a possibility. So I took a deep breath, accepted my assignment and stepped confidently onto the plane.

It was a standard US C130 cargo plane. Designed to haul cargo, it was bereft of the luxuries of modern planes. I had a nine-hour flight ahead of me on an uncomfortable bench. There were around twenty soldiers sitting there when I stepped into the dark interior, most of them already sleeping or making small talk with each other. I shifted my one bag on my shoulder and looked around for a seat, my eyes adjusting to the gloom.

"English!" My eyes snap to the far end as my eyes fall upon Trent. "What the hell are you doing here?"

The brash tone of the Scot means I get more than a few odd looks as I step my way carefully to the far end. "Going on holiday," I reply sarcastically as I walk. "I need a suntan." I get a few chuckles and grins from the other blokes. I note that some of them are officers. I need to be more careful with my tone. "What do you think I'm doing, Scotty?"

Trent stands up and pulls me in for a big hug. "Ah hell, they've assigned you too? Must be getting desperate over there."

Despite his words, I know the man well enough to detect concern for me. I draw back. "No need to go all macho on me, Trent. I've been doing just fine without you, you know. Is Welshie assigned too?"

"He's on leave this week, visiting his girlfriend back home. But he'll be heading our way next week. Rhys will be psyched you're with us." Trent grins and sits back down on the already full bench.

"Here." The dark-haired lieutenant who had been sitting next to Trent stands up. "You can take my seat next to your friend."

"Sir? Are you sure, sir?"

"Definitely, or I'm guessing the private here will shout your conversation across the plane." As he passes me, he says quietly, "Plus, he hasn't stopped talking since I got here, not sure I can handle nine hours of that."

I resist the urge to laugh, but smile instead. "Thank you, sir, much appreciated."

The lieutenant smiles and heads back down the plane to find another seat.

Trent pats the bench beside him with a wide grin. I return the grin; it is going to be a good nine-hour flight.

*

I spend the next nine months in almost, but not quite, front line civil engineering situations. My unit, which included support from Trent, Rhys and other combat soldiers, rebuilt roads and buildings destroyed in the bombings. As the only woman on my unit, I often found I was the one explaining to the community what we were doing. Local men, and women, just responded to me better than anyone else, despite my awful Arabic.

Iraq itself was hot, dusty and contained some of the worst poverty I had never imagined. The streets were dangerous, even for fully combat-ready troops. It was also home to some of the most amazing historical and architectural buildings I had ever seen, and a lot of the people, especially the women who had been deprived under the fallen regime, were simply lovely to me. All they wanted was peace so they could raise their children. I hoped that by rebuilding critical infrastructure I was helping them do that. I was under no illusions that we were the outsiders in their society though, and I always watched my back. Despite all this, I loved my work. I loved being in the army. I couldn't imagine doing anything else.

When I returned to the UK, it was like another world. No longer did I have to study everyone who approached me for possible weapons, or carry a gun with me at all times, or wear heavy combat uniform in the sweltering heat. Everyone spoke English. It took a little getting used to.

After my leave, which I spent with Jason in London, I spent a month in Wales on a training exercise with Trent and Rhys, then another six weeks at Chatham once again, including a project management and leadership combat course.

I had glowing references from my commanders in Iraq, and with my additional qualifications under my belt I was quickly promoted to corporal. Once again, shortly after this promotion, I received new orders. Another overseas deployment. This time, Afghanistan.

*

I'd been in the country less than a month when my commanding officer indicated to me I should be expecting new orders at any time. I was concerned and asked if I was being transferred because I wasn't doing a good job. He gave me a secretive little smile and replied cryptically, "You've been doing too good a job, Corporal. Someone has noticed and pulled some strings." But he wouldn't elaborate further than that. So I was left to wait. The orders had arrived yesterday morning, an unexpected twenty-second birthday message along with the cards from my friends and family back home. I'd been shocked at what exactly they contained. As much as I'd miss my unit, Trent and Rhys and the rest, this was new and exciting for me, and a great opportunity.

So I sat in the back of the supply truck, in a long convoy, and I watched as the run-down houses and small markets passed by outside. The dust and sand got in my mouth and nose. The tight braid at the back of my head, which I always wore to keep my shoulder-length hair out of the way and off my face, allowed air to circulate on my neck, but I could feel the sweat run down my spine. The many layers of camouflage and protective clothing, though designed to be as cool as possible, just weren't satisfactory in this heat. By now, I was used to this. The sweat, like the sand, got everywhere.

I rocked with the motion of the truck as it turned a corner, and I readjusted my helmet as it fell slightly to the left. We were heading out of the towns now, down small dirt but well-maintained roads. The convoy paused as it passed through another security checkpoint; we weren't far from the largest US army base now.

I stare out the back as the truck pulls through the gates. A uniformed soldier with an auto M90 appears around the truck and I show him my British Army ID and orders. He takes them from me, glances through them briefly, then moves towards his tiny office. After a few minutes, he comes back out, hands me back my papers and a US ID card. The card has my name and a barcode on it, nothing else. "This is a temporary pass," he states in a broad American accent. "You'll need to see security and get a permanent one A-sap." I nod that I understand. The soldier waves the truck through and smiles at me as I pass. "Have a nice day." I guess I'm going to have to get used to the accent.

I'd never been to the US military base outside Bagram before; it was a long way from Camp Bastion. There were US troops stationed there too but we kept pretty much to ourselves among the lower ranks. I'd met US units out in the field, of course, but we each had our own assignments and orders to be getting on with. Chit-chatting was not permitted, nor wise in the open streets.

The truck stops jerkily in the shade of an aircraft hangar. I grab my bag and jump out, slinging it over my shoulder. Now we are behind the security fence, I remove my helmet and strap it to the bag, placing my baseball cap on my head instead in an attempt to keep off the sun.

"Do you know where you're going?" The supply truck's driver comes round to me, a friendly smile on his face. Americans are always eager to smile; I like that.

I shake my head. "I have to report to Colonel Jenson."

The driver nods and points to a cluster of low buildings on the other side of the airfield we have parked next to. "His office is in a building over there, near the far end. The airfield's pretty busy so I'd stick to the sides."

I want to reply, *well, duh,* but I don't. He wouldn't take kindly to my sarcasm, and you never piss someone off when you don't have to. "Thank you," I reply instead, nodding once, then turn on my heel and walk away.

I follow the edge of the airfield towards the buildings. It is late afternoon, and I can see army teams starting to return from the field on the other side from where I walk. The sun is high and hot, the air dry and dusty.

The army base is one of the largest in the country, with a high perimeter fence and at least a kilometre of empty land in every direction. I spot several off-duty personnel in army shorts jogging around the fence line and am glad they did do that here too. I need to run to work off my adrenaline after a day in the field. I leave the airfield perimeter and head into the shade of the low white buildings. I glance between and into them as I pass. Mostly supply stores, vehicle maintenance, truck and Humvee parking. At Bastion, the sleeping and personnel areas are in the middle of the base; I suspect they will be here too. There are no signs, as expected. I pass an open doorway and see a soldier, a private judging from his insignia, sitting down on a box, reading a book.

"Excuse me," I say loudly. The soldier jumps up quickly, as if I had just caught him doing something he shouldn't have. "I'm looking for Colonel Jenson's office. Can you point me in the right direction, please?"

The soldier looks me up and down. "Please may I first see identification, Ma'am?"

"Of course," I hand him my temporary US ID, "and it's Corporal, Private."

The private looks sheepish. "Apologies, Corporal. Let me show you to the Colonel's office."

"Thank you, Private." I follow the soldier down between the buildings. He takes a left, then a right.

"Through here." He opens a door for me into a nondescript building which could have housed anything.

"Many thanks, Private." The soldier nods and heads away.

I enter a small, cosy office and immediately feel the refreshing blast of the air con unit. I remove my cap and smooth back strands of hair from my face. There are two soldiers sitting casually on chairs in the small room, but I pay them no attention. A young woman in a pressed uniform looks up from her desk and smiles. "May I help you?"

"Good afternoon, I'm here to see Colonel Jenson. I'm Corporal King. He should be expecting me."

The young woman glances down at her computer monitor then up again. "Yes, Corporal, you can go right on through." She stands and opens the door to her left, standing to the side to let me pass.

I nod my thanks and step into the room.

A greying, middle-aged man sits behind a long metal desk. Two chairs are perched in front of the desk. The floor is light blue and makes the room seem bigger despite the lack of windows. Several photos and framed pages sit on the few surfaces in the room. The Colonel glances up as I enter. I drop my bag by the door as the woman closes it, and stand to attention.

"Corporal Emma King. Reporting as ordered, sir."

The colonel comes round the desk and nods. "At ease, Corporal." I relax into the ease posture.

He holds out his hand. "Michael Jenson. Pleasure, Corporal King. Welcome to Bagram Air Base." I shake his hand formally.

"Thank you, sir."

"Please take a seat, Corporal. I trust your journey here was uneventful."

"It was, sir." I sit in the left-hand chair, keeping my back straight and head high.

"Excellent. Tell me, Corporal, were you expecting the orders that you received yesterday morning?"

"I was expecting new orders, sir. Colonel Mayfield told me several days ago I was being reassigned. But no, I did not expect my reassignment to be a secondment to the US Army."

Jenson smiles slightly. "And I trust you understand the reasons why?"

"I think so, sir, but it might be clearer if you explain in detail."

"Of course. As you should be aware, the US Army, as part of our mission in Afghanistan, is undergoing a radical rebuilding of crucial infrastructure. Mainly roads, industrial buildings and schools." I nod and he continues. "We have several key projects lined up which will help the country to get back up and running, but we have been encountering resistance in some of the local communities. Communication is key. However, a lot of the local men do not trust our soldiers, and the women are culturally unable to speak to our men. It has therefore been decided that a female officer or soldier is to be assigned to each unit to enable this communication, and preferably be able to work on the projects as well. It is… unusual to find a female soldier with technical engineering abilities, especially one with experience. We are increasing our intake of female engineers, of course, but that takes time." The colonel smiles faintly at me. "When I heard about yourself, a female British soldier and engineer on her second tour in the Middle East, I realised you would be perfect for several of our more crucial projects." He tilts his head. "I had to pull in quite a lot of favours to have you assigned to us, Corporal."

"I see," I reply, at a loss as to what to say. "Well, I hope I can help, sir. In Iraq, I was assistant project engineer on several key infrastructure projects."

"Yes, Corporal, there is no need to go through your resume. I have it here." He holds up a piece of paper briefly. "You'll be assigned to our 6th Battalion, Unit Bravo, operating under Major Jonathan Xavier. A mixture of engineers and soldiers, officially not assigned to the front lines," the colonel states. Female personnel are technically not permitted on the front lines, though I have seen myself how often that line can be blurred. "As of now, you are formally assigned to the US Army for the remainder of your tour. Therefore, you must abide by its rules and regulations." He holds up a thick A4 folder. "I imagine they are similar to the British Army, but I expect you to have studied this thoroughly before going out in the field." He passes over the folder to me.

"Yes, sir."

"There is one other thing, Corporal. You may be aware that there has been increased chatter regarding female US, British and NATO officers among insurgents, especially ones doing crucial community and engineering jobs." I raise an eyebrow and nod. I had seen that on the security briefing yesterday. "I don't know what the Brits are doing regarding it, but orders have come down from high up that under no circumstances are we to allow our female personnel to become targets. Therefore, every female soldier in critical community roles such as yours will be assigned male soldiers as a security detail."

I narrow my eyes as his words sink in. "I'm to have bodyguards, sir?" My tone of disgust must register, because the colonel leans forward, his expression stony.

"No point arguing with me, Corporal, it will be done. I have no doubt you do not need it. But as I see it, when you are doing your job, building these schools and talking to the local women, you don't need to be constantly watching over your shoulder for danger, that's what they will do. Watch your back."

"With respect, sir," I say politely but firmly, and with just a tab of cheek, "who will watch their backs?"

The colonel's mouth twitches. Apparently, he likes my attitude. He presses a button on his desk phone. "Cindy, send them in, please." The door behind me opens and I hear several heavy boot steps stop just behind me.

The colonel rises and looks behind me. "Corporal. These are the men from your unit who will be assigned to watch your back." I stand slowly, turning to see two hulking great men in full camo standing to attention behind me. One has bright blond hair and is very tall, at least 6'3". The other has dark features and stands at 6 foot.

"This is Sergeant Rick Tavern." The blond nods at me. "And Sergeant Paulo Vega. Gentlemen, this is Corporal Emma King, assigned to us from the British Army."

The blond catches my eye and I think I see a hint of amusement on his face before it vanishes.

"Pleasure to meet you, Ma'am," he says as I shake his hand in greeting.

"Corporal King will do, thank you, Sergeant Tavern," I say formally. I really hate being called Ma'am. This time, the blond can't hide his smirk, his light brown eyes dancing with laughter. The other man nods in polite greeting as I shake his hand also.

"I have already briefed Tavern and Vega," the colonel says to me, and I turn back to him. "At all times in the field, one of them will be within 5 feet. I will leave it up to the three of you to decide how that will work." He nods between us all. "The unit will meet at zero seven hundred tomorrow to discuss projects and strategy and you will be introduced to the rest of the unit. Tavern will take you around the base tonight, get your paperwork in order and such."

"Yes, sir. Thank you, sir." I nod and follow the men out of the room, stooping to pick up my bag from the floor. We step into the dusty heat and the men each place their caps on and start walking. I heft my bag and the folder, place my own cap firmly on my head and follow them.

"May I take your bag for you, Corporal?" Tavern asks. I give him a sideways glance; he is definitely smirking at me.

"No, thank you," I reply coolly. "I think I can manage." Tavern smirks widely at my response. Clearly an arrogant jackass.

"So how do you guys feel about babysitting duty?" I ask. I'm curious. It's not exactly front line, exciting work.

Vega shrugs. "We follow orders."

"Way I see it," Tavern says, all trace of humour gone, "you're doing important work, rebuilding for these people, liaising with the community where others can't. We need to make sure you can keep doing that." He shrugs. "It's what we do."

Good words; I guess my initial first impression of the blond has been off.

"So you were at Camp Bastion?" the other one, Vega, asks over his shoulder, and sees my nod. "How did you get here?" Vega has cropped black hair, light brown skin and a strong jawline under a perfectly sculpted black beard.

"I hitched a ride on a supply truck," I tell him, then smile, deciding to test the waters. "I was going to get a taxi, but you know, so unreliable around here."

Tavern laughs. "Who knew the Brits had a sense of humour?" he says to Vega, who is smiling broadly. He turns to peer at me from under his cap. "Are you sure you're a Brit?" I take back my good thoughts and scowl.

"As sure as I can tell you're American by your cocky attitude," I shoot back.

Tavern laughs again. "A bit defensive, aren't we?"

I glare at him and press my lips together to bite back my response. This guy is clearly rubbing me up the wrong way on purpose. I am going to be spending a lot of time with him, so I need to quell those urges to be snarky.

"Well, catch you later, Rick," Vega says, starting to head between two buildings away from us. Then tips his cap at me and smiles widely. "Corporal."

I nod in response as Vega walks away.

Tavern keeps walking steadily forward. We are moving into a busy part of the base. Men and women in uniforms scurry past holding clipboards, boxes or weapons. It is all very relaxed but clearly organised. I examine the uniforms as I walk. Everyone has the same light beige and green camouflage pattern, with black t-shirts underneath. Worn in different styles depending on their jobs. Almost everyone wears a baseball cap, if they aren't wearing a helmet. I get a few glances as I walk next to Tavern. British army camouflage is a slightly different shade to that of the US. Not enough to look different from far away or to a novice, but enough that in this crowd I stand out like a sore thumb.

"I suggest I show you the women's bunk house first," Tavern says, nodding and smiling at a group of jogging marines we pass. "Then you don't have to carry your bag around while we do the admin tasks."

"That's fine," I reply.

We don't make small talk, and after a few minutes of walking, Tavern turns left down a wide stretch between large sturdily built warehouses. We move aside quickly as a group of camouflaged large men run past, weapons shining in the sun. Special Forces, I presume. Tavern turns again at the end of the left warehouse and points ahead. "The living quarters are here, in the centre of the base, as is the mess where meals are served." Tavern points to his right where a huge, low white tent stands, looking out of place among the large steel buildings surrounding it. There are a number of benches outside, where a few off-duty soldiers lounge with mugs. The tent itself appears sealed, no doubt to keep the air conditioning in, and through the transparent airlock I see many tables and a long food counter on the far wall. "There are several of those dotted around the base, and a few restaurants as well. The menus change constantly so there is lots of variation in cuisine."

We pass the mess quickly and head towards a group of buildings indistinct from the others. They are set around a square and lots of people swarm about. Tavern points directly ahead. "The gym, laundry and computers are in that building," he states calmly, looking straight ahead. "Washroom facilities and showers are in cabins down that alley and behind it. Separate male and female, of course." He seems to smirk to himself. "That is male bunk room Alpha," Tavern gestures to the right, where I see several men enter a set of double doors, "and the female bunk rooms are directly opposite. There are three sets of bunks on the base: Alpha, Beta and Delta." Tavern turns to the left, where an identical set of automatic double doors sit at the entrance to the building. He enters and turns immediately to the wall next to it. There is a white board pinned to the wall, with names and numbers scrawled in different coloured pens. I look behind me and around. The building is about five stories high and contains what looks from the outside like shipping containers, but I see is actually prefab construction. A double door is behind me and I peer down the corridor to see bedroom doors coming off it at regular intervals. The corridor is very long and winds to the right at the far end. A winding metal staircase sits a few metres to the left of the doorway, leading up to four floors above.

Tavern expertly scans the board. "King, King, King..." I hear him mutter. I go up on tiptoes and peer over his shoulder as I scan the board myself. He is annoyingly tall.

"There." He points at my name scribbled in red pen amidst a sea of black. "You are in bunk 15 on the second floor. Sharing with a Second Lieutenant Grenal." He steps back. "I'll wait here for you. Don't be too long."

I raise an eyebrow at his tone but don't reply, instead turning towards the stairs. I feel his eyes on me as I head up to the second floor. The corridor is drab and unexciting; the floor lino is quiet under my boots. I watch the door numbers as I pass, looking in curiously at the open doors, smiling when a woman catches my nosy gaze. I reach 15 and see the door is open. A young redheaded woman sits on the left bunk, making notes in a large black book.

"Hi," I state, and she looks up in surprise. "Room 15?"

The woman smiles widely. "Howdy. You must be King, my new bunkmate." I think her accent is southern US.

I smile and hold out my hand, slinging off my baseball cap with the other and running my hand over my tight brown braid. "Emma King, nice to meet you."

The woman stands up and shakes my hand, a curious look on her face. "Alison Grenal. Hi."

I smile and place my bag at the foot of the empty bed opposite Grenal's, tossing the folder on the sheets. There is less than a metre of space between the two bunks, each side of the room identical. The bed is single, with starched white sheets and a pillow with a reading lamp over it. The foot of the bed is tall and is suitable for hanging towels over. A small bedside table with a drawer sits next to the head. A small open pine wardrobe is at the foot of the bed, and I can see stacks of cammies, t-shirts, vests and shorts, along with a towel and some jackets. Grenal's side is neat and tidy, with a few books perched on the floor outside the wardrobe and clothes hanging on the end of the bed.

"So how has your day been?" Grenal asks, perching on the edge of her bed.

I shrug. "Hot and dusty, of course," I reply, taking off my field jacket and hanging it on a hook on the wall. "But fine, thanks."

Grenal glances at my uniform and looks confused. "Are you British?"

"I am," I reply, smiling down at her as I shed my t-shirt and replace it with a fresh one. I had long ago lost my modesty about stripping in front of strangers. I check to make sure my dog tags stay around my neck and my standard issue 9mm is safe in its holster on my hip. "I've been seconded to the US Army due to my engineering skills and female attributes."

Grenal laughs. "Cool. That should make things interesting at least. My last roommate was such a bore."

"What do you do?"

"I work in media relations," she states. "So if I sleep talk and it sounds like I'm being interrogated, it's just a radio or TV interview I'm dreaming about." She smiles widely.

I laugh and shrug. "At Bastion, I shared with five women. This is luxury." I grab my papers and ID and place them in my trouser pocket, shrugging into a US-issue lightweight jacket I know will be suitable for wearing about the base.

Grenal smiles widely. "Do you have someone to show you around?"

I nod. "Yeah, he's waiting downstairs."

"Who?"

"Sergeant Tavern."

Grenal smiles knowingly. "He's a cute one."

I glance at her. "Is he? I can't say I noticed." I actually hadn't.

Grenal just keeps smiling, so I change the subject. "Anything I should know? About being here?"

Grenal looks thoughtful, and she tosses her red locks over her shoulder. "There are restrooms just down the hall for washing your face, and teeth, etcetera. Showers are outside behind the gym. Dirty laundry is collected from the end of the hall and done en masse, but there are washing machines in the shower rooms too for your underwear and stuff. Everyone comes and goes a lot so if you don't want to be disturbed, close the door." She gestures to a key on the bedside table. "We can lock the door if you want but I have never had any problems." I nod. "Men aren't permitted in here after nightfall, same for women in the men's bunks." She shrugs. "I think that's about it."

"Great, thanks." I look at my watch. "I should probably go meet Tavern."

Grenal smiles and waves her hand. "I'm sure he's having a great time watching the ladies come in and out."

That made me pause and I ask slyly, "You're giving me the impression he is a bit of a ladies' man."

Grenal smiles. "That's his reputation."

"Is it justified?" I didn't take much stock in rumour.

Grenal looks thoughtful again. "He flirts a lot," she says slowly. "Though now you mention it, I have never actually met anyone who says they've done more than that with him." Grenal smiles widely. "But then that's not exactly allowed around here."

"I'm sure," I reply. "Well, I will see you later probably."

"You betcha."

I smile at her and leave the room. I come out of the second-floor door and start down the stairs. I see Tavern leaning on the wall, arms crossed, right where I left him. He has rolled up the sleeves of his jacket and tucked it behind him, holding his baseball cap in hand. His short, scruffy blond beard covers a neutral but alert expression as he watches around him. Without thinking, I glance down at the rest of him; slender waist, strong shoulders and arms, one with a bold black geometric tattoo circling it, all under that form-fitting black t-shirt. That bright blond hair stands out a mile away. Grenal is right; he is good-looking. Then he glances in my direction and his eyes do the same inspection down me as I descend towards him. The jacket I am wearing is open, and not as bulky as my field uniform. I suspect my black t-shirt is equally as form-fitting as his. His eyes narrow as they skirt back up to my face, and a smirk plays on his lips as I clear the last step and walk towards him.

"All done?" he asks as I stop in front of him. I barely reach his chin, and I'm taller than average. I nod once. "Took you long enough, King." I note the drop of my rank and more casual use of my surname, but I don't mind.

I shrug. I hadn't been gone more than ten minutes and he knew it. "I was chatting to my new roommate, Alison Grenal. Do you know her?"

"Don't think so. Should I?" He gestures outside and I fall into step beside him.

"She knows you, Tavern," I reply, then cast a look at him. "She called you cute."

Tavern frowns at me. "Cute? What am I, a puppy?" I chuckle and his eyes take on a playful gleam. "And what do *you* think, King? Am I cute?"

I make a show of looking him up and down. I shrug. "I guess, if you like that cocky American sun-bleached bad boy attitude of yours," I shoot him a look, "which I don't."

Tavern laughs and steers me around a truck unloading boxes into a warehouse. Before he can respond, I change the subject. "I need a security pass, then you can show me the rest of the base," I say. "Then I'll probably be hungry so you can show me what American military cuisine is like."

I hear Tavern chuckle behind me. "Yes, Ma'am." I stop walking to turn and scowl, but Tavern just meets my eyes and smiles.

"Hey, Tav." A deep masculine voice sounds behind me but I don't break eye contact. "How's it going?"

Tavern smirks, his eyes still on mine. "I'm having fun, as always." Then he raises his eyes to the newcomer. "I'm showing our new teammate around the base." He gestures at me as I turn. "This is Corporal King, on secondment from the Brits."

The approaching man is tall, with clear blue eyes and tanned features. A baseball cap sits on his short dark hair. The man tips his cap at me and sticks out his hand for me to shake, surveying me with undisguised interest. "Second Lieutenant Seth White," he introduces himself politely. "Always good to meet a fellow ally. Not many around these days. I hope Tavern is showing you the best of our American hospitality."

I raise my eyebrows and look in mock surprise at Tavern. "Is that what you're doing?"

Tavern frowns at me. "Don't listen to King. She's got attitude."

"Good." White looks amused at our banter. "Someone needs to put you in your place. You be in the main mess later?"

"Depends on how long King here keeps me waiting," Tavern replies snarkily.

"Which depends on how long you whine about it," I shoot back. I just can't help myself, even in front of an officer.

"I'll take that as a yes. Corporal, I look forward to hearing all about you." White tips his cap at me again and shoots me a wide, charming grin. "And watch out for this one." He points at Tavern. "Fancies himself a right ladies' man."

Tavern sticks his middle finger up at White's retreating back. Now it is my turn to smirk. Tavern catches my look and looks mildly embarrassed.

"Sorry."

"No need to apologise," I say simply as we continue walking. "My best mates are a Scot and a Welshman. There's nothing you can do I haven't already seen, or say that I haven't already heard."

"Oh yeah, want to bet on that?" His words come out quickly, and I get the feeling he didn't think before he spoke.

I stop walking again and regard him. "Was that a sexual innuendo, Tavern? Because that would be seriously inappropriate." Tavern looks taken aback and embarrassed again, then I smirk. "And you don't have a thing on me. Bring it on."

*

The next five months passed in a blur of sand, heat and hard work. As ordered, either Tavern or Vega stuck close to me whenever I was out in the field. At first, it was an irritating annoyance, constantly having someone at my back all the time. But as I got to know the men, I got used to their presence. I began to teach them some basic engineering techniques, how to produce an optimal building design, how to calculate the load-bearing capability of a wall, the best materials for each part of the building, and they humoured me. At all times, they were vigilant around themselves and me. Even when I was lecturing them out loud, they had one ear and eye on me and the other to any possible dangers. An attack and attempted abduction of a female NATO officer in Kabul made me surprisingly jittery the next day, though I kept those feelings locked down. Despite this,

Tavern seemed to recognise it and stuck even closer. I didn't let it show just how much that comforted me.

We often stayed in nearby secure camps at night, especially if the site was a long drive from the base. Whenever we came back to base in the evening, I went running or I had a session at the gym. My average run was five laps of the perimeter fence, around ten miles. Running had always been a way for me to release pent-up physical and emotional energy. I had competed in several long-distance runs as a teenager, but I enjoyed it for fun rather than seriousness. Occasionally, Tavern, Vega or White joined me. Those were fun laps; they liked to up the pace until I couldn't take it anymore. I had no doubt they were taking it easy on me. I was fit; they were super fit.

I didn't have much work contact with Seth White. He was an officer and wasn't assigned to our unit. But he, Tavern and Vega had all completed basic together so they knew each other like brothers. Forever getting on each other's backs about all sorts of shit, but I could see they were all extremely close. It was very common for us all to eat together. White loved football, or soccer as they called it, was a big movie fan and hated Chinese food. He had a great sense of humour and was very smart; he was the only one really interested in my engineering chat. White had an intensity about him that made him an excellent officer. He loved to tell stories, usually about Tavern or Vega and the trouble they had got into.

Vega was a relaxed, chilled-out guy. He came from a mixed Indian and Spanish heritage, an interesting contrast to the mostly white American army guys I met. He had been an American football star in high school before joining the army. They all told me with amusement that this was a big deal. Vega liked heavy rock music, played the guitar and had a three-year-old son he sent his pay home to. The boy's mother and he weren't married, or even together. Vega described his son as the beautiful outcome of a 'massive equipment failure', which I took to mean the condom had broken. Vega treated me with an annoying amount of respect at first, but soon started throwing in cheek once he got to know me.

Tavern was hard to read at first. He didn't seem to like talking about himself that much. Gradually, he loosened up, and I found out he had been on the track team at high school so was a serious runner, liked video games, cartoons, drinking beer, and omelettes. Tavern had three older sisters but he didn't like to speak about his parents very much, admitting to me one day that his mother had died when he was a baby and his father had pretty much left the parenting to his eldest daughter, Jessica. Tavern clearly loved his sister, and spoke about his young niece and nephews a lot.

Tavern slowly became a close friend, though we bickered all the time, throwing flirtatious and even sexual comments back and forth, especially when no one else was around. It was similar to the relationship I had with Trent and Rhys. Everything was fair play; everyone got ribbed about anything. In all the time I had known them, they had never once toned down their language in front of me, or stopped themselves from making a comment that I might find offensive. I had that with Tavern, and it was fun.

My contact with those I had left back in the UK was limited, and mostly by emails. My childhood friend Janine was one of the few friends who kept in touch regularly. Jason and Mum also kept in contact via email, and my grandparents wrote me letters. Mum never understood why I couldn't come home for Christmas.

One of my projects was working on fixing a road bridge which had been damaged by an explosion a few weeks before. The work had come in via a request from the newly elected civilian government, so it was a big deal we got it right. I was the primary combat engineer on each of my sites, and I reported to several higher-ranking senior project engineers, who oversaw the entire programme of works in a given area. The day-to-day work was all down to me.

Today, I'm standing in the temporary site office, basically a big field tent, talking with one of the local women about what we are doing and how fixing the road bridge will help her family. I am showing her drawings and designs on a folding table in the middle of the tent. Tavern stands inside the doorway with an escorting private, watching us chat. When Tavern is my watcher, and I am with our personnel inside, he tends to walk around the perimeter, always keeping me in view. When I am with locals, or out on the street, he never leaves my side. The woman, Fariba, is a local mother, who speaks enough English for me to be able to forgo my rough Pashto. My Pashto is okay for basic conversation, but I often need a translator for more complicated communication.

The temporary site office also includes the unit commander's desk and the duty soldier. Private Fred Collins, a young dark-haired man with an enthusiastic outlook on life, is the duty soldier right now. We all have radios on our vests, but mine is turned down low so I don't get interrupted. When we are on site, only the duty soldier answers queries to base; it makes communication efficient.

"Bravo Alpha 113 calling Charlie Alpha 54. Over." I can just make out the British Army call sign.

Collins taps the headset over his ears and speaks into the microphone attached to his radio.

"Charlie Alpha 54 reading you. Over."

"Be advised, Charlie Alpha 54, we are approaching your position from the south, ETA four minutes. Over."

"Roger that, Bravo Alpha 113." Collins stands and heads outside, no doubt to tell Major Xavier the situation.

I turn away and continue speaking with Fariba. The woman is very gentle, but also firm. Being mother to five boys will do that to you. She is really smart, and pretty. Even under the dark blue headscarf which covers everything but her face, I can see that. After a few minutes, she has all the information she wants, and promising to pass on the details to others, the private escorts her out.

The tent material to my left moves loudly in the breeze, and sand particles fly everywhere. I rub my head in thought, feeling the sand and grime on my forehead, and head for my desk at the far end of the tent. I have some load calculations to finish before the end of the day.

"You look knackered," Tavern comments from the tent entrance. "Late night or something?"

I glare over at him as I sit down. "Yeah, some bastard took all my money at poker."

Tavern chuckles. "Don't play if you can't win."

"Don't worry, I won't be playing you again," I mutter.

"You've never really played me," Tavern comments with a smirk, moving towards me. "If you had, you'd want it over and over."

I roll my eyes in exasperation. "Such a big head, Tavern, I'm surprised you fit in that uniform."

"Well, these are extra-large pants."

I snort. "Please, there's nothing extra large about you." I give him a scornful up and down look. "Nope, first impressions say it all."

Tavern takes a seat on my desk, sitting on my sketches because he knows it annoys me. "Maybe we should give it a go and find out."

I look up at him, all mock innocently. "I think that would be crossing a line, don't you?" We have an in-joke that sometimes our comments to each other cross a line of decency and appropriateness, which they often do, but that's part of the fun.

"But talking about it is fine, is that right?"

"We were talking about poker, weren't we?"

Before Tavern can respond, Collins walks back in. Tavern stands up slowly, keeping his back to the private so the other man can't see the sparkle in his eyes and the playful grin on his face.

"Corporal King, there is someone outside who would like to see you."

"Thanks, Collins." I stand and walk around the desk. "Hopefully, they will have better manners than you."

"My manners are very gentlemanly," Tavern protests. "I just make an extra effort for you."

I smirk and leave the office, grabbing my helmet off the peg as I walk outside. The sun is glaringly high in the sky; hot and bright.

I squint as Collins points me towards the entrance to the construction site, where I can just see a couple of British Army Humvees pulled up alongside the US ones. As my eyes adjust, I notice several figures talking to the unit CO Major Xavier, who is pointing in my direction. The figures are familiar, and it takes me a few seconds to work out why.

A slow grin spreads over my face, and I start walking towards them. "Okay, I take it back. You probably do have better manners than these blokes." Tavern looks confused at my almost compliment.

"English!" Trent's Scottish voice echoes around the site as he walks towards me, causing several surprised glances from the American soldiers. "Bloody hell, what are you wearing Yank colours for?"

I shake my head but choose not to yell a reply.

"I work with the US Army now, moron," I say back when they are closer. "Or did you hit your head again?"

"I take it you know these guys?" Tavern asks low in my ear.

"Sure do, biggest idiots on the planet," I say as Trent comes into earshot. He catches me in a big sideways hug, which is as much as our bulky uniforms allow, and bends down to wetly kiss my cheek. I see Tavern raise his eyebrows in surprise.

"English, I thought you'd disappeared off the face of the planet, or at least got out of this hellhole," Trent booms. Clearly, nothing about Trent has changed.

I punch him in the arm as I wipe my face in mock disgust. "Don't you read your emails? I told you where I was."

"Scotty thinks emails are for pansies." Rhys catches me in another sideways hug. "You know I've replied to you."

"I did, and thank you for enlightening me with tales of Trent's idiotic adventures. Makes excellent toilet reading," I reply with a grin, looking at my two good friends. "You guys look good, very high spirits." I frown and glare. "You haven't replaced me, have you?"

Trent laughs loudly. "If by replace you, you mean have we found another fit bird to laugh at our raunchy jokes, then no. There'll never be anyone else like you, English." I grin widely.

I hear Tavern clear his throat behind me, and turn. He is standing a metre or so back, legs casually placed apart, hands resting together on the butt of his automatic weapon. It's what I call his classic watcher pose. Tavern's face is carefully neutral under that big bushy blond beard, but he is eyeballing Trent and Rhys with more than simple curiosity.

"Guys, this is Sergeant Tavern," I say to Trent and Rhys, suddenly feeling wary as I see Trent and Rhys eyeball Tavern right back. "Tavern, this is Private Trent McTavish and Lance Corporal Rhys Jones." Trent looks Tavern up and down and smirks widely.

"Nice to meet you. King has briefly mentioned you both before." Tavern's words are said politely, but there is challenge in them.

"And you, laddie," Trent replies. I inwardly sigh. I know what is coming next. "So Sergeant Tavern, have you been looking after our girl here?" I punch him in the arm again, and Trent jumps back. "Not that she needs looking after, mind. She has a wicked right hook, you know. Plus, you should see her on the monkey bars."

"And a wicked mind ta boot," Rhys jumps in. "Maybe you've seen some of that." Rhys pauses and tries to look thoughtful, even though I know it is all an act. "Or maybe you haven't. Not sure you Yanks are clued into the British humour."

"I think I understand enough," Tavern replies, his eyes glinting as he casually shrugs and steps forward. "At least, the *English* humour I seem to manage."

As expected, Trent jumps right up to that one; he takes a step forward. The big men are feet apart now. "Ah, I see, Sergeant Yank. Think you're clever, huh? Think you can take advantage of our girl English? Well, you have to come through us first." Trent goes to step forward again, but I use my fingers to whistle loudly enough to get their attention, and step in between.

"Enough, boys! Jeez, what has got into you? Scotty, put it back in your trousers." I point at him then turn to Tavern with a glare and another pointed finger. "And you, put it back in your pants. This is not a pissing contest." Tavern looks shocked, and Rhys just laughs until I glare at him too. "Now, please, let's play nice. Tavern, I did basic with these guys, and we've been deployed in the same units several times. They're arses, but they're fine soldiers, and my friends." I glare at Trent. "For now anyway. Trent, Rhys." I nod over my shoulder at the American man. "Tavern is responsible for my safety in the field, and we have been working very closely together. He's a good man, and an excellent soldier, and in case you didn't notice his rank, he outranks you. So a little respect, please."

Trent steps backwards away from me and hangs his head. "Sorry, English, got a little carried away." He juts his head towards Tavern. "No offence, mate. I just want to make sure English is being treated well and looked after."

"No problem, buddy." Tavern inclines his head. "And she is, I make sure of it."

"Hey, fellas, I don't need looking after." I try to interrupt but they are all on a roll now.

"English is very special to us, you know," Rhys continues. "She gets us into trouble, but then, you know she gets us out again, which is the important part really."

"I understand. She is unique." Oh boy. I roll my eyes at Tavern's sincere tone. I just know he is mocking me.

"And, you know, she's well fit. I've heard stories of you American men and your smooth accents and hairless chests seducing our women to your shores – ow!" I have punched Trent's arm again. No other man provokes as much violence in me as he does. "What was that for, English? I'm just defending your honour."

I glare at him. "My honour is not for you to defend." Trent and Rhys try to look shameful, which is ruined by the playful smiles on their faces. Tavern chuckles and I turn around to glare at him too. He meets my eyes and sobers, but a smirk still ghosts his face. I turn back to the Welshman and Scot in front of me. "Now, not that it hasn't been lovely catching up," Trent grins at my sarcastic tone, "but do you boys have a reason for bugging me? I've got a lot of work to do, you know."

Trent gestures over his shoulder. "Our captain had to speak to your captain about some jurisdictional thing. Every US unit we meet, I ask after you." Trent shrugs and now looks faintly embarrassed. "This time, they said you were here." He brightens. "So here we are, distracting you from your work and meeting your new... buddy." He gives Tavern an up and down look again.

"And it looks like you're off now," Tavern says, then points behind them. The British army vehicles are filling up with personnel, and the driver is motioning for them to hurry. "What a shame."

Trent and Rhys begin to back away. "Good to see you again, English. Glad you haven't disappeared to America yet," Trent yells. "Watch out for the smooth chests!"

"Check your bloody emails," I call back.

"Emails are for pansies!" Trent winks at me, then blows me a kiss before they leg it back to the Humvees.

I feel Tavern move up next to me as the convoy pulls away, Trent manically waving from the back seat. "I would apologise," I say to him, "but there really is no excuse."

Tavern chuckles. "They seem like good fun."

"They are. They also seem like arses, which they are." I shake my head and eye him. "You were acting like one too, you know."

Tavern shrugs. "I guess they brought it out of me."

I'm confused. "Brought what out?"

Tavern turns towards the office with a grin. "Whatever it is I have in my pants."

*

Sometime later that month, I was showering after a long hot day in the field and a good run. I was thinking about that day, and I found myself comparing the three men in my head. Rhys and Trent were like brothers to me; best friends I could be playful and smutty with, but still punch in the arm when they annoyed me. Tavern was different; he was playful and smutty too, but it just wasn't the same and I was trying to think about why it wasn't. Tavern and I had been bantering as usual, and as I thought back over the conversation I found myself wondering what it would be like to take our relationship beyond the sexual comments and actually do something about it… I froze mid-hair shampoo as I realised I had totally drifted into a sexual fantasy about him. As the images grew in my mind and my body responded, I suddenly knew that I was extremely attracted to this man. I wanted him. I had no idea when this had snuck up on me, and it shocked and scared me. Fraternisation within the ranks, and on an overseas base, was strictly prohibited under British Army and US Army rules. Not that I would ever do anything about it. I wouldn't be jeopardising my career for any man, no matter how much attraction I felt towards him. Which, I argued to myself, was likely a null point, as I doubted it went both ways. Still, these thoughts echoed around my brain all night and made for some very interesting dreams.

The next day, we head out to the site of a school we are halfway through constructing. We are in a standard two-Humvee convoy, weaving our way through the early-morning streets. Tavern is sitting next to me in the Humvee; Vega is on my other side. I have told myself to act normal with him, despite my shower realisation of the night before, but I am suddenly acutely aware that my thigh is brushing his whenever the Humvee bounces. I shift slightly to remove the contact and look out through Vega's window. I feel Tavern shift as well, but I don't look over at him.

To distract myself, I lean forward to speak to Captain Marks, who is the senior programme engineer on this project. He is coming with us to check out the status of the school, something he does on all the projects every couple of weeks. "Sir." Marks turns slightly in his seat. "I presented to the tribal leaders last week on our progress, and afterwards a few of the younger women expressed interest to me about teaching there. They seem to assume it will be a girls' only school." I wasn't aware that decision had been made; the main building was replacing a boys' school that had been destroyed by a missile several months ago. Another, smaller building was also being constructed next to it and the layout had also been designed as a school.

Marks grimaces. "That's always a risk with these kinds of projects." He turns back to the front.

Well, that's vague. I sit back and consider his words as the Humvee slows outside the site.

I follow Tavern out and look around at the construction site in the early-morning light. I feel a cold tingle up my spine and I glance around. All is quiet. The site is some distance from residential houses. The plot where the previous school had been situated was unusually large in this part of the city. Usually, when we arrive, a gaggle of interested school children, both young boys and girls, run to me and shout English words they know, and I would say Pashto words back. It was a little game we had which I enjoyed immensely. Male workers, who all lived locally, and some curious women following their children would also arrive. This morning, there was nothing.

I see Tavern start to move forward but I grab his arm quickly. "Wait," I say quietly.

Tavern pauses and turns towards me with a curious expression on his brow. "Where are the children?" I ask, my hand tightening on his jacket as I meet his eyes. "The children are always here."

Tavern frowns, then understanding dawns and he glances up and around. Slowly, he raises his weapon. Then he grabs my arm and pulls me towards him. I glance past him to see Marks, Collins and a few soldiers begin to walk towards the partly constructed building. "Captain, wait." Tavern, his grip on my arm not flinching for a second, moves towards the other men.

Marks stops and watches us approach, a curious look on his face. I see Vega come up behind him. I step past Tavern quickly and study the building shell. It just feels wrong.

"Captain, something might be—"

The explosion catches me completely off guard. One minute I am standing there looking towards the shell of the new building, the next I feel the heat and force of an explosion on my face. I'm not sure if it is the force of the blast, or Tavern's body weight that knocks me to the ground. I lie there on the warm sand, my face scrunched up with a great weight on top of me as my head spins. I can't move, there is a ringing in my ears and everything feels muffled. Then I feel fingers on the back of my neck, and on my face, pulling my head up roughly. I blink several times to clear my vision and Tavern's anxious face comes into view. His light brown eyes are wide as he studies me. His fingers move under my helmet, around my ears and down my neck. Then he moves his hand down my heavily clothed body frantically, looking for injury. I take quick stock. Nothing hurts, and I can move.

"I'm fine," I yell, my hearing muffled. I shake my head and grab his hand as it lands on my hip, squeezing it tight. "I'm not injured. Are you okay?" For a second, his eyes meet mine and I see my own fear for his safety reflected back, my own desire for this man mirrored in his eyes. I take in a shaky breath but don't have time to process this before the look is gone and he quickly looks around us, effortlessly getting to his feet, his weapon scanning the area. I do the same and take out my sidearm, holding it in front of me as I scan for danger. The cool hard metal of the gun feels oddly surreal in my palm, while at the same time the weight comforts me. I've never had to fire my gun in the field before and I feel the adrenaline pumping through my system as I turn to study the building in front of me. The work of several months is now on fire. Huge orange flames lick into the sky, pouring black smoke high into the air above us.

I see Marks and Vega get to their feet, weapons drawn. It's pretty usual for insurgents to fire on survivors of an IED attack. Tavern, his weapon high and his face stern, reaches one hand behind him and presses it onto my stomach, using that and his big body to provide cover and push me back towards the armoured Humvee. I'm capable of defending myself, I want to argue, but one look at his face and I don't resist, but I do keep my gun up. I see Vega and Marks and the rest of the unit retreating towards the Humvees, away from the flames.

I hear Private Collins on the radio, reporting the situation. Within minutes, a heavily armoured security patrol has arrived to cover us, search the area and put out the fire.

Without a word, Tavern pushes me into the Humvee, sitting beside me. Vega shuts the door on Marks at the front and slides in next to me. Without further instructions, Collins drives away. My eyes follow the flames over my shoulder. Just before we turn a corner, I think I see a small girl hiding in the shadows of a nearby building.

Back at base, the medics check us all out. Vega sustained a minor abrasion to his face, and Collins received some cuts and bruises but otherwise everyone is fine. I can feel the adrenaline wearing off now. Shock and fear start to creep in but I push it away. It's not the time for that.

We are quickly whisked away to a briefing room for debrief. Colonel Jenson is there, sitting at the top of the table. I stay silent as Tavern, sitting next to me, explains what happened. I see Jenson's eyes rest on my face as Tavern says how I stopped everyone from going into the building, and he holds up his hand for Tavern to stop.

"Corporal. How did you know?"

I inhale swiftly and meet his gaze. "I didn't, sir. It just felt... wrong. Those kids always came up to me when we arrived. We had a language game which they loved. When they didn't show up, I just knew something wasn't right." I couldn't explain it properly so I shook my head in frustration. I can feel my hands shaking so I clench them into fists. "I told Sergeant Tavern that I thought something wasn't right, and despite not having any evidence he didn't hesitate to stop Captain Marks, Private Collins and Private Waals from walking into that building." I glance at Tavern to see him watching me closely. "He saved their lives, sir."

"No, Corporal, you did," Tavern replies quickly. "It was you, not me."

"I agree," Jenson comments. I don't know what to say to this. "Corporal King, without you there today, no doubt we would be in mourning right now." I glance at Marks, who looks solemn. "But, Sergeant Tavern, you also saved their lives. You worked as a team today."

Jenson stands and we all follow. "I expect written statements by nineteen hundred. But given what's happened, you can all take the rest of the day off."

I nod in thanks, but I feel numb. I feel like I'm viewing the world through a bubble. Captain Marks stops in front of me. "It feels inadequate saying this, but thank you, King." He takes my hand and I find I have to blink back tears. I will not cry in front of these men.

I shrug and force a smile. Marks nods and walks out. Collins also stops and thanks me, making a quip that he will always try and drive me from now on. I smile and nod in response as he moves past me.

"Hey. You okay, King?" I realise everyone else has left the room and it's just Tavern standing in front of me. I need to get a grip right now but I can feel my control slipping away.

I pull myself together, ignoring my increasing heart rate, and look up at him. "Of course, Tavern." I take a step back. "I'll see you later, okay?"

He barely has time to nod before I turn away. Tavern is the last person I want to show my emotional breakdown to. I walk quickly and hurry towards my bunk. I need to run, I need to work my feelings out before I explode and embarrass myself. Running is the only way I know how to do that. Luckily, Alison isn't around when I get there. I strip out of my uniform and into shorts, a sports vest and trainers. Not wanting to draw attention to myself, I walk, rather than run, to the perimeter. Then I start running, slowly at first, warming up, but as the images and feelings of the morning float to the surface, I run faster and faster. I manage two laps before I feel the emotions start to overwhelm me. In the distance, I see the overflow storage buildings, close to the back perimeter fence on the south side of the base. The normal running route cuts in front of these buildings. I know if I can get behind them, no one will see me. I sprint, flat out, knowing I am overdoing it but frantic to get out of sight of everyone. Closer, closer, closer...

As I pass the corner, into the shadows, it all overwhelms me, and I collapse to my knees on the hard sand. Tears stream from my eyes as I lean into the building. I can barely breathe with the exertion; I think my heart might explode out of my chest, it's pulsing so hard. As I pull air into my lungs, I cry and cry, allowing the shock to overwhelm me as I know it must. The images and feelings flow through me as I clench my fists into the sand and bend my head down. All I feel is the fear, the pain, the uncertainty of being so close to death.

I'm so involved with myself that I don't hear him until he is kneeling beside me. I feel soothing strokes across my back. Without looking, I know it's him. It could only be him. I angrily wipe my tears away and bite out, "Go away, Tavern."

Tavern chuckles. "I don't think so."

"What, you've come to taunt me here too?"

"No, I've come to see if you are all right. I could tell you weren't when you practically ran out the briefing room." I can feel the smile in his voice. "I saw you almost flying out the women's bunk. Quite an impressive few laps, by the way."

I grunt and wipe my face with the back of my hand. "It's just shock," I say roughly. "I'll get over it."

"I know you will, King, because you're strong. It's okay to have shock, you know, after what happened. Perfectly normal."

"I know."

Tavern chuckles again. He is still rubbing my back gently; the sensations of his touch start to distract me. "I've had it too, you know." His tone makes me glance at him for the first time. He meets my gaze sympathetically.

"You have?" I find it hard to believe this man has any kind of weakness.

"Yeah, several times."

"But not now?"

Tavern narrows his eyes and glances away. "Shock is the body's way of dealing with traumatic events that threaten your life. In this case, I wasn't so much concerned for my life, as for yours." His gaze slides back to mine. "The thought that anything should happen to you." He swallows hard. "I was so scared, when you were lying so still under me right afterwards…"

I can barely breathe, and it's not from shock this time. "Tavern…"

He nods. "I know. It's against the rules." His gaze slides down to my mouth. "It really is crossing that line."

I nod. "It is." I can't break rules like that, no matter how much I want to.

He smiles sadly, then brushes away a tear from my face. I try not to lean into his hand as he whispers, "Yeah."

Then he stands and pulls me up gently, holding my arm as I wobble slightly. I smile up at him. "Bet it would be fun, though." Tavern looks surprised for a second, then laughs loudly as his eyes sparkle.

"Oh yeah."

*

A few weeks later, we are travelling back to base after a long day. I'd got over the shock of the explosion pretty quickly, as I knew I would, and was back in the field the day after. I thought that Tavern's revelation, that he felt this attraction too, would make things awkward between us, but surprisingly it didn't. We both acted like it hadn't happened, and simply picked up where we left off; banter and flirting.

It had been a long day on site, and we were heading back to the base later than usual. The sun was starting to set and the temperature had dropped slightly. We had eaten field rations on site for dinner, due to the lateness, so I was planning on doing some further work that evening. I had another three weeks before my tour ended, when I would be sent back to the UK, so I still had lots to do and not much time to do it in. I was both looking forward to it and dreading it. I was looking forward to some time off, seeing my friends and family, and being out of a war zone. But I wasn't looking forward to leaving my work here, which I really enjoyed, or Tavern, which I tried not to dwell on.

I'm going through some papers in the Humvee on the way back to base. Tavern and Vega are talking quietly over my head, but I'm not really paying attention. As the Humvee pulls through the gates and into the parking area, I catch the end of Vega's sentence.

"… one more left then that's it, Tav."

I glance up at him. "One more what?" Vega looks at me in surprise, then his dark gaze slides over my head to Tavern and realisation dawns in his eyes.

"You didn't tell King."

I glance to my other side at Tavern. He shakes his head and looks out of the window.

"Tell me what?" I ask. Vega looks really uncomfortable as the Humvee stops, and he quickly piles out. I follow as he scowls at Tavern. The men stand there looking at each other; Vega annoyed, Tavern embarrassed. I'm really not going to let this drop.

As the other men leave, I drop my pack and plant my feet in front of them, crossing my arms. "Told me what? What's going on?"

Vega looks at Tavern expectantly, who clears his throat. "Well, do you remember I told you a few months ago we had applied for special ops training?" I nod. Tavern wanted to be a Ranger. Vega and White had also applied.

"Well, we all got past the initial application process," Tavern says slowly, not meeting my eye. "We start training in the States."

I smile. I'm so pleased for them both. I look between them. "That's excellent. Well done, guys."

Tavern bites his lip and I frown. I'd never seen him do that before. "Uh, we leave tomorrow." I freeze. "Tomorrow night, we get a plane back to the States." My heart starts pounding as my arms drop to my sides. I suddenly feel cold despite the temperature. Tavern is leaving, tomorrow.

After a second, I recover from the surprise and push those feelings right down. "I see," I say slowly, trying not to sound like I am affected. "So you have one more day in the field with the unit?"

"Yeah." Tavern reluctantly meets my gaze.

I blink, swallowing hard, and force a smile at Vega. "That's so great for you." I force myself to meet Tavern's eyes. "So great for you both."

Tavern's gaze searches mine. "We found out a few days ago, I should have told you sooner…"

"It's fine," I force out. "It doesn't matter about me. You are both capable of so much more than babysitting me." I laugh slightly, but it sounds high-pitched. I look at Vega. "I assume there will be some kind of goodbye thing in the mess tonight?" Vega shoots a look at Tavern and nods. "Great, then I will see you there later, okay?" I force another smile at Tavern, pick up my bag and sling it over my shoulder as I turn to head away.

I hold my head high as I walk away. Over my shoulder, I think I hear Vega swear loudly at Tavern, which I think is harsh. It has nothing to do with me; it's his life, his career. He is worth so much more than babysitting me, which is what he had been doing. As I walk out of sight, I move faster, wanting to get away from these irrational feelings choking my insides. I take a deep breath and let it out slowly. I am consumed by the urge to run, to let it all out in the only way I know how. I hurry to my bunk. Alison is sitting on her bed reading a magazine as I come in.

"Hey, Emma, how was your day?" she asks brightly as I begin to undress.

"Long, hot and sweaty," I reply, then it bursts out before I can stop it. "Tavern has just told me he is leaving tomorrow."

Alison gasps. "Oh no. Hon, I'm sorry."

I shrug as I pull on my shorts. "It's no big deal. It's good for him. It's what he wants."

"But what do you want?" Alison is looking up at me with big soulful eyes. She always has a way of getting right to the issue that is bothering me.

I force a smile as I drag on my sports vest. "I want to run."

She smiles kindly. "Of course you do." Then she gets up and gives me a big hug, which I return. "Have a good run."

My mind turns over and over as I pound out a few laps, the light getting darker and darker. I go through various stages of wanting, fantasising, denial, anger and eventually acceptance. I accept he is leaving and there is nothing I can do about it, so I deal with it. As I complete my third lap and approach those additional storage buildings, I feel someone move up beside me. One glance and everything I have told myself flies out of the window.

Tavern grimaces at me. He is wearing running gear now too. "I thought I would find you out here."

I sigh. "What do you want, Tavern?"

"I want to say I'm sorry."

"For what?"

"For not telling you I'm leaving tomorrow."

"It really doesn't matter."

Tavern grabs my arm and pulls it so I stop next to the building. "Yes, it does."

"Why does it matter, Tavern?" Panting from the run, I move

behind the building, not wanting anyone to see our argument from the base. "Why are you chasing me in the twilight?"

The light from the security fence lets me just see his features. "I didn't tell you because I didn't want to upset you." I don't recognise his tone of voice.

"Upset me? That makes no sense. I have no expectations where you're concerned, Tavern."

"I didn't tell you because as much as I want to go, the thought of leaving you makes me sad, Emma." I suck in a hard breath, at his words, and at the use of my first name. He has never called me that before. "Every day I stand and watch you. I get to see an incredible woman do an incredible job," he whispers, "and I want to stand with you all the time, but…"

"It's not enough for you," I finish. "The role you do here, you could do so much more. I understand."

Tavern nods. "I want to do more. I've been putting it off, but I can't do that anymore." There is a look in his eyes as he says that, a hidden meaning behind the words.

"What are you talking about now?" I murmur.

Tavern's breath hitches at my words and he moves in closer. "Would it be totally crossing the line if I kissed you, Emma? Just once?"

He is so close that I can feel his breath on my cheek. I swallow hard as desire jolts through me. "Yes, but you should do it anyway."

The words are barely out before he crushes his lips to mine. He cups my face in one hand and moves the other to the small of my back, pulling me into him hard. I wind my arms around his body and melt into him. I'm on fire from his touch.

Distantly, I hear someone approaching. Before I can react, Tavern has broken the kiss and pulls me in between the buildings, deep in the shadow, where only the barest light illuminates his features. He pushes me against the wall and we hold our breath as a security guard walks by. I let out a sigh of relief as the guard passes without incident, then look back up into Tavern's face. In an instant, he is kissing me again, and I forget about everything else. I caress my hands under his t-shirt and up his bare back, feeling hard muscle and warm skin against my palms. Tavern winds his fingers around the back of my neck and angles my head, holding me in place with his lips while his other fingers explore my bare skin under my own vest. Excitement rushes through me, my skin tingling wherever he touches me. Tavern releases my lips and starts kissing my jaw and throat softly, the contact making me shiver uncontrollably.

"Rick…" I moan into his hair, and he growls low in his throat.

"Say it again, Emma," he whispers hoarsely. I smile. Apparently, I'm not the only one who likes hearing my first name.

"Rick…" My voice is far huskier than I have ever heard it.

"God, I want you," he whispers into my neck, his hands skimming up my stomach and over my sports bra lightly. "I've fantasised about this so many times."

He pushes his pelvis into mine and I moan softly at what I feel. I slide my hands down and under his waistband, feeling his hips in my hands. "I think we have leaped over the line," I murmur, saying what I want before I change my mind. "We might as well leave it behind."

He growls again and his lips find mine, crushing them beneath his. In one movement, he has stripped me of my shorts and pants, and I kick them off. I'm going to just go with it. I grip his waistband and pull it down too, and he cups my arse in his big hands, lifting me against the wall as I wind my legs around his waist.

The strength he shows only heightens my feelings. I'm not petite in any way, yet Tavern doesn't let it bother him; he just pushes his hips into mine and locks me in place against the side of the building.

The sex is quick, raw and passionate. Beyond anything I have ever experienced. As it ends, our lips locked together to muffle the sound of our pleasure, our breathing is ragged. Sweat glistens on both of our bodies as we stay locked in that position.

"Damn…" Tavern replies, pulling his lips from mine slowly.

"Yeah…" I pant, resting my head back against the building. "That's a good word for it."

Tavern chuckles, the sound reverberating through my body. He slowly lets me down and steps away, keeping hold of the wall with one hand as he pulls up his shorts.

My legs are shaky, so I lean on the building as I pull on my clothing, then slide slowly to the ground. Tavern sits down next to me, his long legs folded beneath him.

"Shit," he suddenly says. "You are… still protected, right?"

"Yes," I reply, and he visibly sags in relief. During one of our more intimate conversations, I had revealed I had an IUS, mostly to control the horrible periods I have. The birth control had always been an added bonus.

"Shit," he repeats softly. "I still should have checked. I should have protected you." He takes my hand and slowly threads his fingers through mine.

I smile wryly. "You won't always be there to protect me, Rick." I remember then. "In fact, as of tomorrow night, you won't be."

Tavern sighs. "I know."

We sit in silence for a few minutes. Our backs leaning on the building, our legs bent in front of us, our hands clasped together.

"Emma." He says it slowly, like he isn't sure how I am going to react. "You know that, despite what just happened, I can't be involved…"

"Really, Tavern?" I say, slight exasperation in my voice. "After all this time, you still think I might be one of those girls…" I raise my voice in a high-pitched attempt at an American accent. "'Oh my God we totally had sex that means you're my boyfriend and I'm your girlfriend and we are totally exclusive and must spend every second of every day together.'" Tavern had started laughing long before I had finished.

"You know, that's a brilliant impression of a girl in high school I used to date."

"You poor thing," I mutter. "Seriously. It's fine. Even if you weren't leaving, we couldn't do this again, no matter how much we wanted to."

"Yeah," Tavern replies. "If we are caught…" I see him glance towards the end of the alley.

"We're screwed," I finish, "and not in the good way. I don't think either of us is willing to jeopardise that, are we? I'm certainly not."

Tavern shakes his head and whispers, "No."

I nod. This conversation has to happen, no matter how brutal it is.

"So, what are you doing after your tour ends?" Tavern asks, abruptly changing the subject.

"Well. I have six weeks' leave when I get back to the UK," I say. "So I plan to chill out, do a grand tour of my friends and family and generally kick back." I nod. I find myself looking forward to that. "Then I will probably be deployed somewhere else, who knows where, hopefully somewhere less sandy."

I kick my foot out and move the sand under my trainer.

Tavern squeezes my hand. "That sounds nice."

"Yeah." I turn to him with a grin. "Maybe we will meet again, like ships passing in the night, forever drawn to the sandy alley."

Tavern laughs, then turns his head to regard me. "We should probably get out of the sandy alley." He stands, then pulls me with him, but doesn't let me go as I stand. I finally allow myself to feel sadness that our time together is ending. I'm really going to miss him.

"You are the most unique woman I have ever met," he states simply. "I will miss you." Then he leans over and kisses me gently. I draw back with a curious look. "Goodbye kiss." He shrugs. "I won't be able to do it tomorrow."

That is good logic. Before I can change my mind, I kiss him too, wrapping my arms around his neck and kissing him hard. After a few minutes, I pull away, smile up at him then step back, letting go of his hand.

"Goodbye, Rick," I whisper.

"Goodbye, Emma," he replies, watching me leave. I glance back as I exit the alley, and he is still standing there watching me, so I wave at him before disappearing into the night.

Chapter 3

University Part 2

July 2007

Jon and I leave Birmingham with Amie the day after graduation, and head down to Oxford. After a lot of discussion, we had decided to use half of my saved money and around £15,000 of Jon's money to fund our trip. We figured we would never have the chance to do it again so it was worth it. Jon wants the rest of the money to go towards a house deposit when we get home. It's his money so I don't argue.

I figure this trip will make or break us. We'll either end up even more in love, or breaking up. That's why I need to keep some money back, just in case.

We would be carrying all our possessions in four bags for over a year. One large backpack each, borrowed from Amie and Mike, and smaller backpacks on our fronts. Jon and I had a rough plan of where we wanted to go; Australia, then New Zealand, then up to Asia, across to India, then back over to Europe for the last few months. We wanted to visit as many places as possible, but it also depended on how much money we had. We would almost always stay in hostels, with maybe an occasional hotel. We'd meet a lot more people that way and it was cheaper. Jon and I had made a decision early on to try and have sex in every country we visited. I thought it was more than plausible; after all, we could always rent a hotel room for a night rather than a bunk room at a hostel. I was looking forward to trying it.

Our flight out from Heathrow was to Sydney, with a stopover in Singapore on the 1st of August 2007.

Our visas were valid for three months, so that's how long we were planning on staying in Australia. We explored the east coast, took a tour across country and then explored the west coast. I loved it all; the different culture, the accents, the sunshine. I loved the hostels we stayed in, the different types of people we met, living with no responsibilities. I loved being with Jon, experiencing everything together. We took several internal flights across the country; Australia is so huge, it was difficult for me to grasp the scale of it. One of our internal flights lasted four hours. After two and a half months, we travelled back over to Adelaide. We booked into a hostel and met a group of travelling Europeans. A French woman, a Spanish couple, several Germans and two Dutch girls. They had been travelling the country as a group, having met in Perth several months previously. I found it so interesting that they all spoke English with each other; it seemed to be the universal common language. The French woman, Monique, was thrilled to speak to Jon in French. I got the feeling she was tired of speaking English. I felt slightly left out of their conversations, which were animated and long. Jon had been teaching it to me slowly, but I was having difficulty picking it up and it was slow-going. I didn't want to cause a fuss so I didn't say anything. We joined them to explore Adelaide, taking in parks, bars and restaurants. Jon and I had managed to secure a semi-private room in this hostel. The room had four bunks, but we had it to ourselves at the moment. It was nice to have a little privacy for once. In Perth, we had shared with eight others one time.

One evening, we ate at a seafood restaurant. Something clearly didn't agree with me, because I spent the entire night throwing up. Jon sat with me in the toilets all night, until eventually I could keep water down and then crawl into bed. I felt really miserable, and homesick, for the first time. I spent the entire next day and night in bed. I had told Jon to go out and enjoy himself with the others. I didn't want him to miss out and I was just going to sleep anyway.

I wake around lunchtime the next day. I glance around as the room comes into focus. There are two sets of bunk beds; Jon and I have been using the bottom ones. His bed is empty, the sheets messy. I spot a fresh glass of water and a cracker by my bedside. I sit up and slowly eat the cracker, wary in case I am sick again. After drinking the water, I stand up and stretch. I feel better, but sweaty and gross, so I grab my towel and head to the showers.

Once I am clean and my hair is washed, I feel much better. I go in search of Jon. I hear French voices coming from the computer room, and peer around the doorframe. Jon is leaning on the wall on the far side of the room, grinning down at Monique. She is sitting at a computer, but looking up at him. Monique is incredibly beautiful; straight shiny blonde hair, long legs and a perfectly curvy figure. When she smiles, her blue eyes light up and I swear she could be a model in a beauty magazine. Jon and Monique are having an animated conversation in rapid French. I am about to say hi to them when my limited vocabulary picks up the words '*sexe*', '*bisous*' and '*séduction*' – sex, kiss and seduction. I frown; why would they be talking about that? Surely Jon doesn't know this woman well enough to be discussing these subjects. A sharp wave of jealousy cuts into my chest as I see

Monique reach over and stroke his leg, her hand moving up under his shorts. Jon laughs loudly, apparently not fazed by this woman touching him. Monique stands slowly and places a hand on his jawline, the other on the wall by his head. Then she leans into him.

I swallow hard and turn away, my back against the wall. I can't see that. I squeeze my eyes shut and try to banish the images, but they just repeat over and over. My mind races. I just caught my boyfriend kissing a beautiful French woman. Insecurities I had long ago thought gone leap to the surface. Why wouldn't he want to kiss her? She is beautiful, exotic and French; something I will never be.

I hear laughter in the room behind me. I can't stand it.

I run back to the room, grab my bag and jacket and head for the exit. I have to get away.

"Emma?" I hear Jon say from behind me. I run through the bar away from him, not looking back as he yells, "Emma, where are you going?"

I run out of the door of the hostel, along the pavement, not thinking about where I am going, only that I need to get away. Tears well up in my eyes as I run. How could I have been so stupid?

I slow as I reach the park, fighting for breath as I look around. There are a few people walking around the large green space; an older couple walk their dog not far away. The day is beautiful. It's early spring here; the days are warm and unfamiliar flowers are poking their heads up through the grass. It's both comforting and alien. I am so very far from home.

"Emma, what's wrong?" Jon is running up the path towards me, alarm on his face. I turn and start walking away, wiping tears from my face.

"Go away, Jon," I snap behind me. Anger replaces the hurt.

"What? What the hell, Emma?" Jon stops in front of me, blocking my path. I try to go around him but he grabs my arms and twirls me. I try and wrench out of his grasp but he keeps me pinned. "What the hell is going on?"

"I saw you," I yell at him. "I saw you kiss Monique."

Jon looks shocked and immediately lets me go. "You what?" I don't want to say it again so I just glare at him. Jon looks thoroughly confused, then his eyes darken and his brow furrows. "What did you see?" I scoff and turn away, but Jon grabs my arm again. "Tell me exactly what you saw." Again, I try and shake him off but he grips me tighter. "Now, Emma."

Anger surges in me and I step into him. "I saw you in the computer room. I saw you leaning on the wall. She touched your leg and face and leaned into you and…" I trail off.

Jon raises a brow in challenge. "And?"

"And I didn't want to see what was going to happen next so I looked away," I bite out.

Jon narrows his eyes at me; his voice is low and dangerous. "If you hadn't looked away, you would have seen that there was no kiss." My heart stops for an instant as Jon continues. "If you had understood what we were talking about, you would have realised that she was telling me, and showing me, how her husband…" he pauses for effect and my eyes widen "…seduced her when they first met. She had been talking to him on Skype and was upset because she misses him, so I was making her feel better. She suggested that I do this seduction with you because apparently women like it."

I swallow hard; there is no lie in Jon's eyes. He lets go of my arm and steps back, his face full of disappointment.

Shame fills me and I reach for him. "Jon…"

"How could you think I would do that, Emma?" He shakes his head and steps back out of my reach. "Do you think so little of me you would think I would want to be with someone like Monique? Why would I want that when I have you?"

"I just thought…" I falter. I don't really have any excuses. "It's just she's so beautiful, and French. You guys have been getting on so well… I just thought you'd got tired of having a plain English girl." Dammit, I didn't mean to say that.

Jon stares at me incredulously for a moment. "Are you kidding me, Emma? Why would I want a high-maintenance French woman, why would I want anyone else, when I have you?"

The look on his face beats me down. I swallow hard; I'm so embarrassed. "I was really stupid, huh?"

Jon nods his head, looking upset. He yanks his hands through his hair and exhales loudly. I step towards him again and am relieved when he doesn't back away. I slowly wrap my arms around his waist and lean my head on him as he stands there. "I'm sorry," I whisper. "I wasn't thinking. I'm so stupid. Please forgive me, Jon."

Jon stands still for a moment, then he slowly brings his hands up and holds me to him. "You're not stupid." He whispers into my hair. "You haven't been feeling well and I guess it must have looked really odd when you couldn't understand the conversation."

I wrap my arms more tightly around him and breathe in his smell. I feel like such a fool for jumping to such an unlikely conclusion. We stand like that for a few minutes, until Jon pulls my face up to his.

"Do you know the lesson to be learned from this?" he whispers to me, his hands gently resting on my face. I shake my head. "You really need to learn French. *Je t'aime,* Emma."

*

At the end of October, we flew to Wellington from Adelaide and travelled around the north island of New Zealand. I had always been a big fan of *Lord of the Rings*, so trekking those mountains was fantastic for me. New Zealand was great fun and beautiful, but also expensive, so we only spent six weeks there. From Auckland we flew to Singapore, where we spent a week exploring that amazing city. Then we got on a bus and headed through Malaysia, staying in Kuala Lumpur for a few weeks. It was December by now. On Christmas day 2007, Jon and I sat on a beautiful beach on the north-west Malaysian coast and ate fresh fried fish and noodles for Christmas dinner. We shared a bottle of rum and got rip-roaring drunk, ending the evening with skinny dipping in the warm sea. It was fantastic.

Our next stop was Thailand. Janine had visited a few years previously and recommended we go to Phuket province for the good beaches. So that's what we did.

We arrived and rented a hut on the beach, a little bit of luxury and privacy for once. We could get up in the morning and step straight out onto the sand. There was a great bar just down the beach which we frequented. We spent a few weeks just lazing around and chilling out. Early one morning, Jon and I sat out on the sand. We'd gone to bed early the night before, rather than stay up partying, so for once we'd seen the sun rise. It was a beautiful day, warm and sunny with a very slight breeze on the air. It was still early in the morning so there was hardly anyone around. The bar we had been at last night was just setting up behind us. We were talking about what to do next, where to go and what we were going to do with the time we had left.

"We could always stay here longer," Jon suggests, his face upturned to the sun. "We've been to so many places the last few months, it would be nice to stay put for a while."

"Hmm, I wouldn't object to that," I murmur, laying my head on his leg and playing with the warm sand under my toes.

"Maybe we should find something to do with our time," Jon says quietly. "Those kids we saw in Singapore got me thinking… maybe there is a local charity we could work with for a while. It feels wrong to just waste away our days all the time."

I smile up at him and close my eyes. Listening to the waves lapping on the shore as Jon gently strokes my hair. After a minute, I become aware of a very angry one-sided conversation just behind us, and glance over. The manager of the bar is speaking into his phone; switching from French, then to English, then to Thai, then back to French. He doesn't look like a local man.

"He seems angry," I say, looking up at Jon, who is turned towards him.

"I think his bartender has just quit," he murmurs, "and someone else has called in sick."

We watch as the manager says something very rude into the phone and then chucks it in anger. The phone lands not far from us. The manager curses at the sky, then shakes his head and moves towards the phone.

"Morning," I say as the man approaches. "Is everything okay?"

The manager looks at me in surprise, then shakes his head and curses in French again. Jon smirks.

"No. It is not okay," the man says in heavily accented English. He sits down heavily on the ground next to us, and I sit up. "My bartender has just quit, and my chef is late this morning. I have to open my bar, and I need to go to town to pick up food for the lunches." He shakes his head. "I have only one other person to help me do the bar today." He curses in French again.

I glance at Jon, who looks back with a 'why not?' expression.

"Can we help?" I ask the man.

He looks over in shock. "You would help me?"

"We have no plans for today," Jon says. "It would be good to do something useful."

"I'm Emma," I introduce. "And this is Jon. We're staying in one of the Pha Ku huts just up there." I point a little up the beach, where our hut sits in the shade of the palm trees.

The manager looks over at us, still surprised. "I am Stefan." He casts us a wary glance. "How long are you here for?"

Jon and I share a look. "We aren't sure yet," Jon replies. "We're backpackers, but we are talking about staying here a bit longer."

I shrug. "I can bartend for you for a few days if you want."

"You have worked on a bar before?"

"Yes."

"Have you, Jon?"

Jon shakes his head. "No, but I can do other useful things."

Stefan narrows his eyes, his look thoughtful. "I can pay you in food and drink."

I smile at him. "That'll do for starters."

Stefan regards us for a moment, then throws up his hands. "Why not? I seem to have no choice. You seem like pleasant English people."

Jon smiles and speaks to him in rapid French. Stefan once again looks shocked, then grins as he replies, "You are French too. Even better."

*

Seven weeks later and I'm serving cocktails to tourists from Stefan's bar. I actually love doing this. I get to be on the beach all day, drink whatever I want all the time, eat local fresh food prepared a few metres behind me, and chat to people. In the evening, the real crowds come down and it's a big party. Everyone is so relaxed. Jon and I stay up all night, sleep until mid-morning, go for a swim and start the day again. It's fantastic fun and hardly feels like work at all.

After a few days, Stefan actually begins paying me too. It's not much, but it's enough that we aren't dipping into our savings for our accommodation while we're here. We might actually be saving money soon if we keep eating for free.

Jon does odd jobs around the place, and he has started doing some local children's charity work as well. Fundraising and giving out food to kids who need it, helping out in a local shelter. He loves it.

Right now, Jon is swimming in the sea. The slacker.

The tourists who come here are really interesting. From all over the world, some just passing through, others staying at a local hut or hotel. I have my regulars too, an older English bloke called Tom, who comes here every lunchtime, sits reading the paper all day, then leaves when the music gets turned up. He doesn't speak much, but at least he smiles at me now.

Stefan is really funny. He is loud and very French, and always seems to be on the edge of losing control. I do wonder how this bar has been running for quite so long.

I'm just pouring a beer for Tom when a couple of young women hesitantly come up to the bar and sit down. I smile at them. "Be with you in a sec, ladies." I hand the pint to Tom, take his offered *baht* and thank him.

I grab a cloth and wipe my hands. "Ladies, what can I get you on this gorgeous day?"

The women look at each other nervously. "Uh, a cocktail?" the brunette says carefully. Her accent is American.

I get the feeling they aren't used to ordering at a bar. I pass them the cocktail menu. "Pick your poison. Personally, I suggest the Mai Tai. It's delicious this time of day, and I love making them."

The women exchange a look. The blonde sits up and smiles at me. "Sure, two Mai Tais, please."

"Coming right up." I turn to the counter behind me and grab the rum.

"There he is," the brunette girl says, sounding excited. "Damn, he's hot."

I turn back to the bar and begin to make the drinks in front of them, but they are looking out onto the beach.

"Ooh, is that him coming out the water?" the blonde asks. I

glance up and do a double take. I think they're talking about Jon. I smile to myself as he emerges from the water, all tanned and toned, and dripping wet.

"Oh my God, he is so gorgeous. When I saw him last night, he was totally wearing clothes as well. I'm totally going to talk to him."

"You should, Hol. He is really dishy. I wonder if he's European. He's got that exotic look to him."

I glance at the two ladies then down to their cocktails, holding in a smile.

"Could be British, oh, I hope he is. I love that accent on guys. Oh my God, he is totally coming this way!" The brunette straightens her back and messes with her hair. I glance up. Jon is looking at me and grinning as he walks up the beach. His green eyes are twinkling. "I think he is smiling at me," the brunette says. "Look at those eyes." I bite my lip to stop myself from laughing. I should probably say something, but this is just too much fun.

"Ladies, here are your Mai Tais." I place the rum cocktails next to them. The blonde hands me some money. "Enjoy." The girls grab the glasses and sip, their eyes on Jon as he comes towards the bar.

I place the money in the till, then grab a local beer from the fridge, crack it open and place it on the bar for Jon. Then I begin to tidy the bottles under the bar behind the girls.

"Hi there," the brunette says as Jon grabs the beer off the bar. Jon looks startled but smiles at her.

"Hello."

"I was just admiring you swimming. You're very powerful in the water."

I lean on the bar behind them, where they can't see me, and grin at him. Jon looks amused, both by the conversation and my amused look. He cracks a smile at her. "Thanks. I get a lot of swimming in right now."

He takes a long drag of his beer, and I swear I hear the brunette swallow hard. It is very sexy, watching his throat move like that as water drips down his lean, sculptured torso. Jon knows it too; that's probably why he just did it.

"What's your name?" she asks with a hoarse voice.

"Jon." He tilts his head. "What's yours?"

"Holly, Holly Collins."

"I'm Josie Wain," the blonde tells him.

"Well, it's nice to meet you, Holly, Josie." Jon takes a seat at the bar, a stool apart from Holly. "Have you been here long?"

"We arrived last night," Holly replies. "We came here, and I saw you, so we had to come back." I can't see her face but she is probably smiling flirtatiously at him.

Jon shoots her a polite smile. "Yeah, I come here a lot."

"Are you going to be here tonight? I will be." Her tone is very suggestive. I move along the bar towards Jon and wipe up, mostly so I can see her face.

Jon nods, and leans back. "I suspect so, but I don't want to lead you on, so you should know, I'm taken." Those words make my heart expand.

Holly's face fills with disappointment. "Really?"

Jon nods solemnly. "Definitely."

"Do you have a girlfriend back in England?" Josie has leaned around her friend.

Jon shakes his head. "No, she is here with me." I lean on the bar casually. The women both glance around the beach, away from the bar. Jon's gaze slides to me and he smiles. "In fact, Emma just served you your drinks."

The girls both freeze, then turn to me slowly. I grin at them, then lean over the bar and peck Jon on the cheek. "I'm sorry, ladies, I should have said something, but I really couldn't resist."

They both look a bit startled; Holly looks absolutely

crestfallen. I take pity on her. I grab the tequila bottle, shot glasses, lime and salt. "How's about a shot of tequila, on the house? To say I'm sorry." I wink at Holly. "It was a good try, though." Holly smiles faintly.

I serve up the tequila, including Jon and myself. The women look at each other.

"Have you guys had a tequila shot before?" I ask. They both shake their heads. I smile. "You guys aren't twenty-one yet, huh?" They both nod. "No matter, here's how it's done…"

Jon and I show them how to do a proper tequila shot. Holly's face is priceless as she swallows the bitter liquid.

"Yuck!" Josie exclaims. "That's nasty."

Holly nods in agreement, then smiles at me. "Let's have another!" She places some money on the bar, which I take. I dish them out another shot, which they throw back expertly this time.

"Watch out," I tell them. "This is strong stuff. It'll make you drunk in no time."

Holly giggles, well on the way to being drunk already, so I put the tequila away and sell them both a bottle of water. With great bartending comes great responsibility. Jon turns and starts talking with a French tourist who has been coming to the bar for a few days. I serve him a beer.

Holly leans forward as I move past. "Are you mad about what we said about Jon?"

"Uh no," I reply, resting my elbows on the bar. "You called my boyfriend gorgeous, why would I be mad? I agree!"

Holly giggles and glances at him. "He speaks French too? Wow." I grin and go to serve a couple of guys. "I really do like the English accent," she tells me as I move around. Josie nods in agreement, sipping her cocktail. "On girls as well as guys."

I laugh as I grab some beer bottles out of the fridge. "Well, that's good to know. How long are you guys staying here for?"

"Eight days here, then we are off to Bangkok," Josie says.

"We're on vacation for two weeks."

I hand the beer to the guys and take their money. "Well, you guys wanna grab food with us tonight? I finish at 7pm and then we party."

Holly smiles widely at me. "We'd love to."

*

Jon and I spend the next week hanging out with Josie and Holly, when they aren't chatting up the cute guys. Holly got over her crush on Jon very quickly and soon moved on to a cute Australian who was more than happy to reciprocate her advances. I find it all very amusing.

I have the Wednesday daytime off work, and Jon always makes sure our non-working days coincide, so we all grab some scooters and head into the city to spend a day wandering around the markets. We show Holly and Josie the clothes market, and advise them on how to bargain for the best price. They don't do very well, giving in way too early, but that's all part of the fun.

We are sitting in a street café having coffee when Holly's mobile rings. She gets it out and frowns, before standing up and moving away.

Josie follows her with her eyes, looking concerned. "She would only answer her cell if it was her mom," she tells us, "and her mom would only call in an emergency."

I glance over at Holly, who is leaning on a wall with her back to us. "I hope nothing's wrong."

Josie shoots us a worried glance and goes to her friend. I watch carefully as Josie's face shows alarm. Holly almost collapses into her arms a second later.

Jon and I rush over. Jon takes Holly carefully around the waist and leads her back to the chair.

"What happened?" he asks softly, kneeling next to her.

Holly shakes her head and bursts into tears. Josie grabs the phone. "Mrs Collins? It's Josie... what..."

Josie's face shows pure horror. "Oh God," she whispers. "Oh God, I'm sorry... I..." She glances at us. "Uh no, we're out... yes... we're here with some friends. Yes, yes, I'll get her to call you later when we are back at the hostel. Okay. Bye, Mrs Collins."

Josie immediately wraps her friend in a big hug, rocking her slowly.

"Her brother has been killed," she whispers to me over Holly's shoulder. "He was in the army, serving in Afghanistan."

I gasp. That's so horrible. Jon stands up slowly and takes my waist. I hug him back. It's really horrible.

*

Josie and Holly leave the next day, to fly back to America. It's nice to see Josie looking after her friend; Holly is just dazed.

The incident seems to have thrown a mood over our time here, and Jon and I decide it's time to move on. We still have lots of places to visit before we want to head back home. Stefan is sad to see us go, but I think he is used to bartenders moving on, and we give him a few weeks' notice so he can find a replacement for me.

We travel through Thailand by bus, via Bangkok, then over to Cambodia, spending two weeks in the beautiful Phnom Penh, before heading over to Vietnam. I thought Singapore was crazy. Vietnam is mental but brilliant. We have a thirty-day visa, so we hire a couple of scooters in Hoi Chi Minh City and drive around the south, heading up slowly to Hôi An, a seaside town in the rough middle of the country. Then we hop on a sleeper train in Da Nang and travel up to Hanoi, the capital city. The soft sleeper berths usually sleep four people in one room; we end up sharing with six others. It is apparently possible to fit two adults, a teenager and two kids on one single bed, if you sleep sitting up. Jon and I couldn't quite believe it.

We spend a few days in Hanoi, visit the wonderful Ha Long Bay, then get another train over to Sapa and do some highly recommended mountain trekking. We hire some scooters again and hop over the Chinese border for a few days, just to say we have been there too. Then we head back to Hanoi. We have a flight out of there to Kathmandu, Nepal. There are many other places in Asia we want to visit, but our extended stay in Thailand means we were running out of time if we want to travel around Europe too, which we do. From Nepal we head into India. We travel on the most horrific journey of our entire lives from Kathmandu to New Delhi. I don't usually get travel sick but I do this time. I am very glad to get to our hostel and just sleep on a non-moving bed.

New Delhi was brilliant, full of life and great people. We met a lot of backpackers, and a surprisingly large number of ex-pats. This was to be our last stop in this part of the world, as our time was rapidly running out. So we looked at flights and where we could fly to in Europe. We would stay here in India for twenty-one days, primarily in New Delhi. We decided to fly into Cairo, then go to Italy via boat.

When we got on the plane in New Delhi, it felt like we were saying goodbye to our travels, though in fact we had another three months left before we were due in France.

From Egypt, we travelled up Italy via Rome and then Florence and Milan. We tried some summer glacier skiing in the Alps, and spent more money in three days than we had our entire time in Thailand. Via train, we travelled up through Austria to Vienna, then Prague in the Czech Republic, up to Warsaw in Poland. We spent two weeks in Berlin, which Jon had been to before but loved. I think it was weird for him, finally being in a place he had been to before. From Berlin we stopped off in Hamburg, then got a ferry to Stockholm. Once again via train we travelled down to

Copenhagen and Amsterdam and Brussels. We arrived in Paris on the 3rd of November 2008. Jon's parents were there to greet us.

We had left London on the 1st of August 2007. We had been travelling for fourteen months. We had visited twenty-four countries, and had sex in twenty-three of them. We had met hundreds of people and taken thousands of photos. I had so many more people on my Facebook than I had before.

It had been amazing. As we reached Jon's parents' house just south of Reims, it seemed surreal. Jon's parents were the same as when we had left them over a year ago. Amie and Mike had had a little girl while we were travelling, and we met her for the first time that day. Her name was Addie. She had black hair and green eyes, and she was adorable.

In three weeks, we would be back in the UK, and our adult lives would begin.

*

In late November 2008, we arrived back in the UK, heading to my parents' house. Being back felt really odd. We'd seen so much, done so much, and yet here we were.

Now we were faced with the reality of trying to find jobs. I was really lucky and got a graduate job in an accountancy firm in Southampton almost straight away. Even for a graduate role the pay was good, but the work was tough and the hours long. I couldn't afford a long commute, so we made the decision to live apart until we knew where Jon would be based. I moved into a cheap house-share with other professionals in Southampton, including my best friend, Janine. It was like uni, only I had to get up at 7am every morning now. I discovered that I was more motivated to get up to BBC Radio 4. I found the deep baritone presenters and their interesting discussions really woke me up, and I got into the habit of listening to it as I got ready for work. Having visited a lot of places in the world, I had found my interests were broader than just dancing cats on YouTube. One morning, I heard the morning presenter grilling a US army media relations officer about the foreign military in Afghanistan. I thought back to Holly and wondered how she was doing. The officer representing the US Army, Lieutenant Grenal, was very fiery and stuck to her guns, hardly getting defensive at all despite the aggressive questions. I wasn't sure if I could ever do that. It was strangely enjoyable to listen to.

Jon moved in with Amie in Oxford for a few months while he looked for work, then landed a graduate position with a firm in London, who would be training him to be a solicitor. When Jon wasn't hunting for jobs, he spent time with his niece, Addie, whom he adored.

It was hard, those first few months, living apart. After spending fourteen months together travelling all over the world, to suddenly be apart from him was a big shock and I missed him terribly. I was head over heels in love with this man; I still felt excitement and anticipation when I knew I was going to see him, even after all the time we'd spent together.

As soon as Jon started work in London, we both agreed that we wanted to live together, so we started to look for a place in Reading. The commute was longer for both of us but Southampton was on the same train line, and Jon's office wasn't far from Paddington Station so it seemed a good place to be. Despite the money Jon had, we both agreed we should leave that as a deposit on a house a little further down the line. So we needed a cheap place to rent that we could afford on our salaries. We found one in Reading in April 2009. It was small, dingy and smelt funny, but it was cheap and it was ours.

Our days are long. We both leave at 7am and walk to the station together. I usually get home around 6pm, Jon around 7pm. But it's worth it to go to bed with him every night, and wake up every morning with him. I can't imagine not sharing my life with him anymore. Our weekends are filled with family, friends and fun trips. We often spend weekends with Amie, Mike and Addie, at their house or at campsites. I bought a bike so Janine and I go cycling. Janine is mad on cycling. Sometimes it's nice to just have some time to ourselves. Jon and I go running together and participate in fun runs to raise money for charity. We often have a romantic dinner at home, which I love. Luckily, we are both good cooks, so we eat well despite our busy lives.

Of course, it's not always perfect. Sometimes we argue; sometimes we are grumpy with each other. But we always make up. We never go to bed angry. I have never been jealous since that day in Australia; I trust Jon implicitly.

When the recession hit, my firm downsized and it looked like I might lose my job. I applied for other positions and landed one in a large international construction company called Gold & Sanchez in mid 2009, based in Salisbury. The commute from Reading was a hassle, but it was doable.

I knew several people who weren't so lucky. Janine was a planner in a development consultancy which folded. My father's work pretty much stopped completely. Abbey, who worked for a marketing firm in Bristol, had to take a pay cut and barely kept her job. Luckily, Jon's job was pretty secure, and he had the privilege of working on several of the London 2012 Olympic contracts at the law firm who was training him.

In early 2009, Amie and Mike had twin boys, giving Addie two little brothers, Josh and James. I would have thought this would mean that their twice-a-year camping trips to the New Forest would end, but no. They were determined to continue the tradition. We always joined them camping, taking in a few walks and pubs during the day. July 2009 was no exception. It was a glorious Saturday and we were all spending the weekend camping near Burley. Amie and Mike were always really glad for the help with the kids. Addie now had a tendency to wander off if you weren't paying attention. I was glad to be on Addie-watching duty, following her all over the place and making sure she didn't get into trouble. It was lots of fun.

Jon and I had been together for three and a half years when we took a camping trip to the Peak District in October 2010. Jon and I had been all over the world, but we'd never been to the Peak District. I love the outdoors; hiking up mountains is my idea of a really good time. Fortunately, Jon got used to it while we were abroad so now he enjoyed it too. I needed the trip as well. A few weeks earlier, my grandmother had passed away after a long illness. We had come to our first campsite direct from the funeral. My grandmother had been a wonderful woman, so full of life and old-world advice. I would miss her a lot.

We are about halfway through our holiday, gradually conquering all the peaks one by one, camping in nearby villages. It is a beautiful autumn day when we climb the highest mountain in the Peak District, an upper moorland called Kinder Scout. The air is fresh and cool and brushes softly over my exposed neck under my short jaw-length hair. The sun is shining high in the sky, gradually burning off the mist in the valley below. The weather is gorgeous despite it being late October. It is so early that there isn't another soul in sight. I am pointing out a large bird of prey hovering overhead when I realise Jon isn't beside me anymore. I turn and send him a questioning look. Jon has stepped back and is looking at me with his twinkling eyes.

"Jon? What is it?"

Jon's gaze locks on mine, his green eyes blazing. "Emma, you are my world. You make me so much happier than I ever thought I would be. My life would be empty without you." He smiles widely, then takes a small box out of his pocket and drops to his knee. "Emma, I want to be with you forever. Will you marry me?"

I stare at him with my mouth open for a long second. Then

I feel my face burst into a smile. "Yes! Yes! Yes!" Jon laughs at my enthusiasm and a second later a beautiful silver ring with a delicate red stone is slipped onto my ring finger. Then I throw my arms around him and start laughing. Jon kisses me; a long, lingering, passionate kiss which I never want to end.

When we break for air, I stare down at my left ring finger, studying the stone. The ring fits perfectly. "How on earth did you get my size right?" I ask.

"I measured it while you were sleeping," Jon admits. "I wanted it to be a complete surprise."

A couple of buff-looking blokes choose that moment to walk by us. They look like they are on a serious hike; with large rucksacks, full army gear and big bushy beards, but I am so excited I want to tell someone.

"Look, look, we're getting married!" I tell them, shoving my ring finger into their faces. The soldiers are surprised, but then laugh heartily and offer their congratulations. One of them even slaps Jon on the back and says in a thick Scottish accent, "If we see ya at the pub later, your beer is on us!"

One of the men, the shorter of the two but equally as stocky, even feigns interest in the ring, which I thought was very polite of him. They walk away with big smiles on their faces, and I hope we have made them a little happier too.

*

In early 2011, I was promoted at my company to account officer, a big step up from my graduate/assistant role. The chartered accountancy qualification I had been working for had helped massively. A month or so later, Jon landed a new position, this time outside London. A small but select law firm in Southampton hired him to work in their environmental law department. This was an area Jon had specialised in, and he was enthusiastic that now he could really do something he enjoyed. Due to the locations of our jobs, we finally moved from Reading and bought a good-sized three-bedroom house in Salisbury. Jon's money, and what I had saved over the years, meant we had a large deposit. The house needed some work so we spent a lot of our weekends doing DIY. It was both successful and not. The can of paint I spilt on the living room floor was a massive failure, as was the power cut when we were painting the hallway. But Jon became very good at putting up shelves, and after a year or so, there were no more horrid feature walls and the house looked just as we wanted it to.

I started growing strawberries and tomatoes in the garden. I tried my hand at baking, first flapjacks because I love them, then cakes and cookies for parties, visits and an occasional birthday. I found I was quite good at baking, and Jon and I would eat my creations with lots of wine. I felt very domesticated, and content.

Jon and I got married on a wonderful autumn day in 2011. It wasn't a big wedding, around fifty friends and family at the registry office in Salisbury, and then a magnificent room in Salisbury Guildhall. There was no pretentiousness, neither of us wanted that, and we paid for it ourselves so the day felt like we had really earned it. Rob was Jon's best man, and I had Janine and Amie as bridesmaids. Addie was a flower girl and so very pretty. My father made a really nice speech, talking about when I was little and what an extraordinary woman I was. It nearly had me in tears.

For our honeymoon, we travelled around South America for three weeks. It reminded me of our year-long expedition all those years ago.

One evening, sometime after we had gone back to work, we were sitting in the garden drinking red wine. The night was cold and frost was setting in, but the sky was clear and Jon was pointing out all the stars to me. I lean back in my recliner and study the bright twinkling lights above my head as I feel the wine ebb through my system and warm me from within. I breathe out and a light mist clouds my vision for a second, then it disappears. I sit doing this for a while until I notice Jon has stopped talking. I glance over to see him watching me with a smile on his face.

I grin back, as if I hadn't been doing anything odd, and innocently take a sip of wine.

Suddenly he leans towards me. "We should have a baby."

I almost spit out my wine on him. "What?" I splutter.

"I want to have a baby with you."

I stare at him as he looks back. "You do?"

"Yes." He nods. "Do you remember on our first date when you said you wanted to make your children happy?"

"I do. I remember other things about our first date too, and our second. Very good things."

"Well, I think you would be a great mother, and I want us to have one." Jon is grinning; he is not letting me derail the conversation.

I blink and look back up at the stars for a second. "Okay."

Now it is Jon's chance to look surprised. "Okay?"

"Yep."

"Just like that?"

"Yep."

He grins at me. "Is it the wine talking, or my wife?"

I giggle. "Perhaps both." Then I smile happily at him. "It just feels right, Jon, now you say it. I want it too."

"It's a big commitment."

"It is."

"You'll have to be pregnant."

"Well, duh."

"You'll have to go on maternity leave."

"Woohoo, holiday!" Jon gives me a look and I grin back.

"There'll be late-night feedings, nappies, throwing up, crying, then teenage angst, of course."

"Wow, you're really selling it to me."

"Still yes?"

"Yep."

Jon grins. "Well, then maybe we should get started right now." With that, he leaps on top of me, and I squeal, my wine glass landing on the grass with a thud.

"Ah, Jon, you know I have to..." I'm going to remind him that I need to have my coil taken out before any babies can be made.

"Shh." He covers my lips with his. "We need to practise."

*

Jon and I had a baby girl on the 3rd of September 2012. We named her April. My pregnancy was easy by the standards of some of my friends. I was sick for the first three months but after that the nausea went away. I often felt bloated and emotional, and was very glad that Jon was there. I couldn't have done it alone.

My company offered a generous maternity package, so I took nine months off work after April was born. I watched as April grew from a very pretty baby into a beautiful little girl. She had Jon's bright green eyes and thick black hair, and a wide smile for everyone. I was often stopped when walking with her; old ladies especially liked to comment on what a gorgeous baby she was. I was even stopped once in the supermarket by a young blonde woman wearing an army uniform. April looked up at her and smiled widely. The young woman almost melted into a puddle in the world food aisle.

We were the first of our friends to have a baby. Rob and Abbey got married just after she was born, and had a big party. Jon and I tried not to change our weekend schedules too much.

We still had friends visit us, though visiting others was slightly trickier. We spent a lot of time with Amie and Mike, though it didn't involve beer festivals anymore. Addie was now four, and the twins two years old. Three kids was a lot of work. We all loved to camp, so we still spent a night or two in the New Forest camping, visiting pubs and doing short walks.

When we had no plans and it was a nice day, we would often go to the local park. There was a large area of open green space a few roads down from us. We would pack a picnic and we would sit on the grass to eat it. April would be enchanted, her amazing green eyes taking in everything she could. April loved the swings, and could happily play on them for hours. Jon would play with her on the grass while I lay and watched, basking in the sunlight. There was something very moving about seeing Jon with April, his platinum wedding band gleaming in the light as he held her in his arms. I was struck by the realisation that they were all mine. I loved them both so much, even when they jumped on me and made me squeal loudly in the middle of the park.

April went through a phase of doing this a lot when she was around two and a half, with Jon's encouragement every time. So I was watching out for the tricksters on one park weekend in late summer.

Jon saw me smiling at the memory and pointed it out to April. "Look, April, Mummy's smiling at us."

April turns her bright face to me and yells, "Mummy Mummy Mummy!"

"April April April!" I yell back, and she waddles to me. Her walking is getting better and better.

"Mummy cuddles," she says happily as she leaps into my arms. Jon approaches with a smile and sits down next to me.

"Mummy cuddles are the best," he agrees.

After a minute, April jumps off me and waddles away in her yellow and black wellies. She sits down in the grass a few metres away on her big nappy-covered bottom and begins to play with the late summer daisies.

Jon leans over and nuzzles my neck. "I love your cuddles too," he whispers. "I love everything about you."

I don't need to be told twice. I wrap my arms around his neck and kiss him. After a few minutes, Jon lays down on his side, facing April, and I move to rest my head on his stomach. He gently strokes my hair off my forehead as he leans on his hand.

"How would you feel about having another baby?" I ask after a moment. Jon's hand stills for just a second, then carries on. "I know we've talked about it before, but it just feels like she is old enough to enjoy a younger brother or sister."

I look over into Jon's face against the backdrop of the blue sky and see he is smiling.

"I think it's a great idea," he says, then he looks serious. "Now we have experienced the late-night feedings, nappies and crying, it doesn't seem quite so scary."

"We still haven't got to the teenage angst, though," I point out.

Jon shrugs. "How bad can that be really? At least we'll have slept by then." I roll my eyes at his optimism and he laughs. "I would love to have another baby with you."

I grin, then a thought strikes me. "Jac will be pissed if we beat him. That will be grandchild number five." I am referring to the money left by his grandmother.

"Ha!" Jon laughs. "Serves him right for living a bachelor life for so long."

"Yep, he doesn't know what he is missing out on." I glance at April again. "Let's give April a sibling."

Jon grins, heat flashing in his eyes. "I can't wait." Neither can I.

Jon had recently been promoted at work and was putting in long hours in a more client-facing role, so I had changed my working time so I could take care of April. She was due to start pre-school next year, which would free up some of our time and money.

It was the Tuesday after that weekend in the park. Jon was often home around 6pm, the latest 7pm. He hated to miss April going to bed; it meant he barely saw her. I gave April her dinner, then she had a bath. By the time I was reading her stories in bed, it was after 7pm and Jon still wasn't home. I thought maybe he had been stuck in a meeting and had texted to say he would be late.

As I turn off April's light and shut the door, I check my phone. No message. I call him, but it goes straight to voicemail.

I rack my brains. I didn't think Jon had said he would be home late tonight, but maybe he had and I had forgotten. I text him to remind him to let me know.

I make a simple dinner of vegetables and pasta, leaving enough for Jon, and watch a documentary about the Arctic while I eat. Jon still isn't home after that finishes so I call him again. Again, the phone goes straight to voicemail. I send him another text.

I'm slightly concerned; it isn't like Jon to not answer the phone when I ring. I peer through the curtains, hoping to see him pull into the driveway next to my car, but of course he doesn't.

I play around on my laptop for a bit, waiting for him. By 11pm, I'm really quite concerned, and knowing I won't be able to sleep, I put on iPlayer again and begin to watch a BBC drama series.

I must have dozed off because a sharp knocking on the door wakes me. The drama has ended and the TV has turned itself off by then. I check the time; it is well after midnight.

Sleepily, I turn on the light in the hallway as I open the door a crack and peer outside. Two policemen stand outside the door. The light from the hallway reflects brightly off their fluorescent jackets.

"Mrs Emma Clemens?" the female officer asks. I blink in

confusion.

"Yes?" I reply. "Can I help you?"

"Sergeants Cox and Willis of the Wiltshire constabulary, Ma'am," the female officer continues, showing me her ID. "May we come in and speak to you?"

I blink again, struggling to wake up. I glance behind her at the empty parking space. A police car sits on the road opposite. "Uh, what about?" Then the fact that Jon isn't home yet registers in my brain, and a cold feeling creeps down my spine.

"Please, Mrs Clemens." The male officer, Willis, gestures to the house. I open the door all the way and allow them in.

"What's going on?" I ask.

"Ma'am, we need to ask, is your husband Jon Clemens?"

"Yes," I say instantly. "Is something wrong? He hasn't come home from work tonight."

Willis looks around the room, not meeting my gaze. Cox takes a step towards me. "Maybe you should sit down."

"What?" I ask, puzzled. "Tell me what's going on."

"Mrs Clemens," Cox says slowly, "your husband was involved in a road accident tonight."

I gasp and my hand flies to my mouth. "Oh my God. Is that why Jon isn't answering his phone? What happened? Is he hurt?" The questions fly from my mouth as I feel dread coiling in my stomach.

"A lorry driver was distracted during a traffic jam, and failed to slow as the traffic in front of him stopped," Cox says slowly, and with sadness. I distantly feel Willis move to my side. "Your husband's car was the vehicle in front of his lorry. I'm very sorry, Mrs Clemens, but your husband's car was hit with such force by the lorry that it was crushed against the safety barrier."

"What?" I whisper.

"I'm really sorry," Cox says softly. "Jon Clemens died instantly."

I stare wide-eyed at the officer, then, as if in slow motion, I feel my knees give out. Willis catches my arm and moves me to the sofa, sitting beside me.

"No." I shake my head. "No, you have to be wrong, it's a mistake," I whisper. "Jon isn't dead, he can't be dead…"

"I'm very sorry," Willis says softly, "but it's not a mistake."

I peer into his eyes and see the truth reflected back at me. Horror fills my chest as I struggle to keep control. My heart pounds in my ears, I can barely breathe, everything around me feels wrapped in cling film.

I vaguely hear someone asking me about April, about someone else they can contact, but as the tears overflow, all I can think about is that my husband, my best friend, is dead.

I will never see Jon again.

I feel my heart shatter into a million pieces.

Chapter 4

Army Part 2

July 2009

I left Afghanistan after the completion of my tour in September 2007. After six weeks' leave, I was assigned back to Chatham where I undertook further training with the army engineers for five months. Colonel Jenson and Captain Marks had both given me extremely strong recommendations after I had completed my work with the US Army. I was considered a first-hand expert and was asked to work with senior officers on our reconstruction strategy in the Middle East. I much preferred the actual work to strategy, but I was honoured to be asked. For a long time, it felt very strange being back in a classroom, or wearing my dress uniform, after what I had experienced abroad.

In April 2008, I was sent to a base in northern Scotland, working with the civilian engineers on several complex military projects. I had a brief relationship with a civilian man, Leo, whom I met there. Leo was fun, and sexy, and we could have made it work, but I realised quite early on that it was doomed simply because he was not Rick Tavern. That man had ruined me, I hoped not forever.

After I returned from Scotland, I finally completed my bachelor's degree in civil engineering, paid for by the Army, based on the work I had undertaken in Afghanistan. So I was now a fully qualified engineer with almost four years of experience in some of the most dangerous parts of the world.

I spent six months in the Falkland Islands as part of the army infrastructure team stationed there. I had a brief fling with a civilian again, but I just couldn't get the American soldier out of my head and it fizzled out. In March 2009, I was sent to Salisbury Plain. I had been assigned as a senior engineer liaison for some of the major refurbishment work they were undertaking on and around the base, before I was due to be redeployed back to Afghanistan in July 2009 for my longest tour yet.

My friend Janine now lived in Southampton, and we loved to go off-road cycling through the New Forest. Janine had been the only friend who had regularly kept in contact over the years I was deployed. Whenever I had come back to the UK, I had visited her, so we were making the most of me being in the country. I was shipping out on my second Afghanistan tour the following week.

Early one summer Saturday morning, I met her in a car park near Brockenhurst, and we geared up and left. I didn't own a bike, for obvious reasons, but Janine was a cycling enthusiast and so I always borrowed one of hers. I'd been looking forward to this for ages, something fun to remember during the hot and sweaty heat I was about to endure.

We liked to change the routes frequently. As a serving British Army corporal, my general fitness level was above hers, but Janine was an avid cyclist so we were pretty evenly matched. Our cycling trips were about fun and enjoying the outdoors. Today we were aiming at our longest yet, a 50km circular route with a stop in the pub for lunch.

By the time we got to the pub in Burley, we had completed 35 km's. Experience had taught us it was always best to get most of the route done before the pub stop.

We order our burgers and juices at the bar and are sitting outside in the beer garden when I notice a little girl wandering around by herself. I glance around. No one seems to be paying much attention to her, but I think that maybe they are just letting her play. I keep an eye on her for a few minutes; she is getting dangerously close to a large stream which runs through the garden.

Janine catches where I am looking and glances around for her parents too. I stand and move quickly as the little girl approaches the stream. I kneel down next to her.

"Hi," I say softly, with a big smile. The little girl, her dark pigtails swinging around her head, peers over at me curiously. "I'm not sure you should be playing quite so close to the water," I continue. "It's dangerous, you know. Where's your mummy?"

The girl looks over her shoulder at the garden, her eyes moving quickly. Then I see her bottom lip begin to tremble, I'm guessing because she can't see her parents.

"Hey, it's okay," I say with a smile. "Shall we go and find your mummy?"

The girl nods and holds out her hand. I place one of my fingers in it and we begin to slowly walk towards the pub door.

A tall black-haired woman runs out of the entrance to the pub and spots us. Janine walks out behind her. "Addie!" she calls. The little girl's face lights up as she runs into her arms. "Addie, you shouldn't scare me like that." She hugs the child close to her and stands up. "Thank you. Thank you," she says to Janine and myself. "You look away for a second…" She strokes the girl's hair lovingly. "I have twins too…" She shakes her head. "No excuses. Thank you."

"Of course," I reply with a smile. "She's an inquisitive girl, huh?"

The mother nods and holds out her hand. "I'm Amie," she says.

"Emma, and this is Janine."

"Thank you, Emma, and Janine. And you," she looks into the face of her little girl, "no wandering off again, okay? Can I buy you a drink, to say thank you?"

I hold up my hands and shake my head, as this last comment was directed at us. "It's fine, don't worry, go back to your family."

The woman nods distractedly and turns away with a smile, talking to the little girl, who waves at me over her mother's shoulder.

"Emma King saves the day again," Janine teases with a smile.

I shake my head and swat her arm. "Hardly, she would have realised soon enough." We go back to our table just as the food arrives.

After lunch, we head back out for the final 15 km. The car park is really filling up as we leave, and we have to carefully wind our way through the cars. The New Forest does not have many hills, but there are some steep technical sections which you have to be careful on. I'm thinking about the cute little girl as we descend a steep tricky section, and the little boys and girls I had met on my tours abroad. I was idly wondering if that's what I wanted for myself, and where I saw my future. I should have been paying attention to my speed and the angle of my tyre on the ground because before I can react, the bike jerks beneath me and I'm flying through the air. I have a second to swear at myself before I instinctively put my arms out to stop the impact. I hit the ground hard on my left side, and immediately my left forearm cracks and goes numb. My helmet-covered head thumps on the compacted dry dirt and I slide downhill for a metre, rolling and scraping along the ground.

For a second, I just lie there on my back, stunned. Then I lift my head up slowly and groan as my vision blackens from the edges inwards. Despite the helmet, I really hit my head hard. I hear Janine yell and drop her bike.

"Emma! Emma, are you all right?"

My vision gradually brightens, returning to normal, and I groan as I sit up slowly. Janine helps carefully, looking shocked.

"That hurt," I mutter. Using my right hand only, I slowly take off my helmet and bend my head down between my knees to stop the blood rushing to my head. I can feel the adrenaline pumping through my system. I don't hurt yet, but I know I will.

"Emma." I look up dazed into the concerned face of my friend. "I'm calling an ambulance." Luckily, in the New Forest, you are never too far from an access road. I can see one just over the gorse. I feel as if I should argue about the ambulance, but I can't bring myself to do it.

I'm not sure how much time passes. I hear Janine on the phone. "Emma, where do you hurt?" She kneels down in front of me, her mobile pressed to her ear.

I point at my left forearm, which is lying uselessly across my legs. It's starting to hurt really badly. "I think I broke it." Janine repeats this into the phone, then replies with, "Yes, she is lucid. Yes, she was wearing a helmet." She picks up my helmet and examines it. "No, I can't see a crack in it."

By now, several cyclists and walkers have stopped beside me. One offers me a drink of water, which I gratefully accept.

Everything goes very quickly after that; it's kind of a blur. A first responder arrives and checks me over. They put me into the car and we head off to Southampton General A&E. I wait for a few hours there, during which time Janine arrives and then I'm seen by a nurse. I'm cut and bruised all over my legs, arms and stomach, and I'll have a black eye where my face scraped the ground. Thanks to my helmet, I only have minor concussion. The only serious injury is my broken forearm and wrist. We wait a few more hours, then they put me in a plaster cast and send me home. Janine drives me back, saying she will sort out my car which is, of course, still in the car park in Brockenhurst.

I feel kind of stupid. I survived two tours in the Middle East with nothing more than mild sunburn and here I am having fallen off my bike in the New Forest. With a broken arm, I will have to delay my next tour. I know I will get mocked relentlessly in the office next week.

I have Monday as a sick day, then am back at work on Tuesday. I live on the base in the singles' accommodation, so my commute is a twenty-minute walk to the site offices, which is lucky, as I can't drive for at least a week. My arm will need to be in a sling during that time. As expected, my colleagues, while sympathetic, mock me. I have to delay the start of my overseas tour until late September, something the commanding officer in Afghanistan is not pleased about.

The next Tuesday, a day after I was supposed to be in Afghanistan, the junior project engineer, Lance Corporal Johnson, rushes into my office with an excited look on her face. "Emma, you'll never guess what I just heard."

I peer up at her. Johnson is younger than me with less overseas experience, and I'm mentoring her so she can take over my role when I leave, which was supposed to be yesterday, but somehow the delay hasn't fazed her at all. She is very excitable and enthusiastic, which makes her great to work with.

"The war in the Middle East is over and everyone is at peace?" I reply ironically. My face is still bruised from my accident, the marks a deep purple and yellow, but my cuts are healing and I no longer feel like I was beaten up by an elephant. My forearm aches all the time; I only take painkillers when it gets really bad.

Johnson makes a face at me. "Don't be stupid, that will never happen." She smirks. "I have something better. You know that there are US Rangers here this week?"

I do know that, it was on our security briefing, they are participating in a training exercise with the SAS. I nod vaguely at Johnson, glancing at my watch to check the time, then realise it's on my right wrist at the moment because of my cast and roll my eyes at myself. When I had heard that Rangers would be here, my mind had drifted to Tavern, who I hadn't heard from since he left Afghanistan over two years ago, but I had quickly dismissed that. I had no idea if he was even a Ranger, and there were dozens of US Special Forces units serving all over the world.

"Well, there is a football game going on right now between the SAS and the Rangers, and the colonel said we could all go and watch." Johnson fans herself. "Let's go and see those hunks."

I sigh. As tempting as it is, I have work to do. Johnson sees my facial expression and glares at me. "Oh no, don't give me that look. You work too damn hard and play too little."

I hold up my plaster cast and state: "This is what happens when I play."

Johnson shakes her head, walks around my desk and takes my unbroken arm. "Come on, Emma, no excuses." I'm tempted to pull rank and stay here, but instead I sigh loudly and lock my laptop as she pulls me away from my desk, shoving my phone in my pocket so I can take calls if I'm needed. It is a beautiful summer day again so I don't grab my jacket, not that it could fit over my plaster cast anyway. I'm just in army cargo trousers, black boots and a plain white t-shirt; my standard attire nowadays.

Johnson leads the way to the sports ground where at least half the base has gathered. She pushes us onto a bleacher and we sit. There is indeed a football game going on. The sun is shining in our eyes from this angle, so I can only vaguely see the shapes in front of me, but I'm not looking very closely anyway.

"Wow. Look at those sex on sticks," Johnson sighs.

"You really need to get out more," I mutter, turning my face to the sun.

Johnson elbows me. "I am out, every Saturday night, getting laid where I can. What do you do?"

I choose not to answer, sometimes I just don't want to go out or get laid. I am happy with my life as it is, uncomplicated.

A loud cheer goes up as the SAS scores, the noise turning to laughing boos as the Rangers score a minute later. The Ranger who scored the goal runs around and around the field, firing up the crowd. There is something very familiar about him and I frown as he passes where we sit, studying his profile. He stops near the west end of the pitch next to two other big guys. They are all wearing a red sash.

"Those guys are the Rangers, right?" I point at the group.

Johnson follows my finger. "Yep, all yummy."

Just then, a cloud covers the sun, allowing me to see them all clearly for the first time. My eyes open wide as I realise why he looks so familiar. I study the others he is standing with in shock.

I feel a smile grow on my face. "I know those guys."

Johnson looks at me in surprise. "You what?"

"Those three." They are dispersing back into the other players, but not before I catch a glimpse of Tavern; tall, blond and tanned. My heart leaps in my chest. "I served with them in Afghanistan, when I was seconded to the US base. White just scored the goal." I laugh, I can't believe it.

"You know those hunks?" Johnson repeats, as if she can't believe her ears.

"Well," I see White emerge from the pack and run to score another goal as the crowd boos in jest, "they weren't quite so hunky back then." My eyes search for Tavern, but the game is moving too fast.

"You should call out to them."

"I don't want to bias the game." I smile. "Don't worry. I'll introduce you."

Johnson rubs her hands together. "Yes, please."

I watch the game with renewed interest now, my eyes searching constantly for Tavern. I catch sight of him a few times, moving through the other men, running up the field, passing the ball. Hunk is definitely the word to use. He had been a big muscular guy before, now he looks like he has bulked up a lot. He wears dark cargo pants and a tight short-sleeved green t-shirt under the red sash. That geometric tattoo that wove from his left wrist to his shoulder looks even better than it did before, with all those defined muscles, complimented by a new crest tattoo I notice on his other arm. His face is covered in light stubble, rather than the big bushy beard I had known him with. It has only been two years, but he looks so much more like a man than before. The last time I saw him he'd been stepping onto a US-bound cargo plane in the Afghan twilight. I feel a familiar longing stirring in my stomach, my thoughts racing through that night we had all those years ago, and I take a deep breath to control my now racing heart.

As the game ends – SAS 5-4 Rangers – the crowd cheers and moves onto the pitch.

I leap up and move towards the Rangers, who have all grouped to one side, laughing and patting each other on the back. Knowing how I can easily get their attention, as I approach, I stick my fingers in my mouth and wolf whistle hard. Every man turns towards me, but it is the light brown eyes under the bright blond hair that open wide with shock that I'm most interested in.

Vega's face practically lights up at the sight of me. "King!" he yells enthusiastically. I wave as I approach, Johnson hot on my heels behind me. All three men run towards me. Vega reaches me first and sweeps me into a big hug. I make sure my plastered arm is safety out of the way. White follows with a slightly less brutal but still enthusiastic hug. Finally, Tavern steps towards me and with a big grin, lifts me into the air and spins me around. It is so unbelievably good to see him again. A shiver of pleasure dances up my spine as he holds me tight to him. As he places me back on the ground, he keeps his hands on my waist and frowns at my face and plaster cast.

"What happened?" he asks, his tone now menacing.

I laugh and punch him lightly on the arm. "Stand down, soldier," I joke. "I fell off my bike last weekend." He gives me an amused look and drops his hands from my waist.

"Fellas, Lance Corporal Irene Johnson. She thinks you guys are sex on sticks." The guys laugh. I feel Tavern's eyes studying me.

Johnson whacks me in the arm. "Thanks for that." She holds out her hand to White. "Lovely to meet you."

"And you, Ma'am. I'm Seth White," White says softly, bringing her hand up to his lips in a classic White charm manoeuvre.

"Are you based here now?" Vega asks as White and Johnson flirt next to us.

I nod. "Temporarily, I was due to go back out to Afghanistan this week but," I hold up my cast, "it's been delayed until September."

"You're going back to Afghanistan?" Tavern asks, sounding concerned. Somehow, that gets my hackles up.

I meet his eyes and something flickers in them. "Yes, it's what I do." Tavern doesn't respond.

"How long are you here for?" I direct my question to Vega. I hadn't paid much attention to the briefing.

"Until Sunday," Vega replies, crossing his arms in front of him. His dark beard is still immaculate, but it's now scattered with light grey hairs. "We're off on an exercise with your SAS boys tomorrow."

"Somewhere remote and mountainous, I imagine." Vega looks uncomfortable. "It's all right. I know you can't tell me." Vega relaxes and smiles widely.

A large dark-skinned man comes up to us. "Guys. We've got a mission brief in five."

"Yep," Tavern replies, his eyes still locked on my face.

The dark-skinned man smiles at me. "Hi, how you doing?"

I smile. "Great, thanks. Good football game, I enjoyed it, especially when I saw these guys on the pitch."

"We call it soccer." Tavern and I smile at each other. He had always 'corrected' me with American words.

The man's eyes widen. "Are you King?"

I'm startled. "I am, you're either psychic, or these blokes have been telling stories." I wonder what kind of stories.

The man laughs. "I'm Frank Wade, and these blokes do tell a lot of stories about you."

"Good ones, I hope."

Wade winks. "You betcha. Look, we've got a mission brief now, but those boys say there is a bar on base. We will probably be heading there later, if you're around."

The way his eyes are shining at me tells me Tavern has not told him about anything I might be worried about. I glance at Tavern; his jaw is set and his fists are clenched. I don't want to step on any toes here. "Maybe. We'll see."

Wade nods and slaps Tavern on the back with a laugh. "Let's go."

Vega and White head off with big waves. I step up to Tavern. "Will you be there tonight?"

Tavern looks down at me and his eyes soften. "Yeah."

"Would it make it difficult if I came along? I would really like to catch up."

An odd flicker passes through his eyes, but he smiles faintly. "Of course not, and I would like that too."

"Great. Then I'll see you later."

I had thought that seeing Tavern today had been one of the greatest things that had happened all year. But now he was just pissing me off. It was like he was protecting me in the field again; like that old habit hadn't left him. Early on, I sat with him on one of the sofas for ages, just chatting. We got back into the usual rhythm of banter and ease of conversation, but something had definitely shifted. The attraction between us seemed to sizzle the air and I was acutely aware of every move he made, every laugh and smile. Tavern's eyes were on me constantly; it made it difficult to concentrate on the conversation when all I could think about was that night all those years ago and the man sitting beside me now. When Vega came over and sat down beside me, I was mildly relieved. I saw Tavern glare at him, his jaw tight and his face pissed. But Vega either didn't notice or didn't care, because he stayed right where he was and talked to me. When I moved away to speak to Johnson and White, who were flirting with each other on the opposite side of the room, it wasn't long before Tavern joined us, lurking behind me.

Wade caught me at the bar getting a drink and within minutes Tavern had appeared behind me again. There were several people I knew on base, and quite a few were in the bar, despite it being a Tuesday evening. He glared at any man I spoke to.

Late in the evening, after he had scared away a good friend of mine, I grabbed his thick upper arm and steered him to the patio.

"What the hell are you doing?"

"What do you mean?" He has the balls to look shocked at my question.

"You're following me around like we're out in the streets of Afghanistan again, Tavern," I hiss. "Cut it out before someone notices."

"Notices?"

I roll my eyes. "Notices that you seem to have laid claim to me in the most primitive way possible."

Tavern smirks. "I have." His tone and look make me shiver in delight.

I scowl at him, forcing control on my overactive body. "No one else needs to know that. You might as well write it on my forehead."

Tavern's next words shock me to the core. "Is that a bad thing?"

I shake my head swiftly. "What the hell? Whatever this is," I gesture between the two of us, "we're not in a relationship, Tavern. That is the last thing either of us can do right now. And you leave tomorrow. I have to work here, with these people, and I'd rather not be the subject of gossip."

Tavern sighs and scuffs his shoe on the ground, yanking a hand through his hair. "You're right. I'm acting like an arse."

"Yes, you are." I run a hand over my face, feeling the cuts and bruises from my accident twinge. My broken forearm aches; I've been using it too much tonight. Despite only having had one beer, I'm tired and it's time to leave. I have to go before common sense leaves me, which might just happen with this man in front of me. "Good luck on your exercise this week, and good luck in the future." I reach up and place a light kiss on his cheek. "It was nice to see you, Rick."

I turn on my heel before he can respond. Grabbing my bag and jacket, I hug Vega and White goodbye, then leave the bar. Damn that man, he has made me so angry tonight, but the annoying thing is my treacherous body still wants him. It's all I can think about. Knowing he is so close tonight is going to be torture.

The residential area encompasses a large section of the base, so it isn't long before I'm home. I'm just unlocking the door to my room, not an easy thing to do with a broken arm, when a movement in the corner of my eye makes me turn. My heart starts pounding as Tavern walks up the dimly lit corridor. His eyes are locked on my face, an intensity swimming in them that makes me swallow hard. He is still so damn gorgeous.

I narrow my eyes. "You followed me?"

Tavern nods, stopping just in front of me. I sigh and unlock the door. "Go back to the bar, Tavern." I push it open and he walks in behind me without an invite. The studio flat is tiny. My sleeping and living area are the same room, with a separate tiny kitchen and small bathroom to the right. I slip my boots and jacket off, heading into the barely used kitchen for a glass of water like he isn't even there. I hope my cool exterior doesn't portray the turmoil inside me, my excitement about what could, but probably shouldn't, happen tonight.

"I didn't want to leave on such a sour note," he eventually says as I exit the kitchen and place a glass of water on the small table. I see he has been studying the large collection of CDs scattered on my small coffee table. *The Very Best of Dire Straits* is the album on the top of the pile. They are actually Jason's CDs; I'm ripping them for my MP3 player for when I'm deployed. I love music; the MP3 player is one of my rare possessions that travels the world with me.

"So you thought you would leave on a stalker note?"

Tavern smirks then gives me a long questioning look. "What the hell do you do to me, Emma?" Damn, I like it when he says my first name.

"Tavern..." I move around him to reach for the packet of painkillers on the dresser.

He grabs my arm as I reach for it and whirls me around smoothly; he's careful of my broken arm. "Say my name again."

"Tavern."

He steps towards me and I move backwards until my elbow bumps the wall. My heart pounds but I don't stop him. Despite my resistance, I desperately want this.

Tavern smirks again. "Tell me, Emma, have you been with anyone else since me?"

My pulse skyrockets. "It's been two years, Tavern." I glare at him.

"That doesn't answer my question."

I fume and bite out, "Yes."

Steel flashes in Tavern's gaze. Was that jealousy I just saw? I turn the tables. "Have you?"

"Yes."

Now it is my turn to be jealous. It winds through my veins like a snake. I tamp it down and narrow my eyes at him.

Tavern steps closer, his hands now either side of my head, backing me firmly against the wall. "And tell me this, when you were with this man, did you think of me?"

I poke him hard in the chest in annoyance. "Don't be so arrogant, Tavern. You're not the only man with bulging trousers."

Tavern sends me a smouldering look; damn, he can see right through me. He moves even closer and my breasts push up against his chest. It's impossible to think about anything else but him. "When I was with her, you were the only one I could think of." He brushes his nose along my cheek, whispering in my ear. "I think of our time together every time I go to sleep, no matter where I am, no matter what my situation is. Your face is the last thing I see, Emma." His voice is hoarse, deep and full of promise. A thrill of delight races down my spine, which I know he feels because he chuckles low in his throat.

"So you want another memory?" I whisper shakily, refusing to say his name because I know that's what he wants. "Something to add to your night-time show?"

Tavern gently nuzzles my collarbone, then my neck, his breath hot on my cool skin. I can feel his hand on my hip, peeling out my shirt from where it is tucked into my cargo trousers, stroking the sensitive skin on my belly. I know I should stop him but I really don't want to. "I want you, Emma," he whispers. "But I can't give you anything else except me, right here, right now."

My fingers flex in the t-shirt on his chest; I can feel the smooth hard muscles beneath. His kisses reach my jawline, and I give in, relaxing into his embrace. "How do you do this to me?" I breathe out as his other hand skims down my arm, landing on my hip and flexing. "No one has ever affected me quite the way you do, Rick."

I feel Tavern smile as his lips reach mine. "I know that feeling." Then he kisses me and nothing else matters.

*

In October 2010, I was back on UK soil after a thirteen-month deployment in Afghanistan, seven days earlier than I should have been. I had received news several weeks earlier that my grandmother had died, so had been given leave to return early for her funeral. Afterwards, I planned to go walking in the Peak District with Trent and Rhys, also back from deployment and on leave.

My grandmother's funeral was at a small crematorium in north Somerset, where she and my grandfather had lived all their lives. When my mother had told me months previously that she was slowly slipping away, I had been given compassionate leave and visited for a few days. I was glad I had had that opportunity to see her a final time. My father was an only child, so losing his mother was hard for him. My mother's parents had died many years previously. It was a small, intimate family gathering. My grandfather had always been extremely supportive of my joining the army, and was proud to see me turn up in my full dress uniform. My father barely looked at me; he had never understood my desire to join the military. It was good to see Jason, though, despite the circumstances, and we spent a night in the pub just catching up. When I was back in the UK temporarily, I often bunked at his flat, and he was one of the few people who knew about Tavern.

After that night in Salisbury, Tavern had started emailing me, keeping up the contact as he had whispered he would when he had crept out before dawn. A night where neither of us had got much sleep. Our communication was easy and relaxed; sometimes we would go months before we responded to each other. But I loved seeing that he had emailed me and I treasured them because they were so rare. We were far away from being together, but we were now so much more connected than we had ever been. I had no illusions that that was likely to be the extent of our relationship.

As planned, Trent and Rhys picked me up from the B&B in Somerset on their way up north, showing surprising respect and restraint for Jason when he came to say goodbye to me.

I had travelled all over the world, but I had never walked the mountains of the Peak District. I had immediately agreed to Trent's suggestion, and we had convinced Rhys together. We were walking six peaks in seven days, wild camping and walking with all of our kit during the day. Stopping off at pubs. Easy compared to some of the things we'd had to do. The nights in the camp were full of cans of beer, cheap food and stories. Trent and Rhys had pestered me for ages about Tavern. They knew I was holding something back. I eventually gave in and told them both what had happened. Trent had been appalled.

"You screwed that American son of a bitch behind the storage sheds?" he repeats with mock disgust. I nod my confirmation and he shakes his head vigorously. "That creepy American jackass, I should have beat his arse when I met him." I get the feeling Trent is only half kidding. "Did I tell you I saw him last year, English?"

I shake my head casually as my pulse rockets, eagerly straining for news of him. Dammit, I really needed to get a grip.

Trent scowls. "Yeah, he was doing his special ops thing in Helmand Province. We were in a convoy passing him, and he spotted me. Actually grinned and saluted at me, the bastard. I really should have kicked his arse."

The news that Rick had been in Afghanistan at the same time as me made me feel funny. I tried not to think about what he was doing as a Ranger, or where he was being sent in the world, or whether he was being shot at. In fact, I tried not to think of him at all. My dreams did not comply with this attitude, though, and our nights together were often relived in graphic detail.

"Well, at least one of us got some action in the sandbox," Rhys points out. He sounds impressed and I'm grateful for the subject change. "Even if it was down and dirty with a Yank." He grins at me. "Certainly more than what I got."

"I'm never going to live this down, am I?" I say with a sinking feeling, already regretting my loose beer tongue.

Trent pops a whole biscuit in his mouth and chews dryly. "Nope, going to be telling this story for years to come." Didn't I know it.

I love hiking, even with 40 kgs on my back there is something free about it. One morning at dawn, we pack up our kit and head up Kinder Scout, the highest peak in the district. The morning is fresh and clear, the sun shining despite the late October date. I breathe it all in and savour the feel of it.

A large bird of prey circles above our heads as we reach a flat plateau. There is no one else around except the three of us.

I stop and stare at the view below me. Peaks rise in the distance, covered by light mist. In the valley, I can see tiny houses, some with smoke streaming out of the chimneys. Trent stops a little further along and admires the view too. Rhys looks upwards, examining the bird of prey.

"It's a buzzard," he announces after a few minutes. Rhys has a thing for wildlife.

I'd been putting something off, but now is as good a time as any. "Guys, I have something I need to tell you," I say, walking to where they stand a little further along the trail. Trent looks at me expectantly. "I've decided I'm leaving the army." Trent's eyes hit his hairline in surprise.

"What?"

I nod. "My mind is made up. I filed the paperwork before I left last week."

"But why? I thought you loved the army."

"I do. But..." How to explain? I look down at the houses below us. "I want a home. I don't mean husband and kids," I wave my hand in dismissal, "but I want a permanent, stable job, and a house which I can go home to every night." I frown. "Do you know that all my possessions fit into two boxes? How sad is that?"

Trent looks confused. "But the army is a stable job, English."

I nod and look at Rhys, who is silently studying me. "Good for you," he says eventually. "It's a brave move, leaving all you've ever known as an adult."

Trent looks at him in horror. "Don't encourage the girl."

"Trent," I step up to my friend, this big brash Scotsman who has a heart of gold, "this doesn't mean you have to stop swearing in front of me, you know." I grin. "I'll always be an army girl at heart."

Trent laughs and shakes his head. "I don't think I really understand, but it's your choice, lass. Now let's finish this peak and get to the next so we can go to the pub."

I laugh and fall into step behind Rhys. The question now is: What do I do next?

That turned out to be far simpler than I could have ever imagined. Speaking with my civilian friends, finding a new job under any circumstances is difficult. I had heard stories about ex-army personnel who were simply unemployable in the civilian world. I discovered my engineering degree and overseas experience made this virtually impossible.

Through various connections of my superiors and colleagues, I was told a position was available as a project engineer at Gold & Sanchez, an international construction company with offices all over the world, including Salisbury. I had never had a civilian job interview before, but they called me back the next day to offer me a position. The catch was there was nothing available in Salisbury or any UK office. But they were recruiting in their Atlanta office.

After some thinking, I accepted the job and moved to the United States in February 2011.

*

Moving to another country is a daunting task. You need to sort out where you are going to live, visas, cars, and get your luggage over to name but a few things, all from thousands of miles away. Luckily, there were people at Gold & Sanchez who did a lot of the work for you. A lovely lady named Melanie booked me a hotel for a week, sorted me out a hire car for the first few days and sent me my visa directly. As I had very few belongings, everything fitted into three suitcases I took on the plane with me. I somehow found this very sad.

I knew about three weeks in advance the date I would be flying out, so I took a trip around my friends and family. As expected, my parents didn't understand why I would be doing this after only just getting out of the army. They wanted me to settle down at home and have babies. Jason was excited for me, promising to visit as soon as he could.

I sent an email to Tavern telling him I had left the army and was moving to Atlanta for civilian work. I had no idea where in the US he was based when he wasn't overseas, as he had never told me, and honestly I had never asked. I had a vague recollection that he had some family in the city, though I did remember he was from New York State originally. I didn't expect a quick reply. I knew he was often deployed for months at a time on special ops assignments.

On my flight from London, I sat next to a chatty American man named Austin. He was on his way home from visiting relatives in Europe and was very excited to be seeing his girlfriend again. About halfway through the flight, he admitted he was going to ask her to marry him. He even showed me the ring. I realised then that I wanted that too. I wanted someone to be so excited about seeing me that he would talk the ear off a stranger. As much as I wanted it, I knew that was something I could never expect from Tavern. So I resolved to finally get into the dating world. It was America after all. There had to be lots of single attractive men over there.

As I landed at the airport, I said goodbye to Austin and wished him luck. I collected my suitcases and headed to the hire car desk. This was all very daunting, but also exciting in a way I had never thought possible.

Within two weeks, I had found a small flat to rent in the city centre, bought myself a car and started work. A lot of the projects I worked on were at a US Army base about 30 miles south of the city, so I soon found myself travelling frequently down long straight highways and through small towns. I slowly got used to the left-hand drive automatic cars.

The work was interesting and challenging; the fact I had experience working under the US Army rules had been a massive plus in hiring me. Working as a civilian was an entirely new experience. Some things were simply engrained in me – respect for senior officers, timeliness, following orders – but I found I had a freedom as well. While I had to abide by their rules on base, I could finish work and go home, or to a movie, or to a bar. My responsibilities were still there, and I had to report to the project director frequently, but I finally had a freedom I didn't realise I had been lacking. So I kept myself busy. I took a cooking course: a 'Masterclass 101'. Since moving out of my parents' house all those years ago, I had rarely had to cook for myself and found I barely knew how to boil pasta. I joined a gym and carried on with my running. I finally upgraded to a fancy smart phone from my old 3310 and set up a Facebook account, something my civilian friends had been bugging me about for years. I finally saw what all the fuss was about. One Saturday, I went on a shopping spree and bought smart civilian clothes and a few pretty dresses, doubling my wardrobe in one day. I spoke to my friends and family on Skype frequently, but sometimes I did find myself wishing that they were closer.

In the back of my mind was the one thing I tried not to think about. Tavern. I desperately wanted to move on. I told myself it had been over four years since I met him, almost two since I had last seen him. Our email contact was nice, but it wasn't enough. I was older now, wiser. I had to get over these juvenile lovey dovey feelings and meet someone else. Someone who would actually be there with me, someone else I could really love. So when a guy at the gym asked me out, I accepted. This happened a few times, with a few different men, getting to various stages of dating, and though I tried to be both physically and emotionally interested in them, I found after a while I simply wasn't, so they all eventually ended.

I threw myself into my work to make up for it, spending long hours in the office. I'd been living in the building about a month when I met a woman who lived on my floor. Her name was Shanna Willows, and before long we were inviting each other over for dinner and chatting over wine. I began to feel a little less lonely.

It was a cold but bright winter Saturday in November of 2011.

I was sitting at my kitchen counter in my fluffy red dressing gown drinking coffee early one morning. I was pondering what to do with my day. It was my rest day, so I wasn't going to exercise. Shanna had promised to show me a 'real English pub' in the city that night, but that wasn't until later. There were several museums and exhibitions I had seen advertised that I wanted to see, but did I really feel like them today? I pondered my options. My laptop pinged, telling me I had a new email. I glanced at it absently after a minute, then did a double take as I saw it was from Tavern. My stomach fluttered in that way it did when seeing something from him. It had been over eleven months since I had last heard anything. I tried not to think about how much I missed him.

The subject line read simply: *Atlanta???*

Emma – seriously – Atlanta??? You are living in Atlanta, Georgia, United States??? Tell me you aren't kidding me. Did you really leave the army? What is your address?
Rick

I frown; it was unlike Tavern's usual style of email. He tends to write a lot, asking loads of questions of me and expecting a reply to each one. He takes his time. There wasn't even a hello in this. I reply straight away, though I know he will not likely see it for ages.

Hello to you too, Tavern. Yes, I am serious. I live in Atlanta now, as in Atlanta, Georgia, US. What's with the ?????? – did your keyboard get sand in it?

I am now a civilian (which I'm still getting used to), no more uniform for me! I'm working on some projects down at Fort Benning – do you know it? If you're in the States soon and want to chat, my number is below.
Emma

I include my address and US number under my name. Maybe he would send me a postcard. I try to not think about the fact we could be on the same continent. The thought fills me with an odd sort of excitement I know is totally stupid.

Still not knowing what to do with my day, I shower and dress. It's cool out, and threatening rain, but I feel like wearing a dress, so I choose a knee-length, long-sleeved dark red one with black leggings, leaving my hair loose. That is another novelty; I'd kept it shoulder-length when I was in the army for ease of putting it in a braid or bun all the time. The fringe I had worn as a teenager had grown out long ago, but I was growing my hair long now and it hung down to the middle of my back. I have another cup of coffee and some toast while answering an email from Janine. She has a new job and a new boyfriend and I want all the details. Then I find an email address for Alison Grenal, and tell her I am in the States. I remember she was from Texas and it would be nice to see her again.

There is a sharp knock on my door and I look up from my mug. The only person I know in the building is Shanna. Maybe she is cancelling tonight. Fighting back a wave of disappointment, I unlock and fling open the door.

My jaw almost hits the floor when I see Tavern standing there. He looks equally shocked as his gaze meets mine. For a second, we just look at each other, then his eyes sweep slowly down me. I do the same, taking him all in. He is wearing boots, dark jeans and a black turtle neck jumper. I've never seen him in casual civvies before. My mouth dries up completely. His blond hair is longer than I have ever seen it, falling over his forehead and curling around the neck of his jumper. He has a few days of beard growth on his face. I feel an excited stab in my chest and my belly flutters wildly as I gaze at him in shock.

Without a word, he steps forward and I step backwards automatically, letting go of the door. My heart is pounding.

Slowly, not taking his eyes off me, he closes the door behind him.

"Of all the cities, in all the world," he whispers, his eyes full of desire, "you come to Atlanta?"

I think that is a quote from a movie, but I'm too shocked to respond. "You know my house is in Atlanta, right?" My eyes widen, and I shake my head slowly. "You didn't know that? I never told you?" Tavern looks as stunned as I feel. "Yet here you are, Emma."

I'm actually speechless. I can't think of a single thing to say.

Tavern's eyes darken as he steps right up to me. He looks down, studying me, then slowly cups my face in both hands and kisses me. I respond eagerly, leaning into him as I wind my arms around him. "Hell, I've missed you, Emma," he whispers against my lips. "I was such an arse the last time I saw you. I'm sorry. I should have told you…"

"Rick," I murmur, and he pulls me in tighter to him. "Rick, I love you." I laugh quietly. "I have tried really hard not to, all these years. But I can't help it."

"Emma, I am totally in love with you," Rick whispers in reply, and my heart leaps in my chest. "I think I have been ever since you called me a 'cocky American sun-bleached blond bad boy' and put me in my place." I laugh softly, reaching up and kissing him again, passionately and with no holding back. Without breaking contact, he picks me up and carries me to my bedroom. Where we stay all day.

*

Less than a year later, Rick and I were married and I was pregnant. Friends of mine back home had been surprised we had done it so quickly, but as far as we were concerned, we'd known each other a long time, and we knew what we wanted now. So why wait? I had moved into his house in the suburbs, and it finally felt like I had a home. We had a small wedding in a local private garden, and travelled the west coast of North America for our honeymoon.

Rick was still a Ranger, so he was often deployed for several months at a time. This was a lot harder than I thought it would be.

Shanna, it turns out, had got together with Seth the night we all went to the 'proper' English pub, which had turned out to be an American version of an English pub, but still fun. They were engaged now, and she had become one of my best friends. Several of the Rangers were married, including Mat Fairthorne, who had joined the unit after the Salisbury Plain training exercise and was married to a lovely redhead called Mari. We all got together constantly when our men were deployed. Shanna had once told me I was lucky. I had been there; I knew what they were doing so it wasn't such a mystery. My response had been the opposite. I had been there; I had seen what it was like. I wish I didn't know now.

Early on, Rick had promised he would be here for the birth of our child. He had arranged leave for around the time the baby was due, but I knew what his duties were like. I knew he couldn't guarantee it. I spent most of my pregnancy without my husband. It was tough, but I had been through tougher. I wrote Rick emails telling him what was going on with us; the first time the baby kicked, for instance. I sent him videos as the baby moved in my belly.

I finished working and went on maternity leave about two weeks before I was due, in March 2013. Rick was still not back from his overseas deployment. Rhys, on extended medical leave after a shoulder injury, was staying with me for a while, so I would have someone around if Rick wasn't here. It was great to have someone else in the house, and Rhys was good company. He helped me finish the baby's room and cooked me dinner, but I wanted Rick more than anything else. I finally understood what my friends and family had been telling me for years when I had missed birthdays or family occasions or Christmas during a deployment. It was hard being away from home, and it was hard being left at home.

It is the middle of the night, a few days before my due date, when I think I hear a noise downstairs. Rick has been gone for seven weeks. I'm not sleeping well lately; the baby is restless. It wants out and frankly I want it out too. I sit up slowly, everything is slow these days, and listen hard. I hear the spare room door open and close, then Rhys' soft footsteps as he goes downstairs to check out the noise. I hear his muffled voice, then silence. The house is quiet, but I know if Rick wants to move silently, he does. Anticipation grows in me, excitement bubbling to the surface. Is Rick finally home? I click on the bedside lamp and wait, awkwardly sitting cross-legged in the middle of the bed.

Thirty seconds later and Rick's tired face appears round the door. As his eyes land on me, his expression brightens, a massive grin spreading across his bearded face. I suddenly feel overwhelmed with emotion. I cover my mouth and fight back the tears of joy.

Without saying a word, he crosses to me and sweeps me into his arms, planting kisses over my face and jaw, finally landing on my mouth and passionately telling me how much he has missed me.

"Damn, you're huge," he exclaims as his hands roam over my belly. I love hearing his voice.

I laugh. "I sure am." I lift my oversized t-shirt so Rick can see the bump. The baby chooses that moment to wiggle, and Rick's eyes widen as my skin changes shape before his eyes. He hasn't seen the baby move so much before. He leans down and kisses the skin softly where it moves as I run my fingers through his hair. I'm so overjoyed to have him back.

"How was it, Rick?" I ask softly.

"Too damned long," he whispers. He rests his face on the top of my belly and I feel his warm breath on my skin. "We were supposed to be back two weeks ago, but orders came through and things changed. I was so pissed. I wanted to come back to you so badly." He lifts his head up to look at my face. "I'm done with that now." He leans over and kisses me again.

"What do you mean?"

Rick takes off his jacket and throws it across the room. Then he leans over, opens my bedside table drawer and takes out his wedding ring. I keep it there when he is away; they can't wear personal stuff on missions. "I applied for a position at Fort Benning as a trainer and analyst." He smiles and slips the plain platinum band on his left ring finger. My heart expands. I love that he wears it. "Which I got, it's stateside full time from now on." My eyes widen in surprise. "I'll still be an active reserve, though, so if they need me I can be deployed, but that won't be my main job."

"But… you love being out there in the field. You love what you do."

"I love you more, Emma," Rick says simply, running his fingers lightly over my jaw. I can feel the cool metal of the ring on my skin. "I want to be here for you, for our child." He caresses my belly. "These last few months have been torture, knowing you were here by yourself, growing our baby."

I study his face, playing with his wiry blond beard between my fingertips. "Is this what you really want, Rick?"

"I want to be a good husband, and a good father. Those are the most important things to me." He kisses me again. "Ever since I met you, I've been leaving to serve my country. I won't do that again."

At his words, I throw my arms around his neck, holding him tight. It is more than I would ever have asked him for. Rick's hands travel over my back, then over my bottom, roaming all over my skin in a way that makes me tingle.

"Hmm, you're sexy too."

I pull back and give him an exasperated look. "I'm an elephant."

Rick laughs, kissing my neck and moving down to my breasts. "A sexy elephant."

I shrug, moaning softly as his hands and mouth continue their exploration. "I guess you haven't gotten laid in a little while…"

"Wouldn't matter if I had. You'd still be my sexy pregnant wife. I would still want you."

At that, Rick casts me a questioning look upwards. "Can we…? I mean… with the baby moving and you being so big?"

I grin and sit up on my knees. "Sex is supposed to be good for inducing labour," I tell him, "and frankly, that would be quite nice right now. It might be difficult logistically, though." I give him a wicked grin. "Are you up for the task, soldier?"

Rick smirks, his eyes sparkling. "Yes, Ma'am."

*

Rick and I have a beautiful baby boy on the 22nd of March 2013. We name him Alfie. The next few months pass in a blur of night feeds, nappies and learning what it is to be a parent. We often comment to each other that Afghanistan was easy compared to this mission. As promised, Rick started at the nearby base as a trainer; he was home every day by 6pm, which I loved. After five months, I went back to work four days a week and Rick took reduced duties for three months, spending his days caring for and playing with Alfie.

Mari, who was currently a full-time mother, offered to take Alfie for two days a week to save us on childcare. She had a little girl not much older. We paid her, of course, but her rates were half the price of anywhere else. When Mari started work again, I enrolled Alfie in G&S's onsite nursery. It was the kind of company that encouraged parents to come back to work after having kids. As such, and because their Atlanta office was so big, they had childcare facilities which had excellent rates. Alfie loved it there.

My days were long, as were Rick's. It was hard work, but we were a team together. I wouldn't have changed anything for the world.

Alfie was just over two years old when Rick was once again called to active duty and deployed overseas. I wasn't sure how long he would be away for, and though I kept busy all the time, I missed him something terrible. There was always that nagging feeling in my mind that he might not come back, but I tried not to dwell on those thoughts. I was confident Rick would always come back to me.

Rick had been gone for six weeks and it was around 6pm on the Wednesday of the 7th week. I'm just playing with Alfie before he has his bath. He is walking very strongly now, running around the house manically. Talking to himself in his garbled little language with the occasional understandable word thrown in. I'm sitting cross-legged on the floor amidst all of his toys, staring up at the photos on the mantelpiece and thinking about Rick. "Mummy Mummy." Alfie plunks a train onto my lap and wipes his bright blond hair off his forehead with the back of his hand.

"Yes, sweetheart? You want me to play trains with you?" I'm very tired, but I try not to let that show.

"Yes, Mummy." He hands me a train and sits on his bottom, pushing his favourite blue train around the carpet as my red one chases him.

My head whirls as I hear a key turn in the lock. Could this be Rick… My heart starts to pound as the door swings open at the end of the hallway.

"Daddy Daddy!"

Alfie, his little face screwed up in excitement, runs towards the door.

"Hey, buddy." Rick drops his bag with a heavy clunk as he falls to his knees and sweeps our son up into a massive hug. He spins him in the air as he stands up, and Alfie squeals with delight. I jump up and run to Rick too, throwing my arms around his neck.

"Hey, baby." We all share a three-way hug, standing in the entrance to the house. I lift my face to his and grin. "I missed you," Rick whispers, kissing me softly. Then he kisses Alfie on the forehead. "And I missed you, little guy." Rick sighs and hugs us more tightly. "I missed you both so much."

"Daddy, bathtime," Alfie says loudly.

Rick laughs. "Did I get home just in time for bathtime?" he asks his son. Alfie nods. "Well, as it happens, Daddy has been on a long flight for a long time, so he could use a bath too. What do you say?" Alfie squeals in excitement and wriggles, so Rick places him on the floor.

As Alfie runs off towards the kitchen, I weave my arms around my husband and hold on tight. Rick kisses my hair softly. "He has grown so much in such a short time," Rick whispers.

"Yeah, he has," I say into his neck. "I'm so glad you're home."

"Me too, baby."

"How was it?" Rick hesitates, which tells me it has been very hard. "It's okay, we don't have to talk about it."

I feel Rick relax in my embrace. We stand like that for a few minutes until Alfie starts climbing the stairs. About halfway up, he looks back at us in exasperation. "Mummy, Daddy, bathtime."

Rick smiles, letting me go, then stops and pulls off his boots. Alfie quickly moves up the stairs as Rick watches him.

"He can do that quickly now."

I grin. "Yep, he's good at running away in the supermarket too. You can have a go tomorrow if you want."

Rick laughs as he takes my hand, and we follow our little boy up the stairs.

"Daddy Daddy." Alfie is hopping up and down on the landing, already naked except for his nappy, in anticipation of bathtime. I laugh and scoop him up.

"Nice undressing, Alfie. I wonder if Daddy can be that quick."

Rick raises his eyebrows at me, his eyes darkening. "I am always eager to get undressed, you know that." He reaches for the bottom of his shirt.

I grin in reply; tonight was going to be a good night. "Bathtime!"

After Alfie's bath, we put him to bed with some books, and he falls asleep quickly. Rick doesn't bother to change into anything other than a towel, which I appreciate, as it makes it easier when he scoops me up and carries me into our bedroom.

Later that evening, we are sitting on the sofa, sharing a beer after I cooked him his favourite meal; ham and cheese omelette. Rick has his head back on the sofa and his eyes closed. I'm snuggled into his side. I don't want to let him go. We quietly chat, but Rick is really tired so I suspect he will be falling asleep any time.

"Do you remember Collins?" he asks me quietly when our conversation drifts.

I frown and think back. "Private Collins, Fred Collins?"

"Corporal now, but yeah." Rick sighs; he opens his eyes and looks at me. "He accidentally shot a teenage girl last month in Afghanistan."

I sit up and gasp in shock. "Bloody hell. What happened?"

Rick takes my hand and brings it to his lips. I glance at the wedding band on his finger. "They were on a security patrol. He thought she had a gun, but it turns out she didn't. Anyway, Collins is up on charges, he'll likely be discharged."

I feel for Collins; I had liked him a lot. "A girl is dead, though."

"That's not the worst part. We believe the girl's three older brothers are high up in the Taliban. They'll likely use this as a reason to rally more to their cause, and step up their attacks on our troops."

"Jeez."

Rick pauses, watching me. "The girl was one of the children you used to play that word game with. We think one of her brothers was responsible for the explosion at the school building site all those years ago when we were there." I look at him in shock and he grimaces, no doubt reliving the memories of that day, just as I am. "He was one of the local builders we worked with back then. I ID'd him from photos."

I bite my lip. Now it makes sense. "That's why you were sent out there, because of your history?"

"Yeah." Rick looks sleepy as he rests his cheek on my shoulder and closes his eyes. "Hopefully, for the last time." I really hope so too. Rick is quiet for a few minutes. "That day was the first time I thought that maybe you cared for me too," he murmurs, and I glance down at him. "Until then, you'd never indicated you thought of me as anything other than an annoying, foul-mouthed jackass who followed you around all day." I chuckle, and he smiles against my shoulder as I relax into him. "You make my life so much brighter, Emma. Even though we were apart for all those years, just knowing you were out there made everything seem a little less lonely. I don't know what I would have done without that hope. I don't know what kind of man I would have become." His voice is so quiet now, he's half asleep. "I love you so much."

As Rick falls silent, I smile and glance at the photos on the mantelpiece. Thinking back to those days which seem such a long time ago now. My favourite photo is one of Rick and myself, taken by an army photographer many years ago. We hadn't been aware of it at the time, but Alison Grenal had sent it to me a few years ago after we got back in touch. It shows Rick following me through a building site, his arms crossed on his weapon in that pose he liked to do. He has a cheeky look on his face, visible even under the helmet. I'm turned slightly towards him, walking backwards, smiling and rolling my eyes. A stack of rolled-up designs under one arm and a spade over my shoulder. I recognise the site, but I don't remember what we had been talking about at the time. The work we had been doing had always been dangerous, but it seemed so much more from a distance than when I was actually out there. Perspective changes it all.

After a few minutes, I look down. Rick has fallen asleep, his head on my shoulder. I brush his blond hair off his forehead and run my hands softly down his now clean shaven face. Damn, I love this man.

*

Several months later, in early April 2016, Rick was once again deployed abroad. As before, I worked long and hard to stop myself thinking of him. It was late Friday afternoon when I was out on site surveying the completion of a project I had been working on for many months. I'm just finishing and completing my on-site notes when my work mobile rings. I don't recognise the number.

"Hello?"

"Hello, may I speak to Emma Tavern?"

"This is Emma speaking."

There's a pause. "Are you British?"

I'm thrown for a moment. "Uh, yes, I am."

"Wow, I'm surprised. I was really expecting an American accent on the end of this call." The caller is British himself, I notice, his voice deep and unusual.

"Well, I'm sorry to disappoint you… who am I speaking to, please?"

"Oh dear, I'm sorry, how rude of me. My name is Jon Clemens. I'm calling from the Salisbury, UK office of Gold & Sanchez. Is this a good time, Emma?"

I glance at my watch. "For me, yes, for you, it's a bit late over there, isn't it?"

The man laughs slightly. "When I call my American colleagues, I find it better to disrupt my own evening, not theirs. Makes things a bit easier."

"I can imagine," I reply. "What can I help you with, Jon?"

"I'm in the finance and accounting department, and I have some of your invoices and purchase orders that I need to go through with you. Is that okay?"

I frown, folding my notebook and heading back towards my car. "Sure, but why is the Salisbury office looking at my financial accounting? Don't we have guys like you over here?"

Jon chuckles. "The accounting department in the Atlanta office is rather undermanned, so the files have been sent to me instead for an audit." He sighs, and I sense exasperation. "It makes no sense to me either, but I still have to do it."

"That sounds reasonable. I'm out on site right now, and I don't have my files with me. Is that a problem?" I open the boot and slide off my safety clothes, keeping the phone to my ear.

"Not at all, we will do what we can now and if there is anything you need to check, you can get back to me."

"Okay, I'm going to put you on speaker, as I need to drive to pick up my son." I get into the car and arrange the hands-free.

"Ah, how old?"

"Just over two."

"Ah, my daughter is a similar age. Cute but trouble, huh?" I pull out of the base and wave goodbye to the security guys.

"Oh yes. My husband is overseas right now as well, so that doesn't make it any easier."

"I'm sure. Right, shall we get down to it?"

Jon and I speak for around thirty minutes on my drive back to Atlanta. I answer most of his queries and promise to get back to him on the others. Then I pick up Alfie and head home. Tonight is the bachelorette party of a girl I know from work, and I have a babysitter coming over at 1900.

I bath Alfie, put him to bed and settle the babysitter in. I quickly pull on a dress then head over to a place I had often gone to before with Rick. It's called Mickey's Bar and is classic American.

The evening is fun. After one drink at Mickey's, we leave and head to another called Mason's. A little after 2200, most of the girls extremely drunk by this point, they leave there and head to some clubs. I bow out then, knowing Alfie will be up at 0600 and not really feeling in the mood to party all night.

The next morning, I'm clearing up after Alfie's breakfast when there is a knock on the door. Alfie runs to it, as usual. Luckily, he is still too small to reach the door handle. I open it wide, coffee mug in hand. Paulo, Seth and Shanna stand on the porch.

"Hey, guys," I say, puzzled. "When did you get back? Where's Rick?" I knew that the men had both been with Rick on his deployment, so if they were here, he should be too. One look at Paulo's face and I know something is wrong. "What is it?" I ask bluntly.

Shanna moves past me quickly, not looking at me. "Alfie, why don't you show me your bedroom?" She takes his little hand and leads him away into the house.

I take a step back, fear pulsing in my veins. "Paul? Where's Rick?" I ask again, sharply this time.

I see him swallow hard as Seth closes the door behind him. "Emma…"

"What?" Paulo isn't giving me answers so I look up at Seth. "Seth? Where is Rick?"

Seth looks me straight in the eye and I know. It's like a punch in the gut. The coffee mug slips out of my hand and crashes to the hardwood floor, the sound so loud in the sudden deafening silence. I step back again, away from these men. "No," I say, pointing at them. "No. No."

"Emma." Paulo gently grabs my upper arms but I twist out of his reach.

I desperately try to cling on to something that makes sense. "Tell me where Rick is. Tell me where my husband is."

"He's dead, Emma." The words enter my brain and spin around and around. "He was shot. We saw it. He died… instantly." Paulo's voice cracks but it's like there is cling film around my ears; he is saying more but I can't hear it.

"No, no, he can't be." My legs are shaking, my vision blurred. I think I'm yelling but there's no control. "No, he is coming back. He always comes back…" My legs give out but I feel strong arms catch me, help me gently to the floor, hold me tight against them.

"Rick is not coming back, Emma." Seth's soft voice in my ear permeates my haze.

My husband, best friend and the man I love more than anything else in this world is dead.

My heart shatters into a million pieces.

Chapter 5

University Part 3

May 2016

The sun is shining high in the cloudless sky, the temperature is a balmy 30C and all around me are signs of happiness and life. Despite all this, I'm feeling especially depressed today. It's exactly two years since that night in my living room. Two years since I lost Jon. Two years since my life turned upside down. Even work today had not allowed me a respite from the sadness. Usually, I could concentrate on my tasks, on the numbers in front of me. I could forget, for a little while, that when I go home and my daughter is asleep, I'm all alone in my cold bed. But today work couldn't distract me. The ache in my chest only seems to grow with time, like a bottomless pit of darkness and pain inside me. This is now my life.

As I drive along the highway from my office, *Brothers in Arms* playing on the local radio, I rub my chest hard, then undo the buttons on my shirt. They are making me feel constrained somehow. I automatically start playing with Jon's wedding ring, on a silver chain around my neck. I don't wear mine anymore; it's too hard to look at. I miss Jon so much, it physically hurts. April is the only reason life is bearable, the only reason I go on living.

I glance at the clock on the dashboard, wondering if I have time to pick up some shopping before I have to get April from kindergarten. I have about forty-five minutes, so just barely, but it is so much easier shopping without her these days, she just wants everything. I would just have to hurry. I smile to myself as I think of my daughter and her excitement as she runs down the supermarket aisle. My smile fades as a memory of Jon chasing her as a toddler in Sainsbury's creeps in and, not for the first time today, I fight back tears.

I signal and move lanes as my exit appears on the right. The high-rise buildings of downtown Atlanta shine in the distance, the sunlight reflecting off the tall skyscrapers. My thoughts wander to what Jon would have thought of this city. It is classic American, flashy and modern, but with a friendliness and character that you couldn't find anywhere else in the world. I would probably enjoy it if I didn't feel so empty all of the time.

I shake myself out of my flunk and pull into the supermarket parking lot. Time to put on my fake face and show the world how fine I am. I pull off my work shirt, so I'm just in a vest and suit trousers, and grab my shoulder bag as I jump out of the car and lock it behind me. My Honda is small compared to the other trucks nearby; Americans like to do things big.

I consult my phone for the shopping list as I walk, keeping an eye out for traffic as I cross to the store. I grab a basket and head in, placing my sunglasses on my head in the dimmer interior of the store. My list is small so I hurry around. Milk, bread, tomatoes... boring, but essentials. Just like me, I guess, going through the essential motions of life. I grab a bottle of wine and some ice cream. As I approach the checkout, I quickly think over the items in my basket, then remember something I forgot. Sighing to myself, I head back in and grab a big box of eggs. I turn away from the shelves quickly.

"Ummph." A deep, masculine grunt is unleashed into the air as I crash straight into a man behind me. He grips my arm to stop me from falling, but my hold on the egg box is dubious at best and it slips out of my grip. The box opens as it falls, the eggs cracking onto the black cargo trousers and work boots of the man and sliding to the floor.

"Oh my God," I gasp in shock as I drop my basket next to my feet. "I'm so sorry."

I look up into the shocked face of a really tall blond man. He blinks sharply as our eyes meet, then he looks down at his trousers with a frown.

"I'm sorry," I repeat, looking down at the mess I caused. "Really sorry."

"It's okay," the man replies. "I like eggs."

I glance up quickly at his tone. He looks amused rather than angry.

"Uh…"

"Now, if you had thrown bananas all over my pants, then we would have had a problem." His mouth curves into a smile as he looks down at me, his light brown eyes sparkling.

I blink. Is he flirting? Woah. I suddenly realise his hand is still gripping my bare arm, and I instinctively glance down at it. Instantly, the man removes his grip, but his smile and the look in his eyes remain. I see he is holding a large carton of milk in his other hand.

"Either way," I say slowly, taking a step back, "I'm sorry."

The man tilts his head at me, looking curious, but before he can say anything, a store employee arrives with a mop and towels. She hands one to the man with a smile.

"Here you go, sir."

"Thanks." He leans over and mops his trousers as the woman starts to pick up eggshells and the broken box.

"Ma'am, I'm sorry but you will have to pay for the damage," she says to me from the floor.

I nod. Great, well done me. "Of course."

"No, it's okay. I'll pay." The man stands up straight. He is really tall, at least 6"3', towering over me, and I'm not short. He's also very well built, like he's just stepped out of a superhero movie or something. My gaze travels from his attractive chiselled face covered in scruffy blond stubble to his chest and his muscular arms under a fitted navy t-shirt. He is a very good-looking man, but I tear my eyes away, back up to his face, and frown at his statement.

"Don't be ridiculous. I'm the one that broke them, all over you. I will pay."

The man looks amused. "Nope. I will."

"Uh." The woman has finished mopping the floor and now looks between us. "I don't care who pays, but one of you has to." She nods then heads towards the checkouts, no doubt to tell the manager that an extra box of eggs needs paying for.

"I really am very sorry," I apologise again. "My mind was elsewhere." That may be a major understatement.

"And I said it's fine. Don't worry about it." The man smiles as he moves out of the way of another customer. "Is that a British accent you have there?"

I blink at the random subject change, but I can't help but be surprised. "Yes, it is."

"You seem surprised I got that right." His voice is deep and smooth, a local accent if I'm not mistaken.

"Because usually people here ask me where in Australia I'm from," I say without thinking. I shrug. "Apparently, I sound Australian to Americans."

The man looks amused again. "You definitely sound British to me. Are you on vacation?"

I turn around and grab a box of eggs, being careful to turn back slowly this time, and place the box in my basket as I pick it up off the floor. "No, I live here." The day and all its meaning crashes back into me, and I suddenly find myself fighting back a wave of emotion.

"Hey, are you okay?" The man has stepped closer and has lightly brushed my bare arm with his hand. I jerk away, feeling exposed to this stranger.

"Fine," I snap. "I have to go." Without another word, I turn and quickly head towards the checkouts. I force myself not to look back as I pay for my shopping on autopilot, including a broken box of eggs, and head swiftly back to my car. I load the shopping into the boot and slide into the driver's seat, pulling my sunglasses over my eyes. I sit there for a minute as guilt washes over me. There was no need to be so rude to that man, especially since I threw the eggs over him in the first place. He was just trying to be nice.

As I replay the scene in my head, I start to feel really bad about my behaviour. I sigh to myself; the sooner I get home, get April to bed and have a glass of wine, the better.

I go to turn the ignition when I see the tall blond man slowly walk past the front of my car, sunglasses over his eyes. He doesn't see me, but I watch him pass by, carrying a brown bag of groceries.

There is no way I can't go after him now. I slam the car door behind me and head over to where he is moving past a large grey truck, which has certainly seen better days.

"Excuse me." The man turns quickly, keys in hand. "Hi, I'm sorry I snapped at you," I say as I approach. "I didn't mean to be rude, especially as you were so nice after I assaulted you with eggs." I shrug. Suddenly I feel the urge to explain myself. "I'm just having a bad day, it's a… it's a bad anniversary for me today and I didn't mean to take it out on you." I have stopped in front of him now, next to his truck, and I take a deep breath. "I'm sorry. Again."

The man raises his sunglasses and perches them on the top of his head. Then he looks down at me with interest in his features. He seems to be considering my words.

"First, my name is Rick Tavern." He holds out his hand. I try not to frown. I don't want to make friends but at this point I don't want to be even ruder so I shake it. His palm is warm and calloused, and makes my hand seem very small. I see a black geometric tattoo encircling his left forearm and snaking up under his t-shirt.

"Emma Clemens."

Rick smiles. "Nice to meet you, Emma Clemens," he says slowly, releasing my hand. "Second, forget about the eggs. I've had worse thrown at me, believe me, and like I said, I like eggs." Rick reaches into his brown bag and holds up a box of eggs. "See, I even bought some for myself."

I smile faintly at his attempt at humour.

"Thirdly. I'm very sorry that today is a bad day for you, made even worse by your apparent guilt for having thrown eggs over an unsuspecting fellow shopper." I narrow my eyes at him; is this guy mocking me? "But I'm not sure I can accept your apology, Emma Clemens."

Now I'm frowning as he leans casually back on the side of his truck, his long legs folded so he is almost eye level with me. I see an emblem tattoo of some sort on his right arm, mostly covered by his t-shirt. I cross my arms in front of my chest, feeling defensive. "And why is that, Rick Tavern?"

Rick shrugs and pins me with a half-serious look. "Because frankly, Emma, you hurt my feelings, and therefore the only way for me to forgive you is for you to come and have a drink with me." He smiles and his sharp brown eyes study my reaction.

I reach for my sunglasses and tear them off. His grin widens as he sees the surprise on my face. "Seriously?" I ask, taken aback by his words and cocky American attitude. "You're blackmailing me into having a drink with you?"

"Blackmail is such a strong word," Rick replies with a hint of cheek. "More, how I can buy you a drink to make your day better and how you can buy me a drink to say sorry." He tilts his head to study me. "What do you say?"

My mind is racing with a million thoughts as I stare back at him. I think this man is asking me out on a date, on today of all days. I really don't know how to process this. On one hand, he seems nice and is definitely attractive, and I was rude to him. On the other… a twinge of guilt pierces my chest at the thought of going out with him, even for one drink. I have been on a few dates with other men since I moved here, though never anything more. I always felt horrible during and afterwards, like I was betraying Jon. I really don't need this today. This is dangerous territory.

"What do you say, Emma?" Rick asks quietly, somehow sensing my internal struggle. "One drink?"

"You said two," I find myself saying without really thinking. I frown at myself.

Rick chuckles at my response. "Two drinks then. Tonight?"

I shake my head, both to clear my thoughts and to say no. I can't get a babysitter this short notice, and going out tonight just feels wrong. "I can't do tonight."

"Okay, tomorrow night?"

I hesitate. I could get a babysitter, but do I actually want to? Somehow Rick can read my mind. "How about this? I will be at Mickey's Bar on Oakland and 5th at 8pm tomorrow night. Join me if you want." Rick smiles and stands up straight. "Now if you'll excuse me, I have to go home and wash my pants." He flashes me a wide grin and heads for the back of his truck. I can't stop my eyes from drifting down him, so I quickly turn around instead and head back to my car. As I once again slide into the driver's seat, my gaze wanders to his truck across the lot. He smiles and waves at me as he pulls out, vanishing from sight quickly. Why do I feel better than I have in a long time? Because some good-looking stranger flirted with me? That's just stupid. I shake my head to clear it and glance at the clock. Dammit, I'm going to be late picking up April. Again.

*

It's twenty past eight when I arrive at the bar, and I hesitate before approaching the door. I eye the car park next to it and spot Rick's truck. I have intentionally walked slowly here. A few times, I even stopped and started to turn back around. Then I chastise myself for being so sad, and a coward. Memories of that night, when I was so much younger and so cowardly, surface and I make my decision. Two drinks, that's all, what am I afraid of exactly? Rick seems like a nice guy. What's the harm in having a one-off Friday night drink with a good-looking man? Plus, who am I kidding? As soon as he finds out about my widowed single mum status, he'll be a goner, which is for the best. I should just enjoy it while it lasts.

I take a deep breath, but I can't quite bring myself to approach the entrance. I can see shapes through the large windows set either side of the door. A few men sit at tables on the patio outside, drinking beer and smoking. A red neon sign advertising Budweiser flashes next to the door. It looks like a classic American bar, not something I have a lot of experience with despite having lived here for a while.

I take another breath and push my fringe behind my ear, a nervous habit I have never been able to break. I assure myself I can leave at any time, and head to the door. It opens as I approach, and a group of women pour out. From the clothing some of them are wearing, it must be a hen party. I stand aside and the last one flashes me a drunken smile before I grab the door from her. I step in and slowly look around. A long wooden bar is located on the long wall directly opposite me, with several men sitting on bar stools in front of it. Clearly selling a huge variety of alcohol, judging from the wall behind it. Multiple tables, chairs and secluded booths are on my left and right. The floor is wood and creaks beneath my feet; the ceiling has wooden beams running across it, which makes the place feel cosy. I breathe in the classic bar smell, stale beer and salt, but it's not unpleasant. If anything, it reminds me of the pubs back home, and I feel a pang for my old life, which I quickly push away. The soft country music playing in the background adds to the atmosphere and helps to remind me this is not an English pub, but an American bar.

A few men at the tables nearby turn to look at me as I step further forward. I feel their gazes apprise me but I ignore them. The bartender, an attractive redhead, shoots me a friendly smile as I approach. The man in front of her turns around and Rick meets my eyes with a wide smile. He almost looks relieved to see me. Unlike the other men in the bar, his eyes never leave my face as I walk over to him. Rick is in dark blue jeans and a black shirt, which makes his short bright blond hair really stand out. Unlike yesterday, his face is now clean shaven. He makes casual look very good. I'm not really dressed up myself; wearing black jeans, sandals and a white vest under a blue shirt. Nothing fancy. His smile widens as I lean on the bar.

"Emma Clemens. Nice of you to join me," he says quietly.

I shrug. "I was in the neighbourhood."

Rick chuckles and gestures to the bartender. "First drink on me, as discussed. What will you have?"

I lean backwards and forwards, looking at what's on offer. "I'll have a pint of the craft pale ale, please," I say to the bartender. She cocks an eyebrow in surprise but nods.

"Ale drinker, huh?" Rick observes. "Of course, you're British. What was I thinking? Maybe I should have ordered you a pot of tea."

"I didn't know bars like this served tea, or good ale for that matter. Americans only seem to drink that Budweiser swill." I can't help myself as I smile at his bottle. "How's your drink?"

Rick grins and takes a sip of his Bud. "Strangely unsatisfying now you've said that."

I laugh at his expression as the bartender places the pint glass on the bar and Rick hands over a few dollars.

"Shall we find a seat?" Without waiting for my answer, Rick stands and heads towards the back and a secluded booth. I catch a whiff of a spicy masculine scent as I follow him across the room and slide in across from him on the worn red leather.

Rick holds up his beer bottle and gestures for me to do the same.

"A toast," he says, mischief in his eyes. "To not smelling like dried eggs anymore."

I can't help it. I have to laugh again. "Cheers." I've laughed and smiled twice in the past five minutes; that's pretty much unheard of for me nowadays.

We each take a sip of our drinks. The cool ale slides down my throat. It's been a while since I shared a beer with someone in a bar. I feel Rick's eyes on me and I meet his gaze head-on.

"So, Emma," Rick says, "did you find the place okay?"

I nod. "I drive past it every day on my way home from work actually. I live nearby." I look around the bar. "I've never been here before, though."

"How long have you lived over here?"

"A little over a year," I reply. Before he can ask anything further, I jump in. "Are you from Atlanta?"

Rick shakes his head. "No, I'm from New York State originally." He takes a sip of his beer. "I moved here when I was twelve. Now, I'm in the army and stationed at a base south of the city."

That made me pause, but also explained a few things about the man in front of me. "You're in the army? Cool."

"I'm a sergeant. I just came back from an overseas tour," Rick says slowly.

I note his hesitation. "Stuff you can't tell me about, huh?"

Rick smiles slightly and nods, but there is something in his eyes I can't quite read. "My work is pretty classified."

"What about the unclassified stuff? Where have you worked previously?"

"All over the place." Rick shrugs, but his posture is far from relaxed now. "I did a tour in Iraq after 9/11 and I did two tours in Afghanistan later in my twenties. Mostly with infrastructure teams, logistics, security and so forth." He pauses. "I've travelled around a lot in the last few years. What about you? Have you travelled much?"

I can tell he is trying to change the subject. "I spent over a year after uni travelling Australia, Asia and Europe," I reply. Rick looks impressed. "Then some time in South America." I don't mention Jon. I find I really don't want to talk about him, so I go back to the previous topic. "Do you enjoy your job? What you do?"

An odd flicker passes through Rick's eyes and his expression closes. "Most of the time."

I shoot him a quizzical look but he avoids my gaze and looks out over the bar. I take a sip of my drink and study him, moving so I sit cross-legged on the seat. After a moment, he looks at me and smiles. Whatever had bothered him just then has been pushed away.

"Can I ask you…" he hesitates and studies me "…what it was about yesterday that made you so upset?"

I blink and grimace but struggle to find the words I want to say. As much as I don't want to say it, I know I should tell him the truth.

"If you don't want to tell me, that's fine." Rick shrugs. "I just saw how upset you were yesterday. Maybe I can help."

My chest constricts tightly as I take a deep breath, my right hand going to my necklace and Jon's ring. I see Rick glance at it. "Yeah, well, I'm not sure anything can really help me... you see, yesterday was the two-year anniversary of my husband's death."

Rick's eyes open wide with shock. Whatever he had been expecting me to say, it wasn't that.

"Oh jeez... I'm sorry."

I nod. "Yeah, me too."

Rick studies me, his expression kind. "What happened?"

I exhale sharply. "Car accident, on his way home from work." I meet Rick's eyes. "A lorry driver glanced at his phone at the wrong time, the lorry went into his car and it was crushed against the safety barrier."

Rick's face is full of pain for a moment, then he leans across the table and takes my left hand in his gently. I freeze, but I don't move my hand away. "I've never been married myself, so I don't know what that feels like but..." he pauses "...I have lost friends. Guys I considered closer than brothers." Rick's eyes focus on the table, and I get the feeling he is reliving a memory as he speaks. "I know what it feels like to lose someone close to you, to have that hole in your chest, that ache that never goes away."

My breath catches as his description fits me so perfectly. He really must have experienced it to know. "I'm sorry for you too," I whisper, squeezing his hand gently. Rick meets my eye and smiles a little, then leans away. But his hand remains clasped to mine.

"Is that why you left the UK?" he asks. "To get away from it?"

I nod. "Yeah, I just couldn't stand being there anymore. I couldn't live in our house without seeing him everywhere, or walking around the city where we lived without remembering all the times we shared. Everything reminded me of him." I glance at our clasped hands. Rick is absently rubbing his thumb lightly over my knuckles. It's comforting, this light human contact. "My firm is international, I'm an accountant," I clarify. "So when a

job came up here, I thought, why not? I could do with a change."
I sigh. "I still haven't decided if that was a good choice or not."

"Sounds like a brave thing to do," Rick replies. "Move halfway across the world to a foreign city to start again."

I have to laugh bitterly at that. "My parents called me cowardly for running away."

"Cowardly? What?" Rick frowns and actually looks annoyed.

I shrug, then decide I might as well tell him. "I think it had something to do with the fact that I was taking away their only grandchild." I watch to see his reaction. His thumb pauses in its motion for a second at my words, and he stares at me. I gently remove my hand from his, though he doesn't seem to notice.

"You have a kid?" Rick sounds intrigued, but I'm wary.

"A little girl, four years old. April."

Rick smiles. "That's a good name." He leans towards me, looking serious. "So you lose a husband and your little girl loses her father and you move halfway across the world to a city you don't know in a country that isn't your own to escape your heartache, and your parents are unsupportive?"

I nod at his summary, marvelling at his sensitivity. But I quickly force that observation away.

"Wow." He shakes his head. "Just wow."

"Yeah, well." I shrug it off, but their reaction still stings. It still stings that they refuse to come and visit, to make the effort to come and see where our lives are now. They want us to come and visit them, to come home, as they put it, but won't make the effort themselves.

"What about other family, Emma? Brothers and sisters?" he asks. I study him for a moment; his interest seems genuine.

"I have an older brother." I smile wistfully as I think of Jason. "I have a sister-in-law and several brothers-in-law as well. They're great, especially my sister-in-law. I don't know what I would have done without her." I fidget with the bottom of my beer. "It was her and April that kept me together after…" I shrug, not really sure how to finish that sentence. "My parents-in-law are good too, very supportive. I'm in touch with them a lot." I remember Amie and her family are visiting in the summer, which does bring a smile to my face. I miss them.

Rick smiles gently. "That's nice, to have supportive family."

The way he says that seems almost sad, so I ask, "What about your parents?"

Rick looks down at his beer, his expression once again shuttering. "My mom died of cancer when I was a baby, and my dad wasn't really cut out for being a father," he states plainly. "He's a good guy, but the responsibility was too much for him. Plus, I think he just didn't know what to do without her, how to live his life without my mom." He shoots me a sympathetic look, but continues. "He worked to support us but that was about it. I was basically raised by my sister." He smiles. "I have three elder sisters."

"Three?" I exclaim.

Rick nods. "Yep. There's Mia and Fiona, who are five and seven years older, and then Jess, who is twelve years older than me, so she took care of me, took care of all of us really. She moved to Atlanta for work when I was twelve and I moved with her. Lived with her. Thinking back, it must have been really hard for her." He pauses, his distant gaze on a spot beyond my shoulder. "Having to care for two younger sisters and a baby brother when she was just a teenager herself. But she never complained, never told me what a burden I was."

"She sounds wonderful," I comment.

Rick nods and plays with his empty beer bottle. "She is. Married now with three kids, all scoundrels but I love them to bits. Her husband raises the kids while she goes out to work. She earns big bucks."

"Good for her," I say with a smile.

Rick grins. "Yeah, Jess's husband is a saint."

I'm curious but don't want to overstep my boundaries, so I ask carefully, "Do you see your dad much?"

Rick pauses; his fingers wrap around the bottle and his face closes. "Not really. He still lives up north. I speak to him on the phone occasionally, but he's not really part of my life."

I nod. I can see that's a sensitive topic for him and don't want to probe anymore.

The waitress appears at that moment to ask if we would like any more drinks. My beer is almost gone so I ask for another, as does Rick. The interruption seems to break the seriousness of the conversation as Rick leans back in the booth and smiles widely at me. I notice he seems to be able to switch between moods easily, though I wonder if it's just a cover, a way not to deal with what hurts him. I find myself intrigued by this man in a way I haven't been intrigued by anyone for a very long time.

"So, Emma, what do you do for fun?" Rick asks. He seems to enjoy saying my name. "How do you spend your free time?"

I have to laugh. "Free time, with a four-year-old?" I give him a look. "What is this thing you speak of?"

Rick laughs with me as he accepts the beer from the waitress. I see Rick reach for his wallet but I shoot him a look and place some dollars on the tray, as we had agreed. I see the waitress smile flirtatiously at him, and politely at me. Rick seems not to notice her interest. But it suddenly dawns on me that the man in front of me is extremely attractive. He could probably be sitting opposite any woman in this bar if he wanted. Could take any woman home he wanted. So why is he talking to me? Insecurity about my personality and body left me a long time ago, but given my situation, I find it hard to believe this man is sitting here out of genuine romantic interest. It's more likely he feels sorry for me. Especially now he knows details. I push my fringe behind my ear and take a sip of my beer. I'm not quite sure how that thought makes me feel.

"Outside of work, I spend almost all of my time with April," I say with a shrug, totally honest. My fingers are playing with my necklace again, and I quickly bring them down to my glass. "Which is fun, I love being with her."

"Exhausting but fun?" Rick says. I nod in amusement that he would get that.

"I've babysat my niece and nephews quite a lot over the years," he explains at my look, then wipes his forehead in mock exhaustion. "Man, they make advanced warfare training seem like a walk in the park."

I chuckle in response, but I feel more cautious about him now.

"But you must do adult things," he says. I hold in a smile at my automatic thoughts then, and his eyes sparkle, telling me he could have been thinking the same thing. "I mean, clearly, you have a babysitter tonight."

I shrug. "Occasionally, I go out with the people from work, but it's not easy to make friends in a new city, especially with a four-year-old," I explain. I have an urge to try and make my life sound less lonely than it is, though I can't explain why. "Mostly, if I do anything, I hang out with my neighbours, a married couple who have two young children, one of whom is April's age. They are also my babysitters." I glance at Rick and he is watching me with what looks like interest. "About a week into April's kindergarten, I started talking to this young mother who has a little boy in the same class. It turns out we live two doors down from each other on the same street. So we do play dates and parties. She sometimes takes April after school when I have to work, and I have babysat for them a few times, and them for me." I smile. "It's lucky they are so close and so nice really."

"What about dating?" Rick asks casually, but I feel an underlying seriousness in his question and I glance at him. "Do you… have you dated much since…?" He trails off awkwardly.

I shrug and look down at my almost empty beer. "A few times, but never more than one date. It's never felt right, just awkward and, well…"

"Like you're betraying him somehow?" Rick finishes softly. I bite my lip and nod. I wonder how he can guess these things; it's a bit unnerving. "Do you feel like that now?"

I glance up at him sharply; his gaze is intense on my face. "I thought this was just a friendly drink, there was no mention of a date," I reply seriously, then smile a little to cover the awkwardness I feel.

Rick laughs. "Well, you have me there." He stares at me for a moment, an intrigued look in his eyes, and I find the attention makes me slightly uncomfortable.

I finish my beer and place the pint glass slowly down. "Well, it's been nice talking to you, but I should probably go."

Rick looks startled. "Go where?"

"Home. We've had two drinks, remember. Your obligation is fulfilled."

Rick narrows his eyes at me. "Obligation?"

I shrug. I'm probably being too harsh. But I realise that I could stay here all night and really enjoy myself. That makes me feel very odd. "You've made me feel better, about the egg assault and my being rude to you, and I thank you for that. It's been ages since I've been out on a Friday night." I smile faintly, but Rick has no humour on his face. "But I should go now." I stand to leave but Rick leans across and gently grabs my hand.

"Emma? You thought this was an obligation? That I felt I had to do it?"

"It doesn't really matter, does it? I've had a good time. I hope you have too."

Rick lets go of my hand and regards me with curiosity. I was expecting relief. I nod at him.

"Good night, Rick." I turn and walk quickly out of the bar, trying to make a quick getaway. As I exit, I exhale sharply. I have these odd feelings circulating through me. They confuse me so I try and shake them off quickly.

"Emma, wait." I'm partway across the entrance to the parking lot when I feel Rick behind me. I didn't hear him approach and I jump in surprise. I turn quickly, wondering if I left something on the table or something. "I want to see you again."

I'm blown away. "Excuse me?"

"I'd like to see you again for more than a few drinks."

"What? Why?" I blurt out. I'm suddenly nervous; I didn't expect this. I shove my fringe behind my ear.

Rick seems surprised by my question. "Why wouldn't I?" His expression appears sincere, but I have to be wary.

"Rick, I'm a widowed single mum with a bad attitude and a tendency to throw eggs over strangers." I look up into his face in exasperation. "Why would you want to?"

He steps forward until he is really very close to me. I realise my forehead barely comes up to his chin, and I can smell that spicy cologne again. I resist the urge to step away and hold my ground.

"Emma," he says quietly, amusement on his features. "Despite, and probably because of, the reasons you just described, I find you fascinating, and intriguing. It's been a long time since I found anyone quite as interesting as you, and you are gorgeous, so why would I not want to get to know you better?"

I tilt my head and study his face in the darkening light. "Rick..."

"How about," Rick states before I finish, "you give me your number, and then we can decide the details at a later time?"

That's a good option. It means I don't have to agree to anything now, and I can choose in my own time whether to answer him. It also means I will have a lot of time to think.

I nod in agreement before I change my mind and hold out my hand. "Give me your mobile."

Rick grins and reaches into his pocket, unlocking the screen and placing it gently in my hand. "We call it a cell phone over here, you know."

I type in my number. "It will always be a mobile phone to me." I hear Rick chuckle quietly. I hand him his phone, careful not to touch him, and step back, turning to walk away. "Good night, Rick."

"Wait, didn't you drive?" he calls.

"Nope, I walked," I say, looking over my shoulder at him. "I told you, I don't live far." Two streets over, in fact.

"Can I give you a ride then?" He sounds concerned but also amused.

"Nope," I say back with a smile, then turn the corner and vanish out of sight.

*

Saturday passed in a blur of child-orientated activities, donuts and glorious sunshine. I find myself strangely upbeat at the world, in a way I haven't felt in a long time. I put it down to the simple fact that a man like Rick might be interested in me; I wasn't under any illusion it would last. I ignore the little clinch in my belly when my phone buzzes early on Saturday night. The only further communication I have had from Rick was a text shortly after I left him in the parking lot where he checked I had got home all right, which I had replied to briefly, thanking him for a nice night.

Have you had a nice day? the text reads. April is in bed and I'm sitting on the sofa drinking a glass of wine and watching an old movie, my usual Saturday night activities.

I smile and text back. *Yes, a lovely day, thanks. But I ate too many donuts. You?*

A reply swiftly follows. *My day did not involve donuts, but exercise and video gaming (two of my favourite things). What kind of donuts were involved?*

I have to smile at that. A grown man liking video games. *The ones with sprinkles on.*

Good choice, came his reply. *Can I see you tomorrow?*

I hesitate. Did I want to see him again? Actually, as I thought about it, I couldn't tomorrow anyway. My phone beeps again. *There could be donuts.* I laugh, then it fades. What was it about this man that made me laugh? It was puzzling.

Despite the donut offer, tomorrow is not so good. I have to be at home all day. Which was true.

I could drop by your house then? I would really like to see you, Emma.

Did I want him to come by? Did I want April to meet him? I lean back on the sofa, this is so hard. I'm so very conflicted. Not for the first time I wish I was young and carefree again. There are so many complications now.

How about, you tell me your address... Damn, he was persistent. I couldn't help but wonder why.

I don't think that's a good idea. Plus... no offence, I don't really know you so I don't think I should tell you my address. What a terrible excuse that was. As I wait for the reply, I bite my lip, not sure if I want to hear his response, but still eager too.

It's good to be cautious, comes his reply a few minutes later, and I breathe a sigh of relief. *But I have 'resources', you know. I could find it out anyway if I really wanted to... in a non-creepy way, of course.*

I smile. He's given me a perfect opening not to make a decision. *Yikes, that is totally creepy. But okay then, mate. You use your 'resources' and if you find my address, you can come by. Deal?*

I had no doubt he didn't really have the resources he was boasting about and he wouldn't come round, which was good, considering what was going on tomorrow.

Rick's reply was quick. *Deal. Have a good night!*

*

The picnic was in full swing by lunchtime. Children ran all over the garden, and their parents sat in garden chairs around tables full of food and drink. The sun was shining high in the sky and the temperature was lovely. I brought out another jug of iced lemonade and laughed as April bounded past me into the house, full of enthusiasm as always, her long black pigtails and bright pink sundress flowing behind her. As I set down the jug and offer it to my guests, I hear the doorbell ring over the background music, currently Dire Straits' *Money for Nothing*. Knowing April is in the house, and her tendency to open the door without me there, I hurry back inside.

I hear the front door open and frown. I really need to have a lock installed higher up.

"April?" I call as I approach, seeing my daughter's small body in the gap of light from the main door. "What have I told you about opening the front door without me?" I take the door from her and pull it all the way open, and my jaw nearly hits the floor. Rick is standing on the front step, a wide grin on his face and sunglasses perched on his head. While I hadn't forgotten about the texts last night, I had not actually expected this.

"Afternoon," he says casually. His eyes are twinkling at me in amusement. "You look surprised to see me, Emma."

"Well, y… y… yes," I stutter. "I didn't actually expect you to—"

"Show up?" he grins. "I said I would." He held a bag up to me, looking pleased with himself. "I brought donuts."

"… you're a giant." My daughter's small voice comes from below and I glance down at her as I accept the donut bag. She is staring up at Rick with wide, fascinated eyes. I kneel down next to her.

"April, this is my… friend, Rick," I introduce. "Rick, this is my daughter, April."

Rick kneels down himself and holds out his hand. "It's very nice to meet you, April."

April blinks, then places her tiny hand in his huge one. "Are you a giant?"

Rick smiles at her. "Not quite, though I am very tall."

"Are you here for the picnic?" April smiles widely. She isn't a shy girl.

Rick shoots me a look and I smile. "There are a bunch of kids and their parents in the garden having a picnic." Rick narrows his eyes. "I told you today wasn't a good day."

"You failed to mention why," he points out.

"Come on, Rick, come on!" April grabs his hand and pulls him into the house. Rick has no choice but to follow. I laugh to myself as I close the door and follow them. April pulls Rick out through the back doors and down into the garden. I follow slowly, watching as April leads Rick to the climbing frame that is set up in the middle of the garden.

My friend and neighbour, Julia, comes up to me quickly as I place the donuts down and take my coffee mug off the table where I had left it. "Who is that?" she whispers in awe, her eyes never leaving Rick.

I smile and murmur. "Just a friend, I didn't expect him to show up today."

"A friend?" she gasps. "He's who you had a date with on Friday night?"

"It wasn't a date," I reply sharply. Julia just gives me a look and I relent. "Okay, yes, it was him."

"Wow, Emma. Just wow." Her eyes go back to him. I have to admit, Rick does look very good. He wears beige cargo shorts, flip-flops and a white t-shirt with a band logo on the front. Those tattoos on his arms make him look like a badass, but the way he is patiently standing next to the climbing frame looking up at my daughter is very... attractive. April is directing him from atop the climbing frame, which is about his head height, and he stands there looking amused. Other children are running around him too, craning their necks to look up at him. He is clearly fascinating to them all. As if sensing our gaze, he glances over at me and smiles widely. My word, is he gorgeous.

"Wow…" I hear Julia mutter. I elbow her. "What?" she asks. "I'm married, not dead."

I look over at the other parents and note with a smile that all the women are watching Rick with fascination. The few men here seem to be in deep discussion with each other over their beers and haven't noticed Rick's arrival.

Shaking my head, I grab a beer from the cooler and head over to them, my coffee mug clutched in the other hand.

"Rick, you need to stand there, no, there. Yes, that's right. Now you need to—"

"April, are you being bossy?" I interrupt. April immediately looks guilty.

"No, Mummy, but Rick wasn't doing as I want."

I try not to laugh at her earnest expression, and look at her with my eyebrows raised. "Well, if you want Rick to do something, you need to ask him nicely, okay?" April nods and moves to the slide. "Here, I brought you a beer." I pass it to Rick. He looks at it with interest.

"You're serving me a Bud? After your scathing remarks?"

"Seems to be what the blokes around here drink," I say with a shrug. "I can't help it if American men have bad taste."

"Perhaps in beer," Rick states, his eyes on me. "Not in other things."

I hold back a smile at his suggestive tone and glance at April, who is now bossing the other kids around. I gesture towards the adults. "You want to play here or over there?"

"Wherever you are," he says flirtatiously, his mouth curving into a grin.

I turn quickly, but I can't resist firing back at him, "Feeling playful today, are we?"

"You have no idea," I hear him mutter as he follows me across the lawn, and I bite back another smile. I really should not be flirting with this man. I need to change topics.

"Okay, how exactly did you find my address?"

Rick shrugs and says vaguely, "Like I said, I have resources."

I shoot him a curious but wary glance, slowing my pace so he walks next to me. Rick sighs. "Okay, I memorised your licence plate at the grocery store and had one of my guys run it to get your information," he flushes slightly and runs a hand through his hair, "which I am not really supposed to do but I couldn't resist your challenge." He meets my eyes with concern. "Do you find that creepy?"

I consider carefully, appraising him. "Surprisingly, no." Rick looks relieved.

Julia and her husband are standing at the end of the table, so I walk over to them. "Rick, these are my friends and neighbours, Julia and Austin," I introduce. "Julia, Austin, this is Rick." There are hellos and smiles all around.

"The little boy there," I point to a dark-haired boy of five who is climbing up the slide behind April, "is Lucas, their son, and they have a little girl, who is asleep on my bed upstairs."

"Tell me, Rick, what do you do for work?" Julia asks, her gaze taking him all in.

"I'm in the army," Rick replies simply.

"Based at Fort Benning?" Austin asks. Rick nods.

"Well, that explains the muscles," Julia comments to me out of the side of her mouth. Rick smiles as Austin clears his throat and shoots his wife a look. Julia sees it and mutters, "I'm just saying..."

"Come on, Jules. Let's get you a snack to drool over instead." Austin grins and rolls his eyes in our direction as he grabs his wife's shoulders and leads her away.

"Despite that little drooling incident, Julia and Austin are very happily married," I whisper to Rick.

"I don't doubt it," Rick replies with a smile. "Austin's reaction said it all."

I nod; a very good observation. I give him a sideways look. "You probably get that all the time, though, right, women drooling over your muscles?" I really shouldn't tease, but it's been a long time since I've been in a conversation like this and it's good fun. Jon and I used to flirt like this all the time. Another thing I miss about him.

Rick nods his head and says seriously, "Yeah, I can't walk down the street without being drooled on. It's a problem." Then he smirks and glances my way. "You don't seem to be affected, though."

"Perhaps I'm just better at hiding it." The words pop out before I can stop them. I really shouldn't have said that.

Rick grins widely at me and our eyes meet for a few seconds before I look away towards April.

"She's a beautiful little girl," Rick comments after a moment. "She seems smart too."

I smile widely at the praise. "She is, a little too smart for her own good sometimes. She gets that from her father." I bite my lip as an image of Jon pops into my head again.

"Does she remember him?" Rick asks quietly.

I shake my head. "Not really, she was not even three when he died. When I show her a picture of him, she says 'Daddy,' but I'm not entirely sure she knows what it means. She doesn't seem to feel like she is missing out by just having me, though, at least not yet." I shrug. "Probably in time when she realises that most other kids have two parents, she will."

"Yeah, she's not quite old enough to know that yet," Rick says quietly. Thinking back on his childhood, I reckon he knows better than most. "But it helps so much for her to have such a good mom."

I smile to myself. He can't know that for sure, but it's nice that he says it anyway.

"I hope I'm not intruding by being here," Rick suddenly says, turning to me. "If I realised you had this going on, I wouldn't have come by, but I just had to accept your challenge."

I laugh and shake my head. "Nah, it's fine. But feel free to leave if you get fed up of kids' games, speaking of which…"

April is running towards me, looking excited.

"Mummy Mummy Mummy."

"April April April," I respond as per usual.

She stops in front of me and pulls the bottom of my light blue summer dress. "Mummy, can we play goose and seek?"

"Do the other kids what to play that?" April nods her head. "Have you asked them?" April shakes her head slowly and I laugh. "Okay, go and ask them, and if they do, then we can play."

April makes an excited whooping noise then runs back the way she came.

"I've been out of the kids' party game arena for a while now, but goose and seek does not sound familiar," Rick comments wryly. "Is this some British game you've brought over?"

I chuckle. "Kind of, so you know duck duck goose?" Rick nods, looking intrigued. "And you know hide and seek?" Rick nods again. "Well, it's kind of a mixture between the two. For every kid playing, there is an adult. The adults all sit in a large circle with their eyes closed. The kids go round and round patting each adult on the head, singing a few verses of a song. When it ends, the kid leans down, whispers their name in the nearest adult's ear and then runs off and hides. The adult then has to find their specific kid. The last kid to be found by their adult wins." I smile widely. "It's really good fun for both kids and adults. April's father made it up when she was small. We've taught it to everyone over here."

Rick grins. "I'll enjoy watching it."

I shake my head. "Oh no, April will want you to be her adult. You'll be playing."

Rick looks surprised and I laugh. "Does that mean I have to know the other kids' names too?" he asks, sounding a little bit fearful.

"Nope, because April will pick you." I tap the side of my nose. "Trust me on that." Rick doesn't look convinced. "Don't tell me a big strong soldier like you is scared of a kids' game?"

Rick frowns and puffs up his chest. "Of course not. I'm fearless in the face of adversary." Then he shrugs and laughs. "Sounds like fun, though why she would pick me and not you, I don't know."

I bite my lip to keep from laughing again; he has no idea. April and the other kids run over to me. "We want to play, we want to play!"

"Okay, kids, everyone grab an adult."

The other parents all stand up as various kids pull them to their feet. April grabs hold of Rick's hand. "Rick, you come and play with me." Rick shoots me an amused look.

"Okay, everyone." I put my fingers in my mouth and whistle, getting everyone's attention immediately. Rick looks impressed. "Listen up. Usual rules apply. Kids can only hide in the back garden or downstairs in the house. Not upstairs or in the front garden – everyone got that?" There are various nods nearby. "If an adult finds a kid that isn't their own, the adult cannot tell anyone else." Lots of nods again. "Today, we'll be singing…" I pause for dramatic effect and the kids giggle "…*Baa, Baa, Black Sheep*. Three verses as you run around." I hold up my fingers to say three. "Kids, please be gentle with the patting on the head, no slapping." Rick looks over at me sharply but I pretend not to notice. "Okay, we also have a newbie today." I place my hand on Rick's shoulder, and try to ignore the hard muscle I feel beneath the t-shirt. "Everyone, this is Rick. He has never played before and doesn't know the house or the garden, so be nice to him, all right?" I wink at Rick and pat him gently on the back. "Have fun."

Rick raises an eyebrow at me in response, looking amused. I point at his head where his expensive-looking eyewear sits. "You might want to remove your sunglasses." Slowly, Rick reaches up and takes the glasses off his head. Before I can react, he has stepped towards me and carefully placed them on top of my head. He adjusts them so they fit comfortably, then moves my fringe gently out of my eyes, his fingertips lightly brushing my skin. I clear my throat and shift on my feet, surprised by my sudden nervousness in his proximity. He smiles as April grabs his hand and he is pulled towards the middle of the lawn.

As expected, April directs the adults into a circle and tells them all to close their eyes. There are nine children playing today, each with an adult, and a few extra adults with babies in tow hang back while everyone gets settled. I check around; all of the parents here have played this game before and know the drill. If you aren't playing, you're keeping watch. I see Austin, with their one-year-old girl on his hip, head for the garden gate, to make sure no one escapes out front. I see Susan, a parent of a girl in April's kindergarten class, head into the house, no doubt to lock the door and keep watch inside. Two other parents whose kids didn't choose them position themselves around the garden. I stand on the patio. Only occasionally does April choose me for this game, as she likes to change around, so I am usually the watch guard, which suits me fine.

"Ready?" I shout, and the kids all yell. I put my fingers in my mouth and whistle sharply. As the song begins, the kids begin running around and through the circle, all chopping and changing with each other at different speeds, patting the adults on the head. I see Rick shrink his head slightly as they pat him not very gently on the head in their excitement. As the third verse begins, I see April manoeuvre herself so she is near Rick, then right at the last line she sprints to him. As expected, she ends up behind him, with a big grin on her face.

"Okay, kids, say your name to your adult. Adults, keep your eyes closed."

April leans over and whispers her name in Rick's ear. I see him grin and nod. I see Lucas, Julia's little boy, do the same with her. The kids always get who they want. It's rare for them to end up with the adult they didn't choose to begin with.

"Right, kids, you have thirty seconds to hide, beginning now." I begin to count down, slightly slower than it would be in seconds. I watch as April runs to her favourite hiding place, behind and inside a large oak tree in the corner of the garden, then see a few other kids disappear into hiding places. Three run past me into the house. Then my gaze drifts back to Rick's face, and I take a moment to study it. Sharp cheekbones, firm jaw, close shaven. His skin is tanned and in contrast to his bright blond hair. If I could pick an opposite for Jon, it would be him. I feel a stab in my chest at the automatic comparison. As my count hits one, his eyes snap open and meet my own. His look is serious and intense as he gazes back at me. I find my stomach flip-flops in a way I haven't felt for a long time.

I pull myself together and whistle again sharply. "Adults, go find your kid," I say loudly. Rick narrows his eyes, grins at me as his eyes sparkle, then stands up slowly as the adults move off. The back garden isn't huge, and neither is the house, so there are limited places to hide. Slowly, one by one, each kid is found and they each receive a big hug. Then the fun is to follow the remaining adults around and taunt them. I failed to mention that to Rick on purpose. He is at a major disadvantage, as he doesn't know the garden at all. He walks around, looking in the obvious places, even checking briefly behind the oak tree, but not seeing the opening at the back where April has hid herself. As the other kids are found, they chase him around the garden. He mock glares over his shoulder at them if they get too close, and the kids giggle and scream as he makes sudden lunging moves. Rick definitely knows how to handle himself around kids. Eventually, April is the only kid not found. Rick has searched the downstairs of the house too, and come up empty-handed. He stands in the middle of the garden with his hands on his hips and looks confused. He scratches his head and looks over at me. I'm lounging on the porch steps now with Austin and little Sammie, holding a beer and watching the fun. The kids are all running around him, taunting him. I catch his eye and his gaze asks – where is she? I laugh and shake my head, then subtly move my eyes over his shoulder to the oak tree, then back again.

Understanding dawns on his face and he slowly twirls around and around.

"Come on, guys, help me out here," he asks the kids. "Do you know where April is?"

The kids laugh and scream. "April is hiding so well, I might not be able to ever find her," he says loudly. "But is there anywhere I haven't looked?" He begins to head for the back of the garden. "I'm sure I've checked this old oak tree, but have I looked all the way around it?"

Most of the kids know April is hiding there, and they scream and giggle – basically giving the game away. Rick smiles widely as he approaches the tree.

"April, where are you…?" Rick sings, then jumps suddenly to the back of the tree amidst lots of giggles. I hear him laugh and April squeal as he finds her. They emerge from round the tree. Rick is carrying her with one arm. April has her arms around Rick's neck as she clings to him with a wide smile.

"I think that makes April the winner," Rick announces, as the other kids run up to him and jump up and down in excitement.

I'm mesmerised by the sight as my heart begins to pound. A similar image, of Jon carrying April out from around a tree as she clung to his neck, assaults me and I gasp softly. Apart from our family, I've never seen any other man pick up April since Jon. It's disorientating. That familiar ache returns as I think of my dead husband, of the fact he can never cuddle our daughter again. That she will never really remember him. April leans in and snuggles closer to Rick, her little face in his neck. He pats her on the back gently and glances over at me with a smile. But Rick must see something in my face, as his smile fades immediately. I blink and try to bury the images of Jon and April, plastering a fake smile on my face. Rick doesn't look convinced and slowly lowers April to the ground. April looks delighted to have won, excitement evident on her face as she runs over to me and throws her arms around my neck.

"Mummy, I won. Mummy, I won," she tells me excitedly.

"Well done, sweetheart," I reply, pulling her in close. "You were very clever at hiding."

"Rick found me. The other kids gave me away." She moves back and pouts.

"That's okay, though. You won and the game is over now."

April wriggles out of my embrace. "Can I have something to eat?" I see Rick walking over but I keep my eyes on April.

"Sure. Rick brought some donuts, would you like one?" I don't usually offer her sweets mid-afternoon, but this is a picnic after all.

April nods as I stand and move to the table, which is currently deserted. I pull out several packets of donuts.

"I brought the ones with sprinkles," Rick's deep voice rumbles from next to me, "but then I thought you might be sick of those so I brought a selection too."

"That's very thoughtful of you, thank you."

I pull out both boxes. There are six in each. I open both and show them to April. She picks a sprinkled one. "Now say thank you to Rick, please, sweetheart."

"Thank you." April looks upwards at him and smiles, then stuffs the donut in her mouth and runs off to play with the kids and adults on the climbing frame. I laugh and place the open boxes on the table. I'm tempted to have a donut myself, but I ate quite a few yesterday and I'm a little podgier around the middle recently than I'd like. I absently rub my belly; I just don't get enough exercise nowadays.

"I hope you enjoyed the game," I say to Rick without looking at him, wiping my hands on my dress.

"I did, it was great fun. Thanks for the tip at the end. I swear I had checked that tree."

"Well, now you know about that hidey hole at the back," I comment, looking over at the climbing frame. "April is always pleased to win."

Rick moves in front of me, blocking my view of the kids. "Are you okay?"

I force myself to look up at him. "Of course."

Rick frowns at me in disbelief. "No, you're not. I saw that look on your face. Was it because I picked April up? I'm sorry if that wasn't all right."

"No, that's not it," I say quickly. I don't want him to think that. "If April's okay then I'm fine too." I sigh and wipe my forehead with one of my palms, swiping my fringe away.

"Then what is it?" Rick places his hands on my upper arms gently.

"It's just... apart from her uncles or grandfathers, I haven't seen any man pick up April since her father died," I say slowly, focusing my eyes on the logo on his t-shirt. "It just startled me. The image was so similar to one I remember of her father." I force myself to look into his face. "You didn't do anything wrong. It's all me."

Rick studies my face for a moment. "Maybe I should go," he says slowly. "I'm clearly making things difficult for you, which is the last thing I want." He sighs and drops his hands. "I'm sorry."

I clasp one of his hands mid-air. "No." It comes out before I think. Rick leaving is actually the last thing I want. "No, don't go. Stay, for a bit longer."

Rick hesitates, studying me, then smiles. "If you're sure." I nod and Rick squeezes my hand.

"Emma." Austin walks up to me and I quickly drop Rick's hand. "I'm busting for the restroom, do you mind?" He holds out little Sammie.

"Course." I take the little girl from her father's arms and place her on my hip. She weighs so little and always reminds me of April at this age.

"Thanks, Em." Austin hurries off.

"This is Sammie. Sammie, this is Rick," I introduce. The little girl has her eyes focused on Rick. He smiles widely at her and she grins her one-toothed grin back. She reaches out to him and he lifts a finger for her to grip.

"How old are your nephews and niece?" I ask.

"Seventeen, fifteen and twelve," Rick replies, his eyes on the baby. "Jordan is the youngest, but definitely the boss of her elder brothers." Rick smiles. "I love them to bits, but they were the most fun when they were April's age. Now the boys are teenagers and don't have much time for their Uncle Rick. Jordan always does, though."

He makes faces at the baby and she giggles. "A lot of my friends have kids too." He smiles. "It happens at my age, everyone is married and having babies. Most of our meet-ups now involve a family outing or party. It used to be just bars and clubs." He chuckles to himself.

"Does that interest you?" I ask curiously. "Being a father?"

"Yes," Rick replies instantly, raising his eyebrows and meeting my eyes. "I just haven't got around to it yet."

"How old are you?" I ask, mostly to change the subject.

"Thirty-five, almost thirty-six. My birthday is September 22nd," he replies, then looks at me coyly. "How old are you?"

"You mean you don't want to guess?"

"Oh." Rick looks horrified. "Heaven forbid, no way."

"I'm thirty-one. Birthday is 19th of February."

Rick smiles but doesn't comment. Just then, Austin returns. "Thanks, Emma."

"Do you mind if I...?" Rick holds out his hands to the baby.

Austin grins. "Go ahead, man. Save my arms for a little longer."

I carefully pass the little girl to Rick, who holds her gingerly but confidently at his side. She looks so tiny in his arms. The baby gurgles and presses into him.

"You're a natural, man," Austin comments. "Do you have kids?" Rick shakes his head. "Well, you should do. It's hard work but totally worth it."

"So I hear." Rick bounces slowly and the baby giggles. "Shall we go for a little walk, Sammie?" Rick glances at Austin, silently asking permission, who nods with a smile. Rick turns, then heads away from us.

Austin laughs as Rick disappears out of earshot. I turn to him with a look. "What are you laughing at?" I'm as good a friend with Austin as I am with Julia. Austin is slightly taller than me, with dark blond receding hair and a big smile. Austin reminds me a lot of Mike; they both have such easy-going personalities. Austin adores Julia, who can be a bit of a handful sometimes.

"He's perfect, Em," Austin states. "Tall, good-looking, fun, great with kids, has that protective military instinct. Marry him before someone else does."

I roll my eyes. "Maybe you should marry him."

Austin laughs. "Tempting, but already taken." I watch as Rick walks around the garden with the baby, stopping at the hedgerow and pointing something out to her. There is something extremely attractive about a man that looks like Rick, masculine and muscular with his big bold tattoos, carefully holding a baby. I see Julia glance over, do a double take, then look over at me and her husband with wide eyes. She fans herself and mock faints. Austin snorts in laughter at his wife. "On second thoughts…" he comments dryly "…maybe I can switch."

"I think you'll have some competition." I gesture to where a couple of the mothers are watching him from the other side of the garden. They all look flustered.

"No way," Austin states firmly. "You're the only competition."

I shake my head. "I'm not competition," I state. "We're just friends."

Austin sighs. "Emma, I have no idea what it's like to have been through what you have," his eyes darken as the thought of Julia dying must fill his head, "and frankly I don't want to. But surely there comes a time when you have to take that next step to get on with your life."

I grimace; I hate this conversation. "It's not that simple."

Austin pokes me lightly on the arm. "Em, open your eyes. That man," he points to Rick, who has now joined Julia and the parents next to the climbing frame, "likes you, a lot. And he's perfect. At least give it a go."

"Nobody's perfect," I mutter, remembering some of the dark expressions that had passed over his face on Friday night. Rick might seem carefree and perfect on the outside, but I'm guessing he has some demons locked away down inside. The question was – did I want to find out what they were?

*

Five days later, I am waiting on the porch in the evening light for Rick to pick me up for what is definitely a date. My house has a long wooden porch which adorns the entire front. As such, there are several chairs where you can sit and watch the world go by. In this street, that means a car every so often. There is even a white picket fence, which is a very American cliché. I don't own this house; I rent it from a private landlord. It's in a good part of the city, good travelling distance to work and big enough for April, myself and guests should we have them.

Financially, I'm more secure than I ever thought I would be. Jon's company had salary-related death benefits, so I received a huge sum of money from them after his death. Jon and I had also taken out a life insurance policy when we bought our house together, just in case. When we bought it, I remember us talking about how we would probably never need it, but Jon had insisted. I didn't want the money when I received it, couldn't even bring myself to think about it. It sat in my bank account for two months before I drunkenly confessed to Amie one night in France when staying with my in-laws. She frogmarched me to the computer straight away, paid off the mortgage on our house and set up several savings accounts, including one for April for when she is older. I also couldn't bring myself to sell our house when we moved out here, so I rent it out cheaply to Jason and his girlfriend, who were moving out of London around the time April and I left the UK. The rent goes into April's savings account. It was the right thing to do, but still made me feel cold. I didn't want the money. I wanted Jon back.

My thoughts skip around as I sit on the porch, thinking about Jon and Rick and what I'm doing in my life. My eyes are closed and I feel the breeze flow over my bare legs. I'm wearing a red strappy sundress and sandals. I washed my hair earlier so it's still damp, curling about my neck in the warmth of the day. It's been hot today and the evening will be warm too. I'm not sure where we are going. Rick wanted to surprise me tonight.

I take a deep breath of the evening air and exhale slowly. Tonight is definitely a date, and I think that's okay. Apart from a few texts setting up tonight, I haven't really heard from Rick all week. Which is fine, of course, but I find I actually want to see him. I want to talk to him and hear his voice. I have been looking forward to tonight in a way I haven't looked forward to anything in a long time. That realisation startles me, but also intrigues me. I'm just not sure I'm ready for this yet.

"Evening." My eyes shoot open and land on Rick. He is leaning on the porch railing, a hint of a smile on his face. Rick is wearing work boots, dark jeans and a red t-shirt with another band logo on it. Sunglasses perch on his blond hair.

"How do you do that?" I ask, glancing over his shoulder to see his truck parked on the street. "You're so damn quiet."

Rick shrugs. "It's what I'm trained to do."

"You mean give a girl a heart attack?"

"Be sneaky."

I stand and walk down the porch steps to him. He leans over and brushes a kiss on my cheek. "You look lovely, Emma." His spicy scent washes over me as he pulls away. "I'm glad we're doing this tonight."

"Me too," I reply, my skin tingling from his kiss. "But what exactly are we doing?"

Rick takes my hand and pulls me to his truck. "Something very American, which I think you'll enjoy."

"Hmm, I'm intrigued."

"As you should be." He opens the passenger door for me to climb in, old-school gentleman style. Then he climbs into the driver's side. It's still weird sitting on the wrong side of a car, even after a year of doing it.

He glances down at my bag and jacket. "We'll be outside so it's good you have a jacket."

"Something American that's outside?" I mutter. I rack my brains but can't think of anything. "I really should have paid more attention to all those American chick flicks."

Rick chuckles as he pulls away. "How is April?"

I smile. "Great, as always. She's with Julia and Austin tonight, which she loves. Oh, and she won't stop talking about you."

Rick glances at me with a small smile. "Really?"

"Yep. It's all 'Rick this' and 'Rick that'. It's very cute."

"You're not worried she might be getting attached...?" Rick trails off.

I shrug. "She loves new people, and she is very affectionate. I'm not worried at the moment. I'll have to keep an eye on it." I had decided I'd be careful with how much April saw Rick, and if she started getting too attached, I would need to limit her contact with him.

Rick nods but doesn't say anything. He seems subdued tonight. Not that I have spent enough time with him to really tell his moods, but he just seems... off. I study his side profile. His eyes have black rings under them, his jaw is set and his body seems tense.

"Are you okay, Rick?" I ask quietly.

He glances at me and his expression softens. "I'm fine. I just had a rough day, well, week, is all."

"Do you want to cancel tonight? We can if you want." I will be disappointed but I understand.

"No," Rick says sharply, then his tone softens again. "No, I've been looking forward to this. It's what has got me through it this week." He glances at me. "Seeing you again."

I'm not sure what to make of that, but I touch his arm gently. "Do you want to talk about it? If you can."

Rick shakes his head roughly. I take that to mean he can't talk about it.

"So how has your week been?" he asks, clearly looking to change the subject.

"Uneventful but busy," I answer. "The world of accounting is not generally exciting."

"What firm do you work for again?"

"Gold & Sanchez. They do engineering and infrastructure services all around the world. I'm a senior accountant in their in-house finance team."

"Ah, okay, I know them. Their offices downtown are huge."

"Yeah, Atlanta is one of the largest offices in the world," I say. "Over 3,000 people work there. The office in Salisbury where I worked had 300. It was quite a change."

"Salisbury? I did a training exercise on Salisbury Plain back when I was a sergeant."

"Really? When was that?"

Rick thinks a moment, his eyes on the road. "Summer 2009, I think."

"I was working in the Salisbury office in 2009. That's interesting."

"Maybe we passed each other on the street and never even knew it."

"Maybe. The office is to the north, near the plain." I was living with Jon in Reading in 2009, getting the train in and cycling to the industrial estate where the office was.

"I like the UK," Rick comments as he takes a right turn. "I never spent a great deal of time there, but what I did see I liked."

"Yeah, I like it too," I say quietly, looking out of the window. A sign on the side of the road catches my eye. "Fulton County Carnival…" I murmur, then I look quickly at Rick. "Are we going to a carnival?"

Rick nods. "Yep. A good ole American carnival. Have you been to one since you moved here?"

I shake my head. "No, but I do remember those from the chick flicks." I clap my hands together. "How exciting!"

Rick smiles widely at my excitement. "A couple of my buddies will be there too, and their wives. I hope that's okay."

I nod. "Of course, I would love to meet them. Are these school buddies?"

Rick shakes his head. "No, from my unit."

"Ah, so will there be lots of drooling then?"

Rick chuckles. "I hope you would only drool over me."

I send him a smile but don't comment.

We pull off the interstate and into an already packed car park. I can see some rides and bright lights over a tall thicket of dark green conifers. As I get out of the truck and shrug on my jacket, I hear laughter and chatter, with soft country music in the background and a dog barking. The smell of sugar and barbequed meat is on the air. As we follow other couples and families through the trees, Rick takes my hand and threads his fingers through mine. I force myself to relax and not think too much. It does feel nice to be holding his hand.

As we emerge from the trees, a short queue is forming next to an entrance gate. I glance over the top and see a multi-coloured brightly lit Ferris wheel nearby. A small roller coaster sits at the far end, and I can hear screams coming from that direction. I can see a merry-go-round turning prettily in the darkening day. Bright lights surround the edge of the carnival and illuminate the various stalls and food stands. Lots of people walk around, all smiling and happy. Children run through the crowds grasping big stuffed bears and candyfloss.

Rick pays a few dollars for us to enter and then we are inside. An open area off the main gate is clear of any attractions. I see a tall man wave at Rick and he waves back as we make our way over to him. Rick lets go of my hand and places it at the small of my back as we navigate through the crowds.

"Tav. Good of you to make it," the tall man yells over the crowd. He is striking to look at, with short dark brown hair and blue eyes within a strong, tanned face. As we break through the crowd, I see he is standing next to a petite blonde woman who smiles widely as she spots us.

"Rick! So good to see you." The blonde throws her arms

around his neck, and Rick has to bend over a lot to hug her back.

"Hi, I'm Seth." The dark-haired man introduces himself with a smile and a handshake. He is slightly shorter than Rick, and slender, but still heavily built. His voice is like Rick's, deep with a gentle accent.

"Nice to meet you, I'm Emma."

"This is Shanna White, Seth's wife," Rick says, gesturing towards the blonde.

Shanna throws her arms around my neck too, throwing me off guard. "It's so lovely to meet you," she says. Her accent is local and strong.

I laugh as she unwinds herself, patting her on the back gently. "Nice to meet you, Shanna."

A man suddenly pounces on Rick and Seth, throwing his arms around their necks. "Gotcha!" he yells in their ears as the men jump. Rick whirls quickly and moves away out of the embrace, his expression stony for an instant until he seems to force a big smile.

"Ruggy, you arse." The man, who I see is actually not much taller than me but built like a tank, grins widely at Rick.

"Emma, this is Mat 'Ruggy' Fairthorne," Rick introduces. "But we just call him arsehole most of the time." I laugh as Mat punches him hard in the arm. "And this is his delightful wife, Mari." Seth steps out of the way and I see a stunning redhead with a large pregnant belly step around her husband. "Ruggy, Mari, this is Emma." I shake hands with them both. Mat is also good-looking, with close cropped dark hair and dark brown eyes.

"And I'm Frank Aldsa." A man comes up behind me and smiles widely as I turn from Mari. "Hello, Emma, nice to meet you." Like the others, Frank is tall, good-looking and has dark skin, darker close-cropped hair and a refined jawline. I shake his hand and it lingers a little longer than necessary, his smile widening as he hears Rick grunt.

"We also call Frank an arsehole," Rick states, moving to stand in between us to break our handshake. He returns his hand to the small of my back, and I feel an odd little shiver of delight at this possessive posturing.

"So you guys are all in the same unit?" I ask, looking at the men. They nod. "I feel like I'm looking at a male model line-up. Is that a requirement of the US Army?"

Mari laughs loudly; her voice is husky. "That's exactly what I thought when I met these guys."

I shake my head. "I don't think I've seen so many good-looking, drool-worthy blokes in one place." I feel Rick's hand tighten on my back as Seth chuckles. "And beautiful women as well." I gesture at Shanna and Mari, as the men nod and grin in agreement.

Shanna giggles. "Ah that's so sweet, and wow, I love your accent, so sophisticated."

"Australia, right?" Seth says. I glance at him to see he is smiling widely. I see Rick look over his shoulder, hiding his smirk. This is clear evidence he has been talking about me. That odd shiver of delight runs through me again.

"How did you guess?" I reply casually, then switch to my best approximation of an Aussie accent. "Was it the 'no worries, mate'?"

Everyone bursts out laughing until Shanna elbows Seth in the ribs. "Babe, you shouldn't tease someone you just met. It's rude." But she's smiling.

"So is throwing eggs over a stranger in the supermarket," I respond. "But that didn't stop me when I met Rick." Rick chuckles, but he is looking over my head at something and doesn't really seem to be paying attention.

Shanna giggles as the others all smile widely. "So it's true? I thought Seth was making it up."

I shrug. "Nope. I totally did that."

"That's not as bad as when I first met Mat," Mari confesses. "I threw up on him."

"Ahh, darlin', why'd you have to say that?" Mat groans; he has a very strong southern accent. "That's not a good story."

"That's funny, because when I first met Ruggy, I threw up on him too," Seth confesses. Mat shoots him a look which tells me that's true.

"And me," Frank says, his voice low and mocking. "Must be something about your face."

I see Seth glance at Rick, clearly expecting him to join in the banter. But Rick is still looking away over the crowds, an odd look on his face. Seth frowns at him.

"Ah, you bastards," Mat cries in a broad southern drawl. "Only two people have thrown up on me when they've met me. You, darlin'," he smiles lovingly at his wife, "and you, you arsehole." He points at Seth. "Both for legitimate reasons which have nothing to do with my face."

Everyone is laughing hysterically now. Rick looks around sharply, clearly startled at the noise, and then joins in after a beat, but I can tell it's forced. Judging from the expression on Seth's face, he thinks so too. Mari is holding her big belly with both hands, she is laughing so hard.

"How about we stroll around the carnival?" Shanna asks when the laughter dies down, swiftly moving to my side and taking my arm. Without waiting for a response, she drags me away. Mari comes up to my other side. I look over my shoulder and see the men following; Rick meets my eyes and smiles, but he still seems distant. There is something in his eyes I can't identify.

"So, have you been to a carnival like this?" Mari asks, dragging my attention back.

"There are similar ones back in England," I say. "But nothing quite like this. It's very American."

"That's the best way," Shanna states with a teasing smile.

I smile in kind. "Seth seems nice. Where did you guys meet?"

"I'm a physiotherapist," Shanna replies. "Seth was referred to me after he injured his hamstring a few years ago. He was a difficult patient, but we got through it." Her eyes light up, telling me there is more to that story than she is saying.

"So do you like it over here?" Mari asks.

I nod. "I do, it's kind of similar, culture-wise, but also different." I shrug. "That probably makes no sense."

Shanna smiles widely. "Well, I guess we speak the same language, so that would make it similar, but there are always going to be differences between every place in the world," she says. "Atlanta is very different from Miami, or LA, and they are on the same continent."

"I agree. And yes, at the moment, I like the change."

"Any reason why you came over here? For work, right?"

I hesitate a second. I guess I can tell them; it's no secret. "Work enabled me to come over here, yes, but the main reason is my husband died and I needed a change." Both Mari and Shanna gasp and stop walking.

"Oh my God. That's horrible," Shanna says, her hand over her mouth.

"Yes." I've had this conversation before, and know I need to bring a positive element to it or they will feel uncomfortable and awkward. "But he gave me a wonderful little girl, so I have that to be grateful for." I really hate that I mentioned it now; the women look so upset.

"How old is your little girl?" Mari asks after a moment.

"Four. Do you have any other children?"

Mari nods. "We have twin boys, almost four. They're with my mom tonight, thankfully. They'd go crazy here."

"Wow, twins. Do you know about what you're having now?" I gesture at her belly. I see Shanna staring at me, a look on her face I recognise all too well.

Mari nods. "A little girl. Not twins, we checked and then double-checked." I have to smile at that.

"Everything okay?" Rick is by my side, the other men crowding around us.

"Yes, it's fine." The two women are smiling at me with a look I have seen before, the one between sympathy, pity and not quite sure what to say. "It's okay, ladies." I pat their arms gently. "Let's go enjoy the carnival."

"Yes, let's go." Rick takes my hand and pulls me away. "See you later." He calls over his shoulder as the others call bye. "What was that about?" Rick asks quietly as we move between stalls.

"I told them why I moved here, and they reacted." I sigh as Rick shoots me a look. "Most people don't know what to say, or how to act, when I tell them, especially the married ones. They begin to think what it would be like for them if it happened, then they pity me. I can't blame them really."

Rick puts his arm around my shoulders and pulls me into him, not quite a hug, but close. His warmth and smell is comforting and I try and shake off the guilt in my chest that comes with enjoying being so close to him. "It's not pity." I wind my arm around his back and grip his waist through his t-shirt; the move feels surprisingly natural. "It's just as you say, they can't imagine what it would be like to lose their husbands." He looks up. "Do you like Ferris wheels?"

He has completely changed the subject, for which I'm grateful. I follow his gaze upwards. "Sure do."

"Great, let's go." Keeping his arm around my shoulders, we head to the line, which is short. In no time, we are being strapped into a car and the ride lifts us up. Rick's legs are so long, they are awkward in the small space. I laugh excitedly as the countryside around us comes into view. It's twilight now, but there is still enough light to see by. As we ascend, Rick seems to relax a little, his posture loosening up.

"That's the city." Rick's voice seems strained as he points out west, where I can see the high-rise buildings and suburbs of Atlanta. "And there are quite a few farm towns that way." Rick points east as the wheel stops, where I can see tiny houses and pinpoints of light in the dusk. "Then there's only farmland." Rolling acres of land surround the carnival, a dusty two-lane highway snaking off towards the city in the distance.

"It's so lovely," I say, looking around as the wheel continues its downward motion. Rick tenses again as the noise and buzz of the carnival becomes louder. I can feel it in his arm resting on the back of the seat behind me, in his leg muscles pressed up against mine. He doesn't say anything, just keeps his eyes on the crowd below us, a troubled expression on his face. We stop a few more times to let passengers on and off, then ascend. As the noise decreases, he relaxes a tiny bit again.

"Rick, are you sure you're all right?" He doesn't seem to hear me, so I place my hand gently on his leg. He immediately jumps and I quickly remove my hand. "Sorry."

"No, I'm sorry," he says softly, closing his eyes and inhaling sharply. "I just feel strange, and tired." We go down again and his eyes open wide, darting around like he is looking for something.

"Do you want to leave?" I ask. "It's okay if you do, if you're not feeling well."

"No, it's fine," he says, placing one of his hands on my bare neck and rubbing gently. Tingles shoot down my spine at the touch. "I want you to have a good time."

"We don't have to be here to have a good time," I say quietly. Rick suddenly focuses on me and he starts to smile widely just as I realise what I said. "Though I didn't actually mean that." I laugh, only slightly embarrassed by my words.

Rick laughs too, but that fades as we once again get to the ground. This time, it's our turn to get off. Seth and Shanna are our replacements. I see Seth's gaze focus on Rick and his eyes narrow in concern. Shanna shoots me a wide smile and waves as they get on the wheel.

On the ground, Rick seems agitated. It's almost dark now and the lights are dazzling. His gaze is darting around, his eyes narrowed. His fingers are twitching by his sides. I reach out and grab one of his hands and he stops fidgeting.

"I'm hungry," I state, hoping that will take his mind off whatever it's on. "What's a classic American meal at a carnival?"

Rick smiles distractedly and cracks his neck. "Hot dogs, of course. Let's go." He starts moving towards a nearby food stand and I follow him at a quick pace. This food cart is next to a wall, and the sound is slightly muffled. Rick focuses on me. "With everything?"

"Define everything."

The hot dog vendor gives me an odd look at my suspiciously asked question, until I explain I've never had one before. He must note my foreign accent because he smiles widely and then launches into a description of what a classic American hot dog should be. I nod along, keeping an eye on Rick, who is staring off towards the crowds. 'Everything' turns out to be a wide variety of sauces, onions and gherkins – which all sounds tasty, so I agree. The vendor whips up two hot dogs and I hand over the money. I move away and pass one to Rick. He takes a bite without really noticing, chewing absently.

"This is so good," I say between mouthfuls. "I guess American food isn't all rubbish, right?" I'm goading him on purpose, but I get no response. I quickly finish my hot dog, while Rick barely eats his. As I move to stand in front of him, I realise that even though I haven't known this man very long, and nor do I think I know him very well, I know enough to know that something is very, very wrong. There is a wild look in his eyes; his body is so tense I think he might pull a muscle from standing. His fists are clenched, and I can see the veins in his neck pulsing really hard.

"Rick, I think we should go." I stand in front of him and look into his face, but he doesn't seem to hear me. A loud bang from a nearby shooting stand sounds in the air and he whirls around, dropping the forgotten hot dog, his eyes frantically searching for the source of the noise. I take his hand and uncurl the fist, but he grabs my right wrist rather than my hand.

"Rick? What's wrong?"

Another loud bang and he drops instantly to the ground, pulling me down with him. There's a hard steel glaze to his eyes.

"We have to get out of here," he bites at me, his voice calm and cold, then takes off running. I yelp as he nearly pulls my arm out of the socket, his fingers biting into my wrist as he drags me along.

"Rick? What the..?" I ask as we duck behind a stall. The people standing there give us odd looks.

"Be quiet, Emma. They'll hear us." Rick puts a finger to his lips as he looks out, then using his free hand he seems to be checking himself for something. "Do you have a weapon in your purse?" he asks quietly after a second.

"What? No."

He doesn't seem to really hear me. "Let's go now."

Rick pulls me at a fast run towards another prize stall. Just as we reach it, a teenager fires a rifle at the assembled ducks. Rick swerves instantly at the sound and crashes into a small food cart. He doesn't tumble, simply bounces off and keeps running with me dragged along behind him. After a few seconds, we are in the middle of the crowd. Rick stops running and looks around.

"Rick. Stop!"

"I can't stop, Emma, they'll find us." His voice is hard, and deadly calm; an extraordinary contrast to his body, which is clearly pumped full of adrenaline.

"Who will find us?" I'm so confused. As if other people know something is wrong, a circle has formed in the crowd, with us in the middle.

He suddenly drops to a crouch, once again pulling me with him. "The Taliban. They want all American soldiers dead, you know this. Why are you questioning me?"

Bloody hell. I realise right then what this might be.

"Rick." I shift so I kneel in front of him and grab his shoulder with my free hand. "Rick. It's okay. You're not there anymore."

He finally looks at me. "What are you talking about?"

"You're at home, in the United States. You're not in danger."

He looks at me, totally confused. "What? I need to keep you safe, Emma." He jerks his head up and looks around. "Where's Vega? Have you seen Vega?"

I shake my head. I don't know who that is, so I decide not to answer. "Rick, look at me." He keeps looking around so I grab his face with my hands and force his eyes to mine. "Rick, you're having some kind of episode. You are not in a battlefield. You're in Atlanta, in the United States. This is a carnival." He tries to jerk away but I hold his head hard, my fingers gripping his temples and around behind his ears so hard, I fear I might be bruising him. "Rick, please listen to me."

Understanding starts to dawn in his eyes slowly, and the hard edge fades away. I feel his body relax a little. "Emma," he whispers. "Emma, what's going on? Where are we?"

"It's okay, Rick. I have you."

"Ma'am, is everything all right?" I look up to my left and see an older overweight security guard standing there. My stomach plummets in dread as I feel Rick tense beneath my hands. He turns his eyes upwards and the hard look begins to return.

"Yes, it's fine. Please leave," I say quickly. The circle has widened around us; a crowd of people are pointing and whispering.

"I don't think I should, Ma'am." The security guard steps

forward and reaches round to his side to undo the clasp on his handgun. He has a handgun at a county fair. Rick's expression hardens as he rises to his feet slowly. I see fear flash in the security guard's eyes as Rick reaches his full intimidating height, towering over the man. I don't know much about guns, but I do know that when the gun holder is scared, really bad things might happen.

"Leave now," I tell the security officer, moving in front of Rick and putting a hand against his chest.

Before I can say anything more, Rick grabs my waist and steps in front of me. "Stay behind me, Emma." Rick pushes me to his side and around his back, his arm strong on my waist. Rick goes to take a step forward as the officer starts to pull out his gun.

"Dude, what's happening?" Suddenly Seth is there, stepping in between the officer and Rick. Relief floods my body. Seth's body is relaxed but his eyes are anything but casual as they focus solely on Rick. Behind Seth's back, I see Mat and Frank talking to the security guard, who is putting his weapon back in its holster. Rick's face changes; he seems annoyed now. "White, where's Vega?"

Shock flashes across Seth's face at the words. "Vega?" His eyes dart to me.

"Yeah, Vega. He was here earlier, now I can't find him. They've been tracking me, trying to get to Emma." Rick holds me more tightly to his side, his voice hard and sharp. "We need to find Vega and get out of here."

Seth tilts his head and steps forward, placing his hands on Rick's shoulders. "Rick, we're not in Afghanistan anymore. We're at a carnival in Atlanta, dude."

Rick shakes his head and shrugs off the contact. "Then why are they after Emma? And where is Vega?"

"No one is after Emma, Rick." Seth blinks hard and swallows. "And Paulo is dead. You know that."

"No." I can hear the pain in Rick's voice, hidden under the denial. "No, that's not true."

"Rick. Listen to me…"

"No, you're lying." Rick takes a step backwards and pulls me with him. His eyes are steel and his voice is deadly. "Why are you lying?"

"Rick," I say quietly, moving in front of him. Rick frowns at my voice. I can see confusion crossing his face as his delusion clashes with reality.

"Emma…" I hear Seth warn but I ignore him.

"Look at me." I place my hands on his face again and pull his eyes down to me. "Trust me. It's okay. No one is in danger, Rick."

The steel retreats from his eyes again and Rick sags in my grip. "Emma…" he murmurs, dropping his forehead onto mine. "What's going on? Where are we?"

"It's okay, Rick, you're fine. I've got you." Reaching up, I put my arms around his neck and hug him close. His arms loop around my back and hold me tight. I can feel his pulse pounding in his neck and chest; his breathing is ragged.

"I don't understand," Rick murmurs. "What happened—"

His question is interrupted by a loud bang all around us. I glance up as I feel Rick go rigid under me. Beautiful fireworks are exploding in the sky above us. Oh no. Rick pulls away sharply and stands up straight, the steel back in his eyes. "Rick, it's okay, it's just fireworks…"

Rick grabs my arms and pushes me behind him again as he turns to face Seth. Before he can do anything, Seth moves forward and punches him square in the face. There are gasps and small screams from the crowd around us. Rick drops like a stone to the ground, out cold. I gasp and leap down to him as he collapses on the scrappy grass. Seth kneels next to him, shaking out his hand.

"It was the only way," Seth mutters. I glance up at him. "Trust me, I've seen it before. We need to get him home."

*

Twenty minutes later, Seth and Frank lay an unconscious Rick onto his bed. I pull his boots off but otherwise don't touch him. I bite my lip in worry. Frank, who turns out to also be a medic, has assured me that the blow to his head wasn't that hard and that he would wake up at any time with nothing more than a headache and a bruise. I feel reassured by that. Seth had driven Rick's truck to his house, and I had had a ride with Shanna. Mat and Mari had stayed to talk to the carnival security guards and the police, who had been called because of the incident.

I follow the men out of the room and down to the living area. Shanna is sitting on the sofa but leaps up as we enter. Seth breathes out hard and shakes his hand again, which looks swollen.

"Is it PTSD?" I ask bluntly to the room.

Frank looks surprised as Seth nods. "I think so. I've suspected for a while that he had a problem. But he's been keeping to himself for the last month and I've only seen him a few times. When I have, he has been irritable, withdrawn, looking like shit." Seth sighs and leans against the wall. "I think he has been seeing a shrink on the base, but he wouldn't talk to me about it."

"This guy he mentioned, Vega. He was a teammate of yours? And he died?" Seth and Frank exchange glances. I get the feeling these guys aren't just average US Army soldiers; they do something else that I don't think I want to know about. "Look," I say in mild annoyance, "I know you can't tell me much, but that's true, right?" Seth nods once. "And Rick blames himself?" Seth nods again. I go for the edged question. "Is that blame justified?"

Seth stands up sharply. "No, not at all."

I admire Seth's defence of his friend. "Okay. So why is he blaming himself?"

Seth looks me straight in the eye. "Things happen, when we get sent out on missions. Sometimes a choice seems easy at the time, but later you analyse it and analyse it again and decide you made the wrong choice. Then the guilt sets in." Seth shakes his head. "Paulo Vega, Rick and I joined the army together, have served almost all of our tours together. We were... are... like brothers. When one of you dies..." He grimaces at me. "I think you know what it can feel like to lose someone that close."

I nod at him once. "I do."

"It's also not the first time he's lost teammates," Seth continues reluctantly. "Many years ago, back during our second tour in Afghanistan, he was assigned to an engineering team who were building a school. One morning, there was an IED explosion and Rick lost three of his unit. It's hard, to walk away knowing how close you were to death."

Shanna walks to her husband and wraps her arms around his waist. I'm suddenly reminded of the American girl Jon and I had met in Thailand who'd lost her brother in Afghanistan. It had been years since I'd thought of her.

"I'm sorry," I mutter. "But thank you for the information. It might help tonight."

Seth looks up at me sharply. "You're not staying, I am."

"No, I'm going to stay." There's no way I'm backing down from this.

Seth shakes his head. "No offence, Emma, but you've known Rick for what, a week? I've known him for fifteen years."

I raise an eyebrow. "Maybe that's the problem, Seth. You said yourself he wasn't talking to you. Maybe I can help him in ways that you can't." Seth looks doubtful. I cross my arms. "Did you notice how he wove me into his delusion? How he was trying to protect me all the time? I got through to him, twice, and if it hadn't been for that bloody security guard and the badly timed fireworks, you wouldn't have had to punch his lights out." Seth is staring at me.

"Emma's right, babe," Shanna says softly, speaking for the first time. "I think she can get through to him in a way you can't." Seth looks down at his wife and sighs heavily, clearly resigned.

"Okay." Seth holds out his hand. "Give me your cell."

I fish in my bag then pass my mobile phone over to him. Seth taps away then hands it back. "My cell number is programmed in. If something happens, or if you need me for anything at all, call me. I'll be back first thing in the morning."

Frank, Seth and Shanna leave a few minutes later. I close the door softly behind myself and lock it. I shoot off a quick text to Julia, asking if April can stay the whole night. I get a reply seconds later with an affirmative but choose to ignore her remarks on why I need an overnight babysitter. It's too complicated to explain right now. I step out of the small hall and into the living room as I peel off my sandals, giving it a good look for the first time. It's a classic batchelor pad; large-screen TV, sound system, movies and video games everywhere. It's messy but not dirty. The paintwork is dark and bold, with light wood floors and bright splashes of deep colour in the various decorations. There are photos scattered around the room; a blonde woman smiling widely, young kids, a very old photo of a young couple. I spot a photo of Rick, Seth and another man posing together in army uniforms next to a large army vehicle; that must be when they were deployed overseas. They are grinning widely at the camera, clasping huge guns. On the far side of the living room there is an open-plan modern kitchen, with a small dining table, separated from the living area by a wall. Stairs lead up on the left of the kitchen, bedrooms and a bathroom. It's small and compact and pleasant. It's very Rick.

I hear a groan from the room above me and quickly hurry up the stairs. I push open the door and see Rick sitting on the edge of his bed, cradling his head.

His bedroom is lighter than downstairs, with light wood floors, white walls, arty photos and dark bed sheets. The bed is against the wall opposite the window. As I push the door fully open, Rick glances up and grimaces at me.

"I feel like someone punched my lights out," he groans.

"Yeah… Seth did," I say slowly, coming and sitting next to him on the bed.

"Figures it would be him," he mutters into his hands, not sounding surprised. "Jackass."

I don't respond; I simply sit in silence waiting for him.

"I'm sorry if I scared you," he whispers into his hands. "I don't know what happened… I just…" he trails off.

"Tell me," I say softly, placing my hand on his back and rubbing gently.

He hesitates, then looks at me. "It's impossible to describe what it feels like to have your life be in danger constantly. When you're over there, it's like you're on alert all the time. Adrenaline pumping at the slightest noise, you have spilt seconds to make decisions. I'd heard that sometimes it follows you home," he draws a deep breath, "but I've been a soldier for sixteen years. You live with it, you deal with it. When you get home, it's no longer there. I had no problems until this last mission. Until I got back last month. Now I'm having trouble sleeping. All I have are nightmares. I feel anxious whenever I leave the house, constantly on alert. Like I feel when I'm on a mission, but jumpy, out of control. So I've barely left the house this last month. Only to run, because I need that, and to attend the counsellor sessions they said I needed after my last psych eval. They make me feel better, for a little bit. I was coming back from one when I stopped at the grocery store last week." Now that Rick had started, it was all coming out. Speaking to the floor, he continued quickly. "After I met you that day, for some reason, I started to feel better, lighter somehow. On that Friday, when I saw you in the bar, I felt something lift off my chest. It's crazy but I can't explain it. On the Sunday, I barely thought about it at all, all those kids cheered me right up. I thought tonight would be like that. That I could ignore the fact I'm so tired, so on edge, but the lights and the noise started to wear me down. I thought I heard gunshots,

Arabic voices on the air. I felt in danger, I felt you were in danger. I had the overwhelming urge to run, to fight, to protect you. It felt like I was back over there. It was so out of control." His voice cracks, so full of pain and hurt. I kneel next to him on the bed and cup his head in my hands, feeling the tears streaking down them. I bring his head to my neck and hold him there as he breathes heavily. He wraps his arms around my waist and pulls me in tight, squeezing me hard against him.

"What was different about this last mission?" I ask quietly after a while.

I feel him take a deep breath. "My best friend was killed," he whispers into my neck. "It was my fault."

"Vega?" I whisper back.

I feel him nod. "Paulo Vega. He was shot, but it should have been me." I pull him tighter against me. "I feel... broken," he says. "Like everything inside me has been ripped out and put back together in the wrong way."

"I know that feeling," I tell him quietly, my heart aching for him. "It gets better." He lifts his head and looks at me with red-rimmed eyes.

"Does it really?"

I nod, then shift so I hug him even closer. I tell him what I am only just realising. "In time, it does."

Chapter 6

Army Part 3

January 2017

Five years after I had emigrated to the US, I fly out of it for the final time, heading back to the country of my birth. It was the day before New Year 2016. I had chosen to spend one final Christmas with Jessica and her family, before finally packing up the house and leaving the country. The men and their wives from Rick's unit; Seth and Shanna, Paulo, Frank, Mat and Mari, had all come to say goodbye to us at the airport. The goodbyes had been another pain I had had to endure.

It had been eight months since that dreadful night. Eight months of pain and anguish. Eight months without Rick.

I had received death benefits from the US Army, and a substantial life insurance policy that Rick had taken out the day before we were married, but never told me about. Financially, I was sorted.

But I didn't want the money; I wanted my husband. I felt like

I had a hole in my chest, a great gaping bullet wound which just kept bleeding and bleeding.

Even though I would never come back to live there, I just couldn't bring myself to sell his house. So I left it in Jessica's care, for her kids to use or to rent out to tenants, for Alfie to use if he ever wanted it. It would stay in Rick's family.

Alfie would be four years old in a few months. He didn't really understand what had happened. He knew something had changed; he'd become very clingy to me. The few times he asked me 'Where's Daddy?' I tried not to cry in front of him, but I couldn't help it. He'd give me a cuddle and a kiss. He stopped asking the question after a while.

As the plane landed at Heathrow Airport, I exhaled sharply. My parents had offered to come and pick us up. We would be staying with them for a few days then I would head to Salisbury to find a house. I was due to start work in the Salisbury Gold & Sanchez office in two weeks and needed to find somewhere for us to live before then. The last time I had seen my parents had been when we had visited the UK when Alfie was two years old. Though we had all spoken on Skype, and Alfie knew their faces from photos, he didn't know them. The relationship with my mum and dad over the years had been difficult. I didn't know what to expect from them.

I had left all the furniture and a lot of personal items with Rick's family in Atlanta. The rest was being shipped over. I had three suitcases with our essential belongings. Our lives in three suitcases.

As I exit through the arrivals area, I push Alfie's pram ahead of me. A nice airport employee is pushing the trolley loaded with the three large suitcases. I spy my mum bouncing up and down and waving, and we make our way over to them. My father smiles a thank you to the employee and takes the trolley off him as my mum envelops me in a big hug. It's very good to see her, and I feel my control slip just a little. After a few minutes, she releases me and bends down to her grandson with a big smile.

My father comes up to me and I'm expecting a rough pat on the arm or something. Instead, he pulls me to him as well. I'm deeply shocked; I don't ever remember him hugging me before. I'm tense at first, my face squashed awkwardly against his shoulder.

"Oh, my darling," he says softly into my ear. "I am so very sorry about Rick."

There is something about the way he says it, and the surprise and shock of it all that is just too much. To my horror, I find tears threatening to release. I struggle for a few seconds, but then the dam bursts. I grip my dad around his waist tightly and cry hard into his jacket in the middle of the airport. He just holds me quietly, brushing my hair softly with his large hand.

I find a house in Salisbury not long after I arrive in the UK. I was renting at first, getting Alfie settled and then looking to buy. I had more than enough money to support us without working for a while. But the thought of not doing anything with my day was horrifying. So I had requested transfer within G&S from Atlanta to Salisbury. There had been an engineering manager position available from January 2017. It was working on civilian contracts rather than the military contracts which I was highly specialised in, but I was fine with that. I'd be happy if I never saw another military uniform as long as I lived.

Though I'd only spent a brief few months in Salisbury, even when I worked here, it was odd being back again. I'd been such a different person back then. Young, enthusiastic, optimistic and simply enjoying my life and work. Now there was a dark cloud over everything. Alfie was the only thing that had kept me going day by day.

I thought vaguely about Irene Johnson, and whether I should look her up. I drove past the army base and could just about spot the accommodation block I used to live in. The little studio flat where Rick and I had had that one night, so very many years ago. I knew the football field, my old office and the bar weren't far away either, but I quickly drove off.

My first day of work at the Salisbury office was filled with meeting lots of new people. The UK processes and company culture were similar to the US, but I would need to put a lot of work in to get up to speed on the UK-specific building regulations and policies before I could be really effective. The thought exhausted me.

My direct manager, Elliot Wise, whom I had met during my original interview five years ago, spent a lot of time going over my work experience. He was particularly interested in my early work while I had been in the army. I still had photos and rolled draft designs, which I had kept at my parents' house all these years but had now brought to Salisbury thinking they might be helpful. I offered to bring them in to show him the next day.

I collected Alfie from nursery on my way home. We had dinner and a bath and then I put him to bed.

It was only Monday and as I collapsed onto the sofa, I despaired in my exhaustion and low mood. How was I going to cope doing this alone every day for the rest of my life?

When I leave the house the next morning, I grab as many photos and designs as I can and stuff them into my red Audi A3 while it's defrosting. I had forgotten how cold the UK is in January. Alfie helps me by throwing them onto the car floor during the drive to his nursery. I drop him off with only ten minutes of fuss and head to the office, realising when I get there that I have probably brought way too many examples. I sling my heavy backpack over my shoulder and shift the books and rolled designs around until I can just about carry them all. The office in Salisbury has around 300 employees in it, tiny compared to the office in Atlanta. The office is a five-floor new build on the edge of an industrial estate near the army base. Because I have been faffing around, I am late, so I run quickly up the steps towards the elevators in the main lobby.

"Hold, please!" I call as I see the doors on one lift closing. A hand shoots out just as I arrive, and the elevator doors fall open again. "Thanks so much," I say to a man who is standing there watching in amusement as I manoeuvre myself delicately into the small space.

Then one of the drawings catches on the hand rail and it all starts to slip from my grasp. "Oh no... I'm so sorry," I say as the rolled designs and books fly everywhere, hitting the poor man, landing on the floor and stopping the elevator doors from closing. The man looks surprised, but then smiles.

"It's fine," he chuckles, placing his briefcase on the floor and helping me collect up the papers and books. "I always like a shower in the mornings." He holds up a photo of an Afghan school. "Usually, water is my preference, though."

I smile. "I guess I should have made a second trip for all this stuff." I bite my lip and glance over at him. "But I'm already late and it's only my second day so..." I trail off as the most dazzling pair of green eyes looks back at me in amusement.

"So you thought you didn't have time to do another trip?" The man smiles widely. There is something oddly familiar about his voice. It's deep and husky, with just a hint of an accent I can't identify. "Bet you are regretting that now, huh?"

"You have no idea," I mutter. Then shake my head. "I'm really sorry. I've probably made you late too."

"Yep." The man smiles and reaches for the last rolled drawing. "But as I'm in charge of my department, I think I will forgive myself." He places the drawing on a pile at his feet and stands up slowly, showing me his 6-foot or so height. "What floor?"

"Third, please."

"Ah. The engineers. So, it's your second day at G&S, huh?" he asks as he presses the elevator button.

"Uh, actually second day at this office. I've worked for G&S for over five years, in their Atlanta office. I just transferred."

The man looks at me sharply. "You're Emma Tavern?"

I step back, taken by surprise. "Uh, yeah…"

"I'm Jon Clemens." The man holds out his hand. "We have a meeting later today, and I think we've spoken on the phone once."

The name sounds familiar, but it takes a moment to process it as I shake his hand. That had been the day Rick died, the day before Seth and Paulo had come to my door. I swallow, and force a smile. "Yes, yes, we have. Nice to meet you, Jon."

"And you, Emma." Jon smiles pleasantly. His eyes flick over my face for a moment before he looks away.

The elevator pings and I reach down to grab my papers and books from the floor. Jon puts his briefcase outside in the corridor and then bends down to pick up the designs at his feet.

"Let me help you with these."

"That'll be great. Thanks," I reply, grateful that I wouldn't have to do another juggling act. Jon follows me to my office, on the far side of the floor.

"Put them anywhere," I say as I swing my backpack onto my desk chair. Jon places them carefully on one of the other chairs. He straightens and I smile. "Thanks so much, Jon, and I'm really sorry about showering you with paper."

Jon shrugs. "Don't worry, happens all the time." He smiles back at me and then waves as he heads out of the door. "See you at eleven."

*

I'm so busy that morning that I'm surprised when Elliot sticks his head in my office just before 1100.

"Emma, we've got accounts on the first floor."

"Ah, yeah." I grab my notepad. "Thanks, Elliot."

Elliot is in the meeting too, so we walk down the corridor together.

"I brought those pictures and designs for you, Elliot. We can have a look at them whenever you want."

"Ah, great, thanks." He pushes the button for the elevator. "I've always been interested in the difference between military and civilian engineering. At home, I drive my wife mad with all my model buildings." He laughs, then turns to me as the doors open and we step in. "Tell me, having been both, what do you find the primary difference is between being an army engineer and a civilian engineer?"

I pause and think a moment as the elevator heads for the first floor. "Well, when I was in the army my job title was 'combat engineer', which pretty much says it all. We were in a war zone. The mission was how quickly we could get the structures designed and built, and the security around the materials and the labour." I feel a pang of loss as I remember my own personal bodyguard in Afghanistan, but I push it aside as we step out of the elevator. "As a civilian project engineer, it's a little bit more relaxed. No one is trying to blow us up for building a school."

"That really happens?" Elliot asks in astonishment as we stop outside the meeting room and he opens the door.

"Yes, especially if it's a girls' school. I was almost caught in an IED explosion once. They blew up a school I was building."

"Well, that sounds like a lively conversation." Jon is sitting at the table with a younger woman, and they are watching us with slight puzzlement.

Elliot smiles. "Just hearing some scary stories from Emma here. She was a combat engineer in the army. Emma, this is our head of accounting and finance, Jon Clemens."

"Jon and I met this morning in the elevator," I say, then shake my head at myself. "Sorry, lift. You'll have to forgive my American words for a while."

"I think we can do that," Jon smiles, "and the army past explains the photos and drawings you were kind enough to show me." I resist the urge to laugh at his polite interpretation of this morning.

"Hi, I'm Fiona Forrester." The young woman stands and smiles at me. "I work under Jon in accounting." Thanks to Trent and Rhys, I long ago perfected the art of taking normal sentences and spinning them into something with lots of innuendo. Luckily, I have also perfected the art of not letting it show when it's not appropriate.

"Emma Tavern, nice to meet you." I shake her hand and sit down.

The meeting lasts about an hour; it's about policy, processes and accounting. It's not very interesting. I find myself studying Jon across the table. He has thick black hair which has just the faintest touches of grey at his temples and above his ears. It's cut short on the sides but longer on top. He has a defined black goatee which suits his strong jawline, and I notice a long jagged scar down from his right temple to his jaw, cutting in front of his ear. Earlier, he was wearing an overcoat and suit jacket, but now his fitted shirtsleeves are rolled up to his elbows, and I can see he clearly looks after himself. He is toned and slender and really rather good-looking. I frown at myself and look over at Fiona, who is talking to me still.

Through his reading glasses, Jon's green eyes focus on me as Fiona points out a process and I make a note of it. Fiona has been doing almost all of the talking. I get the feeling Jon is here simply to observe her. I glance up and meet his gaze, and he smiles just a little before glancing away towards his colleague.

The meeting ends just after 1200, and I swear I hear Jon's stomach rumble.

"Anyone want to get lunch?" Jon asks the room, confirming my observation.

"I've got a call now, Jon, rain check?" Elliot nods at me and waves at Jon as he leaves.

Fiona grimaces as she packs up her notes. "I'm meeting a friend. Thanks, though." Her eyes linger on Jon a moment longer than they should as she smiles and leaves. I find that interesting.

"How about you, Emma? Do you have plans too?" Jon asks me as he takes off his glasses and puts them away.

I shake my head and stretch as I stand up. "Nope. What did you have in mind?"

Jon's eyes linger on me, and I realise I stretched a little too enthusiastically. "Well, did anyone take you to the premier G&S lunch station yesterday?"

"Nope, someone brought me a sandwich yesterday." I had been in meetings all through lunch.

Jon and I exit the room, Jon turning out the lights after us. "Great. Let's do that. I'll meet you in the lobby in fifteen minutes."

The wind has picked up over the morning, and I pull my inadequate coat tighter around me. I'm really not used to this biting wind.

"Cold?" Jon comments. He is wearing a hat and scarf and his large overcoat, and doesn't seem cold at all.

"Yes, Atlanta has mild winters and hot summers," I say, pulling my thin hat down over my ears. "It's been about five years since I experienced a UK winter."

Jon laughs and eyes my unsuitable headwear. "You should have come back during the summer, then you would have got used to the cool temperatures."

I shrug, though he probably can't see that under my coat. "That would have been a good plan. Where are we going?"

"There's a deli about five minutes' walk, it's on the industrial estate and services all the businesses." He gestures with his gloved hands around him. "It's actually good food, not just sandwiches either. You can sit in there or get takeaway, and they do larger orders for meetings."

"Sounds great," I reply. After a few minutes, we arrive at the little deli. It's busy but not heaving. I order a jacket potato and Jon gets a chicken wrap. We decide to sit in, as there are still tables free.

"How long have you worked for G&S?" I ask as I tuck into my potato.

"Since 2007," Jon says, waving at someone over my shoulder for a second. "I started on their graduate programme straight out of uni. Originally in the Birmingham office, but I transferred down here in 2010 when a position became available." He pauses. "My... now ex-wife wanted to live down here, it's where her family is."

"You're divorced?" I ask slowly.

Jon nods. "Divorce finalised four months ago, so thankfully, yes."

I choose not to comment on that.

"So, did your husband and son move over with you?" Jon asks. I freeze, wondering how he could know about Rick. I don't wear my ring anymore. Rick's and my wedding rings are on a silver chain around the folded American flag from Rick's memorial service. They sit on Alfie's bedside table.

Then I recall our telephone conversation last year; he clearly has a good memory.

"Ah... my son is here with me," I say cautiously.

Jon nods. He's tucking into his wrap and doesn't notice my hesitation. "Your husband is American? Did he stay over there?"

"Ah, no." I push away my half-eaten potato. "No. No, he died."

Now it's Jon's turn to freeze. He studies me for a moment, then shame floods his cheeks.

"Oh my... uh, I'm sorry." He places his lunch down. "Sorry, I put my foot right in that, didn't I?"

I shrug. "It's okay. You couldn't have known."

Jon just shakes his head. "How long...?"

"Eight months," I say quickly. People always ask the same questions so I just say it all to get it over with. "He was a special forces soldier. He died on a mission abroad." Jon is staring at me, horror on his face. "Actually, it was the day after we spoke on the phone. That's why I had my assistant send over those documents you wanted."

"Jeez." Jon is leaning back in his chair. "I'm really sorry, Emma, that's so horrible."

"Yeah, well, it is what it is." I force a smile and run my hand over my head and down my long ponytail. "I've had this conversation quite a few times, Jon, and it always makes things awkward afterwards. You don't know what to say, I feel bad because I mentioned it. So how about we skip over that and talk about something more pleasant?"

Jon studies me, his eyes flicking over my face. It's an interesting look which I've never seen from anyone before. I wonder if he realises he does it. After a moment, a hint of a smile appears on his face. "Okay. How old is your son?"

"Almost four years old. His name is Alfie. Do you have any kids?"

Jon nods. "I have a little girl, just over four, her name is Stephanie."

"Do you have a photo?"

Jon smiles. "Of course, shall we swap?"

I nod and we both pull out our phones, scrolling to the photos. Jon's daughter has light brown hair and those bright green eyes. She is wearing a big cheeky smile as she sits on a swing.

I show Jon a picture of Alfie in an Atlanta play park from before Rick died. I realise I haven't taken many since then. I should do.

We finish our lunch and head back to the office. The walk is mostly silent. Just before we reach the steps, Jon stops and lightly swipes my arm to stop me from walking. "Emma, I'm sorry about earlier."

"Jon, it's okay, really. It's my problem, not yours."

"Yeah, but I feel bad." He pauses. "What are you up to this weekend?"

I eye him and step back. "Uh…"

Jon must see my expression because he laughs. "Don't worry, I'm not asking you out. I just thought, you're new in town, maybe you don't know Salisbury very well. I have Stephy this weekend and on Saturday we're going to a teddy bear ball hunt in one of the local activity centres. Might be the kind of thing your son could enjoy too."

I'm really not sure this is a good idea. I eyeball him and he laughs again. "Don't be so suspicious, Emma. It'll be fun." He begins walking towards the building, pulls open the door and we enter the warm lobby. "How about I email you the details?" I stand next to him outside the lifts, undoing my coat. I study his profile as he takes off his hat, running a hand through his hair. "It should be fun, for the adults too." He turns to me and grins, clearly expecting an answer, so I give in.

"Maybe, no promises."

*

I walk through the streets of Afghanistan. Everything is silent. The tarps on the buildings move in the wind, I can feel sand biting at my cheeks, local men pass me and their mouths move, but it's all silent. I can feel the hot, dry sun burning my head. I'm not wearing my helmet, and my long hair is loose over my shoulders. Sweat runs down my spine, pooling in my layers of clothes and making them stick to my skin.

I walk to the construction site, slowly, one boot in front of the other. There is no one around. Suddenly I feel a presence behind me and I whirl. Tavern is there, standing in his watcher pose. He is grinning and trying to say something but because the noise is gone I can't hear him. I am frozen as I look into his face. His bright blond hair pokes out from under his helmet. A big blond beard covers his jawline. Rick looks young, like when I first met him. There are no shadows under his eyes yet. I feel overwhelming joy. He is alive, I can talk to him again, touch him again. He can kiss me and make love to me and everything will be okay. Then I see a shadow approach from behind him. I try to warn Rick but there is no sound. I slowly move my arm up and point. Rick tilts his head in question, then his beautiful brown eyes widen and he turns, his weapon moving upwards.

BANG!

The gunshot rings all around me as suddenly there is sound again. I can hear the wind and sand and tarps, hear the voices in the air. In slow motion, Rick falls to the ground. I feel someone push me from behind and I fall beside him. I land on my hands and the sand grits into my palms. I look over at Rick, not caring about who pushed me. He is staring at me with flat dead eyes. A single bullet wound is in the centre of his forehead. The red blood is slowly running down onto the sand.

I hear screaming and I realise it's me. I'm screaming.

I bolt up in bed, my body covered in sweat and my heart racing. I know what comes next so I leap upwards and run for the bathroom. I reach the toilet just before I retch. Hot bile splashes into the toilet as I'm sick. After a few moments, the feeling passes and I flush the toilet. I sit there, on the bathroom floor, in my thin pyjama top, the sweat cooling on my skin, and shiver. Trying to push the image of Rick's cold dead face out of my mind.

It's not the first time I've had this dream. I just wish it would stop. I wish I had never asked Seth for details, and I wish that he had followed his orders and not told me. I wish I didn't know that Rick had been killed by a single bullet to the head on the streets of Afghanistan. I wish I wish I wish...

I sit there and rock for a while, tears sliding down my face. Then I get up and brush my teeth. I pull on my dressing gown and silently go downstairs. I pour myself a glass of whisky and sit on the sofa in the dark. When I have finished my whisky, I rinse out the glass and put it away, silently climb the stairs and slide back into my cold bed.

I try to sleep, but I know I won't.

*

On Saturday morning, I arrive at the Warehouse activity centre and am greeted with mayhem. Kids of all shapes and sizes, all between three and six years old, run screaming and shouting around the room. Tired-looking adults follow them. There is a large ball pit in the middle of the large room, with slides and padded climbing frames surrounding it. Everywhere is covered in teddies, and kids, and more teddies. I see one little boy has taken his clothes off and given them to an assortment of teddies sitting around him.

I stand on the edge of the mayhem and laugh at the scene. My bag is in the locker already, I'm wearing my special padded shoes. I have no excuses. Alfie looks up at me excitedly, waiting for me to tell him he can go and play.

"Emma." I glance around as I hear Jon's voice. I spot him in the ball pit nearest me, covered to mid-chest with balls and teddies. A little brown-haired girl is trying to balance teddies on his shoulders and head, but they keep falling off. As I meet his gaze, he smiles and waves, which knocks even more of the teddies off him. The little girl puts her hands on her hips and seems to tell him off.

"Let's go, Alfie."

My son runs excitedly to the entrance and jumps straight in, narrowly avoiding a smaller boy. Alfie waits for me as I carefully enter, manoeuvring him towards where Jon sits.

"Nice of you to join us," Jon comments as I sink into the plastic balls by his side, Alfie clinging to me.

"Well, when you said there would be a ball pit, how could I resist?" I reply, snickering to myself as my dirty mind once again conjures up hidden meanings. Jon catches my snicker and looks surprised, then laughs himself. He recovers quickly then pokes the little girl next to him in the belly.

"Stephy, this is my friend Emma."

Stephy shoots me an interested look. "Hi, Stephy. It's really nice to meet you. This is Alfie."

I glance at my son. He can be shy sometimes. "Alfie, this is my friend Jon, and Stephy. Are you going to say hello?"

"Hello," Alfie whispers in his soft American accent. I wonder if that will fade with time.

Stephy studies him with wide eyes. "Hi. How old are you?"

Alfie holds up three fingers. "You're almost four, Alfie. In March, you will be four years old."

Alfie nods.

"I'm already four," Stephy replies proudly. "My birthday is nine December." She grabs a teddy. "Do you want to help me put teddies on Daddy?"

Alfie frowns and looks up at me with concern. I peer down at him, confused by his reaction, until I realise Alfie now associates the word daddy with me crying. I feel a stab of guilt in my chest. That's not fair to anyone.

"Not your daddy, sweetheart, Stephy's daddy." I gesture at Jon. "Stephy's daddy is Jon."

Alfie looks at Jon. Jon, who has been watching our exchange with interest, holds out a teddy. "Do you want to put a teddy on my head, Alfie? It's great fun."

Alfie slowly reaches out and takes the teddy, a small brown one wearing a pink apron. Carefully, he moves over and places the teddy on Jon's head. Almost immediately, it slides off onto Jon's lap.

Stephy moves around and takes it. "You have to put it on a flat bit." She places it on the crown of Jon's head, pushes it down and lets it go. It stays for a few seconds then slides off. Alfie giggles. They do this a few times, the teddy always sliding off. Then Jon grabs a big gold bear from nearby.

"Why don't we put him on your mummy's head, Alfie?" He reaches out and places the teddy face down on my head, grinning at me the whole time. Stephy and Alfie watch with fascination as Jon presses it down, then lets it go. The teddy stays in place on my head.

Now I can't move. Alfie claps in excitement. "Looks like we have a winner," Jon announces. Alfie moves closer to me and pokes the bear's fur just above my eye. It doesn't move and his eyes widen.

I meet his gaze. "Ready?" I whisper. "Three, two, one." I suddenly grab him and start tickling, the bear falling off my head. Alfie squeals and falls into the balls, but I'm relentless in my tickling and don't stop as he squirms and screams with laughter.

Jon's laughing at us and Stephy is creeping closer to me, looking like she wants some tickling action too. Then Jon grabs her around the waist and throws her into the ball pit, emerging from the teddies like a monster and trying to run after her.

When they get tired of that game, Stephy takes Alfie by the hand and begins to lead him through the maze of slides and tunnels. You can only get out of the tunnels through the ball pit so Jon and I simply sit in the corner and watch them, our jean-clad legs covered in squidgy balls and teddies.

"I wasn't sure if you were going to show up," Jon says quietly.

I shrug. "I figured you were right. I don't know Salisbury very well, or many people here. So why not?" I see Alfie following Stephy down a wide tunnel. "I was stationed at the army base for a few months in…" I think "…2009. But I never really came into the city."

"It's nice here, it's a beautiful city," Jon comments. "There's lots of child-friendly stuff." He smiles. "Lots of adult-friendly stuff too."

I chuckle. "I bet. Do you live here then?"

"Yep. My ex-wife got the house in the divorce but I bought another here."

"How does it work with Stephy?" I ask. "The whole custody thing?"

"We have shared custody, so I get her Sunday night through to Wednesday morning, and then every other weekend. Sarah has her Wednesday evening to Friday night and then the other weekend."

"Does it work?"

Jon smiles, his eyes focusing on his daughter. "Yes, it's not easy for Stephy but then neither was living in a house where her parents weren't happy." He frowns and I can see memories wash over his face. "I wish it had been different, but as you said, it is what it is." He glances at me and smiles. "How have you found your first week at work?"

"It's been okay, but mostly admin stuff and getting back on my feet in this country. I'm looking forward to actually getting on with the proper project work." I glance at him. "Not that the accounting meeting wasn't proper work or anything…"

"You found it fascinating, huh?" Jon smiles and waves his hand randomly in the air. "Don't tell anyone in my department or you'll be having one every day."

"Didn't I just tell the head of the department?"

"That's right, you did. I will schedule them in first thing Monday."

I laugh; it's been a while since I felt this relaxed and carefree. Jon is easy to talk to.

After all the morning excitement, we go for lunch at a nearby café. Alfie loves his food so he sits there munching away silently while Stephy sings to herself and picks at her lunch.

Jon and I make small talk over our sandwiches and coffee. Basic stuff like school, where we grew up and our families. I find out Jon is half French, which explains the interesting accent. I tell him about my army career.

"So why did you leave the army?" Jon asks. "It sounds like you loved it."

I swallow my bite of sandwich. "I did. But I'd been doing it for a while and I fancied a change." I shrug. "Honestly, I wanted a bit more stability in my life." I thought back. "I worked out that in my eight-year army career, I spent more than half of the time abroad in various locations. And that doesn't count my time in Scotland, or my training in Wales. I had three tours in the Middle East. My last one in Afghanistan was thirteen months. I had leave in between them but it's just not the same. I lost contact with a lot of friends over the years, and I just don't know my family as well as I should. When I moved to the States, I thought that was it, I wouldn't have to move anymore." I glance at Alfie. He is watching Stephy sing to herself. "But things just don't work out the way you plan."

"No, they don't," Jon says sadly.

I don't want to talk about this any longer. Luckily, Alfie saves me. "Mummy, can I go play?" He is pointing across the room, where a train set and building blocks are set up.

"Are you finished with your lunch?" Alfie nods. I hand him a baby wipe and he almost expertly wipes his face.

"Good boy. You can go play now."

"Daddy, I wanna play too." Surprisingly, Stephy has hardly any mess on her face.

"Okay, honey." Jon grabs the remainder of her sandwich and puts it on his plate. "You stay with Alfie, okay, and over there. No wandering off." Stephy nods and slides down her seat, taking Alfie's hand and running across the room. We watch them go, munching on our lunches.

"Where did you meet your wife… ex-wife?"

"Birmingham University," Jon replies, his eyes still on his daughter. "We went out for about two years. Then she cheated on me so we broke up." He glances over at me. "She tried to get back together with me a few times, scared quite a few possible girls away, but I resisted." He smiles grimly. "Then I didn't see her for… three years or so. One day, I ran into her in a supermarket. I could see she had changed, grown up, was no longer so petty. So we got back together. Eventually, we moved down here, got married, had Stephy."

I glance to the play corner. "But it didn't work." It's a statement rather than a question.

Jon sighs, glancing over to our kids himself. "No. It took me a long time to realise I didn't love her the way I wanted to, and that she didn't love me that way anymore." Jon shakes his head. "In fact, it took a car accident to make me see it."

I shoot him a quizzical look. Jon puts down his sandwich and taps the side of his face. "This scar, and another here." He points to his left ribcage, hidden under his scruffy green t-shirt. "Came from a car crash I was in in May 2014. Pretty bad, I was in hospital for five weeks." I gasp and Jon continues. "I was driving home from a client meeting in Southampton, traffic slowed suddenly, the lorry behind me clipped my car and sent it into the safety barrier. I was lucky the lorry driver was paying attention. Otherwise, I would likely have died." Jon nods, and glances over at the kids again. "Anyway, so I'm sitting in the remains of my bashed-up Ford, I can feel adrenaline pumping through me, keeping me alert. It's a really weird feeling." He shakes his head. "I have pain everywhere, I can't feel my legs, my face is wet and sticky. And all I can think about is: I'm not happy in my life. My wife doesn't make me happy. I don't love my wife." He is staring at the table now, lost in his memories. "Then who should stick his head through the car window, my wife's brother, a police officer." He smiles as I laugh. "Afterwards, in the hospital, I think those thoughts are shock from the accident, but when I get home, I realise it's probably the most honest thing I've told myself in years."

He glances up at me. "I try for a while with her, but Sarah can see it and becomes even harder to live with. We decide to separate, and, eventually, divorce." He leans back in his chair and takes a long drag of his coffee. After a moment, he flashes me a faint smile. "Sorry, that was probably a bit heavy for a fun kids-orientated Saturday."

"No more heavy than my story."

Jon raises an eyebrow and nods in silent agreement. We both glance over at the kids, still playing quietly with the toys.

"I don't know why I told you that," Jon says suddenly. "I've only told a few people that before."

"Maybe you are trying to beat my story," I joke quietly. Jon looks at me sharply, then relaxes as he sees I'm kidding.

"I'm not sure I would want to," he replies solemnly.

We are silent for a few minutes as we finish our lunch, watching the kids play together.

"Stephy is lovely," I praise, changing the subject. "Great language skills."

"Yeah, she is way ahead in her class," Jon says proudly. "I'm teaching her French too. Alfie seems smart, a bit shy."

"Yeah, he is. He wasn't always that way, though." I hope everything that's happened hasn't adversely affected him.

Jon shrugs. "Kids change all the time." He leans over and taps my hand knowingly. "They are resilient. They bounce back from anything."

I bite my lip nervously. "I hope so. I would hate for Rick's death to have damaged him somehow."

Jon doesn't reply, simply glances over at the kids.

"We should do this again," he says. "They seem to get on great, and you and I, well…" he chuckles and shrugs, "we've known each other less than a week and we've already had several deep and meaningful conversations. I think that says something."

I smile, and actually mean it. "Yes, it does."

*

The next month flies by in a continuous stream of work projects, engineering schematics, play groups and visits by friends. Now I was back in the country for good, loads of old friends were arranging meet-ups and I found every weekend booked up.

There were several key people I wanted to see, though, and they got priority. Janine, who still lived and worked in Southampton, came over to see us three times in the first two weeks. Rhys, who was out of the army now and also living in Southampton, drove up on a Sunday and spent the afternoon wrestling Alfie on the living room floor. Trent and his wife of two years, Milly, lived in Edinburgh now and were due to come down the weekend of my birthday.

I'll be thirty-two. Both Trent and Rhys had ganged up on me and basically invited themselves over for dinner on Saturday night, with a zoo visit planned for the Sunday. I think they were worried about me. This will be the first birthday since Rick died. I had met him ten years previously, the day after my birthday. The irony of the anniversary was not lost on me.

The previous Thursday, Jon and I had lunch together again. We had started doing this every week, randomly asking the other for lunch. Sometimes we were free and sometimes we weren't. We'd also met up the Sunday before for a play date with the kids, and spent the afternoon hanging out in a leisure centre indoor playground.

I liked Jon. He was funny, with a smutty sense of humour that he was slowly letting shine through. He had a good outlook on life and he was attractive, but clearly not interested in starting anything. I liked that a lot; it made things easy. I knew I wasn't ready for anything romantic.

A few days before my birthday, we were eating lunch in the deli and making small talk.

"So what are your plans for the weekend?" Jon asks me around his chicken and bacon wrap. He always bought the same thing here, something I had started teasing him about.

"Well," I swallow a bite of my salad, "it's my birthday on Sunday." Jon smiles. "So my old army buddies have 'invited' themselves over for dinner." I use inverted commas in that sentence. Jon looks at me, puzzled. "I think they are worried about me because it's my first birthday since Rick died." I shrug. "They don't want me to be alone, which is stupid because I have Alfie, so I would never be alone but…"

I trail off as Jon studies me. "It's nice to have friends who care," he says simply.

"One of the guys is even coming down from Scotland with his pregnant wife," I tell him. "Milly is so patient, it's unbelievable." Jon chuckles.

An idea hits me then. "I know. Why don't you come too?"

Jon looks startled. "Uh, I wouldn't want to intrude…"

"Oh, you won't be." I wave my hand. "I'm also inviting my friend Janine. I'm actually going to try and set her up with one of my buddies. They both live in Southampton and I think they would work well together."

Jon looks thoughtful. "I have Stephy this weekend."

"Well, bring her then. Come earlier in the afternoon, she and Alfie can play and have dinner together and go to bed. I can move a spare mattress into Alfie's room and they can have a sleepover until you're ready to leave." Jon looks hesitant. "Did you already have plans, Jon?"

"No…"

"Well, there you go then." I lean back and smile. "Don't be so suspicious, Jon, it'll be fun."

*

Despite the obvious connotations of my birthday this year, I found myself actually looking forward to dinner on Saturday night. Rhys was close by, so I'd seen him recently, but I hadn't seen Trent since last year when he and Rhys had attended Rick's full military funeral in the US. I hadn't seen Milly since their wedding in Edinburgh two years before, where I had flown over by myself to be one of his two 'best men'. Rhys and I had given a hilarious two-man speech which massively took the piss out of Trent and praised Milly. They had loved it.

Trent and Milly had arrived that morning, and after lunch we had all been sitting in the lounge drinking coffee and chatting. Milly was six months pregnant, and we were comparing pregnancy stories while Trent sat on the floor with Alfie, building a big Lego structure. They would build it as high as they could until it fell over, then they would start again. I was making the obvious engineering comments to help them, while Trent shot me dirty looks. Trent was great with Alfie, and always minded his language. He would be a great dad.

They are building it up for the third time, using a big base to increase its structural stability as I had suggested, when the doorbell rings. Alfie jumps up and runs to it with enthusiasm. Now he can reach the door handle, Alfie likes to open the door without me, so I hurry down the hall after him.

"Stephy!" I hear Alfie say loudly as the door opens.

"*Bonjour*, Alfie. How's it going?" I hear Jon say brightly as I reach the door.

"We have visors," Alfie replies. He means visitors.

"Hey, guys," I say in greeting. I smile warmly at Jon and gesture for them to enter, then look down at Stephy. "Wow, that's a really pretty dress, Stephy."

The little girl grins and twirls. "Daddy bought it for me this morning. *J'aime bien!*"

"Well, aren't you lucky?"

"Hey, Emma," Jon greets as he passes me. "We're here, as promised." He lays a bag down by the hall table. I assume it contains Stephy's sleeping stuff. "Stephy is very excited about sleeping here tonight, aren't you, honey?"

Stephy nods. "I love sleepovers."

Alfie's eyes had got really wide. "Me too, Stephy. I'm building Lego with Tent. Wanna play too?"

"Yes." Alfie grabs Stephy's hand and pulls her down the hall to the living room. The house was a good-sized three-bed with boring bland decoration and old carpets. The stairs were on the left of the front door as you came in, with the kitchen through a door to the right. The hallway was the length of the kitchen, with a small toilet under the stairs, opening out onto a large dining/living area. The house had come furnished, and the set-up was the living room on the left and the dining room on the right, near the kitchen. It seemed logical to me so I hadn't changed it. Large windows and a single patio door led out into a small back garden. I expected to buy a place here within the next year, and I wanted a large back garden. There was one downstairs toilet and a family bathroom on the first floor, unlike US houses, where almost all of them had at least two bathrooms and an en suite.

"Here, I brought you this." Jon hands me a bottle of French red wine as we stand in the hall.

"Thanks, Jon, that'll go great with dinner. Come on through." Jon follows me down the hall and into the living room.

Alfie and Stephy are already sitting next to Trent on the rug as we enter. Trent looks up, smiles widely and stands. Milly manoeuvres her way off the sofa too, treading daintily across the floor.

There are introductions all around. Trent gives me a suggestive look, which I return with a glare. He wisely keeps quiet.

"Jon, would you like tea? Or coffee?"

"Tea would be great, just milk. Thanks."

I lower my voice. "Would Stephy like juice?" You never know what parents give their kids. Jon nods with a smile.

I grab Trent's and Milly's mugs to refill them and head into the kitchen to put the kettle on. I had become far too used to real coffee while living in the US, so I had bought myself an expensive coffee machine a few weeks before. I wasn't drinking that instant stuff, and I couldn't stand tea; a fact which had been almost blasphemous in the army.

They're making small talk as I come back in carrying a tray loaded with drinks. Trent immediately leaps up and begins handing them out.

"Right, that's my mug, that's Milly's," Trent mutters. "Jon, I think this must be yours. American swill for English." Trent can't stand coffee and calls it an awful American import. I'd long ago given up correcting him. "And who is this juice for?" At his words, Alfie and Stephy look up.

I crouch down on the rug, showing them the two plastic cups of apple juice with straws. Alfie looks at me wide-eyed and I nod. He doesn't get juice very much. Stephy's eyes open wide as well, and she glances hopefully at her dad.

"Go ahead, honey, special occasion today." As one, they rush to me and carefully lift the cups.

Jon and I share a knowing look as I place the tray on the floor by the sofa. I sit down next to Jon on the sofa, carefully folding

my legs together, as I'm wearing a short light blue dress. Trent
retakes his position on the rug with the Lego.

"When are you due, Milly?" Jon asks.

Milly smiles and rubs her hand over her belly. "15th of May,"
she replies softly in her light Scottish lilt. Milly is one of the
quietest women I have ever met. She is almost bordering on shy
but has a wicked sense of humour, and so much patience, which
you would need being married to Trent. "Which is two days
before Trent's birthday, so he's hoping she's delayed to then."

"I'd love to share a birthday with her," Trent says with a
smile, placing a Lego block in position on the tower and poking
it to make sure it's in place. "That would be wicked."

"So you know you're having a girl?"

Milly nods. "Trent's not big on surprises."

"Neither would you be, laddie, if you'd seen the things I
have." He nods and winks at Jon, as if sharing some top-secret
information. "Just some advice, never open a briefcase you
haven't x-rayed first."

Jon looks puzzled. "Yeah, or you get a face like Scotty's," I
reply innocently, sipping my coffee.

Trent smiles widely. "I see the smooth American accents and
their hairless male chests have ruined your humour, English.
Better work on that."

"More hair than your chest anyway," I shoot back. Trent
looks taken aback, then pulls out the neck of his t-shirt and
examines his chest hair. Alfie and Stephy look up at him
curiously.

"Nah, not possible. An army could get lost down there." He
sends me a wink which tells me he isn't just talking about his
chest hair and I laugh.

Jon looks very confused. Milly pats his arm reassuringly.
"You'll get used to it, Jon, they always do this. It's worse when
Rhys is here too."

"When is Welshie turning up?" Trent asks me as he places a Lego man on top of their tower.

"Around eighteen hundred," I tell him. I glance at my watch; it's almost 1600 now. I need to get started on dinner soon. "My friend Janine is arriving about then too."

"Ah, this is the lass you are trying to set our boy up with, huh?"

I nod and shrug. "Yeah, but keep quiet. If they know that, it'll be biased."

"Is she fit?" Jon almost chokes on his tea as Trent glances at him innocently.

"Yep," I reply. "Red hair, long legs, great boobs. Not as great as Milly's or mine, of course." I shoot Milly a suggestive glance and she laughs. "But, you know, better than most."

"Excellent. It's about time that boy got some…" Trent glances down at the kids "… cuddles."

Milly and I burst out laughing. Jon chuckles too. I meet his eyes and he looks extremely amused. I shrug. "Sorry, Jon, Scotty brings it out in me. And it's worse with Welshie here too."

"Worse?" Trent repeats. "How can you say that, English? Worse. We had some great times. Do you remember that time we…"

"No." I hold my hand up to stop Trent. "You can tell your obscene stories later. We have sensitive ears around us. Alfie is repeating a lot of what he hears now, and I'm sure Stephy is too."

Trent nods in reluctant agreement, looking solemn, then he brightens. "Great, that means I can tell them with Welshie's input and graphic detail. He always remembers all the boring sh… stuff."

*

Janine arrived just before 1800. I hadn't been kidding when I described her; she was still as gorgeous and free-spirited as she'd been when we were younger. We hadn't been cycling together in years, but I knew she did long-distance rides with her cycle club.

I'd known Janine since we were very little, but I'd never had a chance over the years to introduce her to Trent or Rhys. They had both been deployed when Rick and I had married, so neither of them had been able to attend and therefore Janine hadn't met them then.

Both the lads had come to stay in Atlanta for three weeks sometime later and had made it up to us then. I think Rick had been secretly relieved that Trent wasn't at the wedding. The big badass Scot really knew how to mess up a party and irritate my husband.

We had just given Alfie and Stephy their dinner, and they were playing with Trent and Jon before bed, when the doorbell rang again. I knew it was Rhys. I flung it open and he immediately picked me up and hugged me hard.

"English! Thanks for the invite, I love your cooking." Rhys grins. He knew as well as I did he had invited himself. Rhys had let his hair grow out after leaving the army, and the longer look suited him.

"Do I hear a little Welshman?" I hear Trent roar. Rhys grins and almost runs into the living room.

"Do I hear a pea-brained Scot?" Rhys roars back as they fling themselves at each other. The guys love each other like brothers, and aren't afraid to show it either. They hug hard, patting each other on the back viciously and each trying to outdo the other. There is a lot of man grunting going on.

"Break it up, guys, or get a room," I tell them as I watch Alfie's eyes widen in excitement and Stephy's with a little bit of fear. "There are kids present, you know."

Immediately they release each other, grinning hard and slapping each other on the back. "Reeeese Reeese," Alfie shouts, and dives at Rhys. Rhys catches him. "Hey there, little fella, how can you have grown so much in two weeks?" He lifts him straight up, then drops him for a second before catching him. "Woah, if I do this all night, my arms might fall off tomorrow."

He places him on the ground and scuffs his hair. "Ladies." He bows to Trent's wife. "My beautiful Milly. How are you? Still putting up with that jack… man," he corrects quickly, then glances down as Milly comes round the sofa to give him a hug. "Wow. Nice belly, don't tell me you're growing a little Scot in there?"

Milly just smiles and hugs him.

"Rhys, this is my friend Janine. Janine, this is my other army buddy, Rhys." Janine stands up and leans over the back of the sofa.

"Hi." She smiles. "I have heard so much about you guys, it's so good to finally meet you."

"And you, my fair lady." Rhys leans forward and kisses her softly on the hand. I make gagging noises as Janine laughs. I notice she doesn't pull her hand away, though.

"And, Rhys, this is a friend from work, Jon, and his daughter, Stephy."

Rhys smiles widely at Stephy and waves, then he looks up at Jon and holds out his hand. Jon eyes him. "You're not going to kiss my hand too, are you?"

Rhys laughs. "Only if you want me to, mate. Or we can man hug you if you want."

"How about we just shake hands to start with, maybe man hug later?" Jon grins.

Rhys winks at him. "You're on."

I laugh and roll my eyes at them all. I go back into the kitchen and stir the chilli con carne. It's Rick's recipe and is great for serving to lots of guests. I turn on the stereo hooked up to my phone and my randomised favourites playlist floats through the living room; I love having music in the house. Then I notice the time.

"Okay, kids, I think it's bedtime." Jon smiles and nods at me in agreement. Alfie, who has dragged Rhys to the rug, looks up and pouts at me.

"Ah, Mummy…"

"Alfie." I look at him sternly. "It's bedtime." I see Jon smirk as Alfie pouts again.

"Daddy, do I have to go to bed too?"

"Yep," Jon replies to Stephy.

"But I'm older."

Jon eyes his daughter. "By three months, honey, that does not give you a later bedtime. Besides, I thought you were excited about the sleepover."

Alfie and Stephy exchange a glance. I can see their little minds working as they consider that they can still play in their room after the lights are turned out.

"There's no bath tonight, though, so you can have two extra stories," I tell them.

Alfie smiles widely. "Can Tent read one? His voice is funny."

Trent laughs and sits on the sofa next to Jon. "Sure, buddy, which one do you want?"

Alfie grabs a book from his crammed bookshelf and climbs onto Trent's lap as I sit down beside him. Stephy leaps onto Jon's legs and curls up. Not quite touching Trent but close.

"The dinosaur that pooped a planet?" Trent is amused. "Sounds… dirty."

"It's a good one," I assure him.

"Sure is. We love these books, don't we, honey?" Stephy nods, putting her thumb in her mouth.

Janine, Rhys and Milly all take seats around the room and listen as Trent reads the book, loudly and with lots of different enthusiastic voices. I glance over at Milly, who is watching Trent with a big loving smile on her face. It is so nice to see. I'm so very pleased they found each other. My thoughts wander to Rick as the book progresses, and that ever-present ache seems to grow wider again. Rick would have loved it here, with these people. Damn, I miss him.

Stephy chooses the next book, *Mister Smelly*, which has everyone in fits of laughter by the time Trent is done.

"Okay, now upstairs for teeth brushing, pyjamas and three more books," I call.

"Do you hear that, Stephy? You get another three books," Jon tells her as an excited Stephy follows Alfie out of the room.

"Does Stephy still have milk before bed?" I ask Jon.

Jon nods. "Yeah. I'll get you her beaker." He moves to the hallway as I move into the kitchen. "Oh, by the way, good stern face earlier. That must have been your army 'don't mess with me' look."

I laugh as Jon hands me the beaker and heads upstairs after the kids. "It works on little boys and grown men, you know," I call after him.

"What's this about grown men?" Rhys asks as he waltzes into the kitchen. "Where are they this evening?" He hugs my shoulders as I laugh. "Anything I can do, English?"

"Yep," I reply as I fill the two beakers with milk and put them in the microwave. "You can get everyone drinks. There is wine and beer around, plus juice and stuff. You'll find it. Oh and stir the chilli a few times, will you?"

"Sure thing." He studies me. "How are you doing by the way?"

I smile at him. "I'm okay, Rhys."

"Really?"

I shrug, it's a loaded question, then hug him back. "It's really great to see you."

Rhys hugs me tight, then the microwave beeps and he lets me go. I grab the beakers, shake them, then head upstairs. The upstairs of the house was decorated in the same faded old style, with light blue faded carpets and stain marks on the lower walls.

The main family bathroom was located over the stairs at the front of the house. Next to it was my room, also at the front of the house. The spare room was down the hall a few metres at the back of the house, and I could see the door was open and Jon's bag was on the floor outside it. Alfie's room was the smallest and in between the two bigger rooms at the side of the house, with a little window overlooking the neighbours.

I place the milk on a high shelf and peer into the room. I see that Stephy is already in her pyjamas, bright pink with cute bunnies on. She is pursuing the selection of books. Jon is helping Alfie with the poppers on his space pyjamas.

"Okay, all done." Jon smiles and Alfie grins widely back; he really likes Jon. "Now teeth."

As one, we all troop down the hall. The kids climb onto the small step in front of the sink and make a half-hearted attempt at brushing their teeth. Jon and I watch with amusement from the doorway.

"Rhys and Trent seem like good guys," Jon comments quietly.

"Oh, they are," I reply. "I met them in basic training… fourteen years ago now," wow, that was a long time ago, "and we've served in a few units over the years. I couldn't have asked for better friends."

Jon chuckles. "I have a few friends who I've known that long, but you guys seem to have something more. Maybe it's you all specifically or because of what you've all been through together."

"Maybe. They've always been dirty-minded buggers, though."

Jon laughs quietly. "I think you give them a run for their money, Emma."

Before I can respond, Alfie turns to me. "Mummy, I'm done."

"Great, okay, three more stories then bed."

As we walk back down the hallway, I grab the milk from the shelf and they take it eagerly.

I sit down on the mattress I have laid on the floor for Stephy. She immediately climbs onto my lap, drinking her milk quickly and holding a small stuffed rabbit to her chest. Jon sits down next to me, his legs close to mine. Alfie gives us all a look over his milk bottle. He is unsure about where to go now my lap is taken.

"Do you want to sit on Jon, sweetie?" I ask him. "Or would you like to sit on the mattress?"

Alfie seems to consider it a moment, then hesitantly climbs onto Jon's lap, his back stiff. Jon grabs the book Stephy has laid out and begins to read. Alfie slowly relaxes into him, cuddling his stuffed green T-Rex toy his uncle gave him, and I'm struck for a moment just how much he looks like his father, and how odd it is to see another man reading to him like this. My eyes drift to the folded American flag, wedding rings and the family photo on Alfie's bed stand, and I feel sadness in my chest. I push the feeling aside and concentrate on Jon's words. I realise we are sitting really close together and I can feel the heat of him on my bare legs. It strikes me as an odd observation, and I turn it over in my mind as Jon reads.

After another two books, it's bedtime. Alfie climbs into his bed as I pull the duvet over him, and Stephy lies down on the mattress. I kiss Alfie on the head, saying good night, and move towards the door. Jon is speaking quietly to Stephy, in mixed French and English, but he stands up too after a minute.

"Now, no mischief," I tell them both quietly. "Go to sleep straight away." They both nod, looking innocently up at me.

I close the door behind them and turn on the child monitor.

"I bet they don't do that," Jon murmurs quietly with amusement.

"Of course not." I give him a look. "Everyone loves a sleepover."

Something flashes in Jon's eyes, but it is gone in a second and he just smiles broadly.

We head down the stairs and into the kitchen. I place the child monitor on the table. "What would you like to drink? Beer, wine?"

"Uh, I better not, I'm driving later," Jon says with regret.

"Why don't you stay here?" The words are out before I realise what I have said.

Jon snaps his head to me. "Sorry?"

I shift on my feet, suddenly a bit nervous. "I have a spare room," I explain as I pour myself a glass of red wine. "If you stay here, then you don't have to wake up Stephy and drive her home, and put her to bed again. I know what a hassle that can be. Plus, the kids will love it." I hold up the child monitor, where we can hear soft voices giggling. I shrug. "I make a good breakfast too."

Jon studies me thoughtfully. He seems to be considering my words, then he shrugs. "Okay."

I smile. "Just like that?"

"Yep."

"Great. Help yourself to a drink then." The wine and glasses are all laid out on the small kitchen table. I hear Jon pour himself a glass as I turn to the chilli.

"Can I help?"

"Nope," I reply as I stir. I look over my shoulder at him. "Go and make conversation."

Jon smiles and leaves the kitchen.

As I stir the chilli and put on the rice, I think over my offer to him. It was automatic, I didn't think, but having Jon in the house will be nice. I'm tired of being alone here. A thought creeps into my head, but I dismiss it immediately. No good will come from something like that.

The table is already laid for dinner, so I potter around the kitchen getting things ready, singing along to *Brothers in Arms*; Dire Straits have always been a favourite band of mine. I open a bag of nachos and pour them into a bowl, heading into the dining area and snacking on a few. I glance over to see everyone standing around a big chest of drawers behind one of the sofas. The cabinet holds numerous photos.

"That's English, Welshie and me on basic." Trent is pointing to a photo. "We're on some training exercise in Wales, I think."

"You look muddy," Janine comments. I know that photo; we had just spent three days wading through mud.

"It's Wales, Wales is muddy," Rhys says dryly, poking Janine in the ribs with his elbow.

"Ah, yeah, this one is from Afghanistan, our second tour together in the Middle East. February... '06?" Trent doesn't sound sure as he puts down the one of the three of us in British army gear. The two men had lifted me up just as the guy had taken the photo, and I looked both surprised and annoyed.

"'07," Rhys corrects with a smile in his voice. "Ten years ago now. A week or so later, English was seconded to the US army to work on some major construction projects. She was really good at what she did, had a great reputation for getting the work done." He points at the photo with Rick, Vega, White and myself in front of the American Humvee, the one where I look tiny, surrounded by the big men.

"We were pissed," Trent says with a smile. "I always warned her that she would be seduced to the States..."

"This is Rick." Rhys reaches over and grabs a photo I have hidden at the back, my favourite one which I can't bear to look at sometimes. "This was taken while they were working together. They served together in Afghanistan. Did you know that?" Jon shakes his head. His back is to me so I can't see his face. "This was... what, four years before they finally became a couple? That was after English left the army and moved to the US."

"What was he like?" Jon asks quietly.

Trent laughs. "The first time we met him, he went all-macho American GI and eyeballed us the whole time," Trent says with a smirk, "and we did it right back. English waded in and told us all off like little schoolboys."

"Which we totally deserved," Rhys says with a laugh. "She ordered us to put it back in our trousers."

Then Trent sobers. "He was a great guy, Rick. He totally adored our girl." Trent points at another photo, the one from the day we were married. "Rhys and I couldn't make the wedding because we were deployed, which really sucked." His voice is filled with regret.

"It was lovely," Janine says. "Small and beautiful." She sounds sad. "And Alfie is a great kid."

"I love that photo of all of them," Milly says quietly. She must be talking about the one of the three of us in his sister's back yard. It shows Rick holding me in his arms with Alfie at around two sitting on my stomach. Jordan, his niece, had bet him he couldn't hold that pose for a whole minute. Luckily, Alfie is actually looking at the camera so it's a great photo.

Jon leans forward and removes something from the dresser which clinks.

"Military dog tags," Trent says. He reaches under his shirt and takes out his own. "They must be both Rick's and Emma's. See the difference in US and British Army design?"

Jon nods and places them back. "Are these Emma's medals?"

"Must be." Trent leans over. "This one is British Army, the Afghanistan Operational Service Medal. I think this is a US Army Service Medal but I don't know the details."

Rhys glances over towards the kitchen and sees me standing there watching. "English, what are these medals for?" Heads whip around in surprise.

I smile and move over to them, not meeting anyone's gaze. I hold up the US one. "This is the Soldier's Medal, which is a US military medal which can be awarded to friendly nations. It's awarded for distinguished conduct and heroism outside of combat situations." I pause and hold up the OSM. "I received this after my second tour for services to the Afghanistan people." I place the medal down and shrug. "I was just doing my job." I turn and smile. "You'll be pleased to know it's almost dinner."

Jon gives me a small smile and turns away, Janine and Milly following him towards the table. Trent, who is standing behind me, leans over and wraps his arms around my shoulders and chest, pulling me against him tightly. He bends over and places a kiss on my cheek, then rests his chin on my shoulder.

Rhys grins. "You're too damn modest, English." He leans to the other side, kisses my cheek softly and wraps his arms around us both. "Remember the monkey bars."

I can't help it, I laugh loudly. Jon, Milly and Janine turn towards us. We must make quite a sight, me sandwiched between these two hulking men. I see Jon regard us curiously then smile widely. He says something to Milly which I can't make out, and she shakes her head and laughs.

"Right, boys," I say after a minute. "Stop copping a feel and let's eat."

The chilli goes down really well. I had made a huge vat of it, knowing how much Trent and Rhys eat, but still expected some leftovers. When I examine the pot, there is hardly anything left.

"You fat bastards," I exclaim to the table.

Trent, sitting next to me, just grins. "You're lucky, Jon. English can cook now. When she first got out the army, she couldn't boil an egg!"

"I could too," I reply, then shrug. "I could boil it all day but I didn't know when I could eat it." Jon bursts into laughter as Janine shakes her head at me from the other side of the table. "Hey, it's not like cooking skills were part of my Royal Corps of Engineering training." I have to defend myself here. "I never needed to do it before. I always lived in accommodation with food included." Rhys sticks his fingers down his throat and gags, to everyone's amusement. I ignore him and continue on. "Luckily, there are a lot of takeouts available in the US so I didn't starve when I got there. I took cooking courses, you know." I nod proudly as I receive amused looks.

"And we are very grateful," Trent acknowledges, just before drinking his beer in a big gulp.

"Chilli is just so good," Rhys responds from my right, now licking his fork enthusiastically. "I'll have to invite myself over more often now you're so close."

"What do you do for work now?" Jon asks Rhys, taking a sip of his wine. Jon is sitting next to Rhys on the other side of the table opposite me.

"I'm a supervisor over at the docks in Southampton," Rhys says. "When I left the army two years ago, I thought it would just be a temporary gig, but it turns out I'm quite good at it so they promoted me." He grins. "The hours are shit. When a boat comes in, no matter what time of night, we have to unload it straight away. But the money's good and I enjoy it." He leans forward, all excited. "Plus, I get to play with big cranes!"

I can see why Rhys likes doing that; he is basically a big kid at heart.

"Do you live in Southampton?" Janine asks.

Rhys nods. "I do."

"Me too." Janine sounds surprised.

Rhys regards her with interest. "How interesting."

"Janine, when's your train tonight?" I ask innocently.

Janine glances at her watch. "The last one is at 11pm. Loads of time."

"I can give you a lift if you want," Rhys offers. "I drove tonight." Bingo. Jon meets my eyes and I can see him trying to control a smirk.

Janine's eyes slide to mine and I control my expression. "Well, that's very kind, Rhys, but I really don't mind the train."

"And I don't mind giving you a lift. If we are both going to Southampton…" Rhys' eyes also move to me and he narrows them with suspicion. "Hang on a minute, you told me I had to drive."

"And you told me I had to get the train." Janine points a finger at me. "This is totally a set-up, isn't it?"

"Uh, no." I shake my head, but I don't think I am very convincing.

"Liar!" Rhys points his finger at me. "You are totally busted, English."

Trent starts laughing, hard. I can't control my laughter anymore either.

"Okay, okay." I hold up my hands. "I admit it." Janine is shaking her head at me in mock annoyance; I can see a big smile on her face. "It's just you guys both live in Southampton and you're both awesome, so I thought…" I wave my hand and lean back in my chair, resigned. "Doesn't matter."

Rhys chuckles. "I'm not saying it's a bad thing, English." He glances at Janine, who shrugs.

"Nah, me neither," she replies with a smirk at him.

"Nice work, English," Trent butts in. "Now, is there dessert?"

Janine had brought a cake for dessert, with candles and everything. One thing I did not do was bake desserts. They sing to me and I blow them out, not making a wish on purpose. I give out slices and refill wine glasses.

"So are there any embarrassing childhood stories about English we should know about?" Rhys asks Janine as he eats his cake. "I think she deserves some embarrassment now."

I raise my eyebrows at him, confident that's not going to happen. "I think you know all the really bad ones, Welshie."

Janine narrows her eyes. "Hmm, there must be something. What about that thing with the two boys and the roses?"

I shake my head, eating the chocolate frosting. "They know that one."

Janine looks disappointed, then her face lights up. "Okay, how about when we got drunk on Malibu and tried to perve on that really hot boy, uh, Peter something from the year above us." I groan and Janine smiles. "We got right up to his bedroom window, but you fell out of the tree and got stuck partway down. We managed to just get you free and run away before his parents found us."

I hold up my right forearm and point to the elbow. "I still have the scar!"

Trent laughs. "We know that one, but it's good. I'm interested in what else you girls got up to when drunk on Malibu."

I punch Trent in the arm. "We were thirteen!"

Trent rubs his arm. "So? Thirteen-year-old girls must be as horny as thirteen-year-old boys."

Milly, Janine and I all share a knowing look.

"Oh, come on," Trent exclaims. "You ladies can't do that and then not tell."

I just smile at him. "I hate to kiss and tell, Trent, you know that."

He gives me a look, and I know exactly what he is going to say a millisecond before he says it. "I know a lot of things about you, lass, like how you like getting hot and sweaty behind the storage sheds on overseas tours?"

I close my eyes as Janine gasps. Rhys chuckles lightly. When I open them, I glare at Trent.

"What the hell?" Janine says, leaning forward. "Why don't I know this?"

I continue to glare at Trent. "Thanks," I mutter. He has the decency to at least look a little ashamed.

"Emma?" Janine says, and I turn slowly to her. "You got laid on a tour? I thought you weren't supposed to do that."

"We're not," Rhys says with a wicked grin. "In fact, it was strictly prohibited and can lead to dismissal."

I glare at him too. I don't often get embarrassed, but this is one story few people know about.

Janine leans forward. "Oh, come on, you have to tell us now. Who was he? Where was it?"

I shake my head. "I don't think I should tell this story tonight." I hunt around for a reason, then I glance at Jon. "I'll embarrass poor Jon. He won't be able to look at me the same way again, and we have to work together, you know."

Jon laughs and waves his wine glass at me. "Oh no, that's not an excuse. I'm very interested to hear this story." He waggles his eyebrows at me, his green eyes twinkling, and I get the feeling he really does want to hear it.

"Okay, I'll embarrass Milly." I glance at Milly with a hopeful smile. Milly just meets my eyes and gives me a 'really?' look. "Damn," I mutter. "You're married to Trent. I bet nothing embarrasses you anymore." Milly just smiles at me as Trent takes his wife's hand and grins widely.

"No excuses, Em. Spill. Now," Janine demands.

"Okay, okay. I give in." I take a long gulp of my wine and look straight at Janine. "It was Rick." Janine gasps slightly. "In Afghanistan, on my first tour there." There is silence as everyone waits for me to go on. I sigh. "Okay, so, it was coming towards the end of my tour. We came back from a day in the field, and Tavern tells me that he is leaving the next day to go and do Special Forces training in the States." I lean back. "Which was great for him, and I was pleased for him, but it upset me. I was upset because he was leaving and because he hadn't told me before. So I did what I always did when I was upset. I went for a run. Tavern catches up to me, we argue. Then he kisses me." I pause and smile, remembering that first kiss. Then I chuckle. "Then we have to hide from a security patrol." Janine giggles. "Which led us into the dark maze behind some storage sheds. One thing leads to another and we have sex up against the wall."

"Which is not easy to do," Rhys points out, to nods all around. "Either a very small girl, or a very strong guy."

"Rick was the strong guy." I smile. "So anyway, that's it, that's the story." I glance around. My eyes land on Jon, who is leaning back in his chair lightly holding his wine glass. He is studying me with interest, his bright green eyes twinkling. There is a slight smirk on his lips, which I find intriguing.

"And you should all know," I continue, glancing away from him, "that I've just doubled the amount of people who know that story." I turn towards Trent. "And that Trent is no longer my friend," I reach over and snatch his beer out of his hand, "which means he gets no more beer." I glare at him again. I'm not really annoyed at him, but I like to make him squirm.

Trent makes a small high-pitched squeal and looks over at his wife. "I did a bad thing."

Milly strokes his arm. "Yes, darling, you did. You'll be lucky if Emma ever gives you a beer again."

There's light laughter around the table. I'm thinking about that night, something I haven't done in a long time.

"Please will someone else tell the table an embarrassing sex story?" I say. Everyone looks around to each other. "Come on, someone must have something they want to share."

"I almost made an accidental porno in an alley once." My gaze shoots to Jon, whose eyes are still on me.

"Accidental?" Janine queries, sounding intrigued.

Jon smiles and glances at her. "Yeah, my girlfriend, now ex-wife, and I were getting hot and heavy in an alley behind a pub in Birmingham. We didn't realise there was a camera."

I laugh as Rhys asks, with complete seriousness, "How far did you get?"

"Far enough that the security guard got quite an eyeful." Jon laughs, and chokes out, "It was the noise from the zoom lens that told us the camera was there."

I laugh loudly as the scene plays in my head. Jon is laughing hard too.

"The important question is," Trent chokes out between ragged breaths, "did you get the tape for future use?"

Jon shakes his head, tears in his eyes. "We never picked up the courage to go back and ask for it."

After that, everyone shares an embarrassing story, and I feel mine is actually not as bad as I always thought.

The evening progresses with more wine and chatting. Milly starts to look tired so she and Trent leave around 2230. They are staying at a local B&B, not wanting to bother me with them staying over. Trent gives me a big hug and asks in a small voice if he could please come back for a beer again, to which I agree sternly. Rhys, with Janine, leaves a little afterwards. Rhys will be coming back for the zoo tomorrow but Janine has other plans. I think Jon had forgotten, but Rhys certainly hadn't as he pulls Jon into a surprise hug that had Jon wheezing and grunting. Jon is taller than the Welshman, but Rhys is much wider and stronger.

Janine gives me a big hug as she leaves, placing a gift in my hand to open tomorrow.

Jon and I cleared up in the kitchen, making small talk about the kids as we did so. We'd had enough wine by then and I made us each a mint tea. We sat on the sofa and chatted quietly. The idea I had had earlier was growing in my mind. It probably wasn't a good thing to mention, but I had always been of the opinion that if you didn't ask, you didn't get.

So I take a breath and stand up quickly, walking to the window. Jon pauses mid-sentence. In the window, I see his curious expression as he lounges casually on the sofa. I also see him glance down at my body with undisguised interest, which only fuels my idea.

"Jon." I turn quickly, and his eyes snap up to my face. "I've got something that I want to talk to you about."

Jon smiles. "Okay..."

"It's a bit unusual, a bit out there, so if you get freaked out, please feel free to run upstairs and lock the door."

Jon gives me a curious look, with a hint of a smile and repeats, "Okay..."

I stand in front of him, separated by the coffee table, and place my mug down. "You and I, we get on really well, don't we?" Jon nods and leans forward, placing his mug on the table. "But, I think it's obvious that neither of us is interested in starting anything serious with anyone." Jon's eyes crinkle very slightly and he clasps his hands together. "I mean, you haven't been divorced very long, and my husband hasn't been gone for that long. From my point of view, I just can't imagine being serious with anyone again ever."

Jon nods slowly, still looking curious. "Yeah, I'm not interested in that either."

"Right." I wave my hands at myself. "So, we both agree that we don't want anything serious or emotional." Jon nods again; he looks very wary. "So why don't we just do the... sex?"

Jon's eyebrows jump to his hairline. "What?"

I hurry round the table and perch myself on the edge in front of him. "Why don't we just do the physical stuff? With none of that annoying feeling stuff? Keep it casual and friendly and just have fun with each other?"

Jon is watching me with an odd look on his face. His eyes flick over my face. "You're saying you want to be friends with benefits?" He has chosen the less crude phrase of what I was thinking of, and I don't correct him.

I smile and wave my hand again. "We don't need to label it."

Jon considers this. "In my experience," he says slowly after a few seconds, "it's hard to separate the physical act from the emotional side." I open my mouth to speak but he rushes on. "I'm not saying I'm not interested, but I think we need to consider this carefully."

I nod; good points. "Okay, Jon. Do you love me?"

"What?"

"Do you love me? Are you in love with me?"

Jon's eyes flick over my face again. "Uh, no."

"Good." I smile. "Because I don't love you either. I doubt I will ever be able to love another man again. But I like you. I think you're funny and smart, you're great to be around and you're very good-looking." I lower my voice. "I find you very attractive."

Jon shifts forward on the sofa so that his knees are almost touching mine. He considers his words carefully. "I like you too, and you're gorgeous…"

"Then, why not?"

Jon is silent for a few minutes, and I wait with bated breath, my pulse pounding. Then he moves forward swiftly, pushes aside my knees and kneels in between my legs. His face comes really close to mine as he places his hands on the table on either side of my hips. A scent of light soap floats over me; we've never been this close.

"Before we agree to this," he says quietly, his eyes twinkling as they move over my face, "we need to do two things. First, we need to share a kiss so we can both know it's what we really want. You can always tell from a kiss." I nod as my belly flutters in nervous anticipation.

Jon leans forward and brushes his lips against mine. He pulls back slightly, studying me for a second, then cups my head in his hands and kisses me deeply. I close my eyes and try not to think of Rick. I just enjoy the feel of these new lips against mine, the amazing sensations I had almost forgotten about. How his beard hair brushes against my sensitive chin, how his tongue explores mine, how his soapy smell and minty taste overwhelm my senses. I place my hands on Jon's waist and grip him tightly with my thighs, pulling myself into him.

After a few minutes, Jon pulls away. His eyes are hooded as he drops his hands from me. I inhale deeply and try and control myself; that had been one amazing kiss. Rick's face pops into my head for an instant, but I push the image away and ignore the feelings of guilt I have for enjoying another man's kiss.

"I think that answers that question," Jon whispers, his eyes twinkling. I'm glad he doesn't see what I'm thinking. "Do you agree?"

I smile crookedly at him. "I do. What was your second thing?"

Jon rubs his beard and moves backwards, sitting back on the edge of the sofa and leaning forward. "We need to set some ground rules."

I nod and lean forward myself. "Good idea. Number one." I hold up my index finger. "No one can know. Not the kids, not our friends, not anyone from work."

Jon nods, looking serious. "Agreed. It's just between you and me. We aren't allowed to tell anyone, and we need to be careful no one sees us or suspects anything. Especially the kids." I nod. I don't want Alfie knowing anything about this. I don't want to adversely affect him any more than I have. "Number two." Jon mimics me and holds up two fingers. "We keep it casual. No feelings, just physical." He smiles at that. "If either of us wants to see other people, or end things between us, we can straight away, with no problems. We just need to be honest with each other."

I nod. "Agreed. Number three." I hold up three fingers. "No cuddling afterwards, and no sleeping in the same bed." Jon hesitates slightly but then nods. "If you stay over here and need to sleep, you can stay in the spare room. Okay?"

"Agreed." Jon smiles. For a moment, we just sit there. Jon is watching me closely.

"Any more?" I ask.

"I have one more," Jon says softly. "But it's really only relevant for tonight."

"Shoot."

"You should know it's been a while since I was with anyone, even longer since I was with a woman other than Sarah," Jon says softly. "But that's okay for me. Can I assume that you haven't been with anyone since…" He trails off.

I nod. "Yes. There's been no one since Rick." I hope I say that with less feeling than I'm experiencing.

Jon nods and I don't think I hid that very well. "So, if at any time, especially tonight, if you don't want to go on, if it becomes too much for you, just say. Okay, Emma?" He reaches out and strokes my hair off my face. The move is so sweet, I have to stop it.

I take his hand then shift off the table. I push Jon back on the sofa and slowly straddle his lap. His face ignites with desire as he looks down me, then back into my face. He places his hands on the outside of my bare thighs, and slowly moves them upwards and inwards.

His feather-light touch feels so good, I close my eyes. A memory of Rick doing the same bombards me. I like that Jon is touching me, but it feels like it should be Rick. I open my eyes and Jon's eyes meet mine. I think he can see my struggle because he hesitates, his hands on my thighs under my dress. I smile and dip down to kiss him as he sits up straighter, pulling me closer. I take his hands in mine and bring them up to my breasts, telling him it's all right to keep touching me. I need to concentrate on Jon, how his hands feel on me, how it feels to be kissing him. No one else. Definitely not Rick. Slowly, I begin to unbutton his shirt, my hands grazing his chest, skimming over his light chest hair, down his ribs to his stomach. I feel an abrasion on my fingertips and look down. I am touching a nasty-looking pointed scar just inside his rib cage. Jon smiles, brings a hand up to my face, tangles it in my hair and kisses me.

I pull back and whisper, "We should go upstairs." Jon nods.

Together, we run silently up the stairs. Before I go into my bedroom, I veer off to Alfie's room. Jon follows quietly, his hand clasped in mine. I open the door a little, just to check on them. The dim light from the hallway illuminates Alfie's bed on the wall opposite. Stephy has crawled in beside him.

They lie facing each other on their fronts, curled up into little balls under their duvets, clutching their teddies. They are both fast asleep.

Jon smiles widely at the sight, then reaches over to close the door behind him softly. He practically drags me back down the hall to my bedroom. I close and lock the door behind me. As I turn, Jon kisses me again, his hands roaming all over me, backing me towards the bed. He swiftly relieves me of my dress, and I pull his shirt all the way off as I fall onto the bed backwards. Jon glances at the clock over my shoulder as he moves on top of me, kissing me everywhere.

"It's midnight," he whispers into my neck as his lips touch my skin. "Happy birthday, Emma."

*

... the sand bites into my palms as I fall to the ground. I look over at Rick; I need to make sure he is okay. I don't care who pushed me. All I see are his flat dead eyes in his beautiful face staring back at me. A single bullet hole is in his forehead, blood already streaking down into the sand. I hear frantic screaming...

I jerk awake and in an instant I've jumped out of bed, sweat running down my body as I leg it to the bathroom. I just make it in time and vomit until my stomach is empty, then I lean on my arms over the toilet and breathe deeply. I don't cry this time; maybe I don't have any tears left. I realise I'm naked, and the night comes back to me.

Dinner, Jon, sex and emotional oblivion. I glance behind me towards the hallway, straining to hear if I woke him up. The house is silent and I breathe a quiet sigh of relief. I don't want him to know this.

Then I remember it's my birthday.

I stand up shakily, quickly brush my teeth and head to the bedroom to grab my dressing gown. The luminous digits on the bedside clock tell me it's 0503, and I see Jon is not in my bed, as agreed. He must be in the spare room, and a quick glance down the hall shows me the door is closed.

I grab thick socks, slippers and quietly place a towel outside the room Jon is sleeping in, so he can shower if he wants. I silently slip downstairs. I feel exhausted, but the kids will be awake soon; no point in going back to bed. I make myself a coffee and quietly begin to prepare breakfast stuff. Rhys, Trent and Milly will be here around about 1000. Then we will head off to the zoo.

When I have done all I want to in the kitchen, I slide on some outside shoes, walk to the sliding patio door and open it quietly. With my second coffee in my hands, I sit outside on the step of the patio. I feel the freezing air on the bare skin of my face and hands, feel the freshness of the darkness as it whirls around me. There is frost on the grass in front of me. I breathe in and feel the ice in my lungs, watching my white breath in the air as I exhale into the empty darkness in front of me. I begin to shiver softly. After the Middle East, I thought I preferred the cold, that I would never undervalue a nice cool day again. But this is real cold, cold that's seeps into your skin to your very core. This is the type of cold where only crazy people sit outside in their dressing gowns and socks.

I imagine Rick in this cold, a big hat on his head and a huge overcoat. I smile to myself as I realise he would have a hard time finding a coat that fits. I feel a stab in my chest, and my breath catches. I miss Rick so much, my chest aches, and I rub it hard with my cold palm. Then I think of Jon, about what we did together last night, and I smile again. The ache in my chest subsides, just a tiny bit. Enough so I can breathe out the white mist again.

But it doesn't remove the fact that it's my birthday and my husband is dead.

I hear the boiler come on inside the house and realise Jon is showering. If he sees me outside in my dressing gown, he will think I'm mad, so I head back inside. I check my phone and find I have several birthday messages. One is from Jason, saying he will call me later.

The clock says it's 0630, and Alfie is still not awake, which is surprising. I'm standing at the counter cutting fruit when Jon comes in. He is freshly showered, with damp hair, wearing his jeans and shirt from yesterday.

He smiles when he sees me, but it's a wary smile, like he's not sure how I am going to react.

"Morning," he says, and his voice rings in my ears. It's a beautiful voice. It whispered sexy words to me last night. "Happy birthday."

"Hi." I lean on the counter with my hip and pop a grape into my mouth. "Sleep well?"

"I did. Comfy bed." He approaches me, and the smell of my soapy shower gel lingers in the air. "So, is this the awkward morning after? When we decide we had too much wine and cake and last night was a mistake?"

I study him – he's difficult to read – then say cautiously, "What do you think?"

Jon smiles, his green eyes twinkling with mischief. "I say, we had just about the right amount of wine and cake last night. But not nearly enough of each other."

I laugh. "I think I can agree with that."

"Good." He leans down and kisses me on the cheek, then pulls me in for a hug. I wrap my arms around him and just feel his body against me for a moment.

"Tea or coffee?" I say after a minute, pulling away.

"Oh, coffee this early in the morning," he says. "Just milk."

"Ah, you're one of these people who drink both," I say, eyeing him as I pour the milk into a mug before I place it under the coffee spout. "Must be the Frenchman in you."

Jon laughs and pulls out one of the stools around the small island in the middle of the kitchen. "Guilty as charged. I like coffee in the morning and around lunchtime, then I switch to tea."

"Figures." I place the full mug of milky coffee next to him.

"Thanks." Jon glances at the clock. "Wow, it's almost 7am and Stephy's not awake yet... I totally missed a lie-in."

"Yeah, Alfie is usually up by 0600, must be the excitement of the sleepover."

"That didn't stop you from getting up early." He shoots me a wicked grin.

I smile widely in response then shrug. "Lie-ins were bashed out of me a long time ago. You get up early in the army."

"Ah ha." Jon eyes me like he knows I'm not quite telling the truth, but he doesn't ask.

Just then, I hear footsteps on the stairs and place my mug down. "Speak of the devils."

"Mummy Mummy," Alfie yells as he rounds the corner and jumps at me. I catch him and hug him close, adjusting my robe so I'm still decent.

"Alfie Alfie! Morning, sweetheart." I kiss him on the forehead, smelling his adorable baby scent.

Stephy has jumped into Jon's lap and is wrapped around his neck.

"We slept in the same bed, Daddy."

Jon meets my eye and grins. "I know, I saw. Do you remember that it's Emma's birthday today?"

Stephy's eyes widen. "What do you say when it's someone's birthday?"

"Happppy birffday," Stephy yells at me.

Alfie giggles and kisses my cheek. "Happppy birffday, Mummy."

I grin. "Thanks, Stephy, and Alfie, that's very sweet."

Stephy leans into her dad and whispers in his ear. Jon smiles and says something in French to her. Stephy nods and glances at me. "Okay then, go and fetch it." I find the two-language thing fascinating.

Stephy wriggles out of his embrace and runs up the stairs. I cast a questioning glance at Jon but he just smiles knowingly. A minute later, Stephy comes back down the stairs. She is carrying a paper shopping bag. I'm really curious now. "Shall we go in the living room?" Jon suggests. Stephy nods and leads the way. She sits on the sofa and tells me to sit next to her. Still carrying Alfie, I sit on the seat and reposition him so he is sitting in my lap facing her. Jon kneels on the floor next to his daughter.

Stephy fumbles with the bag, then with a big smile she produces a badly wrapped gift.

"I wapped it myself," she explains. "And I picked it out with Daddy."

I smile widely. I hadn't really expected any presents this year. Alfie is too young to get anything himself.

With a long look at Jon, I gingerly take the package. Slowly, with Alfie's help, I unwrap it. Stephy sits up on her knees and watches with excitement. Inside is a thick and very colourful winter hat. I gasp. It has ear protectors and a bobble on top, with a swirling geometric design of intricate colours flowing over its surface. Inside is a soft fleece lining of pale purple.

"Oh wow," I murmur. "It's so beautiful."

I glance at Jon, who shrugs. "I thought you needed a new hat for our lunchtime walks. Stephy chose the design."

"It's so lovely. Thank you, guys." I lean down and kiss Stephy's cheek, who giggles. Then I lean over and kiss Jon's cheek too. He doesn't giggle, but he does smile. Then I place it on my head and grin widely.

"Will you wear it today? At the zoo?" Stephy asks.

"I will." I take it off; it's a bit warm for inside.

"Might be good for your early-morning outside coffee as well." I glance up at Jon, who is smiling at me in humour, and I realise he must have seen me through his bedroom window.

"Mummy?" Alfie's voice is small, and I look down. He looks sad.

"Yes, sweetie?"

"Reeees helped me pick out your gift, but he didn't bring it last night. He is bringing it today. Is that okay?" His big brown eyes look up at me in concern.

I smile at him and hug him tight. "Of course, Alfie, I really look forward to opening it. Now how about I read us all a book?" There are cheers all round.

*

The zoo was busy but great fun. We saw all sorts of big scary animals, lots of bugs and spiders, fishes and birds. It was a cold but dry day and with my new hat on, I felt very warm.

I'd been nervous that Trent or Rhys might pick up on the fact that Jon and I had slept together. But apart from the obvious crack about having spent the night, they didn't seem to suspect. We had a late lunch at a nearby pub, then came back to the house for tea and coffee.

Stephy had loved the zoo, pulling her dad and me this way and that. She even grabbed Trent's hand at one point to show him something. Trent had smiled widely.

I took birthday calls from my parents and Jason as we walked around, and it was nice to hear from them all. When we got home, I opened the rest of my presents. Trent and Milly had bought me an expensive bottle of single malt Islay whisky from a distillery in Scotland. Rhys gave me a set of socks with monster faces on them, his excuse being that my socks were boring. Rhys had also helped Alfie with his present for me. A large stuffed pillow with Alfie's cute smiling face on it. It was adorable and I hugged it to me. Alfie looked so pleased I liked it. Janine's present was a framed picture of us on a cycle tour years ago. It went straight on the living room dresser.

Rhys had brought another cake and I blew out the candles the second time, again not making a wish. We were just sitting in the living room, eating, drinking and talking about the zoo, when the doorbell rang.

I put down my plate and hurry to the door. A courier wearing a bright yellow coat smiles at me.

"Emma Tavern?" he asks. I nod and he hands me a pale envelope. "Sign here, please."

I scribble my name and glance curiously at the front of the envelope as he leaves. My heart skips a beat as I recognise the stylish whirls of Rick's handwriting on my name. The rest of the address is written in different handwriting and pen colour.

Glancing behind me to make sure no one else is here, I back up and sit on the stairs. Frantically, I tear open the envelope. The picture on the card is of two cows in a dairy field. It's odd, and I frown. I open the card slowly, and Rick's handwriting jumps out at me.

My dearest Emma,

Every year I start with the same words on the chance that this is the one you will read first. So here goes again. Ever since I met you, I have written you a card, to be delivered on your birthday if I'm no longer around. I keep it in my locker on the base. Seth or Paulo will have delivered this to you. There are ten now. The others are all stored in an old box of personal stuff in our house. If you are reading this now on your 32nd birthday, then I'm gone, and wherever I am, I miss you.

It's February 23rd 2016. It's mere days since your last birthday, and once again I wasn't around to share it with you. I'm so sorry for all the birthdays I have missed, my love. I picked this card up at an airport in Germany (hence the silly cows), and am writing it to you on our way back from my first deployment in two years. It was long and hard in a way I never remember the others being. I used to enjoy them. Now they are a burden. How I have missed you and Alfie. I have missed your smiles and your laughter, missed waking up next to you every morning, missed just simply being with you. You make my world a better place. I couldn't ask for a more loving, caring and understanding partner in this life.

Happy birthday, my darling. My birthday wish for you this year is for you to be happy wherever life takes you, and whatever might happen, know I will love you always.

Love forever
Rick

My eyes fill with tears as I reread his words again and again. I drop my head and cry into my hair as I sit on the stairs.

"Emma?" Jon's soft voice brings my head up sharply. He's looking at me with real concern. "Emma, are you okay?"

I hold up the card, and he glances at it. "It's from Rick," I whisper, and his face fills with shock and sorrow. I hear Alfie's voice and footsteps and my heart leaps into my throat.

"I can't let Alfie see me cry," I whisper in panic as I stand and run up the stairs, leaving Jon staring after me.

Once in my room, I sit on the bed and read the card again, choking back the tears. Then I take my phone out of my pocket, find the number I want, and dial.

The phone rings a few times before Seth picks up, his voice solemn. "Hey, Emma, happy birthday."

"Seth..." I start crying again. His voice and his accent remind me of Rick so much.

"You got the card, huh?"

"Yeah," I sniffle.

"I'm sorry. It must have been quite a shock." He sounds really sorry. "But Rick made us promise years ago not to tell you about them."

"Oh God, Seth..." I put my head in my hands. "I thought I was... I just..."

"I know," he replies gently. "Paulo and I debated extensively whether to send it to you. We had lots of arguments about it. But in the end, it was Rick's wish."

I nod and try to pull myself together. "There are others? The card says there are others."

"Yeah, he wrote one to you every year. He made us promise to get them to you if he died. The old ones he stored in a box in your house."

I feel panic. "I didn't find them when I cleared everything out. I didn't bring them back with me. What if I chucked them?"

"Hey, hey..." Seth makes soothing noises. "Didn't you give a load of stuff to Jess?"

"Yeah."

"I bet they are in one of those boxes. Let me talk to Jess, we'll find them." His voice is confident and reassuring; the accent so familiar, it makes me ache.

"Okay," I whisper.

"Hey, Em, it's good to hear from you. We should Skype soon. I know Shanna is eager to see you."

"I'd like that." I wipe my nose with the back of my hand.

"Are you having a nice birthday?"

I laugh. "I was. Trent, Rhys and some friends took us to the zoo."

Seth chuckles. "That sounds great. Okay, I'll let you go. Em, we really miss you and Alfie."

I feel my eyes fill up again. "I miss you guys too."

"Bye, Em."

"Bye, Seth."

I hang up the phone.

A second later, the door opens and Trent peers around. He had clearly been waiting for me to finish my call. He sits on the bed next to me.

I look behind him. "What, no Welshie?"

Trent shrugs. "We figured two of us would be too much for you to handle. We flipped a coin." He grins. "I won."

I shake my head and dip it down between my arms, staring at the floor.

"Jon said there had been a card from Rick…"

I hold up the card. "Yep."

"Damn."

I hold it out to him. "Read it." Trent doesn't take it so I look at him. He looks nervous. "Seriously, Trent, it's okay. Read it."

Slowly, as if taking a poisonous snake, Trent reaches out and takes it. He frowns at the picture then opens it up. As he reads it, his face grows thunderous. He closes it with a snap.

"I always said he was an arsehole Yank."

I chuckle, which slowly turns into a crying snort. Trent puts his arm around my shoulders as tears fall down my face. "I mean, it's sweet and everything," Trent concedes after a moment, "but he had to know what effect something like this would have on you. To send it to you on your birthday, for you to read it if he had died." Trent shakes his head, resting his chin lightly on my head. "I totally should have beaten his arse when we first met."

I laugh through my tears. "I would have paid to see that."

Trent chuckles. He holds me for a few minutes then says thoughtfully, "I think there is a movie about this. Guy dies and he sends his wife letters written before he went. Don't think I've seen it, though."

I nod. "Yeah, it's a chick flick."

"Ah, that would be why then. Has it got a hot girl in it?"

"Yep." I pull away and wipe my eyes. "Sorry I wrecked your t-shirt."

Trent looks down at his red t-shirt; there is an obvious wet patch where my face has been. Trent shrugs. "It'll dry. At least you don't wear mascara."

I give him a watery smile and wipe my face with my hands, pushing my hair back off my face. I rub my wet hands on my jeans vigorously, trying to get control over myself. "Dammit, Trent. Why is this so hard? Every time I feel I'm moving on just a little, something happens that reminds me of him, or us, or whatever. It feels like I'm taking one step forward and two steps back. I still miss him so much." I exhale sharply. "I feel like I could flood Afghanistan with the amount of tears I've cried so far. I think I have no more left and then... bam!" I gesture at my red-rimmed eyes.

Trent shakes his head. "Emma, it's been less than a year. No one expects you to move on overnight." I knew he was serious because Trent never calls me by my first name. "Don't put so much damn pressure on yourself either. It's okay to cry, it's okay to be upset, because the love of your life freaking died." He pulls me into a hug again. "I have no idea what it feels like for you, but I know if I lost Milly, I wouldn't be able to cope like you have." He takes a deep breath as his voice wavers just a little. "You're so strong, English. Just take one day at a time."

Chapter 7

University Part 4

June 2016

On Sunday morning, I pack my daughter into the car and head off. I had left Rick's around 7am on Saturday; I had needed to get back for April. Rick had fallen asleep with me curled in his arms, sleeping all through the night. There had been nothing sexual about it. I doubt he had even realised I was there. I had liked it; it was a long time since I had slept in the arms of a man. For one night, I hadn't been alone. I wrote him a note explaining why I had left, and that I would come and visit him on Sunday morning. I wanted to give him some time to feel better. Seth had arrived a little before I left, giving me a quick hug and telling me he'd be in contact with specialised people to help Rick.

I texted Rick several times on Saturday afternoon to ask how he was, but had received no reply.

I didn't think to let him know I was on my way over, so about 10am I pull up in front of Rick's house. I had told April we were

277

going to see Rick, and she had been talking non-stop about him on the way over.

As I turn off the engine, I swivel in my seat to my daughter on the back seat. She claps her hands in excitement.

"April."

She smiles widely, her pigtails falling about her face as she looks out of the window towards the house. April is at the age where she chooses her own clothes, and has absolutely no shame about what she chooses. Today, she is wearing a bright pink dress and orange leggings combination; a great clash of colours for a Sunday.

"April, can you listen to me a moment?" She looks back at me, all wide-eyed innocence.

"Thank you, sweetheart. You need to know that Rick has not been feeling well this weekend, so he may not be as playful as he was last week." April blinks and studies me intently in a way only a four-year-old can do. I wasn't sure what I'd find with Rick, and I didn't want April to be disappointed so I was preparing her. I had considered not bringing her along, but I didn't want to impose on Julia again. Plus, I thought she might cheer him up.

"So, can you promise me you will be really nice to him? Try and make him feel better?"

April nods. "Yes, Mummy, I understand. I don't like not feeling well so I'll be really nice."

"That's my girl." I smile then get out of the car and unbuckle her from the car seat. As I grab my bag from the front seat, she skips down the path towards his front door, pigtails swinging madly. Too short to press the doorbell, she knocks on the door with her little fist as I hurry up the path behind her. The door opens as I reach the bottom step, and a surprised-looking Rick glances down at April.

Rick looks scruffier than I've ever seen him. A light purple bruise is present around his left eye and cheekbone and his hair is a mess. He has days-old stubble, and wears a white vest and navy sweats, with bare feet. I can see the tattoos on his muscular arms clearly now; the geometric pattern on his left arm winds all the way up to his shoulder and circles all around his arm. On the right upper arm is a black crest I don't recognise. It's the bare feet and tattoo combination that catches my attention and I feel my pulse kick up at the sight of him. I swallow hard and plaster on a smile.

"Hi, Rick," April says brightly. "We've come to make you feel better." With that, she basically launches herself at him. Rick looks startled but immediately reacts as April flings herself into his arms. He scoops her up and smiles a little as I laugh. "When I don't feel well, Mummy gives me a cuddle because it makes me feel better," April says as if it's a well-known fact. "So I will give you one." She curls her arms around his neck and puts her head on his shoulder, pushing her little body into him. After a second's hesitation, Rick wraps his arms around her.

Unlike before, no memories assault me. I stand and watch as my daughter hugs this man, and I feel something stir inside me. Rick meets my eyes and cocks an eyebrow.

"It's Sunday morning," I say softly. "I did say I would come round."

"Yeah, you did." His voice gives nothing away, but I get the underlying feeling he hadn't thought I would.

Suddenly I feel awkward, like we have intruded. "If this isn't a good time..." Rick shakes his head but doesn't meet my eye. "No, it's okay. I just wasn't expecting anyone." He smiles down at April, who is still hugging him. "Come in, please."

He steps aside as I enter. "I like your house, Rick," I hadn't had a chance to tell him on Friday night. "How long have you lived here?"

"I bought it eight years ago, cheaply, because it was in a right state. I've done quite a bit of work on it."

"It's really nice. It suits you."

April pulls her head up. "Do you feel better now?" she asks, her tone expectant of a positive answer.

Rick chuckles softly. "I do, thank you." Slowly, he bends and places her on the floor.

The room is dark, the curtains still drawn. A *Tom and Jerry* cartoon plays silently on the television, which I find very funny. Rick sees my expression and shrugs defensively. "I like cartoons."

"Cartoons!" April exclaims loudly, then turns to me with wide eyes. "Mummy, please can I watch too?"

I try to limit April's television watching; it's only for a special treat like a movie or an occasional cartoon. But I want to talk to Rick and it seems like an excellent distraction.

"You can for a little while, if Rick says it's okay." I smile at him, but he doesn't look at me.

"Please, Rick, can I?"

Rick nods, his eyes on April. "Sure you can. Take a seat on the sofa. Can I get either of you a drink?" His question is directed at me but again he doesn't meet my eyes.

"Do you have juice?" I ask, as I place my bag down on a table and shrug out of my jacket.

Rick nods. "April, would you like some juice?" April jumps up and down on the floor in front of the sofa excitedly.

"Yes, please!"

I chuckle. "Juice it is."

Rick nods, turns the volume on the TV back on and heads for the kitchen. "I don't often let April have juice, or watch TV," I explain as I follow him. "So today is exciting for her."

Rick smiles as he pours orange juice into a small glass. "What would you like? Coffee, tea?" He pauses. "I don't have any English tea, I'm afraid." He sounds genuinely sorry.

"Actually, I don't like tea," I admit. "I go against the stereotype there." Rick smiles a little. "Coffee will be great. Thanks." I grab the juice and take it to April, with instructions for her to stay there and watch the cartoons. This instruction is met with great enthusiasm.

I head back to the kitchen and see Rick turning on the coffee machine. "So, how are you?" I ask, foregoing any more small talk.

Rick opens a cupboard above his head and removes two mugs. "I'm fine, thanks."

I feel a surge of annoyance at his automatic reply. "Seriously? That's what you say to me after Friday?"

Rick glances over his shoulder in surprise, then places the mugs down and turns around, leaning on the counter with his arms crossed. "Okay," he says slowly, his voice firm and controlled. "I'm not fine. But I'm better."

I raise an eyebrow at him and cross my arms too, mimicking his body language. Rick sighs and drops his arms. "Okay, maybe not really better. But I feel better." He runs his hands through his hair; he seems almost embarrassed. "Better than I have for ages actually."

"Have you been sleeping?"

"I slept really good on Friday night," he admits, looking at the coffee machine. "And okay last night."

I wonder if Friday night was because of the emotional outlet or the fact I was sleeping with him. I don't voice this question aloud. "What did you do yesterday? Seth was just arriving as I left." Rick looks up at me then glances away. "I'm sorry I couldn't stay longer," I continue. "I had to get back for April." He nods, not meeting my eye.

"Seth and I went to the base yesterday, and I had to go and give a statement to the police, though they say no charges will be filed." I'd had a phone call from the police station yesterday too, saying I needed to go and give them a statement about Friday night. I would go tomorrow morning before work. I don't mention this to him; he doesn't need to hear it. "I spent most of the day being cross-examined by shrinks." He sighs. "What happened on Friday night was pretty bad by their standards. I'm considered high risk so I'm off the active list for at least two months, and I may never be reinstated." He sounds pretty unhappy about that. "They gave me meds to help me sleep and to take if I start hallucinating again. I have to go in every day next week for counselling sessions and so they can put a plan together to help me." He sighs again and closes his eyes, rubbing them with his hands. "I still can't believe I have this trauma so bad, I was delusional." He shakes his head at himself. "I could have hurt someone." The coffee machine beeps and he turns away to it, filling the two mugs. "How do you take your coffee? Cream? Sugar?"

"Just black, please."

Rick shoots me a quick look of surprise. "You really do go against the stereotypes, don't you?"

"How do you mean?"

"Well, you are an ale and black coffee-drinking English lady who doesn't like tea." He smiles a small smile to himself as I laugh quietly.

Rick turns and hands me a mug. As I take it, he freezes, his eyes on my right hand. I glance down and realise he is looking at my wrist. The wrist with very clear and very finger-shaped purple bruises. His eyes open wide and I see the second he realises what it is. "I did that, didn't I?" he whispers. His startled eyes meet mine.

"Rick..."

His face collapses for a second at my non-denial. Then he hastily places his mug down on the counter so coffee sloshes out over the surface.

"You should leave," he says quickly. "You need to take April and go."

"What?"

He gestures at my wrist as I place my mug down. "I hurt you. I'm a danger to you. You need to leave." He moves past me but I grab his arm to stop him.

"I'm not leaving, Rick. I know you won't hurt me."

He whirls around sharply, and I break my grip. "I did hurt you."

"You were trying to protect me."

"I was delusional," he says loudly, then lowers his voice, shame flooding his features as he bites out. "I lost control, at the carnival, and then here. How can you be so sure I won't do that again? How can you want to be here with me after that?"

Something about his words, and his actions, clicks in my head. I frown. "Is that what this is about?" I ask. "Are you ashamed for having cried on Friday night?" Rick looks away and swallows. "There is nothing shameful about crying, Rick."

"I lost control," he whispers, then firmer, "I don't lose control."

"Even big strong men cry," I shoot back, annoyed at the male obsession with ego. "Everyone does, there's nothing to be ashamed of. Sometimes you just need to let go. Crying makes you feel better. Bottling up all your emotions in here," I poke him in the chest, "just makes it worse."

"It's weakness," he says bitterly, and anger swells in me. "It's all weakness. I'm not supposed to have weakness. I'm a US Army Ranger for Christ's sake. I'm supposed to be strong."

"Bloody hell, do you hear yourself?" I reply angrily. "You've been through so much more than anyone ever should. Do you think you're the only one who feels like this? I bet half the men in your unit go home and cry to their wives. You're not a robot, Rick. You're a man. You are the strongest man I have ever met."

Rick shakes his head and I've had enough. Words aren't getting through to him, actions might. So I do what I've been thinking about doing since the picnic last week. I reach up and push my lips against his, sliding my hand to the back of his neck. Rick freezes and I pull away a little, looking up into his eyes. I see hesitation on his face so I kiss him again, gently, pushing my body against his to show him I mean it. After a second, he responds to me, slowly at first, then passionately, until he is the one controlling the kiss. He threads his fingers through my hair and holds my head in place against him, while his other hand slides sensually down my back. I moan against his lips as the kiss deepens. It's been so long since I was kissed, the sensations all come back to me. How my breasts push into his chest as his body presses against me, how his stubble brushes my skin as his lips slide over mine, what he tastes and smells like. I feel his body shaking as he adjusts our positions and pushes me back into the kitchen counter, holding me in place as he kisses me deeply.

"Mummy Mummy!" April's call from the living room drags me back to reality. Rick pulls away an inch, his breathing shallow. I'm gasping for breath myself, my heart racing. I keep my eyes closed and take a deep breath, trying to calm myself.

"Yes, April?" I call shakily, my eyes still closed. I can feel Rick's warm breath on my cheek.

"The cartoon is over. Can I watch another?"

"Maybe, hang on a minute, sweetie." I exhale slowly and open my eyes, looking up into Rick's face. Rick is still pressed against me, one hand wound in my hair and the other grasping my hip. He studies me for a second, then slowly pushes off and steps back, watching me cautiously. Cool air circles between us, making me miss his presence.

"Did you do that to prove a point?" he whispers hoarsely. "Or because you wanted to?"

I swallow hard. "Both, Rick."

"Mummy!"

I reach out and take his hand. "Shall we watch a cartoon?" We sit and watch cartoons for a while, drinking our coffee. I can't concentrate. I keep thinking about my life with Jon, and Rick and that kiss we just shared. I don't regret it, but I do feel guilty. I feel like I'm betraying both of them. I am betraying Jon for kissing someone else like that, and I am betraying Rick for feeling betrayed about Jon.

April perches herself on Rick's lap as soon as we're sitting down. As the cartoon ends, she says loudly, "I need the loo," and jumps up.

"Go through the kitchen door and it's immediately right," Rick tells her. April yells thanks and runs off. She is old enough to do most of that by herself.

"The word loo is a strange one," Rick comments. "Very British."

"Yeah, it is," I murmur, not really listening.

"You okay?" I glance at Rick to see him looking at me in concern.

I smile a bit. "Yep. Just thinking."

Rick's face becomes even more concerned. "Do I want to ask?"

"Probably not." I reposition myself on the sofa, tucking my legs under me. Rick lifts his arm and places it around my shoulders so I can lean on him. We sit like that for a few minutes, the back of my head on Rick's shoulder, his hand on my arm stroking it very softly. It's nice to sit like this. To feel his warmth so close to me.

"Is it me or does April sound American sometimes?" I'm glad Rick has changed the subject.

I smile. "I notice it depends who she talks to. To me, or when we speak to my family, it's a British accent. To anyone with your accent, it's American." I shrug. "I guess it's only natural she'll pick it up. She's in kindergarten all day with kids who speak like you do."

I feel Rick silently nod. Then he sighs. "Do you regret kissing me earlier, Emma?"

Slowly, I turn on the sofa so I'm looking straight at him. He keeps his arm where it is, placing his hand on my back.

"No," I reply honestly after a moment. I feel him relax next to me. "I just…" I hesitate, trying to put a sentence together "…I just need to work out a few things in my head, that's all."

Rick studies me, his eyes intense. "I guess I do too, about a lot of things. But not about this." He gently caresses my face. "This just feels right." He moves his thumb over my lower lip softly, the sensation sending butterflies to my belly. "Being here with you is the only thing that feels right at the moment, which is probably a crazy thing to say because we've known each other less than two weeks… but…" He shrugs and moves his hand away. "But I want to be honest with you."

I want so badly to comfort him, to reassure him, but caution makes me swallow hard and say instead, "Just give me some time, okay?"

Rick looks like he is going to say something else when April runs back into the room. I slowly move so I'm sitting upright as April jumps onto Rick's lap. Rick catches her and positions her across his thighs so she faces me.

"I want to watch another." April's demand is directed at Rick, but I see her glance at me.

I eye my daughter. "We've already watched three. Don't you think that's enough?"

April turns her innocent face to Rick. "Rick, do you want to watch another one? I will watch with you if you do."

"I think I've had enough of cartoons for today." Rick smiles widely at her as she pulls a face.

There is a loud knock on the front door which makes us all jump. Before we can even move, the door bursts open.

"Rickie? Are you here?" A cheerful older blonde woman strides into the living room. She pauses, then her mouth opens in shock to see April on Rick's lap. Her gaze darts to me and her mouth curves into a smile. "I'm sorry, I didn't realise you had company."

Rick rolls his eyes. "Thanks for knocking, Jess." He moves April slowly onto the sofa and stands, moving round the furniture towards the woman.

"Emma, this is my sister Jessica Fletcher. Jess, this is my… friend Emma Clemens and her daughter, April."

Jessica strides up to the back of the sofa, her hand outstretched. "Lovely to meet you, Emma."

"And you, Jessica."

"Ah, call me Jess. It's much nicer." She looks down at April. "Hello, April. Lovely to meet you. My daughter's here too. She's a tad older than you are, and currently listening to her iPod in the car. It's blasphemy to stop mid-song apparently." Jessica shrugs then turns to her brother.

Rick leans down and captures Jessica in a big hug. The woman is even taller than I am, but Rick still dwarfs her. The hug is long; I can see Rick burying his face in his sister's hair. As they part, I smile. The resemblance between brother and sister is startling. Both with bright blonde hair, light hazel eyes and similar features.

"Uncle Rick!" A short blonde girl wearing bright purple leggings and a red dress pushes past her mother and captures Rick around the waist with so much force that he has to take a step back to keep his balance.

"Hey, munchkin." Rick returns the hug and kisses the top of her head. "Looking good as always. Is that a new dress?"

Rick's niece looks up at him and grins. "Yes! Mom bought it for me last week." Her eyes land on me and they widen. "Uncle Rick, is that your girlfriend?"

Rick meets my eyes for a second, awkwardness filling them, then he glances back down. "This is Emma, honey, my friend.

Emma, this is my favourite niece, Jordan."

"Hi, Jordan," I respond with a smile. I'm still sitting on the sofa. I don't want to intrude. "This is my daughter, April." April is standing on the sofa watching everything with wide eyes; my hand is resting on her back. "Say hello, sweetheart."

"Hello," April says in her little voice.

"What are you doing here, Jess?" Rick asks as Jordan finally lets him go.

"Seth called me." Jessica looks annoyed as Rick mutters under his breath. "Why didn't you, Rick?"

Rick hesitates and Jessica nods towards the kitchen. "Let's go."

As the siblings move off, Jordan stands awkwardly in front of us.

"So," I say to her, "do you live nearby?"

"In Marieta," Jordan replies, watching me carefully. That's a suburb of Atlanta on the other side of the city. April starts to climb off the sofa and I watch her out of the corner of my eye.

"Ah, that's not too far away."

Jordan looks at me for a moment then bursts out, "You talk funny. Where are you from?"

I smile. "The UK."

Jordan's eyes widen. "Like England? Where the Queen lives?"

"Yes, that right."

"Cool. I want to go to London next year. There's a school trip, but Mum says I'm too young." I choose not to comment on that.

"Well, London is a good place to visit. But there are tons of other places in England you would enjoy."

Jordan gives me a look which says she wouldn't be happy anywhere but London. "Are you from London? You sound posh. Isn't London posh?"

"Some parts are posh, and, no, I'm not from there, but I've

visited."

Jordan opens her mouth to ask another question when April tugs on her hand. Jordan looks down in surprise. "Are there any toys?" April asks her.

Jordan looks confused. "Toys?"

April nods, her eyes wide. "I want to play with toys."

Jordan looks thoughtful then smiles. With a sly glance at me, she heads towards a cabinet on the far side of the room. April follows, her hand still clasping Jordan's finger. I watch as Jordan opens a bottom cupboard and removes a cardboard box. Then she upends it all over the nearby rug. A wide selection of trains, cars and building blocks scatter over the floor. She smiles at my questioning glance. "We stay here sometimes. Uncle Rick kept this from when we were little. It's all boys' stuff but it's still fun."

April takes Jordan's hand and drags her down. "Play with me." Jordan looks surprised again, then shrugs and sits cross-legged on the floor next to April.

I watch them play, my arms crossed on the back of the sofa with my chin resting on it. After a few minutes, I become aware of the voices from the kitchen.

"...why didn't you tell me, Rick? Why didn't you call?" Jessica sounds pissed off.

"What would you have done, Jessica? It was the middle of the night."

"Come over."

"That's why I didn't call. I don't need to be mothered."

"Are you kidding me?" Jessica's voice is low and threatening.

I hear Rick sigh. "Sorry, I didn't mean that."

"Yes, you did, that's why you said it." There's a pause, then Jessica continues in a hurt voice. "You're my baby brother, Rick. If you're in pain, I want to help." I feel a stab of guilt for listening in on their conversation, but I can't tear myself away.

"What I need is a new head," Rick says bitterly. "What I'm

getting is shrinks and pity looks, followed by not being able to do my job." Rick's words before our kiss come back to me. He is a US Army Ranger. That's what these guys all are. I don't really know what that is, but it sounds like Special Forces, like the British SAS. It sounds dangerous.

"Isn't that for the best, though? Jeez, Rick, you thought you were back there—"

"I know." Rick cuts her off harshly, then more softly. "I know. It's just hard. I feel so weird, not like myself at all. I'm off the active list, Jess. It's on my record, I may never be able to serve again. What am I going to do? What if this doesn't go away?"

"We'll deal with it, together. Like we always have." Jessica's voice is strong and confident. "There are other jobs you can do with your skill set and experience." I admire her resilience. I can see where Rick gets a lot of his strength from.

"I've been in the military for sixteen years," Rick says. His voice is quiet and sad. "I don't know how to do anything else."

"You'll learn, you'll adapt," Jessica replies confidently, then more slyly. "Maybe you can finally have a life outside the army."

Rick doesn't say anything for a moment. "Maybe." I hear the coffee brewer start.

"What about Emma? Is she really just a friend?" I find myself straining, waiting for the answer.

"It's complicated."

"Is it worth it? The complication? Given what's going on with you?"

After a pause, Rick replies. "Yes."

My heart is pounding in my chest. The confidence and utter certainty in his voice scare me. What am I doing? Eavesdropping on this private conversation, interfering in a family I know nothing about and am not part of. Do I want to be part of it? My chest constricts in mild panic as my thoughts race.

I look at my watch. I have a call with Janine this afternoon.

She has a new Welsh boyfriend that I need to hear the details about, among other things. It's a good excuse to leave.

Rick and Jessica continue talking as I hear cupboards open and mugs placed on counters. I stand up quietly and grab my bag.

"April," I call softly. She looks up at me from the floor. "We need to go now, it's almost lunchtime and Mummy has a call with Janine today."

Her little face falls. "Can we stay just a little longer? Please, Mummy."

"No, sweetheart, we need to go now."

"You're leaving?" Rick's voice makes me jump. He has emerged from the kitchen with his hands in his pockets and is staring at me. I can see disappointment in his eyes, and that's the last thing I want to do to him, but I'm feeling very awkward about being here.

I smile at him. "Yes, it's almost lunchtime so we should get home."

"You should stay here for lunch." Jessica steps around her brother. "I brought food already."

I smile at her kindly. "That's a very nice offer, but I don't want to intrude. Thank you, though."

"You won't be intruding," Rick says quickly.

"I think we are. Besides, I have a friend in the UK I need to call this afternoon. April, let's go."

April looks sad but stands up without argument from her seat on the floor. Jordan watches us all with interest.

"Thanks for the coffee, Rick, and the cartoons," I say as I turn to leave. "It was lovely to meet you, Jess, and you, Jordan."

"I'll walk you out," Rick murmurs, following us out of the door.

April takes his hand as we walk down the steps towards the car. "Rick, will you come to my birthday party?"

"When is your birthday party, April?"

"My birthday is on the 3rd of September," April says. "It's a Saturday. I will be five years old." She stretches out her palm to him to show him all five fingers. "Mummy says I can have a birthday party."

"You know, my birthday is in September too," Rick replies, and April makes an excited noise. I reach the car and turn, worried about how Rick will answer my daughter's question. "But I'm not sure if I can come to your party, April," Rick replies reluctantly.

"Oh, please come, Rick," April begs. "Please come to my birthday party."

Rick kneels down in front of her, taking her shoulders. "I will try, but I can't promise."

April seems to accept this as a good answer as she walks into him and hugs his neck. "Okay, Rick. Bye. I hope you feel better after cuddles and cartoons."

"I do. Thanks, April." He stands and holds the car door open as I help April into her seat, then softly closes the door.

"I'm glad you're feeling better," I say to him, turning away from the car.

Rick smiles, and without a word gathers me into a tight hug. I wrap my arms around his waist and hold on. "I wish I could make you feel better too," he whispers into my ear, his breath tickling my skin.

"You do, Rick," I reply into his neck. "I'm just not sure what to do with that right now."

Rick lets me go and places a soft kiss on my cheek. "I'll call you, okay?"

"Sure." I move away from him and slide into the driver's seat. As I pull away, I glance into the rear view mirror. Rick is still standing there, watching until we turn the corner out of his street.

*

Over the next few weeks, we see Rick quite a few times. April and I go with him to an 'all-American' baseball game, to a barbeque with Jessica and her family, and to a Sunday afternoon picnic with his friends. Rick keeps his distance from me, with only minimal flirting. It's always both April and myself he invites. There is no mention of a date, or of anything other than a friendly peck on the cheek. I appreciate his restraint, especially as I begin to be concerned that April is getting too attached to Rick. How would April react if he was no longer around? Rick is so good with her, and April clearly adores him. I don't want her to be hurt because of me.

Rick has been seeing the military therapists almost every day. I notice a difference in him; he is more relaxed, especially in crowds and noisy environments. He has started talking about some of the things he has seen, about his tours in the Middle East, about his friend Paulo Vega. Rick is understandably anxious about his future. He isn't sure if he will ever be able to serve his country again.

There are so many conflicting thoughts in my head which I'm trying to figure out as I head to a pool party at Mat and Mari's house. When we arrive, Rick is already in the pool with Seth, Mat, Frank, a few other guys and an assortment of kids. April runs straight to the pool and I make sure Rick is fine with her there before I move to chat with Shanna, Mari and a few other girlfriends on the deck. As we talk over a pitcher of lemonade, my gaze keeps going to the pool, and not just to keep an eye on April. As Rick moves around in the water, playing with April and the other kids, I see his naked upper body for the first time. Defined muscles and hard abs, a few other tattoos I find I want to take a closer look at. All wet and glistening. The sight makes me want and think things I haven't in a long time. The other men are all very attractive too, but it's Rick who captures my attention and I can't help but stare. At one point, he looks over at me and catches my eye. I quickly shutter my facial expression and look away, but his suggestive grin tells me I wasn't fast enough.

I'd searched online and read about US Army Rangers. As I glanced around at the men in the pool, I had a new-found respect for them all. These were strong, tough men, the best of the best. To see them playing with their kids like this, loving their wives and partners, laughing and smiling together, was very powerful, especially as I knew they'd just come back from overseas a few days earlier. But I kept these thoughts to myself and chatted casually with the women.

"Ladies, are you going to sit up there all day?" Seth calls out to us after a while. "The water's great and these kids are hard work."

He captures his three-year-old son under the arms and lifts him over his head as the boy yells in excitement, "Come and join in the fun."

"I'm game." Mari, her belly even larger than the last time I saw her, slowly manoeuvres out of the chair and waddles over to the pool entrance. She flicks away her husband's help and slides into the water, a look of relief passing over her face. I wouldn't want to be pregnant in this heat either.

Shanna and I share a look then shrug and nod. We remove our dresses and walk quickly to the pool steps. As I descend the steps, I look up and spot Rick's face, the only part of him visible above the water. He is staring at me with an undisguised look on his features and I get an excited flutter deep in my belly. He watches me closely as I wade into the pool, desire burning in his eyes.

"Mummy, you came in!" April splashes up to me. The water comes up to her shoulders in the middle of the pool. I can easily stand but am enjoying the coolness of being submerged. "Rick has been throwing me around. I bet he'll do that to you too. It's so much fun."

I laugh as I swim closer to her. "I'm good, thanks, sweetheart. I'm just going to… ahhhh…"

I feel large hands grab my waist and lift me. I have a second to realise it's Rick before he throws me across the pool towards the deep end. I land with an undignified splash and submerge under the water. The deep end isn't actually much taller than me, so I easily kick off the bottom. As I surface, I flick my hair from my face and throw a glare his way. April and Rick are laughing really hard.

"Oh, I'm glad you found that so funny," I say to them in mock annoyance. A look of concern crosses Rick's face before I throw a wink at him, letting him know I'm not really annoyed. He grins like a schoolboy as he swims up to me, slicking his wet hair back off his face. I see April move to join the other kids and parents in the shallow end.

"If only I could throw you like that," I say to him. "Then you'd get a taste of your own medicine."

Rick snorts. "Good luck with that."

I narrow my eyes and glare at him, then suddenly change position so my feet are facing him, and kick at the surface. He splutters as water covers his face, then in a smooth move grabs my ankles and swiftly pulls me towards him. Before I can react, he has wrapped my legs around his waist, and my ankles lock at his back, my heels against his skin. I can barely breathe as I float with my head just above the surface.

"I like your bikini," he mutters softly as heat burns in his eyes. His hands are on my lower legs under the water. They aren't moving, just loosely holding me in place, but this still feels so intimate.

"Thanks. I like your… swimming shorts." Not that I've seen them at all, but I can feel the waistband on my calves. It seems the safest thing to say. I glance towards the shallow end, where April is playing with the other kids and Seth. No one is paying us any attention.

Rick's gaze studies my face and he moves in closer. "Emma..." he says quietly "...I need you to know something, and I'm sorry if it makes things hard for you." I tilt my head questioningly at him, trying not to think about just how close we are under the water, and he continues. "My life has always been pretty dark and lonely, and I've been okay with that, I had accepted it. But since I met you... there's been a light and a hope that I've never had before." He meets my gaze head-on, his chin resting on the water. "Spending time with you and April..." he pauses "...has been so amazing, I never realised I was missing anything before. Now I can see that I was." He hesitates again, glancing around to make sure no one is nearby. He whispers huskily, "If we start something together, I know it will be amazing... and it will be forever. If you're worried about April getting attached to me, well, I'm pretty attached to her already." I swallow hard, my heart pounding. I can hardly believe he is saying these things to me. Rick studies me, a serious look on his face. "But I'm not sure how long I can be this close to you and not be kissing you senseless."

My breath catches in my throat at his words. I don't know how to reply. "Rick..."

"I don't expect an answer." Rick releases my legs, pushes himself away and floats backwards. "I just wanted you to know." Keeping his eyes on me, he swims towards the shallow end.

The choice is mine. Now what do I do about it?

*

I invite Rick over for dinner on Friday night. We had texted briefly during the week but hadn't seen each other since the pool last Sunday. My thoughts are still in turmoil. I'd had a long discussion with Amie, which had helped me think about a lot of things. I think I knew what I was going to do, and I was still filled with indecision, but I wasn't being fair to anyone, and I knew I had to do something about it. This evening I would, somehow.

It was around 6pm when the doorbell rang. April knew Rick was coming to dinner and was super excited. She bounded up from where she had been playing with her dolls and ran to the door. I heard it open as I put down the dishcloth.

"Hi, Rick!"

"Good evening, April." Rick's voice drifts through the door, and my belly clenches in anticipation at the sound of his voice. I peer around the door as Rick kneels in front of April. "These are for you and your mom." Rick holds out a small bunch of red roses.

"Roses," April breathes, taking the flowers delicately. She peers back at me. "Mummy, Rick gave us roses, they're so pretty."

"They are beautiful," I agree with a smile. "Thank you, Rick."

"Yeah, thanks," April repeats. She is staring at the roses like she has never seen them before.

"Sweetie, why don't you find that plastic vase that you keep the Smarties lids in? That'll be perfect."

April smiles widely and runs off into the house. I smile and turn to Rick, who is still standing on the porch. He is wearing a black shirt and dark blue jeans, his blond hair falling over his forehead and curling around the collar of his shirt.

"For us, I bring beer." Rick holds up a six-pack of bottled American ale and grins at me. "The good stuff, of course."

I laugh. "Looks great. Come on in."

As Rick passes, he leans in and brushes a kiss across my cheek. That spicy masculine scent of his fills my nostrils and makes my stomach flutter in excitement. I quickly turn towards the kitchen. "It's good to see you," he says quietly to my back as he takes his shoes off. "I was worried I had scared you off with my confession last Sunday."

"It's good to see you too," I reply as I grab the dishcloth again and turn to him, intentionally not addressing his other words. I'm not ready for that conversation yet. "How have you been this week?"

Rick studies me for a moment then shrugs as he places the beer on the kitchen table. "I spend all day talking to shrinks about how I feel, what I think. It gets boring."

"Is it helping, though?"

Rick grabs a bottle of beer. "Well, I don't feel that carnivals are war zones anymore." He hands me an open bottle. "And I'm sleeping again. No more nightmares." He sends me a look. "Now I dream about other things."

I grin and say in a teasing voice, "Reruns of *Tom and Jerry?*"

Rick chuckles, and his eyes sparkle. "Nope, definitely not that PG." I could guess exactly what he dreams about, because I was dreaming about it too.

He takes a swig of his beer. Instead of answering, I gesture with my head towards the living room. "Why don't you go and play with April for a bit? She's been very excited about tonight. Dinner will be another fifteen minutes."

"Cool." Rick turns and heads out of the kitchen.

A few minutes later, I peer out to see what is going on. It is suspiciously quiet; all I can hear is the soft background music of Dire Straits' *Romeo and Juliet* from the speakers. The living and dining room are open-plan at the back of the house, with large patio doors which swing out onto the back porch. There are two red sofas, one next to the window and one to its left, which separate the dining and living area. The TV sits on the wall opposite this sofa. Between the sofas and the TV is April's play area. It is always messy and covered with toys. I had long ago stopped tidying up after her in that area, and she knew to keep her toys there.

A low pine table sits next to the window. I have placed lots of family photographs on it, and April and I often sit on the floor and go through the family members. I feel it is important she knows her family, given we are so far away. There is a picture of my parents and Jason, Jon's parents and his brother, Amie, Mike and their kids. All in various poses or action shots, sometimes with us and sometimes not. In the middle of the table in prime position are two photographs. One is of Jon and myself during our long stay in Thailand. We're sitting on the sand in front of the bar. I'm in a bikini and my long hair is drawn over one shoulder. Jon is behind me with his legs either side, and his arm around my waist. We are both holding a beer and laughing at something Stefan said as he took the picture. We look so very young, carefree and happy, which is what it reminds me of and why it is one of my favourites. The other photo is of the three of us, taken by Jason when April was less than two years old. Jon and I are on our backs on the grass in our back garden grinning up at the camera. April is spread out over both of us, her head on Jon's chest, her feet on my stomach, a wide grin on her face. It's one of those rare family pictures where she is looking at the camera.

I see that April is taking Rick through the family members. He sits cross-legged in front, attentive to her. April stands to the side and is pointing. I watch with a smile, leaning on the door frame.

"This is mummy with my daddy and this is me when I was littlier." She pauses. "My daddy had an accident and he couldn't come home. Mummy says he loved me very much and that I should remember him always." She points at the family photo and Rick leans forward to study it. Then she leans over and takes something off the table. It's Jon's and my wedding rings on the silver chain. Last week, April and I placed it over the family photos. I realised I hadn't been wearing the necklace very much, and rather than keep it on my dresser, I want April to know what they are. April holds up the chains with the rings on it.

"Talking about daddy makes mummy sad. Mummy only used to smile with me but now she smiles with you too." April hands the necklace to Rick, who takes it carefully. He studies the rings for a moment. I can't see his face from this angle. "Do you know what they mean?"

"Yes," Rick replies quietly, studying Jon's ring. It's an interesting sight, seeing Rick holding in his hand what Jon used to wear on his finger. "It means your mummy and daddy loved each other very much." He slowly places the necklace back on the table, then turns to April. "That is something to always remember, April, no matter how you feel. Your parents loved each other and you."

April smiles widely at him, then she spots me over Rick's shoulder and waves. "Mummy, I'm showing Rick the photgrafs."

Rick turns slowly and meets my eyes. His expression isn't awkward, or filled with pity, but with understanding and... something else which I don't want to think about right now.

I clear my throat so my voice isn't shaky. "That's lovely, sweetheart. It's almost dinner. Time to wash up."

"Yay!" April bounds towards the downstairs bathroom under the stairs. "Mummy has made s'getti cabonra, it's my favourite."

Rick swings me a questioning look as he gets up off the floor. "Spaghetti carbonara," I translate with a smile, turning and heading back into the kitchen.

We all make small talk over dinner. Rick tells us about growing up in New York State, and about his other two sisters and their various kids. April is sitting in her booster seat at the table; I always try and eat my dinner with her. Sometimes it means she goes to bed a little later than a four-year-old should, but she almost always sleeps through the night now so I take that as a bonus.

Rick seems to really enjoy his spaghetti, having a second helping while April watches in amazement. I bring out flapjacks for dessert, and Rick teases me about baking.

"Mummy, can I go play now?"

I eye April. She has only eaten half her flapjack but has almost emptied her pasta plate. "Are you finished?" I ask her. April nods vigorously then uses her napkin to wipe her face clean. "Go on then." April slides from her seat and runs to where she had left her dolls earlier, sitting heavily on the rug and mumbling to herself.

Rick grins at me. "Leaving dessert? What kind of four-year-old is she?"

I laugh and pop the flapjack she had left in my mouth. "She really loves carbonara." I stand and begin to clear the table. Rick stands too and grabs the leftover pasta bowl. As I head into the kitchen, I hear April say something loudly to her dolls, and I smile to myself.

Rick pauses outside the kitchen and stares back at her, then follows me to the sink. "Was that... French?" he asks slowly.

I take the bowl from him and smile. "Yep, she is telling her dolls off for being naughty."

Rick looks puzzled as he moves plates into the dishwasher, leaning over to grab a dirty plate. "I didn't realise they taught French to four-year-olds in school nowadays."

I shake my head and turn on the water. "They don't. Jon was teaching it to her. He used to read her books in French and they talked in it together a little. She only does it very occasionally now."

I feel Rick pause next to me. After a second, I glance at him. He is staring.

"What?" I ask.

Rick stands and closes the dishwasher, leaning on the counter next to me. "That's the first time you've ever said his name to me."

I stare right back at him. "It is?"

Rick nods. "Yes." He has an unreadable expression on his face, and his eyes study me closely.

I sigh and turn back to the sink, turning off the water and looking out of the window. "His name was Jon Alfred Lucian Clemens. His mother was French, his father English. He grew up in France, moving to the UK to go to Birmingham University to study law. That's where I met him. I was twenty-two and he was twenty-three. It was so quick and easy how we got together, so relaxed. After we graduated, we travelled for a year, to Asia and Australia, then around Europe. When we got back, we got jobs, eventually buying a house and moving to Salisbury. We got married in 2011 and April was born less than a year later. I'd fallen in love with him so quickly, I was so happy with him. When he died, I wished I had died too. I couldn't see how I could live without him, and I didn't want to. April was the only reason I carried on, feeling empty and alone in the world but knowing that was how I had to live. I couldn't stand to be over there anymore, so I ran halfway across the world to try and get away from the hole inside me, but it only got deeper and deeper until all I had was a chasm in my chest." I finally pause and take a breath. It feels like a great weight has been lifted off me. I shake my head and smile to myself. "Then I threw eggs over a man in a supermarket on one of the darkest days of my life and suddenly everything changed. The ache started to go away, the chasm closing. I still miss Jon, but it's somehow bearable now. I can see myself living again, even being happy again." I shift my gaze from the window, whispering, "You did that." I meet Rick's beautiful eyes and they blaze at me. I turn towards him and smile. "Jon would have liked you."

"Oh yeah?" Rick's voice is rough.

"Yeah. You have similar temperaments, a similar sense of humour, a smutty mind you're not afraid to share." Rick chuckles.

"He would have liked what you did, helping and protecting people, putting others first. How you care for April, he would have really liked that." I swallow hard and mutter, "Jon would be so pissed at me, you know."

"Why?"

"Because I've been a coward. I ran away and I haven't been living my life since the night he died. I haven't been happy for such a long time. Jon always said that was the most important thing in life, to be happy, to enjoy life. To move on from the past and embrace the future. That's what he would want for me." I feel a tear slip from my eye and run down my face. In an instant, Rick has wiped it away, his thumb gently brushing over my skin.

"Are you saying what I think you're saying?" Rick's voice cracks just a little. I nod, but I'm not looking at him. Rick cups my face with both hands, gently but urgently tilting my face to his. "If I tell you I love you, will you run away again?" I laugh quietly and shake my head, not trusting myself to speak as I place my hands on his waist. "I love you, Emma," he whispers hoarsely, then leans down and kisses me softly. After a few seconds, he pulls back and wipes my remaining tears away with his thumbs.

"Mummy, are you okay?" April's small voice comes from next to us. We both glance down at the same time. April looks worried.

I smile. "Yes, sweetheart, I'm fine." I look up at Rick. "I'm really fine."

I release Rick's waist and bend down to pick her up so she can see for herself. Rick wraps his arms around us both, pulling us into him. We stand there for a moment until April wriggles slightly.

"Mummy?" she says, in a hesitant voice I recognise. She is about to ask something she's not sure I will agree to.

"Yes, April?" Rick still has his hand on my back, and I lean into his side.

"Instead of a bath tonight, can I watch a cartoon with Rick?"

I control my laughter and look at her closely. "Well, do you smell?"

April lifts her arms up and sniffs. Rick can't control his laughter and looks away, covering his mouth with his hand. April puts her arms down and shakes her head seriously.

"Are you sure?" I sniff her as she nods. All I smell is April.

"Rick, what do you say? Are you up for some more *Tom and Jerry*?"

Rick considers it. "Well, personally, I'm a big fan of bathtime." He shoots me a cheeky look and I grin. "But yes, I would love to watch a cartoon with you." April claps her hands in excitement.

"Okay, first, go and change into your pyjamas and brush your teeth." I set April down on the floor and she runs off.

As soon as I hear her reach the landing upstairs, I turn towards Rick. In an instant, he is kissing me, hard and passionately. I kiss him back with the same intensity and desire, pouring all my emotions and wants into him until all I can think and feel is Rick. I find bare warm skin under his shirt and feel every inch I can touch, pulling him closer to me. He curls one hand into my hair and holds me to him. The fingers of his other hand travel from my face down my neck, over my breasts and to my belly, making a shiver of pleasure dance along my spine.

I hear April run back down the stairs and I pull away, panting hard. Rick grins at me, equally out of breath, then swivels towards the sink as April comes back in, dressed in cute blue bunny pyjamas and carrying her favourite soft toy, a bright green T-Rex, a gift from her Uncle Jason many years ago.

"Right, let's set up your cartoon," I say, catching my breath, as I lead April out of the kitchen so Rick can compose himself.

I swipe toys off the sofa so they can sit together and set up the DVD. April looks excited, but I can tell she is also sleepy. I wonder how long she will last, and a part of me hopes not very long.

Rick comes in after a few minutes and shoots me a look which tells me he is thinking the same thing. April makes an excited noise as she settles on Rick's lap, cuddling her T-Rex.

"I'm going to finish clearing up," I say with a smile. "Enjoy."

Once the kitchen is clean, I head back in. The cartoon is still playing and Rick is watching it, but I can see April has fallen asleep. Her head leans on Rick's chest; her long hair is fanned over his shirt and her legs are curled into him. They look so very cute together that I just stand there for a moment watching them. Rick notices me and smiles. Quietly, I turn off the TV as Rick scoops April into his arms, her head flopping against his shoulder. We head up the stairs and tuck April into bed, her T-Rex right there with her. Rick is so tender with her, I feel my heart expand in a way I never thought possible again.

I close her door softly behind me and take Rick's hand. Silently, I lead the way to my bedroom.

Once inside, Rick pulls me into his arms and hugs me. "I can make you happy," he whispers. "I promise to spend every day making you happy." I smile against his neck. Then he pulls back and shoots me a cheeky grin filled with heat and promise. "Starting now, in the best way."

I shoot a grin back; no way I can resist anything to do with this man. "Oh yeah? Sure about that, are we?"

Rick starts nuzzling my neck, kissing and nipping me lightly. "As sure as I was that you'd agree to those drinks with me after assaulting me with the eggs."

"If I recall, you blackmailed me."

Rick chuckles and kisses me deeply and thoroughly, his hands exploring under my clothes as he mumbles against my lips. "It still worked."

I'm not really interested in talking anymore, but I manage to smile and murmur, "Cocky American..."

*

A month later, Amie, Mike, Addie, Josh and James fly over from the UK to visit us. I'm super excited. Though I talk to Amie all the time, on the phone and on Skype, I haven't seen them in person in almost two years. They'll be staying with me for a week, then driving down to Florida to explore the theme parks and beaches. I'm also excited that they will be meeting Rick. The last month has been so amazing; I haven't felt this alive for a long time. Rick makes me feel special and adored. I really love him. It's a different love than what I felt for Jon; it's hard to explain why. I just know I will always love Jon in one way, and I love Rick in another.

It's doubtful Rick will ever serve on active duty overseas again, and he has admitted that actually that's okay. He is currently a temporary instructor at the training base, which means he works almost regular hours.

Amie texts me, telling me they have landed and bundled into their hire car, and I call April and Rick outside to the front to wait for them. They both seem apprehensive. Even though April has always been included on my calls to them, she doesn't remember them herself. She was too little the last time we saw them. I think Rick is anxious because it's the first of my family he has ever met.

I sit on the strip of grass and watch as April climbs all over Rick. She loves that he is so strong and can lift and throw her around. I love watching them do that. It reminds me of how Jon used to do the same when she was smaller. I don't feel that deep ache when I think of him anymore. I can remember Jon and smile.

After about twenty minutes, a large hire car pulls up outside the house. I jump to my feet and hurry over as I spot Amie in the passenger seat. A back door opens and a whirl of bright colour runs towards me.

"Auntie Emmy!" Addie yells as she sprints towards me. I feel a rush of pleasure that she is so excited to see me. I grab her under the arms and swing her round in a big hug, quickly putting her down again, as she is surprisingly heavy. Addie is nine now, almost ten.

"Wow, you're so tall," I exclaim. "You're almost like a grown-up."

Addie laughs but wrinkles her pale nose at me. "I'm only nine."

"Nine going on twenty," Amie says as she approaches. I grin and throw my arms around her, hugging her for a long time. It's so unbelievably good to see her.

Rick, holding April in his arms, approaches cautiously. "Hi. I'm Rick," he says. "You must be Amie."

Amie smiles and shakes his hand. "I've heard so many good things about you, Rick. It's so great to finally meet you."

Rick smiles and puts April down so her aunt can talk to her. April is suddenly surprisingly shy and buries her nose in Rick's shorts.

"April." I kneel before her and take her hand. Amie crouches too. "This is your Auntie Amie, and your cousin Addie. We used to all play together when we lived in England."

April moves closer to me and studies Amie in detail. "You look like my daddy," she says quietly. "Like in the photos."

Amie nods and smiles sadly. "Your daddy was my little brother, April." April pauses, then slowly she moves to Amie and gives her a cuddle. Amie looks like she might cry, so I stand up to give her a moment.

Mike chooses that time to appear, with Josh and James in tow.

"Little sis." Mike wraps me in a big hug. He always used to call me that. "It's been too long."

I smile into his neck then draw back. "It has."

"Mike, this is Rick. Rick, Amie's husband, Mike."

Mike is tall, but Rick is of course even taller. Mike shakes his hand and chuckles. "Wow, talk about making a guy feel insecure, mate." He shoots me a glance and we all laugh.

"Hey, boys," I say to Josh and James, who are hiding behind their dad's legs. They are seven, and they look at me with interest, and up at Rick with pure fascination. They probably only remember me a little. "I'm your Auntie Emma. Do you remember me at all?"

All I get is little giggles so I just smile at them. "Right, tea, coffee, beer?"

"Yes, please," Amie replies, holding April's hand as she is dragged inside. "I brought some proper tea from home just to make sure."

Rick winds his arm around my back as we walk inside, kissing the top of my head. "All okay?"

I look up at him and nod. "All okay."

Seeing my UK family with Rick was the final moment of closure for me. After that, life was fantastic. Rick and I bought a house in Atlanta and we all moved in together. I was promoted at work, and Rick officially retired from active duty and became a full-time army instructor.

On New Year's Eve, Rick proposed. I said yes, and we eloped to Vegas within the month.

Rick officially adopted April just after we were married. The first time April called him Daddy, I cried. When April was seven years old, we gave her a little blond-haired baby brother.

Rick and I called him Alfie.

Chapter 8

Army Part 4

April 2017

Over the next few months, I began to slowly feel like I was living my life again. I did what Trent had suggested, and took on one day at a time. I was getting used to living in the UK again. The massive grocery stores, the right-hand drive cars, the rain.

I spoke to my US friends as often as I could. Their accents and our history together still reminded me of Rick, but I knew I needed to get over that if I wanted to remain friends, which I did.

Jason and Kate, his girlfriend of three years, and my parents visited us over the long Easter bank holiday weekend. We visited parks and gardens, tea shops and pubs. My parents loved being able to spend time with Alfie, and he was getting used to them too, which was lovely to see. Jason had begun to talk a while ago about moving out of London. Jason was still a graphic designer, but he freelanced now, which meant he could work from home. Kate was a psychologist and was looking for work in the area.

They were undecided on whether they would be moving to Salisbury or Winchester, or somewhere in between, and we all discussed it as a family. I realised this was the first family event I had been here for since my grandmother's funeral so many years ago. Alfie loved being the centre of attention of so many adults, especially ones who doted on him so much.

The first anniversary of Rick's death, 22nd of April, passed without ceremony. It was a Saturday. I played with Alfie as normal and I explained to him what the day meant. We looked through photos and I showed him Rick's dog tags, medals and our wedding rings. I'm not sure he understood, but he doesn't look at me with concern when he hears the word Daddy anymore. When Alfie was in bed, I drank wine and spoke to Seth and Vega on Skype. We reminisced about the old days, told stories about Rick and just simply remembered him. Then I called Jess and we had a similar conversation, except this one ended with tears. Jess had decided that the family holiday next year would be to come and tour southern England, so they would be coming to visit us. It was a long way away and I looked forward to it immensely.

Always in my mind were these birthday cards from Rick; I was so anxious to see what he had written. But Jess and Seth had not been able to locate them, though they both assured me there were still so many boxes to go through. I had left a lot of boxes with Jess.

I began to slowly relive our time together, looking through photos of all that had happened, mostly without bursting into tears. The ache was always there, but it was growing less painful with time. I figured I was accepting I had to move on as time passed, even though in my heart I didn't want to.

The best thing was that Jon and I continued our liaisons with success, keeping below everyone's radar. We even had meetings together at work occasionally and were very professional towards each other, though Jon found it amusing to throw in some work-related but potentially dirty sentences to see if I would crack. I never did. We got into a pattern; he would usually come over on Wednesday nights after Alfie had gone to bed, staying until the early hours then leaving. If it wasn't his weekend with Stephy, he would often do the same on Fridays too. We had lunch during the week, usually with other colleagues, but sometimes just the two of us.

We often had playdates on the weekends he had Stephy, usually with a sleepover for the kids, and for us, at one of our houses. Alfie and Stephy loved spending time together and having sleepovers.

I really looked forward to those, not just because of the sex, which was amazing, or the fact I felt less lonely when he was in the house, but because I really enjoyed being with Jon. I was still having the nightmares, but being with Jon seemed to decrease their occurrence. I only occasionally had one so severe that I threw up, though rarely coinciding with our nights together. I was glad we still weren't sleeping in the same bed if we stayed over. If Jon had noticed my nighttime runs to the toilet, he hadn't said anything.

It began to occur to me sometime in mid-May that maybe I was breaking one of our rules; maybe I was starting to have feelings for this man. At first, I dismissed this. How could I when I still loved Rick? Jon and I were just having fun, enjoying each other's company. But when a guy I met asked me out, I found myself saying no, not because of Rick but because of Jon. I heard on the gossip grapevine at work that a woman had asked Jon out, but that he had said no because he was seeing someone. I began to wonder if this rule-breaking was going both ways, but we were both too scared to admit it. Not wanting to break what we had, I kept quiet.

One day at lunch, we were sitting in the deli. It was just the two of us. I had finally persuaded Jon to buy something other than a chicken and bacon wrap.

"See, I told you it was worth it," I tease as I eat my pastrami wrap.

Jon slowly chews his chicken tikka sandwich, then swallows. He shrugs. "It's okay." I send him a look. "The chicken and bacon wrap is still the best."

I roll my eyes at him as he puts down his sandwich. "Em, I have something to ask you."

"Shoot."

"Well, you know next Saturday I said we couldn't have a sleepover because there's this party my ex is throwing and Stephy and I have to be there?"

"Yeah, bet you're really looking forward to that one, huh?"

Jon sighs. "Like a car crash," he replies. "And I know what that is like. Well, do you have anything on that Saturday?"

I pause in my chewing. "Why?"

Jon meets my eyes. "Do you?"

"I don't think so," I say slowly. "Why, Jon?"

"Sarah has requested I bring you along, and Alfie, of course."

My jaw drops. "Requested?"

"Yeah. So, it turns out Stephy has been talking about you, a lot, and, well… Sarah wants to meet you. Her argument is that her daughter is spending a lot of time with a woman she doesn't know and she's not comfortable with that."

I nod, fair enough. "Okay, I can understand that, but can't I just meet her some other time? Why does it have to be at the party?"

Jon scratches his neck and plays with his hair, something he only does when he's nervous. "Actually, Sarah suggested we all go for dinner, but trust me when I say that would be really awkward. The party will be better, there will be lots of other people there for her to bug. She'll probably make some polite conversation, some choice comments, and then forget about you."

"She sounds like a dream," I mutter. Jon smiles. "What kind of party is this?"

"Sarah owns a PR firm. They did really well last year so it's a celebration of that. Plus, a lot of her friends and family will be there. Basically, she is showing off her fabulous life to anyone who cares."

I smile at Jon's ironic tone. "Does Sarah have a fancy boyfriend by any chance?"

Jon glances at me. "Yes. They started going out almost as soon as Sarah and I separated." Jon shrugs as if he doesn't care, but I think he does a little.

"Right, so just so I'm clear," I lean forward and lower my voice, "am I the hot girlfriend you're using to show your ex-wife, her fancy boyfriend and everyone else that you're moving on with your life?"

Jon frowns then leans forward too. "You're not my girlfriend."

I smile at him. "That's my point, Jon. Do you want me to act like it? Or say I'm a friend but imply I'm more? Don't tell me the only reason you are inviting me is because she wants to meet me."

Our faces are inches apart on the table now, both of us leaning over our lunches. Jon's eyes flick to my lips and for just a second I think he's going to kiss me right here in the deli. Instead, a smile curls his mouth and he leans back. "Which do you think would have more of an impact?"

"The 'I'm a friend' but imply I'm more. Then we are only partially lying." I smile widely. "I knew it."

"You're just too smart, Emma, I can't get anything by you." Jon shakes his head then sends me a grin. "Speaking of which, you know it's Wednesday, right?"

"Of course." I swallow the last of my sandwich and smile innocently at him. But I know my eyes are full of promise. "It says it on my calendar."

Jon contains a laugh and glances away, but not before I see the twinkle in his eyes. "And I don't think I have plans this Friday either."

"Well, I think I do." I glance at my watch, hiding my smile. The fact he said that makes me feel warm inside. "I have to get back. I'm due on a site in an hour."

"Yeah, I have a meeting too." Jon smiles and gets up. "Let's go." I wave and nod at a few of my colleagues as we pass the long late-lunch queue.

As we head back to the office, we are silent. Just walking and enjoying each other's company in comfortable silence. We pass a few colleagues, a married couple who are holding hands and nod at them in greeting. I look back over my shoulder at them. It would be nice to be able to do that with Jon and not hide anymore. I frown at myself and push those thoughts aside. As I glance back, I see Jon is watching them too, a wistful expression on his face. He gives me a small smile.

"So, see you later?" he asks just before we get to the building. For some reason, he's hesitant, and his eyes search mine.

I smile at him, then wink as I open the door. "Of course. It's Wednesday."

*

The next Saturday, I drive to Jon's house with Alfie just after lunchtime. After the party, Jon has suggested we come back to his for dinner and a 'sleepover'. That's the word we use for our overnight stays now. Alfie, as always, is super excited to be seeing Jon and Stephy.

As I open the car door and unbuckle his seat, he leaps out of the Audi and flies up the drive towards Jon's house. I see the front door open and hear Jon's voice, so I lean into the car and start grabbing Alfie's and my overnight bags. I pull them out of the boot, stand up and I hear a noise behind me. I glance over to see Jon standing at the end of the drive, staring at me with fire in his eyes.

"Wow…" he mutters. His eyes do a long, slow sweep down, then back up again. The look in his eyes makes my spine tingle and my belly flutter. "You look incredible."

I smile, brushing off the compliment. "You told me to make an effort." I'm wearing a dark red halter neck dress which falls to just above my knee. The dress is stretchy and sits tightly over my boobs and waist, flowing out on my hips. Rick used to love this dress, but I haven't worn it for ages. My hair is long now, down to the middle of my back, and I washed and styled it so it curls in little ringlets. I'm even wearing eyeliner today. Jon is still staring. I glance over at him and do a perusal of my own; he's wearing a very elegant and tailored black suit, a bright blue smart shirt and a white tie. Jon seems to have two styles of dress: either scrappy jeans and a loose t-shirt, or a suit and shirt. He looks really good in suits, even the ones he wears to work, but this one is superb on him. I can't help but remember that Rick used to hate wearing suits, or even his army dress uniform, calling them stuffy and overrated. But he was always on the smarter side of casual, even in jeans.

The difference between the two men pings around my thoughts for a second, until I shake my head and look up to find Jon still staring at me. "Hello." I wave at him. "Earth to Jon, do you read me?"

Jon looks startled. "Uh, yeah, sorry, I just… can't believe how stunning you are."

I shrug. Now I'm embarrassed. I pick up the bags. "Is it too much? This dress is actually quite casual…"

"No, no, not at all." He takes Alfie's bag off my shoulder as we walk towards his house. "No, you are definitely not overdressed. You're just so gorgeous."

I used to be uncomfortable when Rick complimented me over and over. I swat him on the shoulder playfully. "No need to keep complimenting me, Jon. You know you're getting laid tonight." I cringe as soon as the words leave my mouth.

Jon stops mid-stride and stares. "That's not why I am doing it." He tilts his head and frowns. "Is that what you think?"

I turn to him. "No. I'm sorry, that was a horrible thing to say. I'm just not used to being complimented quite so much." I shrug. "Hell, I didn't even own a dress until I was twenty-six, Jon, and the only skirts I wore were formal dress ones. I spent my late teens and early twenties trying to be as unfeminine as possible, I just…" I gesture down at myself "…you said to make an effort and be your fake hot girlfriend, so here I am." I point at my face. "Look, I even wore eyeliner for you, it's been years. I had to look on YouTube for how to apply it, you know."

Jon stares at me for a second, then bursts out laughing. We walk up the rest of the drive. Just before we reach the door, he stops me, leans over and kisses me softly. "You may not be my girlfriend in name," he murmurs against my lips, "but you are not my fake anything." He gives me a look then disappears into the house, leaving me to ponder his words.

The party is in full swing when we arrive. The house looks huge from the outside, with a long sweeping front lawn and gravel drive, a large stone frontage and big open windows.

"This was your house?" I ask in amazement.

Jon grins as he parks his BMW on the road opposite. "No, I'm well off, but not that well off." He leans to look out. "This is Max's house. He's some kind of stockbroker in London. Sarah still lives in our old house, but she pretends to live here. This is where they throw all their parties." He gives me a look. "It's all about the Joneses."

Ah, I get that reference. In the States, I always had to have the cultural references explained to me. Rick used to find it very amusing.

Jon glances at his watch but doesn't make a move to get out of the car. "Sarah will be annoyed we're late…" he mutters, then smirks at me as he fixes his tie. I wonder what kind of woman she is to make Jon act petty like this. While I really didn't want to come here today, I'm very curious about Jon's ex-wife. I find I want to know what makes him tick, and this is another piece of the puzzle.

"Daddy, let's go. I wanna have party," Stephy insists from the back seat. Alfie squirms in his car seat.

"Okay, honey, let's go."

Jon and I unbuckle our respective kids and we all walk towards the house. Stephy clearly knows the house and is trying to run to it, but Jon holds her hand firmly. Alfie walks by my side, his hand tight on my finger, his eyes wide. Jon opens the large front door and waltzes in like he knows the place. "Honey, we're home," he calls with a chuckle. A stunningly pretty blonde woman steps into the hallway from the room at the far end. I assume this is his ex-wife from the look she gives him. She is wearing a sheer white cocktail dress, pearls and stilettos. Everything about her screams money and elegance.

"Jon, you're late."

"But I'm here now, Sarah," he says back. He lets go of Stephy's hand and she runs to her mother. Sarah kneels down and carefully hugs her daughter. Jon puts his hand on the small of my back as we approach up the hallway. "Mummy, this is Alfie and Emma who I've been talking about. They are really great."

Sarah rises slowly. I see her eyes look me up and down, but her facial expression gives nothing away.

I stick out my hand. "Emma Tavern, nice to meet you. I've heard a lot about you from Stephy."

The woman nods and limply shakes my hand. "Sarah Willis. Hello, Emma. Nice to meet you after all this time. Stephy here just can't help but talk about you and your son." She smiles down at Alfie, who has hidden himself behind my legs. It's a genuine friendly smile, I'm pleased to say.

"Alfie and Stephy play really well together," I say pleasantly.

Sarah nods absently and turns to Jon. If I were speaking to a superior officer, I would have been dismissed. Instead, I just smile. No one wearing pearls could ever intimidate me. "Jon, you could at least have dressed Stephy in a party dress."

Jon shrugs. "She chose it, Sarah. Who I am to argue?"

Sarah raises a perfectly manicured eyebrow at him. There is obvious tension between the two of them and I feel Jon's fingers press onto my back. Before Sarah can respond, a dark blond man appears behind her.

"Jon, glad you could make it." He sticks out his hand and Jon shakes it. Their postures imply they don't like each other at all. He must be the boyfriend.

"Max. Thanks for the invite. This is my friend Emma Tavern."

Max looks at me and smiles widely, sticking out his hand. "Nice to meet you, Emma."

I shake it, but he holds it for slightly too long, and his gaze sweeps down me as he looks away to his girlfriend. I suspect he is the kind of man who gets gropey when he has too many drinks.

Stephy is clearly growing bored with the adult conversation.

"Mummy, I want to go in the garden."

I lean down to Alfie. "Alfie, would you like to go with Stephy to the garden?" He nods. "Okay, you stay with Stephy. I'll be out in a minute." Stephy takes Alfie's hand and they run up the hallway to the large lawn I can see out the back.

We head up the hallway and emerge into a huge kitchen, following the kids. I can see lots of people standing around, inside and outside, making polite conversation and drinking. "Can I get you a drink, Emma?" Max offers.

"Do you have beer?" I ask.

"Of course, a wide variety, help yourself." The man gestures towards a large selection on the counter, and I head over. I grab a bottle of beer, and a sparkling water for Jon.

I pour the beer into a glass and glance over at Jon. Sarah is talking rapidly to him, hands waving all over the place. Jon stands with his arms crossed over his chest. He doesn't look impressed. I give him the water and nod I'm going outside. He gives me a look which tells me he really wants to come with me.

I head outside to follow Alfie. He doesn't know the house and I don't want him getting lost.

I can see kids playing on a large climbing frame in the middle of the lawn. As I study it, I see Stephy, then Alfie following her around it. There is a bunch of well-dressed adults standing nearby with drinks in hand; they are simultaneously talking to each other and watching the kids. I go up to the climbing frame and wave.

"Mummy Mummy, look what I can do!" Alfie proudly shows me how he can climb the steps, move on his belly down a narrow tube and then slip face first down the slide.

"Looks like so much fun, sweetie."

Alfie doesn't reply, as he is really involved in his play. I move away and look back at the house, then around to the perfectly manicured gardens. This place screams money, and a pretty poor use of money too. This kind of extravagance makes me think of all the poverty I've seen in the world. It makes me kind of sick. I wonder what Rick would have thought about this.

"Emma King?" I whirl as a familiar voice says my old name. I spot a pretty blonde walking up to me. She has a baby boy on her hip. "Oh my God, it is you, isn't it?"

I blink and try to place her. As I study her face, the name slips into my mind. "Johnson, Irene Johnson?"

"Oh wow. Emma. My word, I can't believe it." Irene awkwardly hugs me; it's not easy with a kid in your arms. "I heard you left the army and moved to the States."

I shrug. "I did, then I came back." I smile. "Irene, it is good to see you. I've been meaning to look you up, see if you're still around here but I haven't..." I trail off, I have no excuse.

Irene shrugs. "Life just gets in the way, doesn't it?" She grins at the little boy.

"Are you still in the army?"

Irene smiles and nods. "Yep, though on maternity leave now." She nods at the boy. "I'm based permanently at the Plain now, senior project engineer." She grins. "That recommendation you gave me really helped. I was going to thank you but I never got the chance."

I shrug. "You earned it. So, married?"

Irene nods. "Yep, to that beautiful man over there. Stan." She turns and smiles at a dark-haired man just behind her, who smiles back widely. "Kept my name, though. This little fella is William. He has a double-barrelled name, the poor thing." Irene looks over at the climbing frame. "You got a kid?"

"Yeah, the blond boy." I point to him. "Alfie."

"Very cute. Married as well?"

"I was married," I reply. Often, it's better just to say it. "He died."

"Oh God." Irene bit her lip. "I'm sorry, Emma."

"You met him, all those years ago," I state with a faint smile. "Remember those US Rangers from the football game?"

Irene looks shocked, then grins. "Tavern, right, the big blond hunk?"

I laugh at her guess. "Yep."

Irene smiles. "I knew you guys had a thing. So you married him, huh? Was he still a Ranger when he..."

"Yeah," I reply, and take a sip of my beer. "Last year." Irene looks at me in sympathy.

"Hey, whatever happened to that other Ranger, Seth? We never did keep in touch."

"He's married now with two kids, living in Atlanta. Still a Ranger."

Irene grins. "Good for him, he was a great guy." Irene had told me the next day that she and Seth had hooked up for the night.

"So, what brings you here then?"

Irene smiles. "I do volunteer work for several charities. It's one of the pro-bono causes the mistress of the house's PR firms works on." Irene rolls her eyes. "If I could be anywhere else, I would be." I was glad to see Irene hadn't lost her sense of humour, or her humility.

I glance back towards the house and see Jon emerge right then. My heart does a little skip as his jacket and tie flutter in the breeze as he walks out, showing off his slender waist and defined physique. I remember a phrase that Irene used to use: 'sex on a stick'. Right now, that describes Jon perfectly. Jon looks agitated and runs a hand through his hair, then his gaze lands on me. His posture relaxes and he starts to head over.

"You, Emma?"

I smile at her and jerk my head back towards Jon. "I'm friends with the mistress of the house's ex-husband." Irene glances over her shoulder and makes an impressed noise in her throat. "Oh, nice one," she replies. "You always did have style, Emma."

I laugh at that. "Let's exchange numbers. I'd love to catch up some other time." I glance over at Alfie. He and Stephy are now playing in the sand under the climbing frame.

"Absolutely." Irene turns to her husband, who eagerly takes the baby. Irene shakes out her arm for a second, a move I can easily relate to, then grabs her phone. We quickly exchange numbers.

Jon silently appears at my side.

"Hey." I smile. "Jon, this is Irene, we knew each other years ago when we worked here at the army base. I honestly can't believe we've just randomly run into each other here of all places."

Jon and Irene politely shake hands. "Small world, huh?" Jon comments. He looks flustered and like he wants to talk to me. Irene seems to notice it too.

"Well, it was lovely to see you again, Emma. I can't believe it either." She throws her arms around me. "Let's get together soon!"

She turns away with a smile and heads back to her husband. I look at Jon. "Are you okay?"

Jon sighs and wipes his hand over his mouth. "Not really, if I had a choice we would leave now. But I gave my word that Stephy would stay until at least 5pm." He glances at his watch. "So, another two hours."

I put my hand on his arm. "Do you want to talk about it?"

Jon shrugs. "Not much to talk about. Sarah is being Sarah, i.e. difficult and highly strung. It's better when we don't spend any time together. Usually, Stephy just runs between the house and the car, so all we have to do is wave and smile politely at each other." Jon shakes his head. "What a mess I have made."

"Hey." I've never heard Jon like this before. "What do you mean?"

"Apart from Stephy," he smiles over at his daughter, who has gathered a few other kids around her, "who I wouldn't change for anything, nothing good has come from my marriage to Sarah, only hurt and annoyance."

I frown. "There must have been good times, Jon."

"Not as many as you would think," Jon says. He sounds miserable. "I haven't done any of the things I wanted to do when I was younger. I haven't really made any sort of difference in the world. It's all been about me me me. If my younger self could see me, he would be so disappointed." I wrap my arms around his waist under his jacket and give him a tight hug. He freezes at first. For obvious reasons, we don't do public affection, but then he hugs me back. We stand there for a few minutes, watching our kids play together.

Stephy looks up, sees her dad and runs over. Jon and I quickly separate.

"Daddy, the girl says there is cake inside. Can I have cake? Pretty please?"

Jon crouches down in front of her. "Sure, but first, I'm feeling a little sad. Can I have a hug to make me feel better?"

Stephy immediately smiles and wraps her little arms around his neck. Jon embraces her tightly for a minute, until Stephy starts to squirm. She pulls away and looks at him in seriousness. "Daddy, are you sad because of Mummy?"

I cringe slightly; that is not a good question to have to answer. But Jon just smiles. "I'm sad for a few reasons, honey, but none of them are to do with you." He pokes her in the belly and she giggles. "Now, cake?" He looks up at me. "Cake?"

"Cake," I agree. "Alfie." I call. My little blond boy looks up from the sand. "Do you want cake?"

Alfie smiles widely and, abandoning whatever it is he was doing, follows us back to the house.

Inside, I meet Sarah's brother, Reggie Willis, who is a police officer with the local force. Jon seems to get on well with him and finally starts to look like he is enjoying himself. Cake in one hand and beer in the other, I follow Alfie as he explores. There must be a few hundred guests at this party, and a good number of kids. The rooms seem endless and always contain lots of people. He finally finds a large room with a huge playmat in the middle of it, covered with lots of toys and kids, and plonks himself down in the middle.

I take a seat on an uncomfortable long chair overlooking the play area and finish my cake, idly chatting to a redheaded woman, Laura, who is sitting next to me, also watching her son play.

Before long, I become aware of a group of men standing behind me, talking loudly. They seem to be discussing everything from politics to foreign affairs to women, and they are doing it in very loud voices. I subtly glance over my shoulder at them, and see the tall blond man who had looked at me with undisguised interest when I had entered the room, following it up with an arrogant smirk, which was not in any way appealing. He is standing with two older gentlemen, all wearing pricey suits and drinking dark beer.

Their voices only seem to get louder, and I note quite a few parents glare over at them. Their opinions are arrogant and condescending on almost all of the topics, full of misinformation I would expect on the front of a trashy newspaper. I try not to listen, instead making small talk with Laura and watching Alfie play, but then their topic moves to something I can't help but listen to.

"... this country sends billions of pounds to countries like that all over the world. Plus, the cost of our military presence... is it really worth it?"

I tamp down my irritation. They are talking about foreign aid and wars against terrorism in the Middle East. It's obviously a subject I know a lot about, but I learnt long ago that everyone has their own opinion and that they simply aren't worth the hassle of correcting.

"Ah, you know I have an interesting fact." I recognise this as the arrogant blond man; he has a particularly irritating voice. "When the men build these schools and stuff, they are only built to last ten years. Why? Because chances are they will get blown up, but also because then there is an excuse for the men and their contractors to go back in and build them again. It's a cycle of spend and buy, spend and buy – it makes the world go round and puts money in our pockets."

I snort with laughter, mostly at his ignorance, but also at the self-assured way he said this 'fact'. Then I realise I did this quite loudly, so I try and cover it with a cough.

There is silence behind me, finally. Then I feel one of them approach me. "Excuse me, love, would you like to join our conversation?"

I peer up at him innocently. "Excuse me?"

"Well, you seemed to find my friend's comment funny, so I wondered what your opinion on the subject was." The man looks annoyed; his grey eyebrows are furrowing. He's wearing an expensive suit, his greying hair is licked back and his cologne is way too strong. There's an air of arrogance about him I find distasteful.

I smile politely at him; I don't make enemies when I don't have to. "I'm fine, thank you. I'm just watching my son play."

The man sneers and turns away. "Typical," he says to his friends. "No opinion on important matters. Women these days just want to make snide comments, look pretty and drink expensive champagne."

Anger flashes through me and I turn quickly in my seat. "Actually, I'm drinking the same beer you are, mate." The three men look at me in surprise as I continue. "Just so you know, I was a British Army corporal in the Royal Corps of Engineers. My work involved building roads and bridges and industrial plants and schools and other critical infrastructure, like sanitation facilities." The blond man's eyebrows reach his hairline. "I did this in some of the countries that you were just talking about. Iraq and Afghanistan, for instance. Where the men, women and children that I met just wanted to live and have enough food to eat." I pause and eye them. "So you asked me whether I want to give my opinion on your conversation. No. Because there are kids present. Now if you will excuse me, I want to watch my son play. And I, along with everyone else in this room, would really appreciate it if you would keep your voices down. We are really not interested in your opinions." I raise my beer to them and turn back around. My eyes go to Alfie, who is still playing on the mat. After a second, my eyes snap up to the room as I realise it is completely silent. Everyone is staring at me, most of them with impressed smiles on their faces. Behind me, I hear the men mutter something about their drinks and leave the room through the other door. My eyes search the room as they widen in shock. I hear whispers, and I glance to the doorway to see about a dozen people all crammed there, watching me. I see Sarah and Max, who look horrified. Then my gaze lands on the man with the blazing bright green eyes. Jon is staring at me intensely, his eyes wide. His face shows an expression I have never seen before. Slowly, his mouth curves into a grin, his face lighting up completely. I swear my heart stops for a second. He nods, very slightly, that grin still in place. Sarah says something to him, but he just shrugs, his twinkling gaze never leaving my face.

I cough and shift uncomfortably. Low voices start again, and the room starts to return to normal. Laura leans over and says, "Nice one, I couldn't have said it better myself."

*

We leave the party at just after 1700. Sarah seems relieved to see Jon and myself go, but sad to say goodbye to Stephy. I can see Jon visibly relax as we drive away. He cricks his neck and the tension leaves his limbs. I'm thinking over my actions, so I stare out of the window silently as the kids play in the back. I feel both proud and annoyed at myself. It's not a long drive back to Jon's house. His living room is at the front of the house so as we arrive Jon immediately says, "Kids! How do you fancy a cartoon?"

"Yay!" Alfie and Stephy yell as Jon sets them up with a *Tom and Jerry* in the living room. I go to sit on the sofa with them but Jon grabs my hand.

"You enjoy that, okay? We'll be right back."

The kids yell in unison, their eyes glued to the TV screen. Jon drags me out of the living room, through the kitchen and into the dining room at the back of the house.

"Jon...?"

Jon pushes me against the wall and covers my mouth with his. His kiss is hard, greedy and full of desire. It makes me melt against him. My skin is burning where he is touching me; I don't want him to stop. This kiss feels different somehow, like something has changed between us.

"Jeez, Emma, I've been wanting to do that for hours," he mumbles against my mouth. "That was so frigging hot."

"What was?" I whisper as Jon starts nuzzling my neck. His hands are skirting up my legs and under my dress. A sharp thrill of pleasure darts through me as his body pushes me into the wall.

"The way you bitch slapped those blokes. So hot." He pulls back and looks down at me. "You are so amazing, Emma. I..." Our eyes meet. A spark flares in Jon's eyes for a second as he looks at me, then he pulls away sharply. I swallow hard. I had felt it too, but I don't understand it.

"Jon..." I say hesitantly. Jon looks at me warily; his eyes are sharp and I see fear in them. I can't talk about this now. "Let's go and watch some cartoons."

Jon cooks us all dinner, a bolognese-type spaghetti dish, and we all eat at the table. Then the kids have a bath together, which they love doing because they can splash us a lot, and then they head to bed.

Alfie has stayed round so often now that Jon keeps the extra mattress permanently on the floor in Stephy's room, as I do in Alfie's room. After the excitement of the day, they fall asleep pretty quickly, clutching their teddies to their chests.

I'm wondering if Jon is going to want to talk about earlier, but as we close the bedroom door he captures my face in his hands and kisses me gently, which I take as a no. Quickly, the kiss turns passionate and Jon lifts me in his arms. As he manoeuvres me to the bed and slowly takes off my clothes, there's a look in his eyes I haven't seen before. And like the kiss earlier, there is something different about the way we move together. But we don't talk. Then I stop all thought.

*

I know I am dreaming but I can't help it. I can't stop it even though I know what is going to happen.

Everything is silent and empty as I walk to the construction site. I feel a presence behind me and I whirl around to see Rick. He is grinning and trying to say something but like always I can't hear it. I'm frozen as I look into his face, as I see a shadow approach from behind. I frantically point behind him, but my limbs are so heavy, the movement is slow. Rick tilts his head in question, then his beautiful brown eyes widen and he turns.

BANG!

The gunshot rings all around me and starts the sound again. I can hear the wind and sand and bells, hear the voices in the air. As if in slow motion, Rick falls to the ground. I feel someone push me roughly from behind, but before I land on my hands in the sand, someone catches me in strong arms. I look up into Jon's bright green eyes. I stare at him for a moment, then together we both look down at Rick. He is looking up at us with flat dead eyes. A single bullet wound is in the centre of his forehead; his red blood is running down onto the sand...

I scream and sit bolt upright, my body covered in sweat and my heart racing. Without thinking, I sweep aside the duvet and run out of the room, towards the bathroom. I run down the hall, throwing open the door and launching myself at the toilet.

I just make it. After a few minutes, the nausea subsides and I flush the loo, resting my head on my arm on the toilet seat. Just breathing in and out.

It takes me a few minutes to realise that Jon is there. He is stroking my back soothingly with his palm, crouching just behind me. I don't look at him. I can't look at him.

I shiver in the cool air as the sweat evaporates off my skin. I'm just wearing a light strap top and pants. Jon repositions himself so he is sitting with his legs either side of me, his front against my back. He brushes aside my hair and puts his chin on my neck, his breath tickling my skin. He winds one arm around my upper arms and chest and the other around my waist. He doesn't say a word. I stop shivering as his body heat warms me. We sit like that for a long time.

"I'm sorry I woke you," I whisper eventually. "I try not to. I have this dream… a lot."

"I know," Jon says quietly.

I close my eyes and shudder. He had heard me. "You never mentioned it."

"Neither did you."

I shake my head. "No, I couldn't."

"Tell me now. Tell me what you see."

I swallow hard and squeeze my eyes shut. I find that I desperately want to tell him. "I'm in Afghanistan, at a school site I worked at. I'm walking down the street, it's hot and silent. Completely silent. Afghanistan is noisy, so much noise from people, animals, vehicles, the wind and sand and everything. But it's always silent when I'm there, it feels like that millisecond between taking a breath and letting it out. I feel someone behind me and I turn. It's Rick, fully kitted out, young, like when I first knew him. He's talking to me but because there is no sound, I don't understand, but I frantically want to know what he is saying. Someone comes up behind him, and I try and tell him but then it's too late. Rick turns and there is a loud gunshot."

Tears are running down my face now. "Then all the noise comes back. All in one go, overloading me. Rick falls to the ground and someone pushes me." I pause, thinking back over the dream. "Then... usually, I land on my hands and knees in the sand. I look over to Rick and all I can see is his dead face. His eyes are cold and flat. There is a bullet hole between his eyes, bright red blood running out." I gasp. "That's how he died, a single gunshot wound to the head on the streets of Afghanistan. I begged Seth to tell me and he wouldn't for ages, but then he did, but I really wish he hadn't." I pull in a deep breath. I do feel better for having shared it. "Then I hear screaming, but it's me waking up, and then sometimes I throw up."

Jon is silent behind me, though his grip on me is very strong.

"You said usually." He asks quietly after a moment, "Was there something different about this one?"

"Yeah," I reply, and I shiver. My voice is shaking. "This time, someone pushed me, but then... you caught me before I landed on the sand. Then we both looked at Rick, dead on the ground." I shudder and frown. "What do you think that means, Jon?"

Jon is quiet for a long time. "I don't know," he eventually says softly, "but you're freezing. Let's get you back to bed."

I nod and let Jon pull me up. I quickly brush my teeth, shivering hard, then Jon leads me back to his bedroom, which I don't protest about. I had been sleeping in the spare room. I get under the covers of his bed but take his hand as he starts to move away.

"Jon?"

"Yeah?"

"Will you stay? Here with me?"

For a second, I hear nothing. I can barely see his face in the half-light so I don't know what he is thinking. Then I hear him move around the bed and climb in beside me. In one move, he pulls me to him, my back against his bare chest. Curling his arm around me and gently kissing my neck.

"Night, Emma."

"Good night, Jon."

When I wake the next morning, I'm confused as to where I am. Then I remember I'm in Jon's bed. I have never slept all night in here before. I always go to the spare room. Jon's room is nicely decorated; pale white walls with lots of deep masculine colours. The curtains are navy blue and the current bedspread is deep red. There's an oak dresser on the wall at the foot of the bed which holds photos of Stephy. Jon's whole house is covered in photos of his daughter and his family.

I stuff my head back into the pillow as last night's confession by the toilet comes back to me. The dream almost feels like it has lost some of its power now. The image in my mind is of Jon's alive face, not Rick's dead one. Then I remember about falling asleep in Jon's arms. I try not to dwell on how good that felt. I wonder if it will change what we have been doing. I glance over at the other side of the bed. It's empty.

I check the time; it's almost 0700. I get up, grabbing a towel and fresh clothes from the spare room, heading for the shower. As I go, I peer into the kids' room. It's empty. I crouch on the stairs to listen. I can hear Jon's beautiful voice talking, then Alfie's excited one joined by Stephy's. I trust Jon implicitly with Alfie, so I will shower before heading down to face them.

I shower and dress in a red vest top with dark blue jeans in the bathroom. Knowing my clothes from last night are still on Jon's bedroom floor, I head back in there as I finger-brush my dry hair.

Jon is sitting on the edge of the bed holding a mug when I come in, and I pause in surprise.

"Morning."

"Hey," Jon replies. He is showered and dressed in a baggy t-shirt and worn jeans already, his feet bare. He gestures at the nightstand. "I brought you a coffee."

"Great, thanks." I quickly pick up my clothes from the floor and place them in a pile by the door. Jon is still sitting on the bed watching me, so I take my mug and a big sip. "Ah, that's so good." Jon always gives me real coffee.

I glance out of the door. "The kids?"

"Watching TV, which they were very excited about." He hesitates. "We need to talk."

Oh dear, I really don't like that tone. I sit softly on the edge of the bed next to him.

"Okay. What about?"

Jon glances at me. "I think you know, Emma."

"Do I?" I suspect I do, but I want him to say it.

"Okay. First, I'm concerned that Stephy is getting attached to you and Alfie, and I don't think that's healthy. She is my priority."

I study him carefully. "I understand that, Jon. I feel the same about Alfie. But you once told me that kids are resilient, they bounce back. Don't use her as an excuse. Please."

Jon swallows and looks away. "We're violating our ground rules, Emma. When you start doing that, it's time to stop."

"You mean rule number three?" No sleeping in the same bed together, broken last night.

Jon nods, not looking at me. "Yes, and rule number two." Ah, that one isn't quite so easy to quantify. "We said we would keep this casual. No feelings, remember?"

I tilt my head at him, my heart pounding. I should be taking this seriously, but I don't want to. "Are you having trouble with that one, Jon?"

He stands suddenly and walks away. "Dammit, Emma, this isn't a joke," he says angrily. "We agreed, no feelings. Casual. Seeing other people." He turns and looks at me finally. His eyes are blazing, his features twisted. "Are you telling me nothing has changed for you?"

I shake my head at him slowly. I can't say that, because something has changed. I just don't know what.

"Have you been asked out by anyone in the last few months?"

His sudden question makes me blink hard. I hold my chin up and answer truthfully. "Yes."

"And?" Jon's eyes are fiery. "Did you go out with him?"

"No."

"Why not?"

"I wasn't interested."

"Why weren't you interested?"

I don't answer. I can't answer. "Have you been asked out?"

Jon clenches his jaw. "Yes."

"And?"

"I said no as well."

"Why?"

"I don't know why," Jon admits, his voice full of frustration as he paces to the window.

I take a deep breath. "You said this would happen," I say slowly. "That it's impossible to keep the feelings from the physical. I didn't believe you. I didn't think I…" Jon is looking out of the window, his hands on his hips. I take a deep breath and pull my courage together. "Jon, maybe we could—"

"We need to end it." Jon interrupts firmly, his back to me. "Right now, no more."

A cold shiver runs down my spine. I swallow and force out steadily, "Is that what you want?"

"Yes."

"Okay." I stand. If that's what he wants, I won't argue. He didn't even hesitate in his answer. "After breakfast, Alfie and I will leave. Anything else will upset them." I grab my mug, and my pile of clothes, which I chuck in my open bag as I pass the spare room. I head downstairs and stand behind the kids as they sit on the sofa watching a morning TV show. After a little while,

Alfie realises I'm there and bounds over to me as I crouch down for a big hug. He is still in his dinosaur pyjamas. Stephy sees me too and joins in, and I find myself surrounded by two little warm bodies as I cuddle them close.

I feel Jon's presence behind me. "Daddy, we're having cuddles. Want to join?"

"I want to have breakfast," Jon says after a moment. His voice is steady. "Who wants pancakes?"

I release the kids as they yell in excitement. As Jon makes breakfast, I read a few books to them, anything to keep me out of the kitchen. We manage through the meal by talking politely without eye contact or just with the kids. Afterwards, I leave Jon to tidy up, and dress Alfie quickly, packing our bags hastily.

"Right, we're off," I yell from the front door as I come back in from having put the bags in the car. "Alfie, time to go."

Stephy and Alfie come towards me from the living room. I see Jon wiping his hands on a dishcloth as he comes from the back of the house. I kneel down in front of Stephy, who is still wearing her princess pyjamas.

"Goodbye, Stephy." She leans forward and hugs me, and I pull her little body towards me. Damn, I hadn't realised quite how attached to her I had become. "It was lovely to play with you."

She pulls back with a curious look and I place a kiss on her cheek. "I'm going to see you 'gain, right?"

I force a smile back. "Maybe, we'll see." Stephy frowns. I look over at Alfie; he is giving Jon a goodbye hug. Jon looks sad and my heart aches.

When Jon lets Alfie go, he comes towards me and I scoop him up. Jon picks up Stephy as I open the front door. "Goodbye, Emma."

I glance back and meet Jon's eyes. "Goodbye, Jon."

❋

That night, I found myself feeling very sad. This time, though, it was for Jon, not Rick.

I hurt, but this was a different kind of pain than I had been used to. This wasn't the pain of loss and heartbreak; this was the pain of regret, of a lost future and the knowledge that he was so close but yet so very far. It felt similar to how I had felt after moving to Atlanta, when I knew Rick was in the world but wasn't part of mine.

I thought about Jon all the time. I thought about what I should have said to him that morning. What I should have done to convince him to give us a chance, because I knew now that I did want that chance. He made me happy, made me feel alive again, and though I wasn't sure I was completely in love with him, I knew it wouldn't take much to push me there.

I missed him. I missed both of them.

I saw Jon at work, usually in passing. We'd nod politely but nothing more. He wouldn't look at me. We didn't send each other emails anymore, or go for lunch together. He didn't come over on Wednesday or Friday nights. We had no sleepovers at the weekend. Life was hard again.

My nightmares had almost stopped, thankfully. I'd only had one since that night with Jon, and it hadn't felt so bad, and I hadn't thrown up. I think this was because I was really and finally accepting Rick's death and that that part of my life was over.

It was a Tuesday night several weeks later when Alfie asked me the question I had been dreading: "Mummy, when are we seeing Stephy and Jon?"

I smiled at him. "I'm not sure, sweetheart. Jon's pretty busy right now, it might be a while."

Alfie looked sad and said in a small voice, "Okay." I felt really bad for my son.

That weekend, I had invited Janine and Rhys over to stay on Friday night. They had admitted to me only a month previously that after my birthday dinner they had in fact started seeing each other. I was obviously enthusiastic about this, and planned to rub in the fact I had set them up.

I was making chicken skewers and salad with Janine while Rhys tumbled around with Alfie in the living room.

"So how's Jon?" Janine asks. I have been expecting the question and take a sip of my beer before I answer.

"He's fine," I say casually, chopping the tomatoes and not looking at my friend. "I haven't seen him for a while, though."

"Really? I thought you guys were good friends."

I shrug, concentrating on the big knife in my hand. "Not really, he's fun and all but he has his own life."

I hear Janine stop tearing the lettuce. "Bloody hell, Emma, you slept with him."

Her words make me jump and the knife cuts through my finger. I curse loudly. Janine is startled and quickly grabs a paper towel to stop the bleeding.

Rhys runs into the kitchen. "What the hell?" He quickly surveys the situation, then grabs the first aid box from the kitchen drawer. With skill, Rhys cleans the deep cut on my index finger, then places a big plaster on it.

"Better?"

I flick it around. "It hurts."

"That'll stop, don't be such a baby." I glare at him.

"Emma. You did, didn't you?" Janine could never let it go.

"Did what?" Rhys looks out towards Alfie in the living room, then leans on the doorframe and peers at me.

"Emma totally slept with Jon."

"You did?" Rhys looks pleased. "Good for you, English. I liked him."

I shake my head. "Can't a girl have any secrets around here?"

"Nope. Spill."

Rhys grins. "It was totally that night, right, when he stayed over after dinner?"

I sigh and look at my friends. "That would be the first time."

Janine smiles. "So, you guys have been having a thing?"

I stand and pick up the knife again; we need to finish dinner. Janine glares at me and takes it, chopping the tomatoes herself.

"We had a casual thing. You know, just sex and nothing else."

Janine nods as Rhys chuckles. "Those are good, but only for very short time periods."

"Yeah, well, ours was clearly too long," I mutter.

"So, you decided you couldn't do it anymore?" Rhys asks, moving to the counter to help Janine.

I laugh ironically. "No, he did."

Janine and Rhys both look at me in surprise. I shrug and plunk down onto a stool. "I like him, I really like being with him. I might even love him, but he's really damaged from his marriage. Maybe I'm ready to move on but he's not." I rub my chest, trying to get rid of the tightness. "I think. I don't know. I'm so confused."

Rhys frowns. "Am I going to have to beat his arse?"

"Maybe."

I see Janine and Rhys exchange a look, but I'm saved from their questioning when the doorbell rings. I sigh and stand up.

"Emma Tavern?" the yellow-jacketed courier asks. I get *déjà vu*.

"That's me."

The man hands me a big parcel. "Sign here, please." I scribble, and mumble my thanks.

I look over the parcel as I close the door and head into the kitchen. Then I note the US originating address and I freeze.

"Rick's letters," I mutter.

Janine looks in concern. "Em?"

Seth had told me last month that he and Jess had gone through all the boxes and had finally found Rick's letters. After everything that had happened recently, it had slipped my mind. I wasn't sure if that was a good or bad sign. "I think these are Rick's other birthday cards. The parcel came from Atlanta."

Rhys smiles. "That's good. I know you've been waiting for those. Want to go upstairs? We can finish this and keep Alfie entertained." I glance into the living room; Alfie is playing by himself on the carpet.

"Uh, no," I say. "I'll look at them later."

Janine furrows her eyebrows. "Are you sure, Emma?"

Actually, I was. I wanted to read them, but I didn't want to rush. "Yeah, I'll just put these upstairs."

Dinner is great fun. I tease Rhys and Janine about what a great couple they are and all the Welsh-speaking ginger babies they are going to have. I tell them some more about Jon; they seem both upset and pleased for me. We all share a bottle of red wine and then go to bed at around 11pm.

I walk into my room and see the parcel still sitting on the bed. I hadn't forgotten about it at all, but the sight surprises me anyway. I slowly sit in the centre, on the duvet cover, and tear open the parcel. There is a large yellow stuffed envelope in the box. On top of it is a piece of folded lined paper. I look at that first. It's a note from Seth.

Howdy, Emma,

I hope this finds you good and in one piece. I'll tell you I've posted this but I'm not sure how long until it reaches you; two or three weeks maybe? Please let me know when they arrive.

These were very well hidden at the bottom of an old box of Rick's army stuff. Sorry it took us so long to find

*them. I guess he didn't want you to accidently find them,
so he put them in the dirtiest and nastiest place he could
think of. Typical, huh?*

*I don't know what Rick wrote in these, obviously, but
I hope it makes things easier, not worse, for you. I found
the photo in another box and knew he would want you
to have it.*

*We miss you and Alfie. It's just not the same without
you here. Shanna has been talking about visiting you in
England when the kids are a little older. I hope you will
consider a visit over here too sometime.*

*Love
Seth*

I smile at Seth's note. Damn, that guy is awesome. There is a
photo I recognise with the note. A framed copy of it is on the
dresser downstairs. It was taken a few weeks after I had arrived at
the US base. It is Rick, Paulo, Seth and myself all in army cammies
posing outside a Humvee on base. Big grins on our faces. I'm
between Rick and Paulo, and I look so tiny in comparison to the
men. I smile at the memory. Rick had whispered something rude
to me just before the photo was taken. This copy of the photo
is tatty. I vaguely remember seeing it in Rick's bedroom once,
just after we got together. It's folded in half, between Paulo and
me, so only Rick and I are visible on one side. I think he used to
carry it in his wallet. We didn't take many photos back then, so
this would probably have been the only one he had of me. The
thought makes me warm inside.

Placing the tatty photo on the bed, I take a deep breath and
slit open the large envelope. Inside are nine cards, all with my
name written on them in Rick's handwriting. In the corner of
each envelope where the stamp should go is a number: 1-9. I

lay them out in front of me in a big arc. None of the cards are sealed.

I stare at them for a few minutes, then reach for the first one and pull the card out. The picture is of a beautiful tropical beach.

Emma,

It is July 7th 2007 and I'm writing you this card on my way to the States after leaving Afghanistan, and you, behind. I'm not sure what I will do with it, maybe send it to you on your birthday? I need to tell you the things in my head, but there is just no easy way for me to do it.

Please know that I didn't mean for what happened last night to happen. I don't regret it at all, despite the problems it could have caused, but it was impulsive and I put us both at risk, which is not what I do, ever. You were right, neither of us can want anything more at the moment, the timing is just not there for us. I do love that you were as enthusiastic as me, though. It makes me smile even sitting here on this really uncomfortable bench.

I wonder if you thought yourself a burden these last few months. At first, my assignment was just that, another set of orders and a way to fill my day. But after a while, as I watched you work, as I saw your mind and your enthusiasm, it became more than that. Those few times I thought you were in danger scared me like I have never experienced before. Knowing you are still there and I'm not makes me cold, but I can't dwell on that now. I think you seemed to warm to me after a while too, and I really loved our banter. I've never had that with a woman before. You are so open and quick-witted. You made the days fly by (despite your engineering lectures).

I'm not sure what I feel right now. I miss you, I think. Do I love you? I'm not sure. I don't think I'm mature or experienced enough to know what that is.

I don't know when, or if, I will see you again. But I suspect you will be in my thoughts for a while.

I'll send this to you on your birthday next year, so Happy Birthday, King. If I could give you a birthday wish, I would take you away from all the troubles in the world, and give you a big chocolate cake and a case of cold beer which we would enjoy together on this tropical beach (with the good kind of sand).

Rick (otherwise known as Tavern)

I read it three times, then place it on the envelope and reach for the next one, emotions rushing through me. I read that a few times, then open up the third one. The picture is of a brightly lit carnival. There is a Ferris wheel and a helter-skelter. The people in the foreground are laughing and eating candy floss.

Emma,

This is the third card I'm writing to you, for your 25th birthday. It seems to be a habit now. I have decided that if I die, they will be delivered to you on your next birthday. The other two are in a storage box in my house. I hope you get to read those too one day and I hope that I will be there.

It is July 29th 2009. I'm on a plane back to the States after a training mission in the UK. You and I met in Salisbury, for one extraordinary night I will never forget. I didn't let myself hope that I might see you in the UK, so when I saw you run up that field I thought I was dreaming. When I saw your injured face and arm, I wanted to pulverise someone for hurting you (I know, a macho overreaction). When we were in that bar, all I wanted was your attention. I'm sorry I was such an arse that night. You're right, of course. Whatever we have between us (and it's something, I'm certain), the timing is still not right. Our lives are too separate, our work takes us away, we have homes in different countries. I hope that one day everything will fall into place but for now you have given me another night of memories of being with you, and I thank you for that.

I sometimes wonder what would have happened had we met differently. When we were younger or older, if our lives hadn't intertwined the way they have, would it be different? Would I still feel this way for you? Would it have been an instant attraction for us both? These thoughts are useless, I know, but I can't help but daydream about it.
I know now I love you. I realised it when I left you that morning as the sun was rising, but I couldn't put that burden on you so I didn't say it.

Happy Birthday, beautiful girl. My birthday wish for you this year, if we cannot be together, for whatever reason, is for you to find someone who can love you and cherish you as I do. It hurts to write that, to think of you with another man, but I want you to be happy in this life, even if it is not with me.

Love always
Rick

The seventh card was of a beautiful starry night; you could just see the sun slipping below the horizon at the bottom. Rick had drawn a rude picture in the outline of the stars which makes me laugh.

My darling Emma,

This is the seventh card I am writing to you, for your 28th birthday. If I die, it will be delivered to you on your birthday. The other six are in a storage box in our house.

It is March 12th 2013. It's five days before your due date and I'm desperately trying to get back to you. You have no idea the amount of shit I am giving our CO. I'm hoping he will send me back just to get rid of the hassle. I know I have been absent these last few months, and you haven't complained once, but I don't want to let you down again by not being there when our baby is born. This is it. I won't be doing this much longer. I love my country, and I love my job, but I love you and our child even more.

Today, I saw something that really upset me. I can't write about it but I can say that we are so lucky to be who we are. To have been born into such wealth and privilege that the people I saw today could not even dream about. I know that you can understand. You have seen it too.

I once again missed your birthday this year. I know you will forgive me, but that almost makes it worse. Maybe you should shout and scream at me, tell me you're lonely and don't understand my commitment to my job. I know, of course, that you won't. Because you are you. I know what you would say to this: some people are worth fighting for, even if they don't realise it.

I wish a lot for your birthday this year. I wish that we will have a beautiful baby and I will be there in the future as much as I can. I wish for you to be happy, have fun and live your life.

I will love you always
Your Rick

As I finish card number 9 for the second time, I open up my dresser drawer and remove the last card from Rick. Number 10. I read it again, then place it next to the others in the arc.

My mind is whirling with thoughts, my chest and belly constricting with all the emotions running through me. But my face is dry. I don't feel like crying. I stare at the cards for a while, then at the wall in front of me in a trance. I read the cards again and as I do, I know what I have to do. I quickly run downstairs and grab a pen and a greetings card from a stack in a drawer, then I sit on my bed and begin to write.

*

Several hours later, I pull up in front of Jon's house and turn off my engine. I sit, in the dark for a few moments, just thinking about what I am about to do. The potential consequences.

After finishing what I was writing, I had knocked on the spare room door, first softly, then harder, as no one answered. Until it had flown open.

"What?" Rhys had snarled. He was not a guy who took kindly to being woken up. He was completely naked, but I didn't even blink.

"I have to go and see Jon," I said.

Rhys looked at me, confused. He was still half asleep. "Huh?"

I poked his bare chest hard and repeated, "I have to go and see Jon."

"What, right now? It's the middle of the night." Rhys blinked hard and rubbed his head.

"Yes, right now."

Rhys mumbled something in Welsh which sounded insulting. I handed him the child monitor. "Are you okay with Alfie? I don't know how long I'll be."

Finally, it dawned on Rhys what I was doing. He grinned sleepily. "Absolutely."

I saw Janine move on the bed, a sheet wrapped around her. "Go, Emma, we've got him."

I grinned, then flew down the stairs. "You go get him, English!" Rhys called after me. I heard Janine shushing him, then laughter as I ran out of the house.

Taking a deep breath, I grab my bag and leave the car. The night air is cool as I hurry up the drive. I knew this wasn't Jon's weekend to have Stephy, for which I'm very grateful as I ring his doorbell and wait. Then I ring it again. After a few minutes, I hear movement inside so I ring it again. I hear a yell and ring the bell again, just to make sure.

A few seconds later, the door is pulled open, and a half-asleep Jon peers out at me.

I smile and he blinks at me. "Emma?" Damn, it was good to see him again, even half asleep with bed hair and an irritated expression on his face.

"Hi, Jon," I say brightly. He looks at me oddly. "Can I talk to you?"

Jon frowns and looks very confused. "It's 3am."

"I know, sorry," I grimace, "but I really want to talk to you." Jon mutters something in French then swings the door open. "Thanks."

The door closes behind him and Jon looks at me expectantly. I can tell he's still half asleep. "Uh, can I have a coffee?" I want him to wake up.

Jon blinks, rubs his eyes and yawns. "Sure. I'm gonna…" He gestures down at his dark blue dressing gown then up the stairs. I smile and nod, and with a lingering and curious look over his shoulder at me, he disappears up the stairs.

I make my way to the kitchen and turn on the coffee machine, grabbing two mugs and milk for Jon, pushing aside the dirty wine glass and empty bottle. I take off my coat and hang it on a chair. I place my bag on the floor. I hear the hot water run briefly, then silence. I make our coffees, then sit at the table and wait. I'm really nervous; this is going to be tricky.

After about five minutes, Jon comes into the kitchen, dressed in jeans and a scruffy t-shirt, his bare feet padding softly on the hardwood floor. My heart rate picks up straight away. Damn, he's sexy. He pauses as he spies me, gives me a look I can't interpret, and sits at the end of the table. I'm so close to him that excitement bubbles in my tummy but I tamp it down. I need to be controlled.

"So where's Alfie?" he asks as he sips his coffee.

"Rhys and Janine are staying at my house."

"Ah ha. And did you wake them up too?"

"Yes. Rhys was about as pleased to see me as you were. Except he cursed in Welsh."

Jon's lips curve slightly. "Good language to curse in, Welsh." He pauses. "And I'm not *not* pleased to see you. Just surprised."

I smile lightly at him, studying his profile. We sit in silence for a moment. Jon takes a sip of coffee again, his eyes on the table. "So, Emma, what is so important that we have to talk about it at 3am?"

I take a deep, steadying breath. "I want you."

"What?" Jon's head snaps towards me.

"I want to be with you, Jon."

Jon stares at me for a moment. "Emma…"

"Hang on, hear me out, please." Jon nods warily. I can see the thoughts churning through his head. "We can go slow, take our time, enjoy each other." I lean forward and grasp his hand, which is resting on the table. He glances down but doesn't move. "These last few weeks have been really hard. I didn't realise just how much you had become part of my life, what you made me feel. I didn't think I could ever be like this with anyone ever again. You pulled me out of it, Jon, and I know you're wary after what's happened…"

"Emma, stop," Jon says softly, but I keep on going.

"… and it's okay to be scared, but we can figure it out together."

"Stop, please."

"We can start again—"

"Stop it!" Jon jumps up from the table and snatches his hand out of my grasp. The chair goes crashing onto the floor behind him. He walks over to the other side of the kitchen, leans forward on the counter and inhales deeply. I watch him carefully.

"Please don't make me do this again." He says it so softly to the cabinet, I can barely hear him.

"Do what?"

"Say no to you. End what we have. Dammit, Emma." He turns to me, and I can see fear and pain clearly on his face. "These weeks have been hard for me too, seeing you at work, laughing and talking with everyone else. Knowing you are so close but I can't go near you." He pauses and swallows. "But it's so easy compared to what it might be."

I can barely breathe. "What do you mean?"

Jon paces the kitchen opposite me. I'm still sitting at the table with my hands clasped tightly in front of me.

"What if it doesn't work out? What if this…" he gestures between the two of us "…isn't real? Your husband died last year. How can you be sure about me? My marriage was agony for so many years, I can't put myself through that again." He stops and leans on the table. "I could fall in love with you so easily… But what if it's rebound, Emma?"

I meet his eyes, and they are filled with confusion and agony. I nod, irritated and sympathetic at the same time. "So basically you're basing your decision on what ifs?" I laugh lightly to a joke Jon won't get yet, and lean back in my chair. "Okay, I can play that game. What if I hadn't made the choice to join the army? What if I hadn't met Rick? What if I hadn't moved to the States? What if I hadn't had Alfie? What if I hadn't moved here?" Jon is staring at me. "What if you had stayed in France? What if you had chosen another university? What if you hadn't met Sarah? What if you hadn't had Stephy? What if you had died in that car crash?" Jon's eyes are wide. "You can't base your life on what ifs, Jon. Life is what you make it, bad choices and good. Bad events and good. It all happens, and there's not a damn thing you can do about it except make the choices you are given." I pause and stand slowly, walking towards him around the table. Jon stands up straight. "I have one regret in my life, that when I was eighteen years old I was too cowardly to go to a party. Maybe it is an insignificant event in my life, but I always wonder what would have happened if I hadn't been such a coward. I am not a coward anymore. I make the tough choices, no matter how much it might hurt." I'm really close to him now and I whisper, "Tonight, that was coming here, Jon."

At my whispered words, he exhales sharply. His bright green eyes are alive with panic and fear, but they contain longing as they flick over my face. A spark of hope ignites in my chest. "Emma..." he murmurs "...I'm not strong like you. I have lots of regrets, and hurt and pain, and I don't think I can put myself through that again." His voice cracks. "Please, I think you should leave."

My stomach drops heavily at his words. I nod and step back. "Before I leave, please can I show you something?" Jon looks like he is about to protest. "Please, Jon."

Jon studies me for a heartbeat, then nods.

"Thank you." I gesture at the table as my heart pounds; this is my final chance. "Please sit."

Jon warily moves to the table, dragging the chair off the floor and sitting on it. He takes the cold coffee mugs and moves them to the side. I grab my bag, then move round next to him. I take ten cards out of the large yellow envelope. I lean over to place them in an arc around the table in front of him, and he stiffens slightly but doesn't move away. I place the cards face up before him and move back, sitting down in my previous seat.

Jon frowns and glances at me for an explanation. "These are birthday cards from Rick," I say softly. "The last one is the one I received on my birthday this year. The others were shipped to me from the States and arrived earlier today." I smile to myself. "Actually, yesterday. I want you to read them."

Jon looks at me in mild panic. "What?"

"I want you to read them, Jon. I want you to understand."

Jon shakes his head. "You want me to read your birthday cards from your deceased husband?" I nod. "I can't do that, Emma. Those words were meant for you."

"Exactly." Jon stares at me. I pick up card 1 and hand it to him. "Please read it."

Slowly, looking uncomfortable, Jon takes the card from me. Reluctantly, he opens the envelope, revealing the tropical beach card. He studies the front, glances at me again and then opens the card.

He reads it, expressionless. Then he reads it again.

With another glance at me, he places the first card down and picks up the second. Again, he reads it twice. He reads every card twice. By the time he gets to card 10, he no longer looks uncomfortable, or fearful. He seems eager to get to the next. Emotions are passing over his face so quickly, I can't tell them apart anymore. I'm standing by this point, leaning on the counter on the other side of the kitchen, watching him read the letters from Rick. It's a strange feeling, knowing Rick once held those same cards in his hand.

Jon reads card 10 slowly. When he gets to the end, he curses loudly in French, which makes me smile. Then he reads the card again. He places the card down next to the others and runs his hands over his face and down his neck. He stares at them.

"This guy really loved you," he says softly. "It sounds like he went through a lot in his life."

"Yes."

"And you made it better."

I whisper. "Yeah."

Jon finally looks up at me. My heart leaps in my throat at his expression, but there is something I have to do first.

"There's one more." I head back to the table.

Jon frowns, glances at the cards then back up. "I thought he only wrote ten."

"Yeah, this one is different." I hand him another card. He glances at the front, then looks up at me in surprise. This time, it has Rick's name on the front.

"Please, read it."

Slowly, Jon turns the envelope over and removes the card. I retreat to the counter again, leaning backwards against it on my hands.

The card has a picture of a cute bunny rabbit on it. I have drawn a moustache on the bunny.

Jon shoots me an amused look, then opens the card. I close my eyes and see the words I have written.

My dearest Rick,

It has been one year and six weeks since the day you died. I miss you, every day. I miss your smile, that sun-bleached blond hair, your wonderful voice, that way you always eat the green vegetables off your plate before anything else. When you died, I didn't know how to cope. I only kept going because of Alfie. If it hadn't been for our son, I would have curled up in bed and died myself. It felt like I had a hole in my heart, one that could only be filled by you, and without you there, I was empty.

I got your cards. Thank you. They allowed me to know you in a way I never thought possible. I see them as your final gift to me.

I once read an article by a woman who had lost her

husband. She said that every morning, for years, she would wake up and think he was in bed next to her. Every morning, she would relive his death. Maybe I'm lucky in some ways. I don't do that. Because for the ten years we knew each other, we spent more than half of that time apart. That's not to be pitied, it's just a fact.

I have met someone else, Rick. He is gorgeous and kind and funny. He makes me feel alive and happy, in a way I never thought I would feel ever again. When I'm with him, that hole in my heart slowly closes. If you ever met him, you would like him. Oh, you would stand there at first, in that intimidating watcher pose of yours. Hands holding that big gun (and I do mean gun), eyeballing him. But then he would smile, and joke, and you would grin. You'd share a beer or two as Alfie and his beautiful little girl run around your feet, giggling.

He has been hurt too, in a different way to me but no less painful. I want to help him, see it's okay to move on. I'm so scared, Rick. What if he doesn't feel it too? What if the pain is too much and he can't see past it? But I guess these questions are silly, right? Because you know me so well, you know I will try anyway. I am not a coward anymore.

Every year, you have given me a birthday wish. This year, I didn't make one, so I make it now. I wish I could see you one more time, to say goodbye. I wish I could tell you what you have meant to me, how I will always love you, and how I will always miss you. I would tell you that I have enough love to share again, and I want to be happy.

So now, I say goodbye to you, my love.

Goodbye, Rick
Emma

Jon swears again, in English and French, then he goes silent. I think he is reading it once more. I keep my eyes closed. My heart is thundering in my chest, my palms are sweaty, my mouth dry. Jon is quiet for a long time, then he swears again, louder this time. After a minute, I hear the chair being pushed back, then silence. Maybe he has left the room, maybe he has decided no again, maybe this didn't work… I breathe quickly. Maybe I need to open my eyes and see?

Then I feel him step close to me. I feel his arms brush my sides as he places them on the counter under my arms. Feel his breath tickle my face as he leans in close.

"What if I hadn't stopped that lift?" he whispers to me. "What if you hadn't come to the ball park that day? What if I hadn't kissed you that night?" My eyes pop open and focus on Jon's face, so close to me. "What if I don't take this chance now? And I regret it forever?"

I bring my hands up and stroke his cheeks gently. "Take the chance," I reply, "and you won't regret it." I really believe that.

Jon's eyes flicker over my face, and my belly clenches as he leans in and kisses me gently. I melt into him as he deepens the kiss.

"No ground rules this time?" he murmurs against me.

"Only one," I whisper back, my voice hoarse. "That it's you and me."

Jon places his forehead on mine and smiles softly. "I think I can agree to that."

"Make love to me, Jon."

Jon physically shudders under my hands. I feel it throughout his entire body. Without a word, we head upstairs together.

*

"Uncle Jon Uncle Jon Uncle Jon." The mass of swirling colour and sound erupts out of the pub garden as we approach the gate. Jon gives me Stephy's hand, laughs and runs forward, catching the girl under the arms and swinging her around, then capturing her in a big hug. He quickly drops her to her feet. She looks about ten.

"Addie! You look amazing!" Jon yells. "All grown up."

We enter the beer garden. I lead Alfie and Stephy by the hand. Jon's niece grins and slips her arm around his waist. She eyes me up and down and I smile at her brightly. She looks like Jon, bright green eyes and black hair.

"Jonny." A woman who looks even more like Jon approaches and hugs him enthusiastically. I see a good-looking man and two little boys at the table behind her. Stephy hugs her aunt, then hurries to her uncle and cousins at the table with excited yells. Amie turns to me.

"Hi, I'm Amie. You must be Emma." She gives me a quick hug, and then steps back and appraises me carefully. "I've been really looking forward to meeting you, and this must be Alfie."

I nod. "Hi, it's lovely to meet you, Amie. Jon has told me a lot about you."

Amie smirks. "Hopefully, he left out the embarrassing stuff."

I laugh and gently ruffle Alfie's hair. "And yes, this is Alfie." He is looking up at Amie with a wide look on his face. I grin. "Go and sit next to Stephy, honey."

Alfie obediently goes to the table.

Amie peers at me curiously. "Have we met before, Emma? You look awfully familiar."

"I don't think so," I reply with a smile.

Jon grins and leads me to the table. "Emma, this is Mike, Amie's husband, and their twin boys, Josh and James." Mike smiles and waves from his seat. The boys just stare at me. "And this" he gestures down to the girl still clutching his waist "is my favourite niece, Addie."

Addie rolls her eyes at him. "Uncle Jon, I'm your only niece."

"That's why you're my favourite." Jon leans down and kisses her on the cheek. Addie giggles and sits down at the table, her eyes still appraising me.

Mike offers to go to the bar so I ask for a local beer. He nods and heads inside the pub with everyone's orders. We have met Jon's sister and her family at a pub in Fritham, in the New Forest. I had been here before many years ago and loved the ale and food selection. We were going to go walking after lunch. I was very excited to meet Jon's family. I see Jon go round to his nephews and begin to tease them; they look a few years older than Alfie.

Amie is looking at me carefully. "I'm sure we have met before," she says.

I shrug. "Uh, maybe," I reply. "I mean, you do look familiar but then you look like Jon so…"

"Well, Amie is very good with faces," Jon says from the other side of the table. He comes round and Jon takes a seat next to me at the double picnic tables. Addie moves so she is sitting next to Stephy. Alfie crawls onto my lap, and I bounce him until he squeals.

Mike returns with a large tray of drinks and some menus. As we sit chatting and drinking, Amie suddenly claps her hands together.

"I've got it, and I can't believe it." She grins. "You were the woman at the pub in Burley. The one that found Addie." I frown, trying to place that. "Yeah, it was… July 2009. You were cycling with a redheaded woman."

"Janine?" I say, then I remember. Jon is looking startled.

"Yes, that's right. We were here camping. Addie was almost three, the twins were newborns. Jon was late." Amie shoots him a look. "Mike had popped to the loo." She shoots her husband a similar look. "Josh was throwing a tantrum and Addie wandered off before I noticed."

I smile slowly, the day coming back to me. "She was wandering in the beer garden by herself," I say slowly, looking over at the pre-teen, who is listening with interest. "Near the stream. I was concerned."

"Yes!" Amie cries. "Wow, I can't believe this!"

Jon is looking between us in wonder. "Hang on, was that the day I had that big argument with Sarah and she refused to come along?"

Amie nods. "Yeah, you arrived about an hour late."

Jon looks at me, a smile on his lips. "You were at that pub, that afternoon?"

"I was," I reply with a smile. "I was stationed at the base on Salisbury Plain. Janine and I used to cycle down here on Saturdays."

"Do you remember, Jon?" Amie says. "Almost as soon as you arrived, we went out to buy them a drink and they had probably left, what, five minutes earlier?"

"Wow." I turn to Jon. "What if you hadn't been late, Jon?"

Jon grins. "And what if you had left later, Emma?"

"We might have met years ago," I say slowly. "Huh. That's an interesting thought."

Jon takes my hand and kisses it gently. "Everything could have been different."

It didn't take long for me to know I was truly in love with Jon. I still loved Rick, that part of me would never fade, but the love was different, my heart felt different. Jon was different.

By the end of the year, Alfie and I had moved into Jon's house. Alfie loved having an almost-sister around, and Stephy loved having an almost-brother.

Jon and I both stayed at G&S for a long time. Eventually, Jon dropped his hours to work on various charitable initiatives. He had found a cause he could be passionate about.

Five years after we first met, Jon and I married in a small ceremony with a big party. By then, we already had a two-year-old little girl, a half-sister for Alfie and Stephy.

Jon and I called her April.

Epilogue

Many years later...

As I finally stop talking, my throat spasms and I cough violently. Grace is there instantly with a glass of water. I take a big gulp, feeling the cool liquid run down my parched throat.

I hear a sniffle, and look up. Grace is looking down at me with a watery smile.

"Granny, that was an amazing story," she says quietly, taking my old leathery hand in her young, supple one. "Dad never told me detail like that before."

I smile. "Of course not. It's my story, not your father's." I suddenly feel exhausted; my body is old and I can feel it. I lean my head back and close my eyes.

"Sometimes, I ask myself if I would change anything," I say softly. "Would I have prevented the heartache of losing my first love if I could? If I had, I would never have met my second love. If I could do it all over again, my dear, I wouldn't change a thing."

"Sleep, Granny," Grace mumbles to me, gently stroking my forehead.

When I wake, I'm groggy and cold. I can hear a storm outside the window, the rain pelting against the glass. The room is dark, but as I look around, light slowly floods the world, and I smile. Around me is everyone I have ever known, men and women who have touched my life in some way. I see old friends, long forgotten, I see family who passed many decades ago, people I barely knew but who changed me somehow. My eyes land on my children, standing all around my bedside. They are young and grown, simultaneously. They smile warmly, their faces full of love for me. Their husbands and wives stand with them, and my grandchildren beside them. The younger ones run around the end of the bed. The older ones, like Grace, stand watching me with smiles on their faces. Grace shoots me a 'you really are going to do this?' look, and I smile widely back at her. I see my parents, the way they were when they were there for me. They are long passed now. I see my grandparents, passed so many years ago that I can barely remember their faces. Jason and his wife, and my nephews, are there. Jason is shaking his head at me, looking like a child, an adult and then an old man. All the faces I have known of him.

Behind them, I see Janine and Rhys, young again, and Trent and Milly. Their children stand with them. Trent is yelling something rude at me. I can see it in the way his eyes sparkle, but his words are blown away on the wind. Rhys simply watches me with a smile, his arm around Janine, who is grinning in mischief like when we were kids. I see Rob and Abbey, arms around each other. I see Seth and Shanna, Mat and Mari, Frank and Paulo. All young, in their prime. Their faces wide as they laugh at me.

I see Jon's family. His parents, middle-aged, like when I met them. I see his brother, Jac, his smile so much like Jon's. I see Amie, and Mike. They are old now, but still carry those same wild smiles, the look that tells me we are about to have some fun. Josh and James stand next to them, and Addie, now all grown up, waves at me widely. I will be her favourite aunt forever. I see Jessica, her hair grey now, her smile the same as always, standing with Jordan and her family, just watching me.

I feel two warm, male hands clasp mine as they rest on the bed. I grin. Jon is to my left. Rick is to my right. They lie on their sides facing me, their eyes bright and playful. They are young, as I knew them years ago. Then I am young too; my hair dark, my skin smooth, my body energised. I clasp their hands tightly in mine and bring them to my chest. These two extraordinary men who I loved, and who loved me. They gave me my children, and a world full of fun and laughter. My first love, who enriched my life and showed me how to live, taken too early from me. My second love, who showed me how to go on living, taken after a wonderful life together.

With a smile on my face, I close my eyes, take a last breath, and fall asleep for the final time.